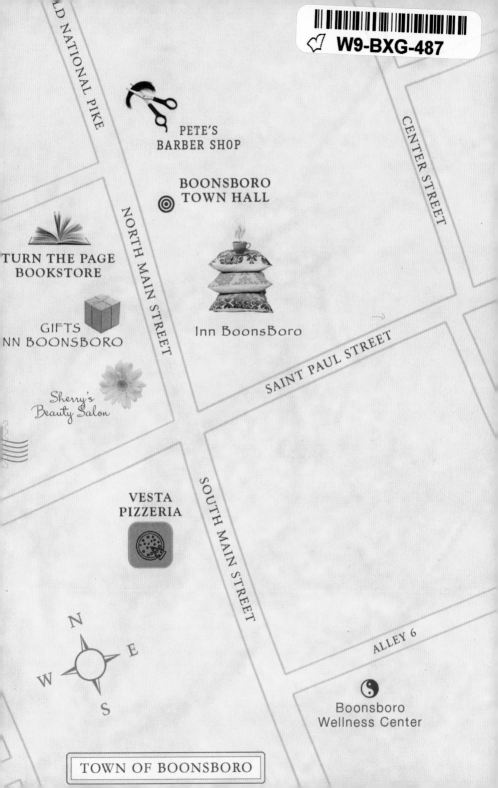

OLD NATIONAL PIKE

CENTER STREET

PETE'S
BARBER SHOP

BOONSBORO
TOWN HALL

TURN THE PAGE
BOOKSTORE

NORTH MAIN STREET

GIFTS
INN BOONSBORO

Inn BoonsBoro

SAINT PAUL STREET

Sherry's
Beauty Salon

VESTA
PIZZERIA

SOUTH MAIN STREET

N
W   E
S

ALLEY 6

Boonsboro
Wellness Center

TOWN OF BOONSBORO

Nora Roberts

Series

THE NEXT ALWAYS

Nora Roberts & J. D. Robb

REMEMBER WHEN

J. D. Robb

THE NEXT ALWAYS

NORA ROBERTS

BERKLEY BOOKS, NEW YORK

THE BERKLEY PUBLISHING GROUP
Published by the Penguin Group
Penguin Group (USA) Inc.
375 Hudson Street, New York, New York 10014, USA
Penguin Group (Canada), 90 Eglinton Avenue East, Suite 700, Toronto, Ontario M4P 2Y3, Canada
(a division of Pearson Penguin Canada Inc.)
Penguin Books Ltd., 80 Strand, London WC2R 0RL, England
Penguin Group Ireland, 25 St. Stephen's Green, Dublin 2, Ireland (a division of Penguin Books Ltd.)
Penguin Group (Australia), 250 Camberwell Road, Camberwell, Victoria 3124, Australia
(a division of Pearson Australia Group Pty. Ltd.)
Penguin Books India Pvt. Ltd., 11 Community Centre, Panchsheel Park, New Delhi—110 017, India
Penguin Group (NZ), 67 Apollo Drive, Rosedale, Auckland 0632, New Zealand
(a division of Pearson New Zealand Ltd.)
Penguin Books (South Africa) (Pty.) Ltd., 24 Sturdee Avenue, Rosebank, Johannesburg 2196,
South Africa

Penguin Books Ltd., Registered Offices: 80 Strand, London WC2R 0RL, England

This book is an original publication of The Berkley Publishing Group.

This is a work of fiction. Names, characters, places, and incidents either are the product of the author's imagination or are used fictitiously, and any resemblance to actual persons, living or dead, business establishments, events, or locales is entirely coincidental. The publisher does not have any control over and does not assume responsibility for author or third-party websites or their content.

ISBN 978-1-61793-374-5

PRINTED IN THE UNITED STATES OF AMERICA

To John Reese,
best job boss ever,
and the crew of Inn BoonsBoro

The song and the silence in the heart,
That in part are prophecies, and in part
Are longings wild and vain.

——LONGFELLOW

CHAPTER ONE

THE STONE WALLS STOOD AS THEY HAD FOR MORE THAN two centuries, simple, sturdy, and strong. Mined from the hills and the valleys, they rose in testament to man's inherent desire to leave his mark, to build and create.

Over those two centuries man married the stone with brick, with wood and glass, enlarging, transforming, enhancing to suit the needs, the times, the whims. Throughout, the building on the crossroads watched as the settlement became a town, as more buildings sprang up.

The dirt road became asphalt; horse and carriage gave way to cars. Fashions flickered by in the blink of an eye. Still it stood, rising on its corner of The Square, an enduring landmark in the cycle of change.

It knew war, heard the echo of gunfire, the cries of the wounded, the prayers of the fearful. It knew blood and tears, joy and fury. Birth and death.

It thrived in good times, endured the hard times. It changed hands and purpose, yet the stone walls stood.

In time, the wood of its graceful double porches began to sag. Glass broke; mortar cracked and crumbled. Some who stopped at the light on the town square might glance over to see pigeons flutter in and out of broken windows and wonder what the old building had been in its day. Then the light turned green, and they drove on.

Beckett knew.

He stood on the opposite corner of The Square, thumbs tucked into the pockets of his jeans. Thick with summer, the air held still. With the road empty, he could have crossed Main Street against the light, but he continued to wait. Opaque blue tarps draped the building from roof to street level, curtaining the front of the building. Over the winter it had served to hold the heat in for the crew. Now it helped block the beat of the sun—and the view.

But he knew—how it looked at that moment, and how it would look when the rehab was complete. After all, he'd designed it—he, his two brothers, his mother. But the blueprints bore his name as architect, his primary function as a partner in Montgomery Family Contractors.

He crossed over, his tennis shoes nearly silent on the road in the breathless hush of three a.m. He walked under the scaffolding, along the side of the building, down St. Paul, pleased to see in the glow of the streetlight how well the stone and brick had cleaned up.

It looked old—it *was* old, he thought, and that was part of its beauty and appeal. But now, for the first time in his memory, it looked tended.

He rounded the back, walked over the sunbaked dirt, through the construction rubble scattered over what would be a courtyard. Here the porches that spanned both the second and third stories ran straight and true. Custom-made pickets—designed to replicate those from old photographs of the building, and the remnants found during excavation—hung freshly primed and drying on a length of wire.

He knew his eldest brother, Ryder, in his role as head contractor, had the rails and pickets scheduled for install.

He knew because Owen, the middle of the three Montgomery brothers, plagued them all over schedules, calendars, projections, and ledgers—and kept Beckett informed of every nail hammered.

Whether he wanted to be or not.

In this case, he supposed as he dug out his key, he wanted to be— usually. The old hotel had become a family obsession.

It had him by the throat, he admitted as he opened the unfinished and temporary door to what would be The Lobby. And by the heart— and hell, it had him by the balls. No other project they'd ever worked on had ever gotten its hooks in him, in all of them, like this. He suspected none ever would again.

He hit the switch, and the work light dangling from the ceiling flashed on to illuminate bare concrete floors, roughed-in walls, tools, tarps, material.

It smelled of wood and concrete dust and, faintly, of the grilled onions someone must have ordered for lunch.

He'd do a more thorough inspection of the first and second floors in the morning when he had better light. Stupid to have come over at this hour anyway, when he couldn't really see crap, and was dog tired. But he couldn't resist it.

By the balls, he thought again, passing under a wide archway, its edges of stone still rough and exposed. Then, flipping on his flashlight, he headed toward the front and the work steps that led up.

There was something about the place in the middle of the night, when the noise of nail guns, saws, radios, and voices ended, and the shadows took over. Something not altogether quiet, not altogether still. Something that brushed fingers over the back of his neck.

Something else he couldn't resist.

He swept his light around the second floor, noted the brown-bag backing on the walls. As always, Owen's report had been accurate. Ry and his crew had the insulation completed on this level.

Though he'd intended to go straight up, he roamed here with a grin spreading over his sharply boned face, the pleasure of it lighting eyes the color of blue shadows.

"Coming along," he said into the silence in a voice gravelly from lack of sleep.

He moved through the dark, following his beam of light, a tall man with narrow hips, the long Montgomery legs, and the waving mass of brown hair with hints of chestnut that came down from the Riley—his maternal side.

He had to remind himself that if he kept poking around he'd have to get up before he got to bed, so he climbed up to the third floor.

"Now that's what I'm talking about." Pure delight scattered thoughts of sleep as he traced a finger down the taped seam of freshly hung drywall.

He played his light over the holes cut out for electric, moved into what would be the innkeeper's apartment, and noted the same for plumbing in the kitchen and bath. He spent more time wandering through what would be their most elaborate suite, nodding approval at the floating wall dividing the generous space in the bath.

"You're a frigging genius, Beck. Now, for God's sake, go home."

But giddy with fatigue and anticipation, he took one more good look before he made his way down the steps.

He heard it as he reached the second floor. A kind of humming— and distinctly female. As the sound reached him, so did the scent. Honeysuckle, sweet and wild and ripe with summer.

His belly did a little dance, but he held the flashlight steady as he swept it down the hall into unfinished guest rooms. He shook his head as both sound and scent drifted away.

"I know you're here." He spoke clearly, and his voice echoed back to him. "And I guess you've been here for a while. We're bringing her back, and then some. She deserves it. I hope to hell you like it when she's done because, well, that's the way it's going to be."

He waited a minute or two, fanciful enough—or tired enough—to imagine whoever, or whatever, inhabited the place settled on a wait-and-see mode.

"Anyway." He shrugged. "We're giving her the best we've got, and we're pretty damn good."

He walked down, noted the work light no longer shone. Beckett turned it on again, switched it back off with another shrug. It wouldn't be the first time the current resident had messed with one of them.

"Good night," he called out, then locked up.

This time he didn't wait for the light, but crossed diagonally. Vesta Pizzeria and Family Restaurant spread over another corner of The Square, with his apartment and office above. He walked down the sloping sidewalk to the back parking lot, grabbed his bag from the cab of his truck. Deciding he'd murder anyone who called him before eight a.m., Beckett unlocked the stairwell, then climbed past the restaurant level to his door.

He didn't bother with the light, but moved by memory and the backwash of streetlights through the apartment. He stripped by the bed, letting the clothes drop.

He flopped facedown on the mattress, and fell asleep thinking of honeysuckle.

THE CELL PHONE he'd left in his jeans pocket went off at six fifty-five.

"Son of a bitch."

He crawled out of bed, over the floor, dug his phone out of the pocket. Realized he was holding his wallet up to his ear when nobody answered.

"Shit."

Dropped the wallet, fumbled out the phone.

"What the hell do you want?"

"Good morning to you, too," Owen responded. "I'm walking out of Sheetz, with coffee and donuts. They've got a new clerk on the morning shift. She's pretty hot."

"I'll kill you with a hammer."

"Then you won't get any coffee and donuts. I'm on my way to the site. Ry should be there already. Morning meeting."

"That's at ten."

"Didn't you read the text I sent you?"

"Which one? I'm gone two days and you sent me a million freaking texts."

"The one that told you we rescheduled for seven fifteen. Put some pants on," Owen suggested and hung up.

"Hell."

He grabbed a two-minute shower, and put some pants on.

The clouds that rolled in overnight had managed to lock the heat in, so stepping outside was like swimming fully dressed through a warm river.

He heard the thump of nail guns, the jingle of music, the whine of saws as he crossed the street. From inside, somebody laughed like a lunatic.

He turned the corner of the building as Owen pulled his truck into the parking lot behind the projected courtyard. The truck gleamed from a recent wash, and the silver toolboxes on the sides of the bed sparkled.

Owen stepped out. Jeans, a white T-shirt tucked into his belt—and on the belt the damn phone that did everything but kiss him good night (and Beckett wasn't taking bets against that)—marginally scuffed work boots. His bark brown hair sat tidily on his head. He'd obviously had time to shave his pretty face, Beckett thought resentfully.

He shot Beckett a grin, and Beckett imagined the eyes behind those bronze lenses were cheerful and alert.

"Give me the damn coffee."

Owen took a tall go-cup, marked with a *B*, from its slot in the tray.

"I didn't get in till three." Beckett took the first, deep, lifesaving gulp.

"Why?"

"I didn't get out of Richmond until close to ten, then I hit a parking lot on 95. And don't, just do *not* tell me I should've checked the traffic report before getting on. Give me a fucking donut."

Owen opened the enormous box, and the smell of yeast, sugar, and fat oozed into the thick air. Beckett grabbed a jelly, wolfed half of it, washed it down with more coffee.

"Pickets are going to look good," Owen said in his easy way. "They're going to be worth the time and money." He cocked his head toward the truck on the other side of his. "Drywall's up on the third floor. They're going to get the second coat of mud on today. Roofers ran out of copper, so they're going to fall a little behind schedule on that, but they're working on the slate until the material comes in."

"I can hear that," Beckett commented as the stone saws shrilled.

Owen continued the updates as they crossed to the lobby door, and the coffee woke up Beckett's brain.

The noise level spiked, but now that Beckett had some sugar and caffeine in his system, it sounded like music. He exchanged greetings with a couple of the crew hanging insulation, then followed Owen through the side arch and into what would be the laundry, and currently served as an on-site office.

Ryder stood scowling down at blueprints spread over a table of plywood on sawhorses. Dumbass, his homely and purehearted mutt—and constant companion—sprawled snoring at his feet.

Until a whiff of donut had his eyes popping open, his scruffy tail thumping. Beckett broke off a bite of donut, tossed it, and the dog nipped it neatly out of the air.

D.A. saw no logical purpose in the fetching of sticks or balls. He concentrated his skills on fielding food of any kind.

"If you're going to ask for another change, I'll kill you instead of Owen."

Ryder only grunted, held out a hand for coffee. "We need to move this panel box, then we can box in this space here, use it for second-floor utility."

Beckett took another donut, considered as Ryder ran through a handful of other changes.

Little tweaks, Beckett thought, that wouldn't hurt and would probably improve. Ryder was, after all, the one of them who lived most intimately with the building. But when Ryder moved to eliminating the coffered dining room ceiling—a thin bone of contention between them—Beckett dug in.

"It goes in, just as on the plans. It makes a statement."

"It doesn't need to make a statement."

"Every room in this place is going to make a statement. The dining room makes one with—among other things, a coffered ceiling. It suits the room, plays off the panels we're making for the side of the windows. The depth of the windows, the ceiling, the arch of stone on the back wall."

"Pain in the ass." Ryder scanned the donuts, opted for a cinnamon twist. He didn't so much as glance toward the madly thumping tail as he tore off the end, flipped it into the air.

D.A.'s teeth snapped together as he caught it.

"How'd it go down in Richmond?"

"The next time I volunteer to design and help build a covered deck for a friend, knock me unconscious."

"Always a pleasure." Ryder grinned around the donut. His hair, a deep dense brown that edged toward black, sprang out from under his paint-stained MFC gimme cap. His eyebrows lifted over eyes of gold-flecked green. "I thought you were mostly doing it to get into Drew's sister's pants."

"It was part of the motivation."

"How'd that go for you?"

"She hooked up with somebody a couple weeks ago, a detail nobody bothered to pass on to me. I never even saw her. So I'm bunked down in Drew's spare room trying to pretend I can't hear him and Jen fighting every damn night, and listening to him complain how she's making his life hell every damn day."

He drained the coffee. "The deck looks good though."

"Now that you're back I could use some help on the built-ins for The Library," Owen told him.

"I've got some catching up to do, but I can give you some time after noon."

"That'll work." Owen handed him a file. "Mom's been down to Bast's," he said, speaking of the furniture store down the street. "Copies of what she's after—with dimensions, and the room they're for. She wants you to draw it up."

"I just did the last batch before I went to Drew's. How fast can she shop?"

"She's meeting Aunt Carolee there tomorrow. They're talking fabrics, so she wants to see if and how what she's got going fits ASAP. You're the one who took off a couple days hoping to get laid," Owen reminded him.

"Struck out, too."

"Shut up, Ry." Beckett tucked the file under his arm. "I'd better get started."

"Don't you want to go up, take a look?"

"I did a walk-through last night."

"At three in the morning?" Owen asked.

"Yeah, at three in the morning. It's looking good."

One of the crew stuck his head in. "Hey, Beck. Ry, the drywaller's got a question up in five."

"Be there in a minute." Ryder pulled a handwritten list off his clipboard, passed it to Owen. "Materials. Go on and order. I want to get the front porch framed in."

"I'll take care of it. Do you need me around here this morning?"

"We've got a few million pickets to prime, a mile or two of insulation to hang, and we're decking the second-story porch, front. What do you think?"

"I think I'll get my tool belt after I order this material."

"I'll swing back through before I head out to the shop this afternoon," Beckett told them, then got out before he ended up with a nail gun in his hand.

❧

AT HOME, HE stuck a mug under his coffee machine, checked the level of the water and beans. While it chomped the beans, he went through the mail Owen had stacked on the kitchen counter. Owen had also left sticky notes, Beckett thought with a shake of his head, listing the times he'd watered the plants. Though he hadn't asked Owen—or anyone—to deal with those little chores while he'd been gone, it didn't surprise him to find them done.

If you were dealing with a flat tire or a nuclear holocaust, you could depend on Owen.

Beckett dumped the junk mail in the recycle bin, took what mail needed attention and the coffee through to his office.

He liked the space, which he'd designed himself when the Montgomery family bought the building a few years before. He had the old desk—a flea market find he'd refinished—facing Main Street. Sitting there, he could study the inn.

He had land just outside of town, and plans for a house he'd designed, barely started, and kept fiddling with. But other projects always bumped it down the line. He couldn't see the hurry, in any case. He was happy enough with his Main Street perch over Vesta. Plus it added the convenience of calling down if he wanted a slice while he worked, or just going downstairs if he wanted food and company.

He could walk to the bank, the barber, to Crawford's if he wanted a hot breakfast or a burger, to the bookstore, the post office. He knew his neighbors, the merchants, the rhythm in Boonsboro. No, no reason to hurry.

He glanced at the file Owen had given him. It was tempting to start right there, see what his mother and aunt had come up with. But he had other work to clear up first.

He spent the next hour paying bills, updating other projects, answering emails he'd neglected when in Richmond.

He checked Ryder's job schedule. Owen insisted they each have an updated copy every week, even though they saw or spoke to each other all the damn time. Mostly on schedule, which, considering the scope of the project, equaled a not-so-minor miracle.

He glanced at his thick white binder, filled with cut sheets, computer copies, schematics—all arranged by room—of the heating and air-conditioning system, the sprinkler system, every tub, toilet, sink, faucet, the lighting, tile patterns, appliances—and the furniture and accessories already selected and approved.

It would be thicker before they were done, so he'd better see what his mother had her eye on. He opened the file, spread out the cut sheets. On each, his mother listed the room the piece was intended for by initials. He knew Ryder and the crew still worked by the numbers they'd assigned to the guest rooms and suites, but he knew J&R— second floor, rear, and one of the two with private entrances and fireplaces—stood for Jane and Rochester.

His mother's concept, and one he liked a lot, had been to name the rooms for romantic couples in literature—with happy endings.

She'd done so for all but the front-facing suite she'd decided to dub The Penthouse.

He studied the bed she wanted, and decided the wooden canopy style would've fit nicely into Thornfield Hall. Then he grinned at the curvy sofa, the fainting couch she'd noted should stand at the foot of the bed.

She'd picked out a dresser, but had listed the alternative of a secretary with drawers. More unique, he decided, more interesting.

And she apparently had her mind made up about a bed for Westley and Buttercup—their second suite, rear—as she'd written THIS IS IT!! in all caps on the sheet.

He scanned the other sheets; she'd been busy. Then turned to his computer.

He spent the next two hours with CAD, arranging, adjusting, angling. From time to time, he opened the binder, refreshed himself on the feel and layout of the baths, or took another look at the electrical, the cable for the flatscreens in each bedroom.

When he was satisfied, he sent his mother the file, with copies to his brothers, and gave her the maximum dimensions for any night tables, occasional chairs.

He wanted a break, and more coffee. Iced coffee, he decided. Iced cappuccino, even better. No reason not to walk down to Turn The Page and get one. They had good coffee at the bookstore, and he'd stretch his legs a little on the short walk down Main.

He ignored the fact that the coffee machine he'd indulged himself in could make cappuccino—and that he had ice. And he told himself he took the time to shave because it was too damn hot for the scruff.

He went out, headed down Main, stopped outside of Sherry's Beauty Salon to talk to Dick while the barber took a break.

"How's it coming?"

"We've got drywall going in," Beckett told him.

"Yeah, I helped them unload some."

"We're going to have to put you on the payroll."

Dick grinned, jerked a chin at the inn. "I like watching it come back."

"Me, too. See you later."

He walked on, and up the short steps to the covered porch of the bookstore, and through the door to a jangle of bells. He lifted a hand in salute to Laurie as the bookseller rang up a sale for a customer. While he waited he wandered to the front-facing stand of bestsellers and new arrivals. He took down the latest John Sandford in paperback—how had he missed that one?—scanned the write-up inside, kept it as he strolled around the stacks.

The shop had an easy, relaxed walk-around feel with its rooms flowing into one another, with the curve of the creaky steps to the second-floor office and storerooms. Trinkets, cards, a few local crafts, some of this, a little of that—and, most of all, books and more books filled shelves, tables, cases in a way that encouraged just browsing around.

Another old building, it had seen war, change, the lean and the fat. Now with its soft colors and old wood floors, it managed to hold on to the sense of the town house it had once been.

It always smelled, to him, of books and women, which made sense since the owner had a fully female staff of full- and part-timers.

He found a just-released Walter Mosley and picked that up as well. Then glancing toward the stairs to the second-floor office, Beckett strolled through the open doorway to the back section of the store. He heard voices, but realized quickly they came from a little girl and a woman she called Mommy.

Clare had boys—three boys now, he thought. Maybe she wasn't even in today, or not coming in until later. Besides, he'd come for coffee, not to see Clare Murphy. Clare Brewster, he reminded himself. She'd been Clare Brewster for ten years, so he ought to be used to it.

Clare Murphy Brewster, he mused, mother of three, bookstore proprietor. Just an old high school friend who'd come home after an Iraqi sniper shattered her life and left her a widow.

He hadn't come to see her, except in passing if she happened to be around. He'd have no business making a *point* to see the widow of a boy he'd gone to school with, had liked, had envied.

"Sorry for the wait. How's it going, Beck?"

"What?" He tuned back in, turned to Laurie as the door jingled behind the customers. "Oh, no problem. Found some books."

"Imagine that," she said, and smiled at him.

"I know, what are the odds? I hope they're as good for me getting an iced cappuccino."

"I can hook you up. Iced everything's the order of the day this summer." Her honey brown hair scooped up with a clip against the heat, she gestured to the cups. "Large?"

"You bet."

"How's the inn coming along?"

"It's moving." He walked to the counter as she turned to the espresso machine.

Pretty little thing, Beckett mused. She'd worked for Clare since the beginning, shuffling work and school. Five years, maybe six? Could it be that long already?

"People ask us all the time," she told him as she worked. "When, when, when, what, how. And especially when you're going to take down that tarp so we can all see for ourselves."

"And spoil the big reveal?"

"It's killing me."

With the conversation, the noise of the machine, he didn't hear her, but sensed her. He looked over as she came down the curve of the steps, one hand trailing along the banister.

When his heart jumped, he thought, Oh well. But then, Clare had been making his heart jump since he'd been sixteen.

"Hi, Beck. I thought I heard you down here."

She smiled, and his heart stopped jumping to fall flat.

CHAPTER TWO

H E HANDLED IT. HE SMILED BACK AT HER, QUICK AND casual, as she walked down the stairs with her long, sunny ponytail swaying. She always reminded him of a sunflower, tall and bright and cheerful. Her gray eyes held hints of green that gave them a sparkle whenever her mouth, with its deep center dip, curved up.

"Haven't seen you in a couple days," she commented.

"I was down in Richmond." She'd gotten some sun, he thought, giving her skin just a hint of gold. "Did I miss anything?"

"Let's see. Somebody stole the garden gnome out of Carol Tecker's yard."

"Jeez. A crime spree."

"She's offering a ten-dollar reward."

"I'll keep my eye out for it."

"Anything new at the inn?"

"We started drywall."

"Old news." She flicked that away. "I got that from Avery yesterday, who got it from Ry when he stopped in for pizza."

"My mother's putting another furniture order together, and she's moving on to fabrics."

"Now *that's* a bulletin." Green sparkled in the gray; it just killed him. "I'd love to see what she's picking out. I know it's going to be beautiful. And I heard a rumor there's going to be a copper tub."

Beckett held up three fingers.

Her eyes widened; the green deepened in the smoky gray. He'd need oxygen any minute.

"Three? Where do you find these things?"

"We have our ways."

She glanced toward Laurie with a long, female sigh. "Imagine lounging in a copper bathtub. It sounds so romantic."

Unfortunately he instantly imagined her slipping out of the pretty summer dress with red poppies over a field of blue—and into a copper bathtub.

And that, he reminded himself, wasn't handling it.

"How are the kids?" he asked, and took out his wallet.

"They're great. We're starting to gear up for full back-to-school mode, so they're excited. Harry's pretending not to be, playing Mr. Old Hat since he's going into third grade. But he and Liam are giving Murphy the benefit of their vast experience. I can't believe my baby's starting kindergarten."

Thinking of the kids always leveled him off, helped him slide her into the do-not-imagine-naked column of MOTHER.

"Oh." She tapped the Mosley book before Laurie bagged it. "I haven't had a chance to read that yet. You'll have to let me know what you think."

"Sure. Ah, you should come over, walk through sometime."

Her mouth bowed up. "We peek in the side windows."

"Just go on around the back."

"Really? I'd like to, but I figured you didn't want people getting in the way."

"As a rule, but——" He broke off as the bells jangled, and two couples came in. "Anyway, I'd better get going."

"Enjoy the book," she told him, then turned to her customers. "Can I help you find anything?"

"We're touring the area," one of the men told her. "Got any books on Antietam?"

"We do. Let me show you." She led him away as the rest of the group started to browse.

Beckett watched her go down the little flight of steps into what they called the annex.

"Well. See you later, Laurie."

"Beck?"

He stopped, one hand on the doorknob.

"Books? Coffee?" She held the bag in one hand, the go-cup in the other.

"Oh yeah." He laughed, shook his head. "Thanks."

"No problem." She sighed a little when he left, and wondered if her boyfriend ever watched her walk away.

CLARE CARTED A tub of books packaged for shipping down to the post office. She breathed in deep a moment as she went out the back and across the gravel parking lot as an actual breeze fluttered over her face.

She thought—hoped—it looked like rain. Maybe a nice, solid soaker that would spare her the time it took to water her garden and pots. If it didn't come with lightning, she could let the boys run around in the wet after dinner, burn off some energy.

Scrub them up afterward, then, since it was movie night, fix some popcorn. She'd have to check the chart, see whose turn it was to pick the flick.

Charts, she'd learned, helped cut down on arguing, complaining, and bickering when three little boys had to decide whether to spend some time with SpongeBob, the Power Rangers, or the *Star Wars* gang. It didn't *eliminate* the arguing, complaining, and bickering, but it usually kept it at a more manageable level.

She dropped off the shipments, spent a few moments chatting with the postmistress. Because the traffic on Route 34 ran a bit thick, she walked back to The Square, pressed the button for the Walk light. And waited.

Every once in a while it struck her that she was, geographically at least, back where she'd started. Everything else had changed, she mused, glancing over at the big blue tarp.

And was still changing.

She'd left Boonsboro as a brand-new bride of nineteen. So young! she thought now. So full of excitement and confidence, so much in love. She'd thought nothing of driving off to North Carolina to start her life with Clint, as an army wife.

She'd done a decent job of it, too, she decided. Setting up house, playing house, working part-time in a bookstore—and hurrying home to fix dinner. She'd learned she was pregnant only days before Clint had been deployed for his first tour to Iraq.

She'd known fear then, she remembered as she crossed toward Vesta. But it had been offset by the wide-eyed optimism of youth, and the joy of carrying a child—one she'd borne back home, at barely twenty.

Then Clint came home, and they were off to Kansas. They'd had nearly a year. Liam had been born during Clint's second tour of duty. When he'd come home again, he'd been a great father to their two little boys, but war had stolen his easy cheer, his quick, rolling laugh.

She hadn't known she was pregnant when she'd kissed him goodbye that last time.

The day they'd handed her the flag from Clint's casket, Murphy quickened for the first time inside her.

And now, she thought as she opened the glass door, she was back home. For good.

She'd timed the visit postlunch, predinner prep. A scatter of people sat at the dark, glossy wood tables, and a family—not locals, she noted—piled into the booth in the far corner. Their curly-headed toddler sprawled over the red cushions, sound asleep.

She lifted her hand in salute to Avery as her friend ladled sauce on dough behind the service counter. At home, Clare walked over to pull herself a glass of lemonade and brought it back to the counter with her.

"I think it's going to rain."

"You said that yesterday."

"Today I mean it."

"Oh, well then. I'll get my umbrella." Avery covered the sauce with shredded mozzarella, layered that with pepperoni, sliced mushrooms, and black olives. Her movements quick and practiced, she opened one of the big ovens behind her and shoved in the pie. She shoveled out another, sliced it.

One of the waitresses swung out of the closed kitchen area, sang out a "Hi, Clare," then carried the pizza and plates to one of the tables.

Avery said, "Whew."

"Busy day?"

"We were slammed from eleven thirty until about a half hour ago."

"Are you on tonight?" Clare asked.

"Wendy called in sick, again, so it looks like I'm pulling a double."

"Sick meaning she made up with her boyfriend again."

"I'd be sick too if I was hooked up with that loser. She makes a damn good pizza." Avery took a bottle of water from under the counter, gestured with it. "But I'm probably going to have to let her go. Kids today?" She rolled her bright blue eyes. "No work ethic."

"I'm trying to remember the name of the guy you were tight with when you got caught hooking school."

"Lance Poffinberger—a momentary lapse. And boy, did I pay for it. Screw up once, just once, and Dad grounded me for a month. Lance works down at Canfield's as a mechanic." Avery wiggled her eyebrows as she took a slug of water. "Mechanics are hot."

"Really?"

"With Lance the exception that proves the rule."

She answered the phone, took an order, pulled out the pizza, sliced it so her waitress could carry the still-bubbling pie to the table.

Clare enjoyed her lemonade and watched Avery work.

They'd been friendly in high school, cocaptains on the cheerleading squad. A bit competitive, but friendly. Then they'd lost touch when Avery went off to college, and Clare had headed shortly after to Fort Bragg with Clint.

They'd reconnected when Clare, pregnant with Murphy and with two boys in tow, had moved back. And Avery, with the red hair and milk white skin of her Scot forebears had just opened her Italian family restaurant.

"Beckett was by earlier."

"Alert the media!"

Clare met sarcasm with a smug smile. "He said I could take a look inside the inn."

"Yeah? Let me finish putting this order together, and we'll go."

"I can't, not now. I have to pick up the kids in . . ." She checked her watch. "An hour. And I've still got some work. Tomorrow? Maybe before things get busy here or at TTP?"

"That's a date. I'll be in around nine to start the ovens and so on. I could slip out about ten."

"Ten it is. I've gotta go. Work, kid pickup, fix dinner, baths, then it's movie night."

"We have some excellent spinach ravioli if you want to cross off the fix-dinner portion."

Clare started to decline, then decided it would be an excellent delivery method of spinach, and save her about forty-five minutes in the kitchen. "Deal. Listen, my parents want the boys for a sleepover on Saturday. How about I fix something that isn't pizza, open a bottle of wine, and we have an adult, female evening."

"I can do that. We could also put on sexy dresses and go out, perhaps find adult males to share the evening."

"We could, but since I'll be spending the bulk of the day at the mall and the outlets browbeating three boys into trying on back-to-school clothes, I'd probably just shoot the first male who spoke to me."

"Girls' night in it is."

"Perfect."

Avery boxed up the takeout herself, put it on Clare's tab.

"Thanks. See you tomorrow."

"Clare," Avery said as Clare walked to the door. "Saturday, I'll bring a second bottle of wine, something gooey for dessert. And my pj's."

"Even better. Who needs a man when you've got a best girl pal?"

Clare laughed as Avery shot a hand in the air.

She stepped out and nearly bumped into Ryder.

"Two out of three," she said. "I saw Beck earlier. Now I just need Owen for the hat trick."

"Heading over to Mom's. He and Beck are working in the shop. I'll give you a ride," he said with a grin. "I just took a dinner order, since Mom says it's too hot to cook."

Clare lifted her bag. "I'm with her. Say hi for me."

"Will do. Looking good, Clare the Fair. Wanna go dancing?"

She shot him grin for grin as she pushed the Walk button on the post. "Sure. Pick me and the boys up at eight."

She got lucky with the timing, and headed across with a wave. She tried to remember the last time a man had asked her to go dancing and meant it.

She just couldn't.

⁓

THE MONTGOMERY WORKSHOP was big as a house and designed to look like one. It boasted a long covered porch—often crowded with projects in various stages—including a couple of battered Adirondack chairs waiting for repair and paint, for two years and counting.

Doors, windows, a couple of sinks, boxes of tile, shingles, plywood, and various and sundry items salvaged from or left over from other jobs mixed together in a rear jut they'd added on when they'd run out of room.

Because the hodgepodge drove him crazy, Owen organized it every few months, then Ryder or Beckett would haul something else in, and dump it wherever.

He knew damn well they did it on purpose.

The main area held table tools, work counters, shelving for supplies, a couple of massive rolling tool chests, stacks of lumber, old mason jars and coffee cans (labeled by Owen) for screws, nails, bolts.

Here, though it would never fully meet Owen's high standards, the men kept at least a semblance of organization.

They worked together well, with music from the ancient stereo recycled from the family home banging out rock, a couple of floor fans blowing the heat around, the table saw buzzing as Beckett fed the next piece of chestnut to the blade.

He liked getting his hands on wood, enjoyed the feel of it, the smell of it. His mother's Lab-retriever mix Cus—short for Atticus—stretched his massive bulk under the table saw for a nap. Cus's brother, Finch, dropped a baseball squeaky toy at Beckett's feet about every ten seconds.

Dumbass lay on his back in a pile of sawdust, feet in the air.

When Beckett turned off the saw, he looked down into Finch's wildly excited eyes. "Do I look like I'm in play mode?"

Finch picked up the ball in his mouth again, spat it on Beckett's boot. Though he knew it only encouraged the endless routine, Beckett snagged the ball, then heaved it out the open front door of the shop.

Finch's chase was a study in mad joy.

"Do you jerk off with that hand?" Ryder asked him.

Beckett wiped the dog slobber on his jeans. "I'm ambidextrous."

He took the next length of chestnut Ryder had measured and marked. And Finch charged back with the ball, dropped it at his feet.

The process continued, Ryder measuring and marking, Beckett cutting, Owen putting the pieces together with wood glue and clamps according to the designs tacked on sheets of plywood.

One set of the two floor-to-ceiling bookshelves that would flank The Library's fireplace stood waiting for sanding, staining, for the lower cabinet doors. Once they'd finished the second, and the fireplace surround, they'd probably tag Owen for the fancy work.

They all had the skills, Beckett thought, but no one would deny Owen was the most meticulous of the three.

He turned off the saw, tossed the ball for the delirious Finch, and noticed it had gone dark outside. Cus rose with a yawn and stretch, leaned against Beckett's leg for a rub before wandering out.

Time to call it, Beckett decided, and got three beers out of the old shop refrigerator. "It's oh-beer-thirty," he announced and walked over to hand bottles off to his brothers.

"I hear that." Ry kicked the ball the dog dropped at his feet out the open window with the same accuracy he'd kicked a football through the goalposts in high school.

With a running leap, Finch soared through after it. Something crashed on the porch.

"Did you see that?" Beckett demanded over his brothers' laughter. "That dog's crazy."

"Damn good jump." Ryder wet his thumb, rubbed it on the side of the bookcase. "That's pretty wood. The chestnut was a good call, Beck."

"It's going to work well with the flooring. The sofa in there needs to be leather," he decided. "Dark, but rich, with lighter leather on the chairs for contrast."

"Whatever. The ceiling lights Mom ordered came in today." Ryder took a pull of his beer.

Owen took out his phone to make a note. "Did you inspect them?"

"I was a little busy."

Owen made another note. "Mark the boxes? Put them in storage?"

"Yeah, yeah. Marked and in the basement at Vesta. The dining room lights—ceiling and sconces—came in, too. Same deal."

"I need the packing slips."

"They're on-site, Nancy."

"We've got to keep the paperwork organized, Jethro."

Finch trotted back in, dropped the ball, banged his tail like a hammer.

"See if he'll do it again," Beckett suggested.

Obliging, Ryder kicked it out the window. The dog sailed after it. Something crashed. Intrigued, Dumbass wandered over, put his paws on the sill. After a moment he tried crawling out.

"I've got to get a dog." Owen sipped his beer as they watched D.A.'s back legs kicking and scrabbling. "I'm getting a dog as soon as we get this job finished."

They closed up, and taking the beer outside, spent another fifteen minutes talking shop, throwing the ball for the indefatigable Finch.

The cicadas and lightning bugs filled the strip of lawn and surrounding woods with sound and sparkles. Now and again, an owl worked up the energy to hoot mournfully. It made Beckett think of other sultry summer nights, with the three of them running around as tirelessly as Finch. With the lights on in the house on the rise as they were now.

When the lights flicked on and off, on and off, it was time to come in—and always too soon.

He'd wondered—and worried a little—about his mother, alone up here in the big house tucked in the woods. When his father had died—and that had been hard—the three of them had basically moved back home. Until she'd booted them out again after a couple months.

Still, for probably another year, at least one of them would find an excuse to spend the night once a week or so. But the simple fact was, she did fine. She had her work, her sister, her friends, her dogs. Justine Montgomery didn't rattle around in the big house. She lived in it.

Ryder nodded toward the house where the porch and kitchen lights— in case they came back in—and their mother's office light shone.

"She's up there, hunting on the Internet for more stuff."

"She's good at it," Beckett said. "And if she didn't spend the time, and have a damn good eye, we'd be chained down doing it."

"You do anyway," Ryder pointed out. "Mister Dark but Rich with Contrast."

"All part of the design work, bro."

"Speaking of which," Owen put in, "we still need the safety lights and exit signs for code."

"I'm looking. We're not putting up ugly." Beckett stuck his hands in his pockets, dug in on the point. "I'll find something that works. I'm going to head out. I can give you most of tomorrow," he told Ryder.

"Bring your tool belt."

❧

HE DROVE HOME with the wind blowing through the truck's open windows. Since the station he had on reached back to his high school days with the Goo Goo Dolls, he thought of Clare.

He took the long way around, driving the back roads in a wide circle. Because he wanted the drive, he told himself, not because that route would take him by Clare's house.

He wasn't a stalker.

He slowed a bit, scanning the little house just inside the town limits, and saw that, like his family home, her kitchen lights were on—front porch and living room, too, he noted.

He couldn't think of an excuse to stop in, not that he would have, but . . .

He imagined her relaxing after a full day, maybe reading a book, watching a little TV. Grabbing a little downtime with the kids tucked in for the night.

He *could* go knock on her door. Hey, just in the neighborhood, saw your lights on. I've got my tools in the truck if you need anything fixed.

Jesus.

He drove on. In his entire history with the female species, Clare Murphy Brewster was the single one of her kind who flustered and flummoxed him.

He was *good* with women, he reminded himself. Probably because he just liked them—the way they looked, sounded, smelled—the strange way their minds worked. Toddler to great-granny, he enjoyed the female for who and what she was.

He'd never been at a loss for what to say around a woman, unless it was Clare. Never second-guessed what he should say, or had said. Unless it was Clare. Never had the hots for without at least making an opening move. Unless it was Clare.

Really, he was better off with somebody like Drew's sister. A woman he found attractive, who liked to flirt, and who didn't make him think or want too much.

Time to put Clare and her appealing boys out of his brain, once and for all.

He pulled into the lot behind his building, looked up at his dark windows.

He should go up, do a little work, then make an early night of it and catch up on some sleep.

Instead, he walked across the street. He'd just do a walk-through, check out what Ry, the crew, and the subs had gotten done that day. He wasn't ready for his own company, he admitted, and the current resident of the inn was better than nothing.

❧

IN CLARE'S HOUSE, the Mighty Morphin Power Rangers waged war against the evil forces. Bombs exploded; Rangers flew, flipped, rolled, and charged. Clare had seen this particular DVD and countless others in the series so often she could time the blasts with her eyes closed.

It did give her the advantage of pretending she was riveted to the action while she worked on her mental checklist. Liam sprawled with his head in her lap. When she peeked over, she saw his eyes were open, but glassy.

Not long now.

Harry lay on the floor, a Red Ranger in his hand. His stillness told her he'd already passed out. But Murphy, her night owl, sat beside her—as alert and as fascinated by the movie as he'd been the first time he'd watched it.

He could, and would, remain up and revved until midnight if she allowed it. She knew damn well when the movie ended, he'd beg for another.

She really needed to pay her personal bills, finish folding the laundry, and throw in another load of towels while she was at it. She needed to start the new book she'd brought home—not just for pleasure, though it was, but because she considered reading an essential part of her job.

Thinking of what she'd yet to check off that mental list made her realize she'd be the one up until midnight.

Her own fault, she reminded herself, for letting the boys talk her into a double feature.

Still, it made them so happy, and gave her the joy of spending an evening snuggled up with her little men.

Laundry would always be there, she thought, but her guys wouldn't always be thrilled to spend the evening with Mom watching a movie at home.

As predicted, the minute good vanquished evil, Murphy sent her an imploring look out of big brown eyes. How odd, she thought, he'd been the only one to inherit Clint's color, and genetics had mixed it with her blond hair.

"Please, Mom! I'm not tired."

"You got two, that's all for you." On the rhyme, she flicked his nose with her finger.

His pretty face with its pug nose and dusting of freckles crumpled into abject misery. "Please! Just one episode."

He sounded like a starving man begging for just one stale crust of bread.

"Murphy, it's already way past bedtime." Now she held up a finger when he opened his mouth. "And if that's a whine about to come out, I'll remember it next movie night. Come on, go up and pee."

"I don't gotta pee."

"Go pee anyway."

He trudged off like a man walking to the hangman's noose while she shifted Liam. She got him up, his head on her shoulder, his body boneless.

And his hair, she thought, the thick golden brown waves she loved, smelling of shampoo. She carried him to the steps, and up, and into the bathroom where I-don't-gotta-pee Murphy sang to himself as he emptied his bladder.

"Leave the seat up, and don't flush it."

"I'm s'posed to. You said."

"Yes, but Liam has to go. Go ahead and get into bed, my baby. I'll be right in."

With the dexterity of experience, Clare stood Liam on his feet, held him upright with one hand, lowered his pj shorts with the other.

"Let's pee, my man."

"'Kay." He swayed, and when he aimed, she had to guide his hand to avoid the prospect of scrubbing down the walls.

She hitched his pants back up, would have guided him to bed, but he turned, held his arms up.

She carried him to the bedroom—the one intended as the master, then laid him on the bottom of one of the two sets of bunks. Murphy lay in the other bottom bunk, curled up with his stuffed Optimus Prime.

"Be right back," she whispered. "I'm going to get Harry."

She repeated the routine with Harry, as far as the bathroom. He'd recently decided Mom was a girl, and girls weren't allowed to be in the bathroom when he peed.

She made sure he was awake enough to stand upright, stepped out. She winced a little as the toilet seat slammed down, waited while it flushed.

He wandered out. "There's blue frogs in the car."

"Hmm." Knowing he dreamed vividly and often, she guided him to bed. "I like blue. Up you go."

"The red one's driving."

"He's probably the oldest."

She kissed his cheek—he was already asleep again—walked over to kiss Liam, then turned and bent down to Murphy. "Close your eyes."

"I'm not tired."

"Close them anyway. Maybe you'll catch up with Harry and the blue frogs. The red one's driving."

"Are there dogs?"

"If you want there to be. Good night."

"'Night. Can we get a dog?"

"Why don't you just dream about one for now."

She gave her boys, her world, a last glance as they lay in the glow of their Spider-Man night-light.

Then she went downstairs to start work on her mental checklist.

Just after midnight, she fell asleep with the book in her hands and the light on. She dreamed of blue frogs and their red driver, purple and green dogs. And oddly, she realized when she woke enough to shut off the light, of Beckett Montgomery smiling at her as she walked down the stairs at her bookstore.

CHAPTER THREE

CLARE PULLED INTO THE GRAVEL PARKING LOT BEHIND
Turn The Page at nine. Since her mother had the boys for the
day—God bless her—Clare had time to work in the quiet before
Laurie came in to open. Shouldering her purse and briefcase, she
crossed over to the back door, unlocked it. She flipped on lights as
she went up the short flight of stairs, through the room where they
stocked sidelines, and through to the front room of the store. She
loved the feel of it, the way one section flowed into the next but
remained distinct.

The minute she'd seen the old town house just off The Square,
she'd known it would be her place. She could still remember the
excitement and nerves when she'd taken that leap of faith. But somehow, investing so much of the lump sum the army provided to the
spouses of the fallen had made Clint part of what she'd done.

What she'd needed to do for herself and her children.

Buying the property, creating the business plan, opening accounts, buying supplies—and books, books, books. Interviewing potential employees, working on the layout. All of the intensity, the stress, the sheer volume of time and effort had helped her cope. Had helped her survive.

She'd thought then, and knew now, the store had saved her. Without it, without the pressure, the work, the focus, she might have shattered and dissolved in those months after Clint's death and before Murphy's birth.

She'd needed to be strong for her boys, for herself. To be strong, she had to have a purpose, a goal—and an income.

Now she had this, she thought as she went behind the front counter to prepare the first pot of coffee of the day. The mom, the military wife—and widow—had built herself into a businesswoman, a proprietor, an employer.

Between her sons and the store the hours were long, the work constant. But she loved it, she mused as she made herself a skinny latte. She loved being busy, had the deep personal satisfaction of knowing she could and did support herself and her kids while adding a solid business to her hometown.

Couldn't have done it without her parents—or without the support and affection of Clint's. Or without friends like Avery, who'd given her commonsense business advice and a wailing wall.

She carried the coffee upstairs, settled down at her desk. She booted up her computer and, because she'd thought of Clint's parents, sent them a quick email with new snapshots of the kids attached before she got to work updating the store's website.

When Laurie came in, Clare called down a good morning. She gave the website a few more minutes before dealing with the rest of the email. After adding a few additional items to a pending order, she headed downstairs where Laurie sat at her computer behind the low wall.

"Got some nice Internet orders overnight. I—" Laurie cocked her brows over chocolate brown eyes. "Hey, you look great today."

"Well, thanks." Pleased, Clare did a little turn in the grass green sundress. "But I can't afford to give you a raise."

"Seriously. You're all glowy."

"Who isn't in this heat? I'm going out, getting my tour of the inn, but I've got my phone if you need me. Otherwise, I'll probably be back in thirty."

"Take your time. And I want details. Oh, you didn't send in that book order to Penguin yet, did you?"

"No, I thought I'd do it when I got back."

"Perfect. Some of these orders take us down to one copy of a couple titles. I'll give you the deets before you send it in."

"Good enough. Need anything while I'm out?"

"Could you box up one of the Montgomery boys?"

Clare smiled as she opened the front door. "No preference?"

"I trust your judgment."

On a laugh, Clare went out, texting Avery as she strolled up toward Vesta. On my way.

Almost instantly Avery came out the restaurant's door. "Me, too," she called out. They stood on opposite corners, waiting for the light— Clare in her breezy sundress, Avery in her black capris and T-shirt.

They met halfway across Main.

"I know damn well you spent half your morning riding herd on three boys, dealing with breakfast, breaking up spats."

"This is my life," Clare agreed.

"How come you look like you never sweat?"

"It's a gift." They started down the sidewalk, ducking under scaffolding. "I always loved this building. Sometimes I'd just look at it out of my office window and imagine it the way it used to be."

"I can't wait to see how it *will* be. If they pull this off, your business and mine, baby, we're going to see a jump for sure. So are the rest of the businesses in town."

"Fingers crossed. We're doing okay, but if we had a nice place for people to stay right in town, boy oh boy. I could lure more authors in, have bigger events. You'd have guests staying here heading over for lunch or dinner."

They stopped a moment at the back, looked over the uneven ground, the planks and rubble. "I wonder what they plan for back here," Avery began. "With those porches, you want something fabulous. Rumors are abundant. A bigger parking lot to an elaborate garden."

"I heard fountain and lap pool."

"Let's ask the source."

When they went inside, into the noise, the clutter of tools, Avery glanced at Clare. "Testosterone level just jumped five hundred points."

"And counting. They've kept the archways." She stepped closer, studying the wide, curved openings ahead and to the left. "I wondered if they could, or would. They're about the only thing I remember from when there was an antiques shop in here. My mother used to come in sometimes."

She moved through the center arch, noted the rough, temporary stairs leading up. "I've never been upstairs. Have you?"

"Snuck in once when we were in high school." Avery studied the steps. "With Travis McDonald, a blanket, and a bottle of Boone's Farm Apple. We made out up there."

"Wild child."

"My dad would've killed me, still would, so no telling. Anyway, it didn't last long. He never made it to second before he got spooked. Doors and floorboards creaking. I wanted to check it out, but he was such a wimp about it. He never did make it to second." She laughed as she started up. "He didn't smell the honeysuckle, either—or never admitted it."

"Honeysuckle?"

"Strong—heady, really—like I had my nose buried in a vine. I guess with all that's going on here now, whoever—you know—walked the night's moved on."

"You believe that? In ghosts?"

"Sure. My great-times-three-grandmother is supposedly still haunting her manor house near Edinburg." Stopping, Avery set her hands on her hips. "Wow. It sure didn't look like this when I kissed Travis McDonald."

Rough-framed doorways led off a hallway on the second level where the smell was dust from wood and drywall. They heard workers above on the third floor, below on the main. Clare stepped into the room on her left. The light, dim and faintly blue from the tarp blocking the front windows, washed over the unfinished floor.

"I wonder which room this is. We should probably find one of the Montgomerys. Oh, look, there'll be a door leading out to the porch. I'd love that."

"Talk about love." Avery gestured. "Look at the size of this bathroom. From the looks of the pipes," she said when Clare joined her, "you've got a tub here, shower over there, double sinks there."

"It's bigger than my bathroom and the boys' combined." Pure and undiluted bathroom envy washed through her. "I could live in here. Could they all be this big? I've got to know which room this is."

She hurried across the bedroom space, and turned through the doorway. And ran straight into Beckett.

His hands came up to steady her. She wondered if she looked as surprised and flustered as he did. Probably more, she imagined, as the hammer slotted in his tool belt probably wasn't jamming into his hip.

"Sorry," they said in unison, and she laughed.

"Me, first. I wasn't looking where I was going. The size of the bathroom in there put stars in my eyes. I was coming to find you."

"Find me?"

"We probably should have before we came up, but everyone seemed so busy. I need to know which room this is before I move in."

"Before you . . . Ha." Jesus, his brain staggered under the scent of her, the feel of her under his hands, the misty lake color of her eyes. "You'd probably like it better when it's finished."

"Paint me a picture."

For a half second he took her literally, and wondered if Owen had picked up the paint yet. Deliberately, he made himself step back. Obviously, his IQ dropped fifty points if he touched her. "Well . . ."

"It's your design."

"Mostly. Oh, hi, Avery."

A laugh danced in her eyes. "I thought I'd swallowed an invisibility pill. I can't believe the transformation here, Beck. The last time I was in here, it had broken windows, broken bricks, pigeons, and ghosts."

"The windows and brick weren't as big a chore as the pigeons, believe me. We've still got the ghost."

"Seriously?"

He winced, adjusted his dusty ball cap. "Don't spread that around, okay? Not until we figure out if she'll be a liability or an asset."

"She. Honeysuckle."

His eyebrows lifted. "Yeah. How do you know?"

"Years ago, brief encounter. It gets cooler and cooler." At his expression, Avery zipped a finger across her lips, then her heart.

"Appreciate it. Anyway, this one's Titania and Oberon."

"The copper tub." With a swish of skirt, Clare beelined for the bathroom space.

"The big-ass copper tub," Beckett confirmed, following her. "Along the wall there. The tiles will accent it, play off it, with coppery and earthy tones. Heated floors. All the baths will have heated tile floors."

"I'm going to cry in a minute."

More at ease, he smiled at Clare. "Shower there. Unframed glass doors, oil-rubbed bronze fixtures. Heated towel rack there, another feature in all the baths. Two copper-vessel sinks, each on this kind of foresty-looking stand, copper drum table between. The lighting picks up the organic feel with a vine pattern. John over there."

"The famed magic toilet," Avery commented. "Word's out on those. It's like a bidet and toilet all in one," she told Clare, "with automatic flush—*and* the lid lifts when you walk up to it."

"Get out."

"At your service." Grinning, Beckett stepped back into the bedroom. "Bed there, facing out into the room. Iron, open-canopy four-poster, in copper and bronze tones with a vine and leaf pattern. She's a beauty."

"Like a bower," Clare murmured.

"That's the plan. We're going to drape it some, or our fabric people are. Dresser there, flatscreen above. Whitewashed nightstands, and these woodsy lamps. We need a bench under the windows, I think. Soft green on the walls, something flowy on the windows— we're doing dark wood blinds throughout for privacy, and we'll work on window treatments. Toss in a few accessories, and that's a wrap."

Clare sighed. "A romantic bower for two, midsummer or midwinter."

"You want to write our brochure copy? I wasn't actually kidding," he said when she laughed.

"Oh." Obviously taken aback, Clare looked around the bare room. "I could help if you—"

"You're hired."

She hesitated, then smiled. "Then you'd better give us a very thorough tour. In stages," she said with a glance at her watch. "I've only got a few more minutes right now."

"I'd really like to see the kitchen space. I can't help it," Avery said. "It's a sickness."

"I'll take you down. We'll work our way up when you've got time," he told Clare.

"Perfect. What's this one?"

He glanced over as they stepped out. "Elizabeth and Darcy."

"Oh, I love *Pride and Prejudice*. What are you—No, no, don't tell me. I'll never get to work."

"Highlights," he said as they started down. "Upholstered head- and footboard, lavender and ivory, white slipper tub, tiles in cream and pale gold."

"Hmm" was Clare's opinion. "Elegant and charming. Miss Bennett and Mr. Darcy would approve."

"You're definitely writing the copy." He turned left at the base of the steps, came up short when he heard Ryder curse from the laundry room.

"Goddamn it."

"It's a problem," Owen responded. "I'll work the problem."

"What problem?" Beckett demanded.

Owen shoved his hands in the pockets of his carpenter jeans. "Karen Abbott's pregnant."

"Didn't your mom ever talk to you about safe sex?" Avery asked, ducking around Beckett's arm.

Owen sent her a bland stare. "Funny. It's Jeff Corver's. They've been seeing each other since Chad started college last year."

"Doing more than seeing," Ryder muttered. "Jesus, she's got to be forty-couple, right? What's she doing getting knocked up at that age?"

"I note you don't question how Jeff Corver could knock her up at his age," Avery added.

"She's forty-three." Owen shrugged. "I know because we've been talking to her about the innkeeper position. We were pretty well set. Now she and Jeff are getting married and picking out baby names."

"Damn it. Well, from our perspective," Beckett said when Clare sent him a disapproving look. "We know Karen, and she and Mom and Owen were working out all the details. Hell, she'd picked out the paint colors for the innkeeper's apartment on the third floor."

"And she had hotel experience," Owen put in. "Working at the Clarion. I'll put some feelers out," he began.

"I know somebody." Avery held up a finger. "I know the perfect somebody. Hope," she said, turning to Clare.

"Yes! She *is* the perfect somebody."

"Hope who?" Owen demanded. "I know everybody, and I don't know the perfect Hope."

"Beaumont, and you met her once, I think, when she was up visiting, but you don't know her. We went to college together, and we stayed pretty tight. She's in D.C., and she's thinking of relocating."

"What makes her perfect?" Ryder asked.

"A degree in hotel management to start, and about seven years' experience at the Wickham—ritzy boutique hotel in Georgetown. The last three as its manager."

"That's too perfect." Ryder shook his head. "What's the catch?"

"No catch with Hope. It's the jerk she was involved with, whose parents own the Wickham. He dumped her for some bimbo with a pedigree and man-made tits."

"She's working out her contract," Clare continued, "and that takes spine. Professional spine. She's looking to move, considering her options."

"From Georgetown to Boonsboro?" Ryder shrugged. "Why would she?"

"Why wouldn't she?" Avery countered.

"Avery and I have been trying to talk her into moving up here, or closer anyway. She likes the area." The more she thought of it, the more Clare wanted it. "She comes up to see Avery now and then, and we got to be friends. We had a girls' weekend at the Wickham last year, and I can personally attest, Hope doesn't miss a trick."

"Do you really think she'd go from managing urban ritz to innkeeper at a small-town B&B?"

Avery smiled at Owen. "I think she might, especially if the rest of this place is going to be as good as Titania and Oberon."

"Give me some more data," Owen began.

"Show me the kitchen space, then you can come over to the shop. I'll give you more, and I'll call her if you want."

"Deal."

"What does she look like?" Ryder called out.

"One of the many reasons Jonathan Wickham is a jerk? Throwing over somebody who looks like Hope, has her brain and energy, for some pinched-nose, big-racked social piranha."

"Confirmed. I've got to get back," Clare told her. "Let me know what Hope says. This would be great." She beamed at Beckett. "Will you be here later? I can probably get back around two or two thirty."

"Sure."

"See you later then. Oh, and you'll be lucky to have Hope if this works out. She really is perfect."

Ryder scowled as she hurried out. "I don't like perfect. Because it never is, but you don't see the trouble until it's too late."

"I've always admired and envied your sunny optimism."

"Optimists never see the boot coming until it kicks their balls into their throat. Optimism is how a forty-three-year-old woman ends up with one kid in college and another in the oven."

"Owen'll fix it. It's what he does."

❧

CLARE MET WITH a sales rep, then chatted with her UPS guy while she signed for a delivery. She loved new shipments, opening the cartons and finding books, the covers that closed in all those stories, all those worlds, all those words.

While shelving, she paused when her phone signaled an incoming text, then smiled at Avery's message.

H will talk to O tmoro. If click H cms up nxt wkend 4 intrvw. :)

She texted back. Fingers X'd.

Wouldn't it be wonderful? she thought. Not only for Hope, but all of them. She'd have a friend right down the street, and another right across. She'd be able to pop over to the inn now and then to see Hope, and all those beautiful rooms. They would be beautiful. She was sure of it now.

Oh! She'd book the Titania and Oberon room for her parents' anniversary next spring. Or maybe Elizabeth and Darcy. A perfect gift, romantic and special. The Montgomerys ought to push that, subtly, in their brochure.

She should make some notes.

She took out her phone to do just that, then tucked it away again when one of her regulars came in with her toddler in tow.

"Hi, Lindsay, hi there, Zoe."

"Need book!"

"Who doesn't?" Charmed, as always, Clare plucked Zoe up, set her on her hip.

"I was a block away," Lindsay said, "and I wasn't going to stop in. But she got so excited, bouncing in the car seat."

"I swear, I'm going to hire her the minute the law allows." Clare kissed Zoe's dark curls as she carried her back to the children's section.

By the time they left—two books for Zoe, one for Mommy, and a pretty plush kitty purse for a niece's birthday—Clare had been filled in on celebrity gossip, town gossip, the niece's mother's recent weight gain, and Mommy's newest diet.

When the door jingled closed, Laurie peeked up from the annex. "I deserted the field."

"I noticed."

"You handle her better than I do. She gives me an earache."

"I don't mind. She just needs to talk to an adult now and again.

Plus she spent more than fifty dollars. Did you take your lunch yet? I can handle things if you want to get out for a bit."

"I brought mine with me. Lindsay's not the only one on a diet. I'm going to eat my measly salad in the back. Cassie just got in. She's getting some net orders together for shipping."

"I'll take the front. I need to go back out about two, but I'll be back before you leave for the day."

"Give a shout if we get busy. One of us'll come out."

She could only hope. The store hadn't exactly bustled with business today. She could use a few more Lindsays before closing, she thought as she got herself a cold drink from the refrigerator.

She carried it into the children's section, tidied up the toys Zoe had played with while her mother had her visit. And thought of Zoe's soft, dark curls.

Clare wouldn't trade her boys for anything in heaven or on earth, but she'd always secretly hoped for a little girl. Pretty dresses, ribbons and bows, Barbies and ballerinas.

And if she'd had a girl, her daughter would probably have turned out to be a tomboy, as into action figures and dirt fights as her brothers.

Maybe Avery would fall in love and end up having a baby girl. Then she could be the doting honorary aunt and finally get to buy all the fuss and flounces.

Now that would be fun, she decided while she tidied books, rearranged stuffed animals. Watching Avery fall in love—the real thing—helping her plan a wedding and on to sharing the excitement of a new baby. Their kids could grow up together. Well, her boys had a head start, but still. Then, *years* from now, Avery's daughter and . . . probably Murphy, considering the ages . . . would fall in love, get married, and give them both gorgeous grandchildren.

Clare laughed to herself, running her finger down the cover of a children's book.

Fairy tales, she mused. She'd always been a sucker for them. And for a happy ending where everything wrapped up as pretty as a bow in a little girl's hair.

Maybe more of a sucker than ever now, she admitted. Now that she'd known real loss. Maybe that's why she just needed to believe in that bright, shiny ribbon tied in a bow around happy ever after.

"Daydreaming about me?"

She jumped at the voice behind her, turned and tried not to wince when she saw Sam Freemont in the doorway.

"Just restoring order." She spoke pleasantly, reminding herself he sometimes actually bought something rather than just pestering her for a date. "I didn't hear the bell."

"I came in the back. You should put some security up, Clare. I worry about you working in this place."

She caught the condescending tone in *this place*, struggled to remain pleasant. "Laurie and Cassie are in the back room—and there's a monitor. In fact," she said deliberately, "they can see us right now. What can I do for you, Sam?"

"It's what I can do for you." He leaned against the framework of the opening. Posing, she noted, in his putty-colored suit—the bold blue tie, she imagined, chosen to play up his eyes. "Got a nice, fat bonus check in my pocket." He patted it, added a wink. "I'll take you to dinner at my club. We can celebrate."

Since he worked—when he chose—for his father's car dealership, and his mother came from old money, she imagined he often had fat checks.

He certainly bragged about money often enough.

"Congratulations, and thanks for the offer. But dinner at the club doesn't work for me."

"You'll love it. I've got the best table in the house."

Always the best, she thought. The biggest, the most expensive. He never changed. "And I'll be at my kitchen table, convincing my three boys to eat their broccoli."

"What you need is an au pair. My mother could help you with that."

"I imagine she could, if I were interested, which I'm not. Now, I need to—"

"I've got some time now. We'll go have a champagne lunch."

"I don't—" The bell jangled on the front door. "Have time. Obviously. Excuse me."

Rather than moving past him, she went out the other doorway to the main room, ready to kiss whoever had interrupted Sam's annoying campaign.

"Justine! I was just over at the inn this morning. Carolee. It's so nice to see you both."

Justine pulled off her red-framed sunglasses, waved a hand in front of her face. "We walked up from Bast. God, the heat! And you look cool and fresh as ice cream—no, lime sherbet—in that dress."

Carolee dropped into one of the chairs at the little table by the windows. "God, I could use some lime sherbet. We're going to treat ourselves to one of your fancy iced coffees."

"Our special this week is Cookie Dough Jo—it's sinful."

"Make it two." Justine dumped her purse on the table, then swung toward the stack. "I didn't know this was out yet." She grabbed a book. "Is this as good as the last one she did?"

"Actually, I think it's even better."

"Well, this stop-by's going to cost me more than the price of sinful coffee." Justine arched her brows at the sound of the back door slamming.

"Sam Freemont, expressing his annoyance. And the coffee's on the house, in gratitude for you bringing the end to his pestering me to go to dinner at the club."

"Sam Freemont's a little prick who grew up to be a bigger one." Carolee's pretty hazel eyes turned hard. "Remember, Justine, how he spread rumors about my Darla? He was after her to go to the prom, and when 'no' didn't work, she finally told him to get lost."

"Or words to that effect," Justine added, and made her sister smile fiercely.

"That's my girl. So, he spread it around she was pregnant, and didn't know who the father was."

"And Ryder kicked his ass. Not that he'd ever admit it," Justine continued, "and my other boys kept the brothers' vow of silence. But I knew, and I bought him this CD player he'd been saving up for. So he knew I knew."

"They've got Riley blood, and Rileys take care of their own. Montgomerys, too." Carolee jabbed a finger in the air. "It's how that Freemont boy was raised. Spoiled rotten. His mother's the worst— never could stand that woman—but his father's just as bad for going along. Anything he wanted, anytime he wanted. And he just lorded it over everybody."

"She got what she deserved, didn't she?" Justine shrugged. "A big prick for a son."

Clare smiled as she started the grinder. Justine Montgomery was exactly what Clare wanted to be when she grew up. Smart, strong, self-aware, an excellent and beloved mother to her sons. An attractive woman with her dark hair scooped up in a sassy tail, the body she kept in excellent shape clad in casual but stylish capris and a thin white shirt.

Carolee, who had stood up to browse with her sister, was pale gold, nearly as tall, delicate in build.

They were bonded like glue, Clare knew.

Justine walked over, set two books on the counter. "You know, honey, Ryder—any of them—would warn Sam off if you said the word."

"Thanks, really, but I can handle him."

"Just keep that in your back pocket. So Owen tells me you and Avery may have a prospect for innkeeper now that Karen's buying baby booties."

"Hope would be amazing. I think the place deserves someone as talented as she is. I only really got the sense of one room—Beckett filled us in on Titania and Oberon this morning. But oh, I'm in love. I can really picture it."

"You and Avery both have good heads on your shoulders, so your recommendation's something I take seriously. That place." She stepped over to look out the glass in the front door. "It's got my heart now. Ours—doesn't it, Carolee?"

"I've never had so much fun in my life. Helping to pick out everything from four-poster beds to soap dishes. We're going to have a smell contest next week."

Clare paused as she added whipped cream to the iced coffee. "Sorry?"

"Scents," Justine explained with a laugh. "You put us on to Joanie—Cedar Ridge Soaps."

"Oh, she's great, isn't she? She did tell me she was going to do your amenities, all locally made. I think that's such a wonderful idea."

"With each room having its own signature scent."

"Now that's a *fabulous* idea. Soaps, shampoos, lotion. Have you thought of doing diffusers?"

Justine narrowed her eyes. "Not until right this minute. Can she do those?"

"She can. I use them at home."

"Carolee—"

"I'm writing it down."

"That does look sinful." Justine took both cups, carried one to her sister. Have you got a minute, Clare?"

"Of course."

"I wanted to talk to you about The Library. We're going to hit the used bookstore for the bulk, I think, but I want to mix in some new. I want romance novels, thrillers, mysteries. The kind of thing somebody might like to read on a rainy day, or curled up in front of the fire on a cold night. Can you put a list together, things you'd recommend?"

"Of course."

"Mix of paperbacks and hardcovers. And some of the local books. Nonfiction on the area. Nobody's got a better spread of those than you. You can put some together now, some closer to the first of the year. Add that to the books for each room. And Beckett said you can get DVDs."

"Absolutely."

"Well, I want DVDs of all the room books, and I'm going to make you a list of what I want us to have on hand for guests. You can add any ideas you have on those, too, if you think of any."

"I will." She grinned at Carolee. "It *is* fun. I'm going back over later, to get a better sense. Beckett asked if I'd help write the brochure copy."

"Did he?"

"If that's all right."

"It's just fine with me." Justine smiled as she licked whipped cream from her fingertip.

CHAPTER FOUR

A RMED WITH A NOTEBOOK SHE'D ALREADY ORGANIZED
and divided, Clare crossed Main Street. Helping out with room
descriptions wouldn't take much time or trouble, but it made her
feel a part of the project. In a minor role. Plus, she'd help select and
supply some of the books and DVDs.

She wondered what the inn's library would look like. Would there
be a fireplace? Oh, she hoped there'd be a fireplace. Maybe, if she
inched her way in, they'd let her help set it up.

She stepped in through the back, into the bangs, buzzes, and
echoes. She heard a voice say "fuck yourself, Mike" in easy, casual
tones—and the answering "I would, but your sister did such a good
job of it last night."

Laughter rolled out just ahead of Beckett.

He stopped, stared at her, then blew out a breath. "Lady in the
house," he called out. "Sorry."

"No problem. I thought there were already ladies in the house."

"Mom and Carolee are checking out the third floor. And they're used to it anyway. So, okay. Ah . . ."

He looked distracted, she realized, and busy. And just a little confused.

"If this isn't a good time, I can—"

"No, just shifting gears. We can start right here."

Relieved she wouldn't have to bottle her excitement for later, she turned a circle.

"Where is here?"

"You're standing in The Lobby—double glass doors where you came in—they'll look out on The Courtyard. Tile floor, nice pattern, with a tile rug centered to highlight the big round table under the chandelier. The light's kind of contemporary and cool, and organic. Looks like white glass pieces that melted. Mom wants big, showy flowers on the table. Couple of slipper chairs there."

"Tell me you're keeping the brick wall exposed."

"Yeah. The chairs, the tile have a French feel to them, straw green upholstery, bronze rivets on the chairs, so it's a blend of rustic and French. Mom's still fiddling with the table for the chairs. Maybe another chair in the corner, and I think we'll need something on the facing wall."

She studied it, tried to get a picture. "A little server, maybe."

"Maybe. Artwork to be determined, but we're going local all the way, and we'll have a list of the art and artists in the room packages, with pricing."

"That's a great idea." He rattled everything off so fast she assumed he was in a hurry. She scribbled down notes as quick as she could, trying to keep pace. "So this is really a pass-through? A place to sit down with a cup of coffee or tea, maybe a glass of wine? You didn't say anything about a desk or counter for check-in, so—"

"That's Reception. Entrance for that'll be right off the sidewalk. I'll take you around. Jog left from here, and into The Lounge." He gestured, vaguely, toward a short hallway. "It's crammed with equipment and materials right now. It's long, a little narrow. It used to be the carriageway."

"A lounge, for . . . lounging?"

"Hanging out. Kind of a contemporary pub feel, I guess. We're going leather sofa and chairs. Big, comfortable, rolling ottomans for the wing chairs. Mom went for yellow."

For the first time, he smiled, seemed to relax.

"I thought Ry was going to have her committed."

"Buttery yellow, buttery leather." She tried to imagine having a yellow leather sofa, thought of the kids. Just couldn't do it. "I bet it's going to be fabulous."

"She and Carolee swear it'll have that upscale pub feel. Some kind of card or game table, with lime green leather club chairs," he continued. "Thirty-two-inch flatscreen. Three ceiling lights—organic feel again—oak leaves. We're still filling in the details."

"I can't believe how far ahead you are, and how you can furnish a place when it's still under construction." She scribbled in her notebook as she spoke. "I should've known Justine wouldn't go for chintz and gingham."

"She wants a jewel, every facet sharp and shiny. We're going to give it to her."

Struck, Clare looked up. "It's nice, the way you are. All of you. It's what I want for me and my boys. The affection, the teamwork, the understanding."

"I've seen you with your boys. I'd say you already have what you want."

"Some days I feel like the ringmaster in a three-ring circus inhabited by demons. I imagine your mother felt the same."

"I think if you asked her, she'd say she still does."

"Comforting and scary at the same time."

Yes, he looked busy, distracted—and flat-out sexy on top of it.

But she'd been wrong about the confused. He knew every sharp and shiny facet of the jewel they were creating.

She remembered she'd dreamed about him one night not long ago, and, flustered, turned away.

"What's down there?"

"The ADA room and the front entrance to the dining room."

"Which one's the ADA room?"

"Marguerite and Percy."

"*Scarlet Pimpernel*. Speaking of French." She flipped through the notebook. Tilting his head, Beckett noted she'd headed sections with the room names. "Can I see it?"

"You can try. It's got material stacked in it, too. It's the smallest," he said as he led her down the short hall. "We had to work with the footprint of the building, and the ADA code. Going with two full-sized beds, night table between, with this great old ornate lamp that was my grandmother's."

"You're putting family things in here?"

"Here and there when they work. Mom wants to."

"I think that's lovely, and special. The beds go in front of the windows?"

"Right. Cane headboards, and we'll dress up behind them with treatments—for style and privacy. Cane benches with fancy fabric pads at the feet, fancy bedskirts. Some sort of big, ornate mirror for this wall as you come in. Cream walls and crown molding, soft blue ceiling."

"A blue ceiling." For some reason it struck her wonderfully romantic. She wondered why she'd never thought of painting her ceilings anything other than flat white.

She supposed she'd forgotten how to be romantic.

"It sounds very French. I never asked what you're doing as far as dressing the beds."

"After considerable, occasionally heated debate, we're going with high-end sheets—white or what is it, ecru, depending on the room. Down alternative, all-weather duvet—covered by another sheet rather than spread or quilts or whatever. Lots of pillows, with neutral-tone linen shams, possibly a bedroll, and cashmere throw things."

"Cashmere throws? I'm so booking a room. Peacock feathers."

"Is that some sort of curse?"

"There should be peacock feathers somewhere. I know they're supposed to be bad luck, but they just feel French, and opulent."

"Note to self. Peacock feathers. It's the most problematic space, but I think it's going to turn out."

"I love it already. Where's the bath?" She managed to step in, over buckets, some lumber.

"Watch your step," he warned, taking her arm. "No tub, but a big luxury shower. We'll do the rain head, the body jets—ORB."

"Orb?"

"Sorry. Oil-rubbed bronze. All the public areas have that accent. Crystal vessel bowl sink on an iron bracket. It's big and it's beautiful. Cream and pale gold tiles, fleur-de-lis accents."

"Mais oui," she said and made him grin.

"I found some iron wall shelves, scrolled. The code and the space equal some limitations."

"That is not good copy. Something more like 'special needs meet spectacular comfort. The grandeur of a bygone age with all the comforts—no, pleasures. All the pleasures of today.'"

She started to make more notes, backed up a step, rapped into a stack of paint cans.

"Careful." He wrapped an arm around her waist to steady her as she grabbed his arm to keep from overbalancing.

For the second time that day they stood close, bodies brushing, eyes locked. But this time the light was dim, filtered through the blue tarp. Something near to moonlight.

Being held, she thought, a little dazed. She was being held by a man, by Beckett, and in a way that didn't feel friendly or helpful. In a way that made something coil inside her, a long, slow wind.

Something that felt exactly like lust.

It spread in a swamping wave as she watched his gaze slide down to her mouth, hold there. She smelled honeysuckle. Moonlight and honeysuckle.

Yearning, she eased closer, imagining that first touch, that first taste, that first—

His gaze snapped back to hers, jolted her out of what seemed like some strange dream.

My God, she'd nearly—

"I need to get back." She didn't squeak it out, but she knew it was damn close. "I have the . . . the thing to do."

"Me, too." He stepped back like a man moving cautiously away from a live wire. "I have the thing."

"Okay, well." She got out, out of the room with its false moonlight and air that had so suddenly smelled of wild summer vines. "So."

"So." He slid his hands into his pockets.

Safer there, she imagined, or she might jump him again.

"I'll play around with some ideas for the rooms I've seen."

"That'd be great. Listen, I can let you have the binder. We have a binder with cut sheets and photos of lighting and furniture, bath fixtures, like that. The one here has to stay on-site, but I have one at my place you could borrow for a couple days."

"Okay." She took a breath, settled a bit more. "I'd love to look through it."

"I can drop it off at the bookstore, or by your place sometime."

"Either's fine."

"And you can come back, when you've got time, if you want to go through more of the space. If I'm not around, Owen or Ry could take you through."

"Good, that's good. Well, I'd better go. My mother's going to drop the boys off at the store in a little while, and I still have . . . things."

"I'll see you."

"Yeah."

He watched her go, waited for the door to close behind her with his hands still in his pockets, and balled into fists. "Idiot," he muttered. "You're a goddamn idiot."

He'd scared her so she could barely look at him, so she couldn't wait to get away from him. All because he'd wanted—just wanted.

His mother liked to say, to him, to his brothers, they were old enough so their wants wouldn't hurt them.

But they did. This kind of want left a jagged hole in the gut.

He'd stay away from her for a few days, until those jags smoothed out. And until she felt easier around him again. He'd have one of the men run the binder over to her—keep clear.

His wants might hurt, but he was old enough to control them.

He caught the scent of honeysuckle again and, he swore, the faintest whisper of a woman's laugh.

"Don't you start on me."

Annoyed, he clomped upstairs to harass the crew.

❧

NOT READY TO face the bookstore and her staff, Clare bolted to Vesta. Behind the counter, layering cheese on a pie, Franny, Avery's second in command, shot her a smile.

"Hey, Clare. Where are my boyfriends?"

"With my mom. Is Avery here?"

"In the back. Is something wrong?"

God, how did she look? "No, nothing. Just . . . just want a minute with the boss."

Striving for casual, Clare strolled around to the closed kitchen area where Avery cut fresh dough into tins for rising. Steve, the dishwasher, rattled around at the big double sink, and one of the waitstaff grabbed glassware from the wire shelves.

"I need to talk to you when you have a minute."

"Talk. I'm not using my ears for anything right now." Then Avery glanced over, saw Clare's face. "Oh. *Talk.* Give me five. Go grab something cold out of the cooler for both of us. I need to get some supplies from downstairs anyway."

"I'll just go down and wait."

She grabbed a couple of ginger ales and went out the door to the back stairwell. Outside again, and under the building—she could hear people talking and laughing on the porch above—and into the sprawling, low-ceilinged basement with its stacked cases of soft drinks, bottled beer, wine.

Cooler, she thought. Cooler here. And opened the ginger ale to drink long and deep.

Moonlight and honeysuckle, she thought in disgust. Just another fairy tale with her. She was a grown woman, a mother of three. She *knew* better.

But really, had she ever noticed, *really* noticed, how strong and wonderfully shaped Beckett's mouth was? Gorgeous—she knew that, too. All the Montgomerys were, but had she ever noticed how deeply blue his eyes were in the moonlight?

"There wasn't any moonlight, you idiot. It was an unfinished room crowded with paint cans and lumber and tarps. For God's sake."

She'd gotten caught up in the romance of it, that's all. Buttery leather, blue ceilings, peacock feathers, and cashmere throws.

It was all so fanciful, so outside her own reality of practical, affordable, childproof. And it wasn't as if she'd actually done anything. Wanting to for a minute wasn't doing.

She paced, then whipped around when the door opened.

"What's up?" Avery demanded. "You look like the town cops are hot on your trail."

"I almost kissed Beckett."

"They can't arrest you for that." Avery took the unopened can of ginger ale. "How, where, and why almost?"

"I went over to see a few more rooms, and we were in Marguerite and Percy—"

"Ooh-la-la."

"Cut it out, Avery. I'm serious."

"I can see that, sweetie, but almost kissing a very attractive, available man who's got the hots for you doesn't rate disaster status."

"He doesn't have the hots for me."

Avery drank, shook her head. "I beg to differ, most strongly. But do go on."

"It was just . . . There was all this stuff in there, and I bumped into something, tripped a little, and he reached out to steady me."

"By which part?"

Clare tipped her head back, stared at the ceiling. "Why am I talking to you?"

"Who else? But really, which part? Did he take your hand, your arm, your ass?"

"My waist. He put an arm around my waist, and I . . . I don't know, exactly, but then we were there, and his mouth was there, and that funny light, and honeysuckle."

"Honeysuckle?" Avery's face lit up. "You saw the ghost."

"I did not, first because there are no ghosts."

"You're the one who smelled honeysuckle."

"I only thought I did. I just got caught up. Romantic room—or it will be, the way he described it, the light, and I felt . . . I felt what I haven't felt in a long, long time. I didn't think, I just leaned in."

"You said almost."

"Because just before contact, he looked at me like I'd kicked him in the balls. Just stunned." Even now, with Avery, mortification and that sneaky wave of lust flooded her. "And I stopped, and we both made excuses. After, he kept his distance, like I was radioactive. I embarrassed him, and myself."

"I'll tell you what I think. I think if you'd followed through, neither of you would've been embarrassed, and instead of running over here looking as if you'd mugged an old lady, you'd have danced over singing."

Really, *really*, why was she talking to Avery about this?

"First, Beckett's a friend, just a— No, first, I don't have room for dancing and singing. My priorities are my boys and my business."

"Which is as it should be, and which—as I've said before—in no way precludes what we'll now call dancing and singing." The teasing smile gone, Avery rubbed a hand on Clare's arm. "Jesus, Clare, that part of your life's not over. You've got a right to sing and dance, especially with someone you like and trust. You felt something, and that's significant."

"Maybe. But now that I'm thinking again, I really think it was just that false romance. The room in my head, the light, the imaginary scent, and being touched. It'll be all right," she decided. "Beckett's not the sort to take it too seriously. It was all so quick, he's probably already forgotten it."

Avery started to speak, then decided to keep her opinion to herself. For now.

"Anyway, the rooms are going to be fabulous, and he's lending me the binder with cut sheets and pictures. I'll be able to pump it up to Hope when she comes up. Honestly, Avery, she'd have to be crazy not to jump at the chance to work there."

"I bet," Avery said, and thought she had a couple of crazy friends.

⁓

BECKETT DECIDED TO give Clare a little time, a little space, so she wouldn't think *he* thought anything about what he supposed he'd call The Moment. He sent his copy of the project binder over to the bookstore with one of the crew and the message he'd pick it up there in a couple of days—no hurry.

He skipped his traditional stop-in for coffee for a few mornings, and split his workdays between the inn and another project in nearby Sharpsburg. By the time he made it back to Boonsboro, the crew had knocked off for the day, and his brothers were locking up.

"Just in time." Ryder strolled over with D.A. at his heels. "We're heading across the street for a meeting over beer and pizza."

"My favorite kind of meeting. You talked to Avery's friend?" he asked Owen.

"Yeah. If you want the details, you can buy the beer."

"I bought the beer the last time."

"*I* bought the beer the last time," Ryder corrected.

"He bought the beer the last time." Owen jerked a thumb at Ryder.

"Maybe." Beckett tried to think back as they made their way down the sidewalk under the scaffolding. "When's the last time you bought the beer?"

Owen gave him a satisfied smile, tipped down his sunglasses. "I'm excused for six turns since I scored the man lift. I've got two more left."

He remembered the agreement struck when Owen had negotiated an excellent deal on a used lift. The machine saved them the time and sweat to warrant it. He started to question, then let it go. If Owen said he had two more rounds clear, Owen had two more rounds.

Beckett glanced down toward Turn The Page as they crossed the street, half listening to his brothers discuss water heaters. He should probably give it one more day, he considered. Stay clear, give her time to go through the binder, keep it all easy, friendly.

As if The Moment hadn't happened.

But it had. It damn well had.

"Have you got a problem with that setup?" Ryder demanded.

"What? No."

"Then stop looking pissed off." Ryder secured the dog beside the front porch of the restaurant. "I'll bring you dinner," he said, then pulled open the door.

They stepped into Vesta at the early-dinner hour. Families and small packs of teenagers crowded in the booths, a few couples scattered at two-tops twirling pasta or studying the menu while two regulars sat on stools at the counter for an after-work beer.

Along with his brothers, Beckett exchanged hails and waves.

"Order me a Heineken," Owen said, then peeled off toward the closed kitchen.

"Let's sit in the back," Ryder suggested. "If we sit out here, we'll end up talking to everybody."

"Fine." Beckett hooked a waitress, ordered the beer, then walked down the hallway to the back dining room. A couple of high school boys competed on the video games with the requisite insults.

"The tile's shipped," Ryder said when Beckett joined him at a table. "Or most of it. A couple of the patterns are still on back order. We're scheduling the delivery in two weeks. Owen contacted them about the install. They can start the end of the next week if the job they're on stays on schedule. Early the following if not."

"That's good for us."

"I want to schedule the install of the rest of the flooring right behind it. This heat's bound to break. We can put the crew back on the pickets, get the exterior painting started."

Owen slipped in beside them right as the beer arrived.

"You all ready to order?" the waitress asked.

"Warrior's pizza," Ryder declared.

"I'm not eating that much meat." Owen shook his head, sipped his beer.

"Wimp."

"You go for the super-artery-clogger," Beckett suggested, then looked at Owen. "Split a large pepperoni and jalapeno?"

"Deal. And some crab balls."

"Gotcha. How are things going at the inn?"

"We're moving along," Owen told her.

She pointed her pencil at him. "Are you going to take that tarp down soon?"

"Sooner or later."

"It's a big tease." She rolled her eyes and went off to put their order in.

"You know that tarp's building a lot of expectation we may not meet."

Ryder shrugged at Beckett. "It's also keeping debris off the street, and the crew out of the worst of the heat. Tell him about the Urban Princess."

"Hope Beaumont," Owen began. "She's smart, savvy. She asked all the right questions, including a lot I hadn't thought of, or we haven't gotten around to dealing with. She's got a sexy voice, one of those dark velvet jobs. Nice."

"Sexy voice. She's hired." Ryder sat back with his beer.

"You're just jacked because we may have to go outside for the job."

"It'd be nice to keep it all local," Beckett mused. "But we need somebody who fits the bill. Besides, if she takes the job and moves here, she'll be local in ten or twenty years."

"We'll know more after Saturday. We're meeting with her Saturday morning," Owen continued. "Taking her through the place. I looked her up online." He took files out of his briefcase, passed one to each brother. "Some D.C. society stuff—her out and about with the guy who dumped her. A solid article in the *Washingtonian* about the hotel, with some stuff about her, some quotes. Ry's dubbed her Urban Princess because she's from Philadelphia originally and won a couple of beauty pageant deals back there."

Beckett started to open the file, take a look, when the sound of running feet boomed down the hall. Clare's three boys burst in like convicts on the lam. Breathless, wild-eyed, they chattered about the Mega-Touch before Harry spotted the brothers.

"Hi! Hi! We all got a dollar."

"How about a loan?"

Liam cracked up at Beckett's question. "We get to have pizza and play games."

Murphy walked up to the table, studied the three men. "You can play if you've got a dollar. Or I can ask my mom to give you one."

Because the kid slayed him, Beckett hoisted Murphy onto his lap. "I bet Owen's got a dollar. Why don't we . . ." He stumbled to a halt when Clare came in.

She looked a little flushed, a little frazzled.

"Sorry. They're slippery as soap. You're talking business," she said, noting the files. "Why don't I just move them out until—"

"Mom!" Harry's response was absolute and horrified betrayal.

"When you sit back here, you expect some noise," Ryder pointed out. "They're fine. Have a seat."

"I was just telling Beck that your friend is meeting with us on Saturday," Owen began.

"Avery just told me, which is why in that two-second window, the trio escaped."

"How's the copy coming?"

"I've got some ideas."

"She's got great ideas," Avery confirmed as she came in. "She's run some by me."

"Just bits and pieces. I'd like to see a little more, get the feel."

"You should go over now. Beckett, you should take her over now."

"Avery," Clare muttered, trying to disguise the shock.

"No, really. It's empty. It's got to be easier and more productive to look at it without the banging." She smiled, winsomely. "Don't you think?"

"Sure." Murphy deserted Beckett to join his brothers in a three-player game. And now he didn't know what to do with his hands. "Yeah, sure."

"I'm interrupting, and I have the boys."

"We'll watch them. I'll get their pizza ordered." Avery made a shooing motion. "This way we can run your ideas by Hope when she drives up tomorrow. Let me have your seat, Beck, and no charge for the beer. I'll finish it." She picked it up, took a sip, smiled. "I'm not working tonight."

Out of choices, Beckett got to his feet. "Okay?"

"Apparently." Clare shot Avery a cool look before she turned. "I'm going with Beckett for a few minutes," she told her sons. "Avery, Ryder, and Owen are in charge. Behave."

"Okay, Mom, okay." Harry's face was fierce as he focused on the screen.

She and Beckett walked through and out of the restaurant together. The wind streamed through her hair as she looked up at the clouds rolling in.

"Storm's coming," she said.

CHAPTER FIVE

CAREFUL TO KEEP A FOOT OF SPACE BETWEEN THEM AND
his hands in his pockets, Beckett led her around the back of the
inn to unlock the door.

The late summer evening had gone gloomy, so he switched on bare
bulbs and work lights as they went. Glare and shadows, he thought,
bare walls and concrete floors. Not exactly a seduction pit. She should
feel safe.

"Do you want to finish up the main floor?" he asked her.

"I'd like to see some more guest rooms. Maybe we could go
through the second level. I don't want to stick Avery and your brothers with the kids for too long."

"You didn't stick. Avery volunteered."

"Yes, she did, didn't she?"

Beckett raised his eyebrows at the dark tone. "Is everything okay?"

"Why wouldn't it be?"

"Okay then." He headed toward the stairs. "We did T&O and E&D," he began. "I guess we'll move on to N&N—Nick and Nora."

"*The Thin Man.*" She ordered her thoughts, aimed them toward the binder he'd loaned her. "I like the lamps you've got for there, and the bed and dresser are beautiful—and very Deco."

"A little sleek, a little glamorous." He made the turn down the hall of the second floor. "So, The Library'll be down there, and—"

"Oh, The Library. I really want to see that space."

"Sure." He turned left down another short hallway, flicked a switch for the work light.

"Pretty dim right now. It's only got the one front-facing window. We'll put a desk there. Built-ins—the bookcases—in those recesses, fireplace with surround between, brown leather sofa facing."

She wandered through. She'd seen his sketch of the bookcases, she remembered, and lusted for them.

Don't think about lust!

"Ah, you and your brothers are building the bookcases."

"Yeah, and the fireplace surround. A few other things."

"It must be satisfying to be able to build something."

"You should know. You built a family," he said when she glanced back at him.

"That's a nice thing to say." She studied him as he stood in the doorway and she in the center of the room. This, she decided, this *space* between them was too weird, too uncomfortable.

Time to fix it, she told herself.

"I can't figure it out."

"Figure what?"

"If you're annoyed with me, avoiding me, or if I'm imagining one or both."

"I don't know what you mean."

"You haven't been in the bookstore since . . . I was here last. And like right now, you're standing as far away as you can manage and be in the same room. Look, Beckett, I'm sorry about what happened, even though it didn't happen."

"You're sorry about what didn't happen," he said slowly.

"Well, for God's sake, I just got caught up in the room and the light, and . . . whatever. It was only a moment, so—"

"The."

"What?"

"Never mind. You're apologizing to me for what happened?"

"And I don't know why I should when it didn't." Temper surged in, only highlighting embarrassment. "I don't know why two adults can't handle something that didn't happen without acting like it did. And even if it had, so what? Oh, never mind," she snapped when he simply stared at her. "Just show me the next room." She stalked toward the doorway. "I need to get back."

"Wait a minute." He took her arm, effectively wedging them both in the open doorway. "Are you sorry it didn't happen?"

"I don't like embarrassing myself."

"I embarrassed you?"

"No." She shook her head. "Now you're confusing me."

Maybe. But she was clearing things up for him. "Why don't we start over?"

Lightning flashed, a bold burst of blue through the tarped window. She jolted in his hold as thunder boomed its cannon fire.

"It's only thunder."

"It just startled me," she said, her eyes on his. "I'm not afraid of storms."

"Let's see."

Still, he moved slowly, taking his time as much to prolong this new moment as to gauge her reaction. He laid his hands on her hips as the rain beat and splashed, sliding them up her body, smooth and easy as he lowered his head, paused—one long breath—then fit his mouth to hers.

This, he thought as he took her face in his hands. Just this, so worth the wait. Soft, sweet, a yielding tremor, and her arms came up to wrap around his waist, to draw him into her.

The next flash of lightning didn't make her jolt. She rolled with the thunder, sinking into that lovely flood of pleasure.

Being held, being touched. Tasted and tasting. Nerve endings coated dull by circumstance, by obligation, snapped hot and sharp to life.

She fisted her hands in the back of his shirt and took what he gave her. No, she'd never been afraid of storms.

Even when he eased back she felt buffeted, wonderfully, by the whirlwind.

"I've been waiting to do that since you were sixteen," he murmured.

She smiled, gave a half laugh. "Come on."

"Okay, since you were fifteen, but that seemed pathetic."

Her eyebrows drew together. "I don't know what to say."

"Why don't I give you more time to think about it?"

He kissed her again, stealing her breath, shooting bolts of heat and ice along those newly awakened nerves.

Think? Impossible.

"Beckett." She nudged him back, just a little. "I'm out of practice. I probably do need to think—should think—but it's hard right here and now."

"How about anywhere and anytime?"

She laughed again, not so steadily. "Maybe if—" She broke off, frowning as she leaned in to sniff his shoulder. "It's not you."

"What?"

"I could swear I smell honeysuckle."

"She likes honeysuckle." He smoothed a hand down her ponytail, something else he'd wanted to do for years. It ran against his skin like sunny silk.

"Who does?"

"Elizabeth. I call her Elizabeth because the first time I was sure she was here, I was in E&D—Elizabeth and Darcy."

"You're seriously talking about a ghost."

"This building—or parts of it—has been here for two and a half centuries. It would strike me odder if there wasn't a ghost. Not everything, everyone, leaves."

That cut straight to her heart, but she only shook her head. "Everything about this strikes me as odd. My kids are over playing video games, and I'm here, with you. I should get back. At this rate it's going to take me a year to see the whole building."

"All the time you want. Come out with me tomorrow night."

"I . . . I can't. I'm having Avery and Hope over for dinner. And before you ask, because I hope you were going to, Saturday I promised the kids a movie marathon. They start school on Monday, and Murphy's starting kindergarten. It's a big deal."

"Sure it is. Soon then. Say when."

"Maybe next Friday. If I can get a sitter."

"Next Friday." He kissed her, lightly, to seal it. "Don't change your mind."

She stepped away because she wanted to step toward. "Sorry, but the kids. I don't even know how long we've been gone. It got fuzzy."

"Not that long." He took her hand to draw her down the hall.

"It's dreamy here," she began. "I can, if I think about it, layer image over image. It's the strangest thing, the way I could picture the rooms when you talked about them, even before I looked through the binder. I should've brought it with me. I have it at the bookstore."

"I could use it. How about we run down and get it?"

"Ah—"

"Hang on." He pulled out his phone as they crossed the main level to the back door. He let them out, relocked, then stood, sheltered with her by the floor of the overhead porch as he called Ryder.

"Hey, kids okay?"

"Yeah, no problem. We sold the older two for twenty each to a traveling circus. Let the runt go for a six-pack. Good deal."

"We'll be about five more minutes."

"Okay by me. They ate your pizza, man. The runt went for the jalapenos like candy."

"Hold on. What do you like on your pizza?"

"I was going to have a salad." When he just stared at her with those deep blue eyes, she sighed. "Just pepperoni works for me."

"Order up a pepperoni," he told Ryder. "Five."

He clicked off, took her hand again. "I'll buy you a pizza, a traditional first date. Your kids ate mine."

"Oh, I'm sorry."

"I'm not. It's giving me the first date. Rain's slowed down. You can give me the bookstore keys, head right over."

"I don't mind a little rain. Plus it'll be easier and quicker if I get it. I know just where it is."

They circled the building. "Did you know Murphy likes jalapenos?"

"He'll eat anything." She laughed when Beckett made a dash for it, pulling her along. Laughed when the rain cooled her skin, dampened her hair. "Beckett? This is already a really nice first date."

BECKETT DOUBTED A traditional first date included a trio of kids begging for quarters, his brothers and the owner of the restaurant playing chaperone—and video games—and people dropping by the now-sprawling table to catch up on news or ask about the inn.

But it suited him fine.

Plus the casual, crowded circumstance would keep everybody from speculating. He didn't mind town gossip; hell, it was part of the fuel that ran the engine. He'd just as soon not have his personal life discussed over breakfast at Crawford's or scooped up like a banana split at The Creamery.

He and his brothers put business on hold until Clare packed her kids up.

"One more game. Please!" Liam, the designated negotiator, put on his best begging face. "Just *one* more, Mom. We're not tired."

"I'm tired. And I'm out of quarters, plus you have to pay off your current debt cleaning your room tomorrow."

She watched his eyes slide toward the Montgomerys and narrowed her own. "Don't you even think about tapping that source again."

"Sorry, pal." Beckett lifted his hands. "Nobody bucks a mom."

"Aw, come on," Liam began before his mother's eyes narrowed a bit more.

"I think you meant to say something else to Beckett, and to Ryder and Owen, and Avery."

He sighed, hugely. "Thanks for the quarters and the pizza and stuff."

"I'll take you down in Space Crusader next time around, shortie," Ryder told him, and Liam brightened with the challenge.

"No way! I'm taking *you* down."

"Come on, troops." Avery pushed to her feet. "I'll walk out with you."

After a chorus of 'byes and thanks, and some foot dragging, Clare wrangled the boys to the stairwell door.

When the noise level dropped, Owen reached for his briefcase, where he'd stashed the files again.

"Hold on," Ryder told him. "Let's take this up to Beck's. God knows who else might drop by and challenge us to a few rounds of Monster Bash."

"Good idea." Owen rose, pointed at Beckett. "Go pay the tab."

"Hey."

"I called it first. We'll meet you up there."

By the time he made it up, his brothers—both had keys—had raided his kitchen for beer and chips before making themselves comfortable in his living room.

D.A. lounged on the floor enjoying leftover pizza.

Ryder sent Beckett a slow smile. "So, you're hitting on Clare the Fair."

"I'm not hitting on her. I'm exploring the possibility of seeing her on social terms."

"He's hitting on her," Owen said around a mouthful of chips. "You've still got that thing you had for her back in high school. Are you still writing bad song lyrics about heartbreak?"

"Suck me. And they weren't that bad."

"Yeah, they were," Ryder disagreed. "But at least now we don't have to listen to you playing your keyboard and howling them out down the hall. You have noticed she comes with three additions."

"It's come to my attention. So what?"

"Just checking. I like them. They're not brats or robots."

Beckett dropped down in a chair, picked up the beer his brothers had set out for him. "I'm taking her out next week. I figure dinner and maybe a movie."

"Old school," was Ryder's opinion. "Predictable."

"Maybe, but I think old school and predictable may be what's called for. I get the feeling she hasn't dated much since she came back to Boonsboro."

"Ask Avery. They're tight as spandex."

Beckett gave Owen a considering nod. "Maybe I will."

"I'd skip the movie and just go for dinner, the kind of place where they're not looking to turn your table in an hour. More face time."

"Might be better," Beckett agreed.

"Now that we've helped launch Beck's love life, can we get down to it?"

In response to Ryder, Owen pulled out the files on Hope again. "You can check her out whenever, get a little background before we meet with her. If she lives up to the hype, she'd be a real asset. Next deal." He tossed out brochures. "We have to settle on the gas logs for Reception, and the gas fireplaces for J&R, W&B and The Library. Thompson's is going to come in, take another look, and we'll talk about where to bury the tank, how to run the lines. That's set for Monday. We're going to meet about The Courtyard—the pavers, the design, and how to deal with accessing the tank, the fencing, the plantings, the whole shot. That's for Tuesday."

"I've been working on that some," Beckett said.

"Which is why you need to be there. Tuesday, four o'clock. Mom and Carolee are in on that, too."

"We've got to deal with some practicalities," Ryder put in. "Like how we're going to set all the HVAC units, and getting them in, set, inspected, and passed before cold weather sets in."

"Yeah, we do. And that's why you need to meet with Mike at Care Services next week. We've got down-the-line details to start. And I'll be meeting with Luther about the railings. But we have to settle on the design and the finish. Then there's the design for the entrance doors," Owen continued.

They divvied up work areas, merged some. Then got into a long, protracted argument over mechanics, which required shifting to Beckett's office and studying blueprints.

By the time Beckett booted his brothers out the door, he figured he could re-create the blueprints—structural and mechanical—in his sleep.

And really, for one night, all he wanted to do was think about Clare.

He'd kissed her. Something he'd wanted to do for nearly fifteen years. Now, in about a week, he'd have her all to himself for an evening. A nice, quiet dinner, Owen had that right. A little wine, some conversation.

What did two people who'd known each other most of their lives talk about?

Then again, there was a lot about her he didn't know.

He stood at his window looking out at the dark, shrouded inn and wondered what he'd find out. And what would happen next.

☙

WORK-RELATED HEADACHES DOMINATED the next day, starting with a visit from the building inspector who, according to Ryder, arbitrarily reinterpreted codes, requiring a change in exterior doors already installed.

After spending half the day in Hagerstown straightening it out, Beckett came back to the site only to learn the tile supplier had misordered the flooring in one of the guest room baths, and apparently— oops—forgotten to order the entire supply of another pattern. And now claimed their installer couldn't begin the job for six weeks.

He'd have booted that nightmare to Owen, but his brother already had his hands full in a meeting with the mechanics about the building's sprinkler system.

He retreated to his home office, and spent the next hour giving the salesman who'd screwed up a bigger headache than his own.

In that, at least, rode some satisfaction.

When he finished, he grabbed a Coke, swallowed some aspirin, then headed back across the street. He caught Owen in the parking lot.

"Where are you going?" he demanded.

"I'm going to put in some time in the shop. Look, Ry told me about the tile screwup. I'll kick some ass in the morning."

"Already kicked. Emergency meeting. Where's Ry?"

"Third floor, last I checked. Hey, I'd better tell you about the gallery space next to the bookstore, and Mom's latest brainstorm."

"Not yet. Let's go."

They found Ryder on the third floor, installing one of the custom panels in the window well. "Fits like a glove," he said, "and looks fan-fucking-tastic."

D.A. thumped his tail in agreement, and probably hoped someone had food on them.

"That's one thing that's gone right today."

"Tell me about it." He glanced over at his brothers. "Did Owen tell you?"

"I'm telling Owen, and you. First, don't get into a pissing contest with the building inspector even if he's being a dick."

"Hey, listen—"

"No. You were right, but you cross cocks with County, it can just bog up the whole project. The exterior doors meet code, were approved and signed off on previously. They stay. But let Owen or me handle the dirty work, if it looks like it's going dirty. Next—"

Ryder set down his nail gun. "Give me that Coke." He snagged it out of Beckett's hand. "If you're going to lecture me, I deserve a nice little treat."

At the word *treat*, D.A.'s tail thumped harder.

Ryder merely glanced at him. "Mine."

"Next," Beckett continued. "I reamed the salesman. Asshole tried to tell me he meant to order that entire run, how it'll only take a week to get in. Which is bullshit," Beckett said before both of his brothers could. "Everything we ordered from them's taking weeks."

Owen grabbed the Coke from Ryder. "They came recommended, made a damn good pitch, and swore they could handle the job. Lesson learned."

"I'm not blaming you—much. The vendor screwed up, big-time. They're expediting the replacement tile and the one he didn't order— at their expense, and we're getting a ten percent discount for our inconvenience. I talked to the owner."

"Nice work," Owen commented.

"I learned from Dad, too. The salesman's ass is in a sling where it deserves to be, the company's on notice, and you're going to follow up every day to make sure they don't screw up again."

"I'm on it."

"And they're not doing the install."

"Wait a minute. Wait—"

"You didn't just spend two hours on the phone listening to excuses, wheedling, and bullshit, while the owner tried to evade and stall. We don't deal with that kind of company. We'll stick with them for the tiles because it's a worse headache to start over with what we're missing, but I'm damned if they're getting any more work out of us."

"I'm with Beck," Ryder said.

"Just hold on. We've got a lot of specialty tile—glass tile, imported, intricate patterns. We need installers with experience handling that kind of work, and a good-sized crew."

"I've got the owner of another company coming in to look the job over. He's one of the guys who dropped off a business card. He's local, he's hungry, and he gave me three references to check out. He checked out. He's on his way. You talk to him," he told Owen. "If you don't think he can handle it, you find somebody else. But we're finding somebody else. It's a matter of principle."

"You know how he is when he's got his panties in a twist," Ryder pointed out. "Besides, he's right."

"Great. Fine." Owen scrubbed the heels of his hands over his face. "Jesus."

Beckett pulled out the aspirin bottle he'd stuck in his pocket on his way out the door.

"Thanks."

"Now, what about Mom and brainstorms?"

Owen swallowed aspirin, chased it with Coke. "You might need these again. Now that The Gallery's moved out of that space, Mom wants a gift shop to tie in with the inn."

"I know that."

"You don't know she wants it now."

"What do you mean, *now*? She can't have it now."

Owen gave him a look of pure pity. "You tell her. She's over there now with a paint fan, a notebook, and a measuring tape."

"Oh, for Christ's sake." Beckett rubbed the back of his neck. Just when the headache had eased off. "You guys are coming, too. I'm not dealing with her alone."

"I like it here," Ryder claimed. "Doing carpentry. I like the quiet."

"Then bring your hammer. We might need it."

They'd owned the commercial space beside the bookstore for a few years. It had, over time, seen many incarnations. The latest, a little art gallery and framing shop, had moved across the river to a bigger location.

Now, as he could clearly see through the display window beside the door, his mother was in the nearly empty space holding a paint fan up to the wall.

Shit.

She looked over as they came in.

"Hello, boys. What do you think of this yellow? It's pretty, it's warm, but quiet enough not to distract from the art."

"Listen, Mom—"

"Oh, and that wall there? That really needs to be taken down to a half wall. It'll open up the space, lead nicely into the little kitchen area. We can leave that pretty much intact, use that for kitcheny things. Pottery, cutting boards, what have you. Then we'll leave that doorway open leading down to what'll be the office. Maybe do a beaded curtain or something for some jazz. Then upstairs—"

"Mom. Mom. Okay, this is all great, but maybe you haven't noticed we're up to our necks across the street."

She gave Beckett a smile, a pat on the cheek. "This isn't much. Mostly cosmetic."

"Taking down a wall—"

"That's just a little wall." She bent down to rub D.A. when he leaned lovingly on her leg. "It mostly needs paint, and the bathroom there needs a new sink, that sort of thing. Freshen it up. You can spare a couple men while the floors are going in."

"But—"

"We don't want to leave this space empty, do we?" She put her hands on her hips as she turned a circle. "We'll need a counter there, for the cash register, for checkout. Small again, nothing fancy. You can build that, can't you, Owen?"

"Ah . . . sure."

"Coward," Beckett muttered as their mother walked back to study the closet-sized powder room.

"Bet your ass, bro."

"Pretty little wall-hung sink, a new toilet, nice little mirror and light—done. Paint and pretty lights out here and upstairs. Oh, new exterior paint. We'll go with what complements what we're doing on the inn."

"Mom, even if we could split some of the crew, get this done, you have to get somebody to run it, stock it and—"

"Already there. Don't you worry about any of that. I've talked to Madeline—from our book club. You know Madeline Cramer," Justine continued in her cheerful steamroll over objections. "She used to manage an art gallery in Hagerstown."

"Yeah, sure, but—"

"She knows all sorts of local artists and craftsmen. We're going to do all local art and crafts, showcase what we have, who we are." Sunglasses perched on her head, paint fan at the ready, Justine beamed at the space. "It'll be wonderful."

He couldn't argue with that. He couldn't argue at all, Beckett realized. He was outgunned. "We're only going to be able to send somebody over to work when we can clear them from the inn job."

"Well, of course, sweetie. Ry, do you have time to help me figure out the wall there?"

"Sure."

"Won't this be fun?" She turned that cheerful beam on all of them. "We'll add a fresh, new business to town, give local artists a wonderful venue, and have a nice little lead-in to the inn before it's done and open."

She put her hands on her hips. "Any of you have dates tonight?"

"Who has time?" Owen muttered. "No, ma'am, not me."

She got shakes of the head from the other two, sighed loud and long before bending to address Dumbass. "How am I going to get girls and grandchildren unless they start hunting them up? Well, why don't you all come to dinner? I'll pick up some fresh corn on the way home, make you a feast."

And rope them into refining details on her latest brainstorm, Beckett thought. But what the hell.

"I'm in." He glanced around as Clare poked her head in the door.

"Hi. Family meeting?"

"Just adjourned," Justine told her.

"Oh, it looks so sad in here now. I'm sorry to see The Gallery go, but I know she'll love having a bigger space over in Shepherdstown."

"It won't look sad for long. You're just what I need." Justine held the paint strip up again. "Tell me what you think of this color for the walls."

"I love it. Sunny. Warm, but not overbright. Do you have a new tenant already?"

"We're the new tenant. I guess you haven't talked to Madeline recently."

"Not since our last book club meeting."

While his mother filled Clare in—surely satisfied with Clare's enthusiastic delight—Beckett walked outside, then sat on the steps leading up to the bookstore porch.

They'd figure it out, he decided. The scheduling of crew and work, the materials. He could eke some time out if it needed a bit of rede-signing. No need for permits if they didn't change anything structur-ally, and since it would remain a retail space.

Owen would deal with the business license, the paperwork, and the rest.

But, Jesus, the timing. Crap timing at the end of a crap day.

At least he'd get a home-cooked meal out of it.

His mother came out with Clare, repeated the process, this time holding a new strip up to the exterior wall before she frowned over at Beckett.

"You look beat, baby."

"Hard day at the ranch. Ironed out," he added before she pecked at him. "We'll fill you in later."

"See that you do. For now, why don't you go ahead and run Clare home."

"Oh no, I'm fine. It's a nice walk."

"Why are you walking?" Beckett asked her. "It's nearly a mile."

"Hardly more than a half mile, and I like to walk. My sitter's car was acting up, so I left her mine in case. I don't want her to have to pile the boys in and come get me."

"I'll drive you."

"Really, you don't have to bother."

"You can argue with me," he said as he pushed up. "But there's no point in arguing with her." He stepped over, kissed his mother's cheek. "Remind Ry and Owen they've got the tile installer coming."

"Will do."

"See you later, slave driver."

CHAPTER SIX

I APPRECIATE THE LIFT," CLARE BEGAN AS THEY WALKED TO his truck. "Especially since you look tired."

"Not tired. It's just been a pisser of a day."

"Problems with the hotel?"

"Irritations equaling a day I'd rather have been swinging a hammer than talking on the phone. It better be worth it in the long run," he added with a glance toward the inn.

"It will be. And now the gift shop. That's exciting."

"It'll be more exciting six months from now." He opened the passenger door of the truck, took a clipboard, a fat notebook, and an old, dirty towel off the seat.

"It's mostly just painting, isn't it?"

He turned, gave her a long look.

"What?"

"First, it's never just painting, not with Mom. Second, you smell really great."

A horn tooted. Glancing over, Beckett spotted one of his carpenters driving by, waved. Clare boosted into the truck.

"Are we still on for Friday night?"

"Alva's free to watch the kids."

"Good." He stood there a minute, just enjoying the fact that Clare sat in his truck, and they were making plans for Friday night. "Does seven work for you?"

"Yeah, seven's fine."

"Good," Beckett repeated, then closed the door and walked around to the driver's side. "So, are the kids up about school starting?"

"Liam's all about it. Murphy's thrilled—especially with his Power Rangers lunch box. And Harry's still pretending not to be."

Beckett pulled out of the lot, caught the light, made the left. "How about you?"

"We've got new shoes, backpacks, lunch boxes, crayons, pencils, notebooks. The Mad Mall Safari is now over, and that's a relief. With Murphy in school full-time, a lot of the child-care issues go away, and that makes life easier."

"I hear the *but*."

"But . . . my baby's going to kindergarten. Five minutes ago I had him in a backpack, now he'll be carrying one to school. Harry's moving halfway through elementary school. It doesn't seem possible. So, I'll drop them off Monday morning, go home, have a good cry. And that'll be that."

"I always figured my mom did a happy dance the minute we walked down the lane to the school bus."

"The happy dance comes after the good cry."

"Got it." He pulled into her short gravel drive behind her minivan. "I can't ask you in to dinner. Avery and Hope are coming."

"That's okay. Mom's bribing us with a meal."

She hesitated, gave him a sidelong glance. "You could come in if you have a minute, for something cold to drink."

"I've got a minute." Testing them both, he leaned over to open her door, stayed where he was, looking into her eyes, into the glimmer of green over gray. "It's nice. Being close to you without pretending I'm not trying to be close to you."

"It's strange knowing you want to be."

"Good strange or bad strange?"

"Good and strange," she said, and got out.

He didn't really know her house. He'd been inside a few times. She'd hired Ryder to do some work shortly after she'd bought it, and he'd helped.

Any excuse.

She'd hosted a couple of backyard cookouts over the years, so he'd been in the backyard, the kitchen.

But he didn't know how the place worked, day-to-day. It was something that interested him about buildings and the people who lived or worked in them. And particularly interested him about her.

She had flowers planted in the front, a nice, well-tended mix suffering a bit from what his mother called the late-summer shabbies. Her tiny patch of lawn needed mowing.

He ought to help her with that.

She'd painted her door a deep blue, had a brass Celtic knot knocker centered on it.

She opened it directly onto the living room with a small-scale sofa in blue and green stripes, a couple of chairs in the green. The remains of a multi–Matchbox car wreck scattered on the hardwood.

The bookshelves he'd helped build took up an entire wall. It pleased him to see she made good use of them by crowding them with books, family photos, a few trinkets.

"Come on back to the kitchen."

He stopped in the doorway of a small room with the walls covered with maps and posters. Colorful cubbies held toys, the ones that weren't littering the floor. He studied child-sized bean bag chairs, little tables, and the debris three young boys made.

"Nice."

"It gives them a place to share, and get away from me."

She continued back, passed the bolt-hole of a powder room under the stairs and into the combination kitchen/dining room.

White appliances and dark oak cabinets. Fresh summer fruit in a wooden bowl on the short run of white countertop between the stove and refrigerator, the refrigerator covered with kids' drawings and a monthly planner calendar. Four chairs around the square wooden table.

"The kids'll be in the back. Give me a second."

She went to the door, called through the screen. "Hi, guys!"

There were whoops and shouts, and from his angle Beckett saw her face just light up.

"Clare! Why didn't you call me to come get you?"

"I got a ride home. No problem."

Beckett heard the scrape of a chair, then saw Alva Ridenour come to the door.

He'd had her for algebra, freshman year, and calculus his senior. As she had then, she wore silver glasses perched on her nose, and her hair—now brilliantly white—pulled back in a no-nonsense bun.

"Why, Beckett Montgomery. I didn't know you were running a taxi service."

"Anywhere you want to go, Miz Ridenour. The meter's never running for you."

She opened the screen as the boys rushed in to assault Clare with tales of the day's adventures, questions, pleas, complaints.

Alva scooted around them, gave Beckett a poke in the shoulder. "When's that inn going to be finished?"

"It'll be a while yet, but when it is I'll give you a personal tour."

"You'd better."

"Do you need any help with your car?"

"No. My husband managed to get it into the shop. How's your mama?"

"Busy, and keeping us busier."

"As she should. Nobody wants a pack of lazy boys. Clare, I'm going to get on."

"I'll drive you home, Miz Ridenour."

"It's two houses down, Beckett. Do I look infirm?"

"No, ma'am."

"You boys." She used her former teacher's voice, and the three kids fell silent. "Give your mother a chance to take a breath. I want to hear all about the first day of school when I see you next. And Liam? You pick up those cars in the living room."

"But Murphy—"

"You brought them down, you pick them up." She winked at Clare. "I'll be on my way."

"Thanks, Alva."

"Oh, I promised them cookies and milk if they didn't fight for a half hour. They made it."

"Cookies and milk it is."

"Did you fight with your brothers today?" Alva asked Beckett.

"Not in the last half hour."

She cackled out a laugh as she left.

Murphy tugged on Beckett's hand. "Do you wanna see my Power Rangers?"

"You got Red Ranger from Mystic Force?"

Murphy's eyes widened. He could only nod rapidly before running from the room.

"Wash your hands," Clare called after him. "Now you've done it," she murmured to Beckett. "Wash up," she told the other boys, "if you want cookies."

They obviously did, as they dashed off.

"Power Rangers are Murphy's current obsession. He has action figures, DVDs, pajamas, T-shirts, costumes, transports. We had a Power Ranger theme for his birthday in April."

"I used to watch them on TV. I was about twelve, I guess, so I said they were cheesy. But I ate it up."

As he spoke he watched her take little plates out of a cupboard to set on the table. Power Rangers, Spider-Man, and Wolverine.

"Which one's mine?"

"Sorry?"

"Don't I rate cookies and milk and a superhero plate?"

"Oh. Sure." Obviously surprised, she went back to the cupboard, chose another plate. "Han Solo."

"Perfect. I dressed up as Han Solo for Halloween."

"How old were you?"

"Twenty-seven."

He loved the way she laughed, and when she brought the plate and four small, colorful plastic cups to the table, he caught her hand.

"Clare."

"I got *ALL* of them." Murphy muscled in a white plastic basket loaded with action figures. "See, we got Mighty Morphin and Jungle Fury and see, I got Pink Ranger even though she's a girl."

Beckett crouched down, took out one of the Green Rangers. "This, my man, is an amazing collection."

Murphy, eyes wide and deadly earnest, nodded. "I know."

❦

HE STAYED NEARLY an hour. Clare would have kissed him again just for the fact he'd given her kids such a great time. He'd never seemed bored or annoyed with a conversation dominated by superheroes, their powers, their partners, their foes.

But he didn't kiss her.

Of course, he didn't kiss her, Clare thought as she slipped potatoes, quartered and coated with olive oil and herbs, in to roast. That would've proved awkward with three kids hanging all over him.

She set her cutting board over the sink—the better to watch the kids, who'd gone back to swarming all over the play set her parents had given them—and minced garlic for the chicken's marinade.

They'd so enjoyed having a man to play with.

They had her father, of course, and Clint's dad when he came to visit, and Joe, Alva's husband. But they didn't really have anyone, well, their dad's age.

So, it had been a nice hour.

Now she was behind in dinner prep, but that was okay. They'd eat a bit later than planned. The evening would be nice enough to have dinner out on the deck, then the boys could spill back out into the yard after for a bit before bedtime.

She whisked ingredients together, poured the marinade over chicken breasts, covered the bowl, set it aside.

Clare enjoyed the kitchen time, listening to her boys' voices carry on the warm air, the bark of the neighbor's dog, the scents from the oven, from her little kitchen garden. Which reminded her she had to do some weeding and some harvesting over the weekend.

And the laundry, she remembered, she'd let go because they'd stayed so long at Vesta the night before.

When she'd kissed Beckett in the shadows of the inn.

Silly to obsess over that, she thought. She'd kissed other men since Clint died.

Well, two, so that qualified as *men*. Her mother's neighbor's son, a perfectly nice accountant who lived and worked in Brunswick. Three dates there, two pleasant enough kisses. And no genuine interest or chemistry on either side.

Then Laurie's aunt's friend, an estate attorney from Hagerstown. Great-looking guy, she recalled. Sort of interesting, but very bitter regarding his recently-ex-wife. One date, one fraught good-night kiss. He'd even sent her flowers, with an apology for spending the evening talking about his ex.

How long ago had that been? she wondered. Idly she counted back as she peeled carrots. Harry had fallen off his trike and chipped his front baby tooth the morning before she'd gone to dinner with the accountant, so he'd been five.

God, over three years ago, she realized. And she'd gone out with the lawyer the day after she'd moved Murphy into his big-boy bed, so he'd been three. About two years there.

Which was more telling, the fact she measured time by little events in her kids' lives or that she hadn't even thought of dating for two years?

She supposed one was the same as the other.

She had the chicken simmering in wine and herbs when she heard the front door open, and Avery's hail. "We come bearing gifts."

"Back here!" Clare took one last glance out the window before hurrying toward the front of the house. "Hope." She grabbed the woman in a hug. "You look amazing."

It was invariably true. She radiated chic in her casual summer skirt and flounced top the color of chili peppers.

"Oh, it's good to see you." Hope returned the hug with an extra squeeze. "It's been too long. God, something smells amazing."

"Dinner, which is a little behind. Oh, sunflowers."

"Couldn't resist them."

"I love them. Come on back."

"Where are my men?" Hope shook the trio of gift bags she carried.

"You know you don't have to bring them presents."

"It's as much fun for me."

"Hey, I brought the wine." Avery tapped the bag in her arm. "Which will also be as much fun for me. Let's go open it, get this party started."

Hope headed straight out the back, laughing as the kids stampeded toward her, and the gift bags. Clare watched through the screen door while Avery opened the wine.

The kids adored Hope, Clare thought, with or without gifts. And she really did look amazing. Sultry looks to go with the smoky voice, the short, razor-sharp wedge of dark hair with spiky bangs suited the knife-edged cheekbones, the long, heavy-lidded smolder of her eyes.

The body Clare knew she trained with vigorous daily workouts managed to be both athletic and intensely female at the same time.

"God, she's beautiful."

"I know. She'd be easy to hate." Avery passed Clare a glass of wine. "But we're bigger than that. We love her despite her beauty. We've got to talk her into taking this job."

"But if she decides she doesn't want it—"

"I've got the gut feeling." Avery pointed at her belly. "The McTavish Gut Feeling. No one dares ignore the McTavish Gut. She's unhappy down in D.C."

"Small wonder," Clare muttered and felt her gorge rise over Hope's miserable prick of an ex yet again.

"She's made some noises about going back to Philly, or trying Chicago, and I know—Clare, I *know* that's not what she should do. She should be here, with us."

"Well, I can do my part, hyping the inn, and the Montgomerys. But it's going to be her call at the end of the day." She slipped her arm around Avery's waist. "But it sure is good to have both of you here."

So good, Clare thought over dinner while the food she'd prepared was enjoyed and the sunflowers beamed at the head of the table.

She let the boys burn off dinner and excess excitement until dusk. "I'm going to put them in the corral for the night."

"Want some help roping them in?" Avery asked.

"No, I've got it."

"Good, because after that meal, *and* the ice cream and fresh strawberries, I'm not sure I can move yet."

Clare called them in, got the expected whines and protests. "We had a deal," she reminded them. "Say good night."

They obeyed, heads hanging, feet dragging like a trio shackled for the chain gang.

By the time she got back, her friends had cleared the table.

"I'd say you didn't have to do that, but I'm glad you did." She plopped back down, reached for the wine Avery topped off. "Boy, does this feel good. It'd feel great if we could do this anytime at all."

"Avery's been pitching this B&B since I got here."

"Well then, it's my turn." Prepared, Clare straightened up, leaned forward. "It's more than a bed-and-breakfast. I think it's going to have that kind of warmth and charm, but combined with the pizzazz of a boutique hotel. I've been through parts of it, gotten a sense of the setup, looked at the cut sheets and photos of furniture and fixtures. I'm still dazzled."

"Living where you work." Hope lifted her shoulders. "There are pros and cons there."

"Come on, Hope, you practically lived at the Wickham anyway."

"Maybe." Unable to deny that singular fact, she blew out a breath. "The Prick and Miss Tits are officially engaged."

"They deserve each other," Avery muttered.

"Oh yeah. Anyway, she actually breezed into my office last week, wanting to discuss wedding plans, as they'll have the event at the hotel."

"Bitch."

"And another *oh yeah*." Hope toasted Avery. "Yesterday, the big boss calls me in. He'd like to discuss my contract as it's nearly up. He offered me a raise, which I declined, explaining that I'd be tendering my resignation. He was, sincerely, stunned."

"Did he really think you'd stay on after his son treated you that way?" Clare demanded.

"Clearly he did. When he realized I was serious, he doubled the raise." One eyebrow arched, she lifted her glass again in toast. "Doubled it without a single blink. That was incredibly satisfying. Almost as satisfying as telling him thanks, but no thanks. Pissed him off, enough for him to release me from the remainder of my contract."

"He *fired* you?"

"No, he didn't fire me." Hope grinned at Clare's outrage. "We simply agreed that since I'd be leaving in a matter of weeks anyway, I could depart the premises on the spot. So, I'm done."

"Are you okay?" Clare leaned over, squeezed a hand over Hope's.

"I am. I really am. I have an interview next week in Chicago, another pending in Philadelphia, and yet another in Connecticut."

"Stay with us."

Hope gave Clare's hand a squeeze in turn. "I'm not throwing it over, or I wouldn't be here. It's intriguing, I admit, what these people are doing. I want to see it, feel it out. Being so close to you and Avery is a big draw, but this job has to be the right fit."

"It's as tailored as one of your Akris suits. Don't take my word." Avery shrugged, leaned back nonchalantly in her chair. And smiled a very smug smile. "You'll see."

"I like the town, or I should say I've always liked spending a day or two here when I've come to visit. So, tell me more about the Montgomerys. Avery's given me the basics. Mom, three sons. They lost their father who started the contractor's business about ten years ago. They own several properties in and around town."

"They saved the inn property. There was talk about just razing it, it had gotten so bad. And that would've been a crime."

"I remember how it looked the last few times I came up," Hope commented. "Saving it's no small feat."

"They have a good eye, and talent. All three are terrific carpenters and cabinetmakers. They built this deck."

"Ryder—the oldest," Avery continued. "He's standing as job boss on this project. Owen's the detail guy, runs the numbers, makes the calls, takes the meetings. Or most of them. Beckett's an architect. Clare can tell you more about him since he's sweet on her."

"Oh?" That eyebrow arched again. "Oh, really?"

"Really," Avery said before Clare could speak. "They shared a big, sloppy kiss in the dark, haunted halls of the inn."

"*Really?* Wait, haunted? No, one thing at a time." Hope waved her hands in the air as if clearing a chalkboard. "Now, tell me everything about Beckett Montgomery. I met him briefly in your place, Avery, but all I remember is an impression of yummy."

"Yummy's accurate, but Clare would have more details there due to big, sloppy."

"I should never have told you about last night," Clare said to Avery.

"As if. He's gorgeous—they all are. He has his office and apartment over the restaurant."

"Oh, that's right, that's right. I remember now. I met Owen long enough to say hi, there. Two out of three, at least, are yummy."

"Ryder carries on the tradition. Anyway, Beckett." Avery grinned at Clare. "He got his degree from the University of Maryland, worked for the family business in the summers, then apprenticed with a firm in Hagerstown for a couple years. He's full-time with Montgomery Family Contractors now, handles the architectural needs, and still straps on a tool belt whenever he's needed. Which looks fine on him."

"Maybe you should go out with him."

Avery just kept grinning at Clare over her wine. "He never gave me the puppy-dog eyes. He's been stuck on Clare since high school. He told her."

"Aww."

Avery gave Hope a light slap on the arm. "I *know*. They're going out Friday night."

"Where?"

Clare shifted in her chair. "I don't know. Dinner, I guess. He's coming at seven. That should be dinner."

"What are you wearing?"

"I don't know. God, I don't know. I don't remember how to do this."

"We're here to help," Hope assured her. "We'll go up and pick something out."

"I don't even know if I have anything that's date-wear. Everything's Mom- or bookstore-wear."

"I love your clothes," Avery disagreed.

"We'll see what's what. And if we can't find anything that makes you happy, we'll go shopping."

"I don't really have time to—"

"Clare, you've been shopping with me." Hope lifted a finger. "You know I can whip together an outfit, including shoes, accessories, and underpinnings, inside twenty minutes."

"She has that talent," Avery confirmed. "See, fun. We can do this all the time when Hope's living in town. You know what you need to do! You need to move up here now. Move in with me until the inn's finished. It's perfect. We could be roommates again. You'll get to know the area, the people, have a real handle on the inn before you really start working there."

"Getting way ahead of yourself has always been one of your talents. I haven't even seen the place. And, even if I decided I wanted the job like I want a new pair of Manolos, there's no guarantee they'll hire me. For all we know, Mom and Sons might take an instant dislike to me."

"Never happen; they're too astute. Especially Justine. Oh, Oh." Avery waved her wineglass. "Did you hear about the gift shop?"

"I was in there earlier," Clare confirmed. "The building next to the bookstore," she told Hope. "Their tenant moved out, and they're going to make it into a gift shop, specializing in local arts and crafts. Tying it in with the inn."

"That's a clever idea."

"They're full of them," Avery told Hope.

"Uh-huh. Tell me about the place being haunted."

"It's a woman with a preference for honeysuckle. That's all I know."

Avery shrugged. "The original part of the building is the oldest stone house in town. Seventeen-ninety-whatever. So she could be from any time. You know what? Owen ought to research her. That's what he does—research things."

"Owen's the one I talked to. The detail man. Has this honeysuckle-loving ghost caused any problems?"

"Not that I've heard of. And I would, or Clare would. The crew eats at my place a lot, and gets coffee or books at TTP. They'd talk about it, believe me. Maybe you'll make contact when we go through tomorrow. Clare, you've got to come."

Clare tuned back in, shifted her gaze from the softening light over the backyard—that needed mowing. "I don't think the Montgomerys want three little boys running around the place. Plus, it's not safe."

"It wouldn't take long. I could get Franny to watch them for a half hour. She's on tomorrow."

"I don't know . . . Let me see. I might be able to drop them at my mother's for a bit. A little bit," she added. "We've still got a lot of back-to-school prep to do, and I've got yard work and housework."

"Walk-through's at ten."

Clare juggled tomorrow's agenda in her head. "Maybe. I'll be there if I can make it."

"Good enough. Now." Hope rubbed her hands together. "Let's go play closet."

CHAPTER SEVEN

A S ARRANGED, OWEN ARRIVED AT VESTA AT NINE THIRTY
sharp to meet and interview Hope. Since she'd promised to
stay out of the way, Avery busied herself with the morning prep—
firing up the pizza ovens, making the sauces in anticipation of Saturday business when they opened at eleven.

When Owen walked in, Hope sat at the counter drinking coffee
as she looked over her notes.

Owen shifted his briefcase to his left hand, held out his right.
"Hope."

"Owen."

"It's nice to see you again. Appreciate this, Avery."

"All for the common good," she said from the stove. "Coffee?"

"That'd be great. I'll get it." At home, he walked around to the
pot she had on one of the twin burners, poured, then added a dose of
sugar. "Why don't we take a table?" he suggested. "So, how was your
trip up?"

"Not bad." She took her seat, gauging him as she knew he gauged her. His eyes, a clear, quiet blue, stayed direct on hers. "I left early enough to miss the traffic."

"I don't get down to D.C. often. Traffic's one of the reasons." A smile shifted, softened the angles of his face. "Things move a lot slower up here."

"Yes, they do. It's a pretty town." She kept her tone carefully noncommittal. "I've enjoyed the area when I've come up to see Avery and Clare."

"It's a big change from Georgetown."

Circling each other, she decided. Well, she knew how to dance. "I'm looking for change. Rehabbing and reimagining a building like the inn, with its long history, must be a big change from the kind of work Montgomery Family Contractors has done in the past. You and your family have rehabbed old buildings before, including the one we're sitting in, but nothing on this scale. It must be a challenge."

"It is."

"And owning an inn, with all its demands, issues—quirks—that's a big change from a more traditional landlord role."

Who was interviewing whom? he wondered, and decided he liked her.

"We thought about it for a long time, blended viewpoints, and came up with a specific vision. We're going to make that vision a reality."

"Why an inn?"

"I'm betting you researched the history."

"That doesn't tell me why you and your family conceived this particular vision."

He considered her while she questioned him. He gave her points—for appearance, to start. Killer looks, and she knew how to play them. The sharp style of her hair set off her eyes. The cut and rusty red color of her suit set off her body, and telegraphed control and authority.

Big, sultry eyes, he noted, offset by an air of coolness.

It was a nice combo.

"It was originally a tavern stand," he told her, "a place for travelers to rest, rest their horses, get a meal. Over time, various owners added on. The name changed, but for more than a century it served as an inn. We'll make it an inn again, respecting that history. While bringing it into the twenty-first century."

"I've been getting the rundown on some of the features." She smiled then, warming up the cool.

He gave her more points.

"We're having some fun there. This area has a lot to offer visitors. Antietam, Crystal Grottoes, Harpers Ferry, and plenty more. Right now, there's no place for those visitors to stay in Boonsboro. Once there is, we'll draw people in, people who'll want to eat, to shop, to sightsee. We want to give them a unique experience in a beautiful place with exceptional service."

"Exclusive, individual, historic. It's an interesting concept, naming the rooms after literary couples."

"Romantic couples. Each room has its own flavor, its own feel. Couples are a major clientele of B&Bs. We'd like to draw honeymooners, couples celebrating an anniversary or special occasion. Give them a memorable stay, so they'll come back, and tell their friends."

And enough about us, he thought, sipped some coffee.

"Your resume certainly qualifies you for the innkeeper position."

"I have a hard copy of the file I emailed you if you want it."

"Sure."

"You'd need the innkeeper to live on-site."

"Can't keep the inn by remote. We'd provide the apartment. It's a two-bedroom on the third floor. Living room, bath, smallish kitchen, but the innkeeper would have access to the main kitchen, and the laundry facilities."

"She—or he—would have to cook."

"Just breakfast."

"I'd think you'd want more than that. If you're providing B&B service, you'd want homemade cookies, muffins, or some other type of thing to offer during the day. Wine and cheese in the evening."

"That'd be a nice touch."

"Avery had an idea about offering guests delivery, if they didn't want to go out."

Owen glanced back toward the open kitchen. "Smart. We could put her menu in the room packs. Smart," he said again, and made a note.

"There are a lot of practicalities, Owen. A list of duties, salary, days off. Housekeeping, laundry, budget, maintenance. Anyone taking this on would need an assistant. Nobody can work twenty-four-seven, fifty-two weeks a year."

"Then let's talk about that."

While they discussed nuts and bolts, Justine came in. Mint green sunglasses today, to match her high-tops. She sent Avery a wave and walked straight to the table.

"And you're Hope. I'm Justine Montgomery." She shook hands before running one over Owen's shoulder. "How's it going here?"

"A lot of questions," Owen told her. "And a lot of fresh ideas."

Hope shifted in her chair to meet Justine's eyes. "You already have a lot of great ones. I'm impressed with how many of the nitty details you've already nailed down. You've got a very comprehensive plan for someone who hasn't worked in the trade."

"We took polls, friends and family, people we know who travel a lot. What their dream list would be in a hotel. I expect there'll be a learning curve once we open, but we'd like to hit most of the notes right off the bat."

"Can I get you coffee, Justine?" Avery called out.

"I'm going to grab a soda out of the cooler. I've been up since six," she said as she did so. "My brain won't turn off. I was thinking, Owen's going over all the details, the job description, and so on. I thought I'd come by for a minute before we went over, and tell you what it is I'm looking for."

"Of course."

"No question we need somebody presentable, who knows how to deal with the public, roll with the punches. But you wouldn't have lasted at the Wickham if you couldn't do all that. I want more."

Watching Hope, Justine twisted off the top on a bottle of Diet Coke. "I want somebody who can put down roots, who'll look at the inn, and this town, as home. Somebody who does that'll be happier in the job, and do a better job because of it. The day-to-day, the this-and-that, we'll work that out. But you've either got the heart for it, or you don't. You're going to have to fall in love, or it won't work for you, or for us."

She smiled. "Now, Owen's thinking it's more important that you can handle the reservation software, keep good records, keep a data-base on guests, know how to turn a room if there's a rush. I imagine you can do all that and more, or Avery wouldn't have suggested you in the first place. But this isn't just a business, not to us. That place needs love. We're giving it plenty. I want to put it into hands that can do the same. And whip up some nice waffles."

"I don't know if I'm the right person," Hope said carefully. "I don't know if this is the right place or situation for me. My life's . . . in flux at the moment. But I do know I'm interested. And I have fallen in love with your concept, and your purpose."

"That's a start. Why don't we walk over, take a look? You and Owen can talk more about details later."

"I'd really like to see it."

"I'll be over in a couple minutes," Avery told them. "As soon as Franny gets in."

"Back door's open." Owen picked up his briefcase as he rose. "Ry and Beck are putting in a couple hours this morning."

"You'll need your imagination," Justine began as they stepped out. "We've come a long way, but there's a lot left to do before she shines."

"It's a big project. Beautiful stonework." Hope studied the lines as they walked down the side.

Justine talked about a courtyard where Hope saw rubble and hard-packed mud. But the porches looked promising with their charming banjo pickets.

They went into The Lobby, and Hope listened as Justine talked of tile and tables, art and flowers, then moved through a wide arch into what would be the dining room. Coffered ceiling—white trim over deep brown, Justine explained. Tables of glossy wood, left unclothed, each with a little vase of flowers. A small arch of the original stone left exposed in the back wall, with a big, carved buffet in front of it. Chandeliers of iron with oak leaf motif and big globes of stained glass shaped like acorns.

Hope nearly saw it in the unpainted walls, the rough floor, the jumble of material. She saw enough to be sure they'd need a couple of server tables, maybe under the wonderful side windows.

They moved down, more exposed stone, exposed brick, passed what would be the laundry room, the office and into the kitchen space.

She listened again, tried to see the cabinets, many with glass fronts to break up the solidity of dark wood. The granite countertops and stainless steel appliances—wall oven, the range in the island done in cream wood to contrast with the dark.

"There's no door on the kitchen?"

"We're leaving it open." Justine, her sunglasses perched on her head, her thumbs in the front pockets of her pants, scanned the space. "We want guests to be at home, the minute they walk in the door. We'll keep the fridge stocked with cold drinks—soda, juice, bottled water."

"Like a big minibar?"

"In a way. Guests should feel free to help themselves. We're not going to nickel-and-dime people. Once they're here, the room charge covers the lot. They want a cup of coffee before breakfast—or anytime—and the innkeeper isn't right on the spot, they can make a cup here, or on the little machine we're getting for The Library on the second floor. We should have a bowl of seasonal fruit maybe. Or cookies."

"She already thought of cookies," Owen pointed out.

"See, same page. That's the idea. Relax, enjoy, be at home."

Something in Hope warmed, and that warmth spread as they moved into Reception. She could barely see over boxes and tools, but she began to visualize. A pair of big barrel chairs in soft green in front of the brick fireplace. No desk, no counter, but a long, custom-made table for the innkeeper. Tile floors, tying in with the kitchen and lobby, and all the windows bringing in the light.

She knew she asked practical questions about check-in, computers, storage, security, but by the time they'd finished the main and started up, she understood why the Montgomerys had fallen in love.

"Sounds like my other boys are up on the third floor." Justine glanced back. "Why don't we start up there, and the innkeeper's apartment? You can meet the rest of the family."

"Perfect."

She felt a little tug from the left as they started the turn toward the third floor.

"Elizabeth and Darcy," Justine told her when she hesitated. "Both these front rooms have access to the porch over Main Street."

For a moment she thought she smelled honeysuckle, turned back to look inside. And jumped when Avery shouted from below. "Are you up there?"

"Heading to three," Owen called back.

"Took longer than I thought." Avery jogged up. "What do you think?"

"It's big, and wonderfully thought-out. I've only seen the ADA room on the main level as far as guest rooms. We're going up to three, working down."

"You can check out your apartment."

With an indulgent shake of her head, Hope continued up, gripping the temporary rail. Imagination, she thought as she pulled her hand away again. She could have sworn she'd touched smooth metal.

"The innkeeper's apartment." Justine gestured. "And The Penthouse, where somebody's busy."

Hope stepped in behind her. She heard the whoosh, thud of a nail gun before she saw him. Sunlight flashed through the window where he worked. For a second, she couldn't see his face, only had the impression of strength and competence as the nail gun thudded again.

He ran his hand down the wood—the same type of panel she'd seen framing the windows downstairs. Then he lowered the tool, shifted.

He stared at her out of cool, assessing eyes. From somewhere nearby another nail gun thudded. Justine spoke, introducing them, but Hope's ears buzzed. She barely heard his name, felt a quick and foolish relief that it wasn't Beckett.

Ryder.

She shook his hand—one with a healing scrape on the back, felt the hard, calloused palm briefly before he dropped it again.

"How ya doing?"

"Fine, thanks." But she wasn't entirely sure. The heat rose, seemed to concentrate right on that spot. Her brain throbbed from an excess of details, images.

She wanted suddenly, desperately, to sit down and drink something—anything—very cold.

"Are you okay, honey?"

She looked at Justine, whose voice came down a long tunnel. "Ah . . . too much coffee this morning," she managed. "I'm a little dehydrated."

Ryder flipped open the lid of a cooler for a bottle of water. When she just stared at it, he twisted off the top. "So hydrate."

"Thanks." For the first time she noticed the dog—the wonderfully homely mud brown dog—who sat with his head cocked, studying her. "That's a lovely detail," she said to keep herself from gulping half the contents in one go. "The side panels."

"Yeah, they turned out."

"Shit, out of ammo. You got any—" Beckett sauntered in. "Oh, hey."

"And here's Beckett," Justine announced. "We're showing Hope around."

"Yeah, hi. I think we met for about five seconds a couple years ago. Welcome to The Penthouse. I was just across the hall in what may be your apartment. So . . . Clare's not with you?"

"I called her before I came over," Avery said. "She had to stop by TTP, some Internet glitch."

"Let's show you the rest of this space before we go through the apartment." Justine gestured. "This will be the parlor, third-floor porch access through the door at the end of the hall. The bedroom's in the back, with the bath between."

Hope followed her down a short hall, then goggled. "This is a *huge* space. I love the floating wall."

"My son, the architect. Counter with double sinks on this side, shower there. The tub, and it's a beauty, on the other side of the wall. We're going for lush here, intricate tile work, some mosaic touches, crystal sconces with brushed-nickel accents. Contemporary with a touch of Old World."

The Penthouse equaled luxury, Hope decided, with a big, ornately carved four-poster showcased in the bedroom, with fancy stools at the foot, a dainty side chair.

She had a sense they'd make the space worth the climb.

She felt steady again when they went through the apartment across the hall. The wonderful windows again. A small-scale kitchen, but Owen was right, she wouldn't need bigger. It jogged off a living room she thought she could make both cozy and efficient. Not nearly the space she had now, even with the second bedroom, but access to the porch—and to the big, beautifully appointed inn.

It was certainly more than adequate, she mused as she wandered through. And more than twice the size of her first efficiency apartment.

Also a third-floor walk-up, she remembered.

Closet space wouldn't be a problem. She'd just use the second bedroom for that as she'd have the office downstairs. If she wanted to have a guest, she could . . .

And when had she decided she wanted this job, wanted this place?

"It's a good, practical space, and again well laid out."

"If we come to terms, you can pick out any colors you like for the walls." Justine smiled at her. "We can go out and see Westley and Buttercup, our other suite. It's got its own outside entrance."

"I'd love to see it."

She loved it all, but she knew better than to leap into something without refining the details, negotiating terms, thinking it through.

This would be a major change—in geography, in lifestyle, in career. She couldn't make a decision like this without giving it a great deal of thought.

"It's going to be amazing." She stood in The Lobby again, taking one last look around. "Every room is special, or will be. And the building has such character, such a good feel to it."

"Could you love it?" Justine asked.

On a half laugh, Hope shook her head. "I think I already do."

"Do you want the job?"

"Mom, we really have to—"

Justine simply waved Owen aside.

"We should both . . . Yes." Saying it felt terrifying, and absolutely right. "I really do."

"You're hired."

Avery let out a whoop, grabbed a shell-shocked Hope, and danced in a circle. Then she grabbed Justine and did the same. When she started for Owen, he threw up his hands.

"That's a girl thing."

So she punched him in the arm.

"I'm so happy. I'm so excited. Hope!" She grabbed Hope again, bounced.

"I— Mrs. Montgomery, are you sure?"

"Justine. We're in this together now. I'm sure. Owen and his brothers will catch up. Now, why don't you and I meet for lunch over at Vesta, say, about twelve thirty? We'll have some wine and talk some more."

"Yes, of course."

Clare tapped on the door, pushed it open. "I wasn't sure you'd still be here. I got hung up. If one thing didn't go screwy this morning, three other things did. Did you already go through?"

"Every room," Avery said, grinning like a maniac.

"Oh well."

"I'll take you through what you haven't already seen if you like." Justine set a hand on Hope's shoulder. "But first, say hello to our innkeeper."

"You— Really? *Really?* Oh, Hope!"

Hope told herself she felt giddy because Clare was squeezing the air right out of her. And not because she'd just made one of the biggest decisions of her life more on the basis of emotion and instinct rather than analysis and intellect.

Since the women were talking a mile a minute, Owen slipped out and headed back upstairs.

He found his brothers discussing the logistics of the sink counter in The Penthouse bath.

"Mom hired her."

"Aesthetically, it plays better if we . . ." Beckett stopped in midstream. "Huh?"

"I said Mom hired Hope Beaumont."

"What do you mean, she hired her?" Ryder shoved his measuring tape back in his tool belt. "She can't just hire her."

"Well, she did." Owen raked a hand through his hair. "On the spot. I couldn't get a word in with all the squealing and dancing, especially after Clare came in and joined the chorus."

"Clare's here?"

"Mind on the target," Ryder snapped. "How the hell did you let this happen?"

"Hey, don't blame me. Plus side, Hope's more than qualified, but—"

"She's qualified to flounce around some fancy hotel in D.C., where she's got staff and money to burn. Jesus, she climbed a couple flights of stairs and looked like she was going to keel over." Disgust laced Ryder's voice. "Probably because she's walking around a damn construction zone in shoes with five-inch spikes. She was wearing a suit, for Christ's sake."

"Well, it was an interview."

"She's city. The innkeeper's going to be key to whether this place gets off the ground. You and Mom talk to her for five minutes, and she's on the fucking payroll."

"I interviewed her for damn near an hour today, not including the phone call from the other day. I read her resume, checked it out." The more Ryder objected, the more Owen sided with their mother. "She's smart, and she knows the business. She brought up details we haven't even thought of yet, and had suggestions."

"Suggestions are easy. Making them work's different. What's going to happen the first time somebody spills their coffee on the floor? Is she going to call housekeeping? We don't have housekeeping."

"Did you even read her resume?" Owen shot back. "She's been working since she was sixteen. She waited tables when she was in high school."

"Big fucking deal. That's high school. This is now. What happened to discussing key elements of this place and voting?"

"Ask Mom," Owen suggested. "But if it came down to a vote, I'd add mine to Mom's." The argument solidified his stand.

"That's just great. What about you?" Ryder stabbed a finger at Beckett.

"Yes, Beckett," Justine said from the doorway, "what about you?"

Everybody froze, including Clare, who'd come up with Justine. Even as she tried to step back and make herself scarce, Justine clamped a hand on Clare's arm. "No, that's fine. This won't take long. Ryder has objections to my choice of innkeeper, apparently. I take it Owen doesn't."

"I maybe would've . . . Not really," Owen decided. Wisely.

"Beckett?"

Stuck, Beckett looked from his mother to Clare, and back again. "I really only talked to her for a second. It's a key position, like Ry said. It's *the* key position. But I did read her resume, and I agree with Owen that she's more than qualified. She obviously made a strong impression on you or you wouldn't have hired her. So . . . I guess we've got an innkeeper."

"Then that's settled. Now, before I take Clare out to see W&B, I'm going to tell the three of you *morons* you're damn lucky Hope didn't come back up with me. She might have changed her mind about working for a trio of rude, bitchy men. And you." She pointed at Ryder. "I'll give you six weeks after she's worked here to apologize for questioning my judgment."

"Mom—"

"That's all I have to say." She cut him off with another point of the finger. "Come on, Clare."

After one apologetic glance, Clare followed in Justine's steaming wake.

"Great," Beckett muttered, scrubbing his hands over his face. "That was just great."

" 'I guess we've got an innkeeper,' " Ryder mimicked. "You only went along like that because you want to get lucky with Clare."

"Jesus, shut up. And it has nothing to do with Clare." Or hardly. "She's qualified; Mom likes her. That's that."

"We don't even know her."

Though he was fairly steamed himself at this point, Beckett nodded. "So we'll get to know her. We've got that apartment across St. Paul. It's vacant right now. We put her up there, have her work with Mom and Owen for a while. Ordering supplies, organizing the inventory, whatever. She gets a taste of small-town living, and we get a better sense of her."

Ryder opened his mouth to protest on principle, then rethought. "That's actually a pretty good idea. If she bails, or is just a screwup, we'll know before it's too late."

"And if I could toss some of the phone calls, the lists, the grunt work to her, I'd have more time here and in the shop. We give her the apartment and a small hourly wage." Owen nodded. "This could work. If she'll agree."

"Tell Mom," Ryder suggested. "She'll get her to agree."

"I'll go run it by her. My idea," Beckett added, and took off.

He caught them at the base of the outside steps. "Hey! Hold on a minute. Did you get the full tour this time?" he asked Clare as he came down.

"Yes. It's going to be wonderful. I've got more ideas." She tapped her notebook. "Justine and I are going to talk about them once I get them in some sort of order. Thanks for taking me through. I really need to get going."

"Can you wait a minute—you could weigh in on this. Mom, how about asking Hope if she'd move up here now, or as soon as she can? We could give her the apartment across the street. It would give her time to acclimate to the town, get to know the area. And she could help you and Owen with the stuff you and Owen do."

Justine tipped down her sunglasses, eyed him over the top. "Whose idea is this?"

"Well, mine, but Ry and Owen—"

"It's a good one. You are, temporarily at least, my favorite son. I'll talk to her about it over lunch. We'll talk soon, Clare. Just email me some of the copy whenever you think you're ready."

"I will."

"I'm going to call Carolee." Justine pulled out her phone as she walked away.

"Sorry about the family drama."

"We have plenty of our own. Does Ryder really not want Hope?"

"He's just pissed Mom didn't consult him." Beckett left out issues like *city*, *suits*, and *five-inch spikes*. "Listen, I thought maybe I'd swing by later, give you a hand with the yard work."

"The yard work?"

"Get the grass mowed for you. I miss mowing grass."

"Oh, that's sweet of you, but I mowed this morning."

"This morning? It's still morning."

"The kids never sleep in on Saturdays, especially summer Saturdays. The advantage is, I can get a lot done before noon. Which is good as Saturdays are my get-it-all-done day, with Sunday for what didn't. But thanks."

"Anytime. Really."

"I'll keep that in mind. I have to go, pick up the kids from my mother's, hit the grocery store. I'm so glad you hired Hope. She's going to be perfect for the inn, and the inn's going to be perfect for her. Well, I'll see you."

"Yeah. Come here." He pulled her around the steps, under the side porch roof. "I missed doing this yesterday."

He closed his mouth over hers, nice and easy. Lingered a moment longer when her free hand curled up around his shoulder.

"That's nicer than help with the yard work," she murmured.

"You can have both, anytime."

She thought both would take some time to get used to.

"I guess I'll see you Monday."

He ran a hand down the sunny tail of her hair. "I'll call you later."

"All right."

It would all take time to get used to, she thought as she got into her car. Phone calls and kisses and Friday night dates. It was almost like being in high school again—well, except for the kids, the grocery store, the laundry waiting to be folded, and the checkbook that needed balancing.

She gave the inn a last glance as she drove away. The place had been there for over two centuries, she mused. And somehow it was changing everything.

CHAPTER EIGHT

SINCE YARD WORK WASN'T ON THE WEEKEND AGENDA, AND he couldn't think of a reasonable excuse to drop by Clare's, Beckett put some extra time in at the family shop. With the dogs and his iPod for company, he set to work building the wood frame that would cap in the stone arch leading from The Lobby to the entrance hallway.

He didn't do as much fine carpentry or cabinetmaking as his brothers, but enjoyed it when he did. And for the moment, he liked having the shop to himself.

He remembered his father teaching him how to use the saws, the lathe, the planer. Thomas Montgomery had been patient, but expected precision.

No point in doing something if you're going to do it half-assed.

A motto to live by, Beckett thought now.

God, his dad would've loved this project. Everything about it would have appealed to him, challenged him. He'd loved the town, the old buildings, its rhythm, its colors and tones. Its politics.

He could sit at the counter at Crawford's over bacon, eggs, and hash browns and bullshit with the best of them.

He'd never missed a parade or the fireworks for the Fourth in Shafer Park, not in Beckett's memory. He'd sponsored a Little League team, and the family business still did. He'd even coached for a few years.

In his way, Beckett supposed, without the bullshit or posturing, he'd taught his sons what it was to be a part of a community. And how to value it.

Yeah, he'd love this project, for the work, for the building, and for the community.

For that reason alone, nothing about it would be half-assed.

Beckett took out his tape measure, the one that had been his father's. Their mother had made sure each of them kept a specific tool. He measured and marked the next piece.

He straightened when his mother came in.

"Putting in some overtime, I see."

"I got into it. Since I'm the one who wanted the archways framed in, I thought I should start the build."

"It's going to look fine, too. Look at the bookcases." She laid a hand on her heart. "That's damn pretty work you boys are doing there. Your dad would be so proud."

"I was just thinking about him. It's hard not to in here. I was thinking how much he'd love working on the inn, bringing it back."

"Rolling his eyes at me behind my back when I came up with some new idea. And don't think I don't know you do the same."

"Just carrying on the tradition."

"You do a good job of that, the three of you."

"Are you still mad?"

She angled her head. "Do I look mad?"

"You can be sneaky about it. Anyway." He grinned. "It was Ry's fault."

"He's got his father's hard head and my temper. Tough combo. But he had a point. I should've talked it over with the three of you first. And if you tell him that, I'll kick your ass."

"He won't hear it from me. Why'd you hire her like that, Mom? Just bam!"

She shrugged, then opened the shop fridge, shook her head at the pair of six-packs, took out two cold sodas. "Sometimes you know something's right, and sometimes you have to accept things happen for a reason. This was both."

Then she laughed, drank. "I think Hope surprised herself taking the offer as quick as it was made. I don't think she was going to, but that's what love'll do to you. She fell for the place. You'll see."

"I guess we'll see soon enough if she moves up."

"She will be," Justine assured him. "She's going to get herself organized. She'll make the move in a couple of weeks."

"You talked her into it?"

"I had help. Avery."

"Secret weapon."

"She's a go-getter, all right," Justine agreed. "I gave Hope the key, let her go over and see the apartment. You're going to need to see it gets a fresh coat of paint."

When he blew out a breath, she lifted her eyebrows. "I know, but it needs to be done. By the way, I ordered the new sink and faucet for the gift shop. And a new toilet while I was at it. I sent you the links. Since Willow Run's coming in to talk about the final design for The Courtyard next week, I'm having Brian take a look at the back of the gift shop. I think it needs a nice patio, and new fencing along the bookstore side. Some plantings," she added, laughing now. "And those old steps can be worked in with stone like the patio."

"Would you turn around so I can roll my eyes?"

"It's going to be nice. Madeline's already talking to local artists. And I've got Willy B signed on."

"Avery's dad?"

"He does wonderful metalwork in his spare time. You saw those candlesticks he gave me last Christmas. So . . . I think we can open toward the end of October."

He felt the swallow of Coke stick at the base of his throat. "Mom, we haven't even started."

"Better get to it then. Oh, and mention the fence to Clare if I don't get a chance."

"Okay."

"You can talk about it on your Friday night date."

He lowered his drink. "What, did somebody take out an ad? I only mentioned it to Owen and Ryder."

"And they didn't tell me? I need to talk to those boys. Avery told me. You sure took your sweet time there, baby boy."

"It's just dinner or something."

"You've been wanting to have dinner or something with Clare since you were a teenager. It broke my heart."

"I didn't think you knew."

"Baby, of course I knew. I'm your mom. Just like I knew the night you came back from a date with Melony Fisher you'd had sex for the first time."

He actually felt heat rush up the back of his neck. "Jesus, Mom."

She laughed herself breathless. "I know what I know, and I trusted you'd been careful as your father and I drummed safe sex, respect, and consequences in all your heads. Make sure you remember all that with Clare."

"Jesus, Mom."

"You're repeating yourself."

"I—" When his phone rang, he snatched at it like a lifeline. "Owen. You don't know why, but I owe you big. I'm out at the shop, why? He what? Seriously. Yeah, yeah, I'll come in."

He shoved the phone back in his pocket. "Ry's sucking up after this morning. He's taking your wall out. They want me to come take a look."

"Go on then. Have you got anything going on tonight?"

"No."

"You could pick up a pizza, come back. I'll go over what I ordered today, and a few things I'm mulling over."

"I can do that."

"If either or both of your brothers hasn't managed a date on Saturday night, I don't know what the hell's wrong with them. But if not, and they want, get more pizza."

❧

BY MONDAY, THEY had crew in three buildings, painting the vacant apartment, prepping for paint at the gift shop, and since the temperatures dropped a little, doing exterior paint at the inn. Copper shone in the sun as the roofers worked on the mansard.

By ten, ready for a break, Beckett walked over to the bookstore.

He found Clare at Laurie's station. "Hey. Where's your crew?"

"Laurie had a dentist appointment. She'll be in later. Cassie's due in any minute, and Charlene's coming at one. I said I'd open today anyway so I wouldn't sit home and brood."

"Brood?"

"First day of school." She walked behind the counter to make his coffee without being asked.

He supposed that made him predictable.

"Did they get off okay?"

"Oh yeah. They were raring to go—that'll last about a week. They're excited about seeing all their friends, using their new supplies. I'm the one having problems," she admitted. "I didn't even go back to the house after I dropped them off because I knew the quiet would kill me. That'll probably last about a week, too, then I'll be annoyed when they have one of those professional days, and the kids have off."

He dug back in his memory, felt a little glow. "I loved those."

"I bet your mother didn't. I've been watching all the activity this morning. It feels like the whole town's buzzing with it."

"We're scattered everywhere. Mom wants to open the gift shop in about six weeks. You knew," he said when she cleared her throat.

"She may have mentioned it. It's great Hope will be here for the opening." Clare handed him the coffee. "She'll be able to meet some people."

"Opening? We're having an opening? I should've figured."

"Your mother will take care of it. I imagine you'll just have to show up." Obviously amused by the worry on his face, she gave his hand a pat. "Consider it a trial run for the opening for the inn."

"I guess I'll need a date. How about—sorry." He pulled out his phone. "Yeah. No, I drew that up. I showed you. Yes, I—no, I didn't. I left them at home. I'll get them and be right there. Gotta go," he said as he shoved his phone away.

"Don't worry about it," she said when he reached for his wallet. "First cup, first customer. No charge on back-to-school day."

"Thanks. Why don't we—" His phone rang again, and the bookstore line jingled along with it. "Later," he said and headed out with his phone to his ear. "What now?"

❧

IT WAS A week of fits and starts, progress and delays, with plenty of frustration mixed in. Beckett found now that he didn't feel as obliged to come up with an excuse to see Clare, he didn't have time. And when he did, she didn't.

"You'd think two people who live and work in the same town could manage more than a five-minute conversation." Beckett installed yet another picket on the third-floor porch.

"You've got it bad. I've got it bad," Ryder decided, "when I know who you're whining about even when you don't use names."

"I'm not whining, I'm just saying."

"Aren't you going out tomorrow night?"

No point in admitting he still felt the need to sort of work up to that. "Yeah."

"Talk then. Hell, go over and talk to her after we knock off. She's open till six."

"She's got to pick up the kids from school. Plus she's got that book club thing she does tonight."

"People talk too much anyway, especially when they don't have anything to say. The woman I went out with last weekend? She never shut up. Great pair of legs, and a mouth that wouldn't quit." He ran his hand along the side rail he'd finished. "Nice."

He looked over at Beckett. "Why don't you go over and check on the crew at the gift shop? Since it's next to the bookstore, maybe you can have the conversation you're yearning for. Plus, it'll get your lovesick germs away from me."

"Good idea. Want me to send one of the men out to work with you?"

"No. I like the quiet."

Beckett went through the building, where quiet it wasn't, and out the back. They'd be taking the scaffolding down soon, he thought as he walked under it. And before much longer, they'd get rid of the tarp on the front.

He ran through scheduling and time lines in his head as he crossed the street. He met obligations first, going inside the gift shop. His mother had been dead-on about the wall color, he decided, and about opening the wall.

He talked with the painters, and went out the back.

His mother was right about that, too. It needed sprucing up. Maybe they could add a little gate to—

He caught himself. "Don't start, man. Just don't give her any more ideas."

He walked around to the parking lot just as Clare came out the back, moving fast, her phone at her ear.

"No, don't worry about it. Just tell her to feel better. Okay, sure."
She sent Beckett a distracted wave. "I'll talk to you later. Bye."

"Problem?"

"Lynn Barney. Called to tell me Mazie came home from school
early. Maybe a stomach virus."

"Sorry to hear it."

"Mazie was on tap to babysit for me—book club night."

"Oh, right."

"I've got to run, pick up the kids, figure this out."

"I can watch them," he heard himself say. Then wondered where
the hell that came from.

"What?"

"I can watch them. It's, what, a couple, three hours, right?"

"Oh, well, thanks, but I'll figure something out."

"Hold on."

Amused at both of them, he took her arm before she could wrench
open the door to her van. Besides, now that he actually thought about
it, he liked the idea.

"You don't think I can handle three boys? I was a boy. I was one
of three boys."

"I know, but—"

"What time do you have to leave for the thing?"

"I should be here around five to help set up. We usually start
around five thirty. We generally go until about seven, then it takes a
while to close up and—"

"So about five to eight. No problem."

"Yes, but they need to be fed and bathed and—"

"I'll pick up dinner at Vesta, come down at five."

"Well . . ."

"It'll be fun. I like your kids."

"God, I'm going to be late."

"So go. See you at five."

"I just don't know if— Okay," she decided. "But not pizza. If you get spaghetti and meatballs, they can split it three ways. And a salad. Just tell whoever's taking the order it's for my boys. They all know what they like. I'll make sure they have their homework done," she added as she climbed into the van.

"If something comes up—"

"Clare, I'll be by at five. Go pick up your kids."

"Right. Thanks."

It would be fun, he thought again as she drove off. And spaghetti and meatballs sounded just about perfect.

⌒⌒

"HOW COME GRANDDAD can't come play with us?" Liam sulked over his chapter book.

"I told you, he's got a meeting with his photography group. Now answer the question. What did Mike find when he climbed the tree?"

"A stupid bird's nest."

"Write it down."

He slid his eyes up with the little smirk Clare found both endearing and infuriating, depending on her mood. "I don't know how to spell 'stupid.'"

"L-I-A-M," Harry sang out.

"Mom! Harry called me stupid."

"Harry, knock it off. Liam, write down the answer. Murphy, how many times do I have to tell you not to throw that ball in the house? Take it outside."

"I don't wanna go outside. Can I watch TV?"

"Yes, please. Go do that."

"I wanna watch TV."

Me, too, she thought when she glanced at Liam. "Then finish your homework."

"I *hate* homework."

"You and me both, pal. Harry—"

"I finished mine. See?"

"Great. Let's go over your words for your spelling test tomorrow."

"I *know* the words."

It was probably true. Spelling had always been a breeze for Harry.

"We'll go over them anyway, then yours, Liam, when you're done with your book."

"How come Murphy gets to watch TV?" Liam managed to look long-suffering and outraged at the same time. "How come he doesn't have homework? It's not fair."

"He had homework. He finished."

"Just stupid flash cards. Baby homework."

"I'm not a baby!" Murphy's furious protest rang from the living room. He had ears like a cat.

"He gets to do anything he wants. It's not—"

"I don't want to hear 'it's not fair.' You know, Liam, the longer you sit here complaining, the longer it's going to take. Then you won't have any play or TV time."

"I don't want Beckett to watch us."

"You like Beckett."

"Maybe he'll be mean. Maybe he'll yell and lock us in our room."

Clare folded her arms. "Has he ever been mean before?"

"No, but he could be."

"If you want somebody to yell, keep stalling over that homework. You'll hear somebody yell." She grabbed Harry's spelling list, began to call off the words.

After he'd finished, she scanned the list he'd written. "That's an A-plus. Good job, Harry. Now scram."

She sat, the better to focus her middle son. "That's good, Liam. See here, though, you wrote a *d* instead of *b*."

"How come they made them that way, so they get mixed up?"

"That's a good question, but it's what erasers are for." She got out his spelling list while he fixed it—grudgingly. "Get a fresh piece of paper."

"I got more homework than *anybody*."

He didn't, but she didn't have time for the lecture about stalling, scribbling, and staring into space. "Almost done." He hunched over the paper when she gave him the words.

His penmanship was better than Harry's, but the spelling? Not so much.

"Pretty good. You missed three, but see here, you wrote *b* instead of *d*. You know how you can remember? B's for butt, and your butt's in the back."

It made him laugh, and she decided to end it on a high note. "We'll go over it in the morning, one more time. Put your things away, and you can watch TV."

She walked out with him. "No fighting," she called out, and dashed upstairs to freshen up before the book club meeting.

She shoved the book and her notes in her purse, grabbed her hairbrush. And heard the doorbell.

Not only on time, but ten minutes early. She glanced at herself in the bedroom mirror. She could've used that ten minutes.

She rushed downstairs in time to hear Murphy ask, "Are you going to lock us in our room?"

"Are you guys planning to rob the bank?"

"Nuh-uh!"

"Then I won't need to lock you up." Beckett looked over, up. And smiled. "Spaghetti and meatballs, as ordered."

"Thanks. You're a lifesaver." She took the bag, then felt a little clutch in her belly as she noted all three boys watched Beckett like they would a strange animal in the zoo.

"Let's take this back so I can show you where everything is. They've finished their homework," she began as they went back to the kitchen.

"They should eat by around six." She got out plates as she spoke. "Don't worry about the bath, I'll get them in the shower in the morning. Their pj's are laid out, they like to get in them at least an hour before bedtime."

"Men of leisure."

"Exactly. I'll be home before bedtime, that's eight fifteen or so."

"Got it. Clare, relax. Those child endangerment charges were dismissed."

"Very funny. I'm actually more worried about you. They know the rules, but that doesn't mean they won't pull something. You've got my numbers. I can be home in five minutes if—"

"We'll be fine. I won't listen if they tell me to run with scissors."

"Okay." She let out a breath. "I'd better go."

He walked back in with her, and once again the boys turned as one, stared. "I'll be home by bedtime. Be good, and no snacks before dinner. Good luck," she told Beckett.

He closed the door behind her, waited a beat. "All right, men, what's the plan?"

As oldest, Harry took point. "We want cookies."

"Gotta say no to that one. Just got a direct order."

"Told ya," Liam muttered.

"We want to play PlayStation. Pop and Nan gave us PlayStation 3 for Christmas."

"What games have you got?"

Harry eyed him speculatively. "Do you know how to play?"

"Please. You're looking at the reigning town champ."

"Nuh-uh."

Beckett just smiled, flexed his fingers. "Bring it on."

❧

THEY WERE PRETTY good, even the little guy. It shouldn't have surprised him to find himself in real competition. He'd been battling his brothers at video games at five. Harry had patience and a knack for strategy while Liam went full-out, a technique that either paid off big-time or went down in flames.

And Murphy? He just lived it.

They bitched and moaned a lot, accused each other or the game itself of cheating regularly. Beckett either ignored them or joined in. Once they got over the shock of not being called out for poor sportsmanship or not being told it was just a game and supposed to be fun, they got louder, and wilder.

"I smoked you!" Harry cackled, shook his fists in the air.

Not entirely pleased at being smoked by an eight-year-old, Beckett scowled at the screen. "Shit."

"You're not supposed to say bad words," Murphy informed him.

"*You're* not supposed to say bad words. I have a license to swear."

Liam snorted. "Come on."

"And it's up for renewal next month. Let's—shit," he repeated when he noticed the time. "We were supposed to eat a half hour ago."

"We've got another Ben 10 game." Harry bounced up to get it out of the case. "We can play it first."

"Gotta fuel up, otherwise your mom will kick all our butts."

"Butts are behind so you know how to write a b."

Beckett studied Liam. "Okay. Let's eat."

He didn't tell them to pick up the games. Harry hesitated, then shrugged and raced to the kitchen.

In the spirit of solidarity Beckett chose a Hulk plate. It amazed him that they ate salad without whining about it, but maybe it was because they rehashed the games while they wolfed it down.

Or they were starving since dinner was late.

They asked for Coke. Murphy broke as Beckett poured it out.

"We're supposed to have milk. We're not supposed to have soda."

Liam shoved him. Murphy shoved back.

"Cut it out. It's a special occasion. Man Night. Sodas all around."

"He hit me."

"I did not."

"Yeah, you did," Beckett said before Murphy could come up with the inevitable "did, too." "And you hit back. It's a wash."

"I'm telling Mom," Murphy muttered.

"You can't do that, man." Beckett shook his head as he scooped spaghetti, without warming it up, onto plates.

Torn between insult and being called *man*, Murphy stared at him, bottom lip quivering. "How come?"

"Code of Brotherhood. It's strictly enforced on Man Night. What goes on here, stays here."

Murphy thought about it as he studied his plate. Nobody cut up the spaghetti or the meatball. Maybe because it was Man Night. He stabbed at the meatball with his fork, and sent it winging across the table to land in Liam's lap.

"Two points," Beckett commented.

Then all hell broke loose.

On a cry of rage, Liam scooped up the meatball, threw it at his brother. He had damn good aim, and bounced the meatball off Murphy's forehead.

Beckett had to give the little guy credit. He didn't cry; he didn't hesitate. He attacked.

He bounded out of the chair, leaping toward Liam. Spaghetti flew like wet confetti. Beckett managed to hook an arm around Murphy's waist, haul him back as he kicked enthusiastically at his brother. Wild to retaliate, Liam made a grab. Beckett shifted to block, bumped the boy into the table.

And the cup of soda dumped all over Harry.

Desperate to stop the war, Beckett scooped up Liam as Harry, fists bunched, jumped up.

"Hold it, hold it. Harry, that was my fault. I knocked it over. Take it easy. Everybody just stop!"

"He did it on purpose!" Liam accused and tried to wiggle around to punch his little brother.

"Did not." Murder in his eye, red sauce on his face, Murphy got in one good kick. "He didn't cut it up. It's *his* fault."

"Everybody stop! Quiet!"

The shouts and accusations snapped off. Three mutinous faces stared at him as Beckett surveyed the damage. "Wow, that's a pretty big mess."

The meatball that started it sat partially smashed on the floor. Noodles and sauce glopped over the table.

"Mom's gonna be mad." And now Murphy's eyes shone with tears.

"No, she's not. Look, kid, these things happen when men eat together without women around."

"They do?"

"I'm looking at it, so they do. Everybody just sit down."

"He threw a meatball at me."

"He didn't throw it at you," Beckett corrected as Liam stared at Murphy with the active dislike only siblings can feel for one another. "It was an accident because I didn't cut it up. It's my first day on the job, so cut me some slack. Go on and sit down."

"But I got meatball on my pants."

"So what? We'll clean up after we eat."

He set Murphy down, then picked up the guilty meatball and tossed it in the sink before sliding Murphy's spaghetti back on his plate. He got a knife, another meatball out of the take-out dish, then set to work cutting it up.

"Big Chief Murphy. You look like you're wearing war paint."

And the boy smiled at him, sweet as an angel. "I like pisgetti."

"Me, too. Want yours cut up, Liam?"

"Okay."

"Gut shot." Beckett poked a finger on the red stain on Liam's T-shirt. "And still up for the battle. Harry?"

"I like to twirl it."

"Good plan." Fairly exhausted, Beckett dropped into his chair. "Dig in, men."

CHAPTER NINE

THEY ATE LIKE WOLVES, BECKETT INCLUDED. MAYBE virtual war followed by a minor meatball fight piqued the appetite. After the meal, the best solution he could come up with was to strip them down in the tiny laundry room off the kitchen. As he tossed his spaghetti-tagged shirt in the machine for good measure, the boys did what naked boys have done throughout history.

They ran around the house yelling like heathens.

He wasn't sure which was more of a mess, the kitchen or the kids, but opted to deal with the kids first. Since he doubted Clare's standards stooped low enough to deck out three sticky, sauce-stained kids in their pajamas, he herded them into the bathroom.

"It's a three-for-one," he announced. "Everybody into the pool."

"Can we have bubbles?" Murphy asked.

"I don't know, can you?"

"We got Spider-Man." Harry reached onto a shelf in the splinter-sized linen closet, took out a Spidey-shaped bottle.

"Very cool." Beckett dumped a hefty dose in the water. "Okay, hop in, and I'll—"

"We need our toys." Liam got a plastic basket out of the closet, dumped in all contents. From the sneaky look he shot Beckett, Beckett figured that wasn't how their mom handled it.

But, it was Man Night.

"Okay—"

"We need our soap stuff." Harry got a pump bottle. "You can wash your hair and your skin with it."

"Handy."

"But you gotta wash our hair," Murphy told him.

"Okay." Beckett studied the bottle. "Let's go for it."

They climbed in. If he hadn't been distracted by Spider-Man, toys, and soap stuff, he'd have considered water displacement.

He switched off the taps, tossed a towel on the floor where the water had lapped over. Because he was currently shirtless, he metaphorically rolled up his sleeves and got to it.

Realized inside of thirty seconds he'd need more towels.

It brought back dim memories of baths with his brothers, the water battles, the floods, the silly fun.

The wheedling protests when it was time to get out.

"Here's the deal about Man Night. Women come back. If your mom comes home and sees this bathroom, the kitchen, men, we are toast. It's better to get rid of the evidence."

He pulled the plug. Between the floor, the walls, the kids, he used half a dozen towels. And now naked boys ran around yelling again, but at least they were clean.

"Everybody go suit up." Beckett grabbed wet toys out of the tub, tossed them in the basket. "I've got to go deal with the kitchen."

He carted the towels down, switched the wet clothes to the dryer, dumped the towels in the washer.

He glanced at his watch. Jesus, how the hell did it get to be quarter to eight? Moving fast now while running feet and shouts sounded from upstairs, he stuck dishes in the dishwasher. He scrubbed off the table, swiped the sauce off the floor, then tossed the dishrag in the washer with the towels.

"Hey, you need to come down and put away these games."

"We're putting on our pajamas!" Harry shouted back.

The hyena laughter followed.

"Yeah, I bet."

But time was running out. He made a dive for the living room, gathering up games, controllers, then charged up the stairs.

They'd pulled on the bottoms, and wore the tops on their heads like war bonnets as they sat on the floor around a small mountain of action figures.

"I can fart with my arm," Murphy told him. "Liam showed me."

He demonstrated to his brothers' hysterical laughter.

"An important life skill, well executed. Tops on, guys. Your mom'll be home any minute."

"She says it's rude to fart in public, even with your arm."

"Words to live by." Taking matters in his own hands, Beckett tugged down Murphy's shirt.

And got that angel smile again.

"Can it be Man Night tomorrow?"

The oddest sensation of pleasure glowed in Beckett's belly. "Can't tomorrow, but we'll do it again."

"We can do it when it's not school, then have a sleepover."

Here's hoping. "I'd like that."

"Mom's home. Mom's home." Murphy raced off, followed by, then passed by, his brothers.

When he started down they surrounded her, Murphy holding his arms up to be lifted, and all of them talking a mile a minute.

She laughed, hitched Murphy up, managed to kiss the top of Liam's head and run her hand over Harry's.

"Man Night, huh? Well, we'll have to . . ." She looked up at Beckett as he came down the stairs. Blinked. "Ah, hi."

"Hi. How'd it go?"

"Really well. Um, how'd it go here?"

"Good. We just played some poker, drank a six-pack."

"Naturally. You boys have to go up and brush your teeth. I'll be up in a couple minutes. Say good night to Beckett."

He got high fives from Harry and Liam, a down low and leg hug from Murphy.

"We're gonna have a sleepover," Murphy told his mother. "Bye, Beckett. Bye!"

Clare set her purse aside as they raced upstairs. "So, everything's okay?"

"Sure."

"You didn't have to give them baths." She tapped the side of her nose when Beckett looked blank. "They smell like their bath soap."

"Oh yeah, well . . . There was a little spaghetti incident."

"I see. Is that why you're not wearing a shirt?"

"Oh, right." He glanced down. "Forgot. I tossed the shirt in the washer with their clothes. They're drying. Ah, there was also some minor flooding, so I dumped the towels in the wash."

It was her turn to look blank. "You did laundry?"

"Sort of. I deserve a reward."

"I guess you do." She stepped to him, kissed him on one cheek, then the other before laying her lips softly on his.

His bare skin was warm and firm, his arms strong as they wrapped around her.

"You smell like an orange smoothie," she murmured. And wanted to lap.

"Sorry?"

"The bath wash I use on the kids. It's different on you. Beckett—"

"Mom!" Liam's shout made her jump. "We brushed our teeth. Harry's got the book."

"Okay. Be right there. Sorry, it's bedtime, and I try to read to them for a few minutes most nights."

"I'll get going. I'll pick you up at seven tomorrow."

"You can't go out without a shirt."

"I don't think anything of yours will fit me."

"But—"

"It's still warm out." He gave her another quick, light kiss.

"Well, thanks." Flustered, she stepped back. She'd actually started to ask him to stay—until his shirt dried. Maybe have a glass of wine with her. Maybe . . .

"Mom!"

"No problem. I had fun. See you tomorrow."

She sighed, locked up behind him. "Coming," she called when Liam shouted again. Probably better this way, she thought. She could hardly—maybe—with Beckett while her kids were right upstairs.

❧

BECKETT PULLED INTO his slot in the parking lot behind Vesta.

When he started down the walkway to the stairwell, Brad, their plumber, called down from his seat on the dining porch. "Hey, Beck! Rough night at the poker table? Lose your shirt?"

"You don't know the half of it."

In his apartment, he went directly to the fridge for a beer, then switched on the TV, flopped on the couch.

"Good God." He felt like he'd just finished running the Boston Marathon.

How did she do it? How the hell did she do all that every day, and probably a lot more? But just the dinner, the squabbles, the mess, the sheer volume of *stuff* that needed to be remembered, done, handled with three kids. It was mentally and physically exhausting.

Fun, he admitted, but exhausting.

And she'd have to get up in the morning, get them up, dressed, fed. *Then* go to work. After work, she'd replay—basically—what he'd just done. And with all that, she still had to maintain the house and run a business.

Did women have superpowers?

Regardless, he was sending his mother flowers in the morning.

⌒

"WHEN I HEARD he came home shirtless, I thought, that Clare. She's a wild woman." Avery leaned back on her elbows on Clare's bed.

"More like wild boys."

"Flying meatballs, bath floods." Avery shook her head. "And he's still taking you out tonight. Shows character."

"Once I convinced Murphy to make me an honorary man, he spilled his guts. Plus I found a couple spaghetti sauce handprints Beckett missed." She picked up the earrings Hope had selected. "He did great, really, and got out fast. Didn't even wait for his shirt to dry."

"Is that code?"

"Not entirely. Though I was going to ask him to stay awhile, maybe open a bottle of wine."

"You are a wild woman."

"You know you can put men and sex on the back burner." To test the earrings, Clare tipped her head from side to side. "In fact, you can take them off the stove altogether. It's not easy to fit them into the schedule anyway. But . . . once I started thinking about Beckett that way, and realized he thought about me that way . . ."

"The heat got turned up."

"The pot's simmering away. It's not as easy to keep it on the back burner now."

"Move it up front. Be proactive."

"I guess I'd better see how it goes tonight first. We're sure this works, right?" She did a little turn.

"You look fantastic. That shade of blue, turquoise I guess, looks amazing on you."

Clare narrowed her eyes at her reflection. She liked the dress's simple lines, just a little flow to the skirt that stopped shy of her knees. "With or without the sweater?"

"Start with, then you can slip out of it later. Yeah." Avery nodded approval. "A very nice end-of-summer look. Nervous?"

"A little. And excited. I'm going on a date, and for the first time with a man I'm actually interested in."

"Proactive," Avery repeated.

"I started back on the pill. Is that proactive or aggressive?"

"It's just smart. I've got to go. I'm closing tonight." She took Clare's shoulders. "Have fun, and call me tomorrow and tell me everything."

"I will."

She took another moment, studying herself from every angle. Three kids, she thought, but she'd kept in pretty good shape. That was a matter of vigilance and lucky genes.

If tonight went well, if the chemistry continued, she and Beckett could—probably would—end up doing what single adults with chemistry did.

"It's called sex, Clare," she muttered to herself. "Just because you haven't had any in years doesn't mean you can't say the word."

She didn't even know if she was good at it. She and Clint had enjoyed a healthy, satisfying sex life, but he was the only man she'd been with. And they'd known each other's rhythm, signals, bodies so well even with, maybe because of, the long separations.

And now, Beckett.

What would it be like with Beckett?

What would *she* be like with Beckett?

Don't think about it, she ordered herself, or you'll never be able to enjoy a simple date. Be in the moment. One step at a time.

She went downstairs. She could hear the boys in the playroom. Loud, but getting along. Saw them ranged around a superhero war as she walked by to the kitchen. Alva sat paging through a garden magazine at the table while the happy sound of popcorn popped in the microwave.

"We're watching *How to Train Your Dragon*."

"Again?"

"Good thing I like it." Alva tipped down her reading glasses. "Clare, you look beautiful."

"It's nice to dress up for a date. Different, but nice."

"You did a good job of it. And he's right on time," Alva added when the doorbell rang. "Want me to get it so you can make an entrance?"

"No, and too late," she said as Harry shouted *I'll get it*. "I'd better go save him from the pack."

They outnumbered him right inside the door, battering him with questions, begging for a game. She realized she'd gotten used to seeing him in work clothes so it came as a pleasant jolt to study him in black dress pants and a steel gray jacket.

He held a bouquet of pink baby roses in his hand as he grinned down at her boys.

She knew, in that instant, she was a goner.

"Boys, let Beckett get in the house at least."

His grin softened to a smile when he looked at her. His eyes warmed. "You look great."

"Mom got dressed up 'cause she's going out," Murphy informed him.

"Me, too. These are for you."

"They're beautiful. Thanks." She saw Harry's solemn, searching look as she bent her head to sniff the blooms. Instinctively she ran a hand down his back. "Come on in while I put these in water. I'll—"

"Mom."

"Just a minute, Liam."

"Mom, I don't feel good. My belly hurts."

As she shifted toward him, he bent over and threw up on Beckett's shoes.

"Oh God." She thrust the flowers back at Beckett. "Harry, go tell Mrs. Ridenour that Liam got sick, and ask her for a towel."

"Wow," Beckett said as Clare crouched to feel Liam's forehead.

"I'm sorry. I'm so sorry. Just let me—Baby, you're a little warm."

"I don't feel good."

"I know. Let's get you upstairs. Beckett, I'm so sorry."

"Don't worry about it."

Alva came bustling out with towels, a bucket, and a mop.

"Liam puked," Murphy informed her.

"I heard. Poor thing—and you, too," she said to Beckett. "Let's get this cleaned up."

"I have to get him upstairs." Clare gave Beckett a distracted smile. "I'll need to take a rain check."

"Sure."

"The flowers—thanks. Sorry. Come on, baby." She hefted Liam into her arms. He laid his pale cheek on her shoulder.

"Can I get in your bed?"

"Sure. We'll fix you up. Harry, sweetie, will you bring up a glass of ginger ale?"

Upstairs, she washed his face—held his head when he threw up a second time. She took his temperature—ninety-nine point three—then urged the ginger ale on him.

"I threw up two times."

"I know," she soothed as she changed him into his Iron Man pajamas. "Do you feel sick again?"

"No."

"I've got the bucket right here if you do and we can't make it to the bathroom." Stroking his head, she picked up the TV remote. "Cartoon channel or Nick?"

"Nick. I feel better since I threw up."

"That's good, baby."

Tears glimmered as he huddled against her. "I didn't mean to throw up on Beckett."

"Of course you didn't."

"Is he mad?"

"No, he's not mad." She kissed the top of Liam's head. "I'm going to change my clothes."

"Are you mad?" he asked as she pulled yoga pants and a T-shirt out of her drawer.

"Why would I be?"

" 'Cause you got dressed up."

She took off the pretty, impractical shoes. "It was fun to get dressed up. And I'll get dressed up again another time." Angling the closet door, she stepped behind it, took off the dress, put on her mom clothes. Because it smelled faintly of vomit, she stuffed the dress in the dry cleaning bag.

Oh well.

"Mom, can I have Iron Man—the new one, not the old one—and Wolverine and Deadpool? Can I have Luke, too?"

Luke was his tattered stuffed dog, named for Skywalker.

"Sure."

"And can I have more ginger ale?"

"You bet." She laid her hand on his brow again, then her lips. Still warm, she thought, and so very pale. "I'll be back in a minute. There's the bucket now. You call if you feel sick before I come back."

"Okay. Thanks, Mom."

She got the toys first, left him curled up with Luke.

"Alva? Thanks so much for—" She broke off when a barefoot Beckett stepped out of the playroom.

"She just left. She said to call if you needed any help. How's Liam doing?"

"Better, I think. He's in my bed watching Nickelodeon with his stuffed dog, Wolverine, Iron Man, and Deadpool for company. Deadpool's——"

"I know who Deadpool is. You keep forgetting I used to be a boy."

"You know who Deadpool is. Okay, anyway, he's just got a low-grade fever, and his color's already a little better so it sounds like the same thing Mazie had. I didn't expect you to stay."

"We had a date."

"Oh, but——"

"So, since you're standing me up, I'm hanging with the bros. It's what men do. I guess you've got some nursing to do. And I don't guess you've got one of those uniforms, with the little white skirt and——"

"Did Liam frow up again?" Murphy asked.

"Yeah, he did, but he felt better after." She laid a hand on his brow. "How about you?"

"I don't feel sick."

"We don't call you Iron Guts for nothing. Harry?"

"I feel okay. We're going to play Bendominoes, but Beckett doesn't know how."

"I'm a quick study. Set it up, prepare to be beaten."

"No way!" Harry grabbed the box.

"Beckett, you don't have to—— Oh, hell, I need to take more ginger ale to Liam. I don't want him to get dehydrated. Just give me a minute."

She hurried into the kitchen. Popcorn sat in a bowl, and her lovely, lovely roses in a vase on the table.

"Am I in the way?"

She turned to see Beckett watching her from the doorway. "No, of course not, but you can't want to spend two evenings in a row with a bunch of kids, including one who threw up on your shoes. How are your shoes?"

"They'll survive."

"He was afraid you'd be mad at him."

"It's not like he aimed for me." He watched her pour ginger ale in the cup she'd brought back down, then put a few crackers in a bowl.

He thought of the kid, stuck in bed while his brothers played.

"Why don't I take them up to him?"

"Oh . . . well."

He solved it by taking the glass and bowl out of her hands. "I hear there's movies and popcorn on for later."

"That was the plan—a bit of a delay now."

"I can wait. I can wait," he repeated, making sure she got the message.

"Beckett," she said when he turned. "How about scrambled eggs?"

"How about them?"

"If Liam keeps those crackers down, he's going to want scrambled eggs. It's his sick meal. Harry's is Campbell's Chicken and Stars and Murphy—though he's hardly ever sick—goes for toast and strawberry jelly. I can make some scrambled eggs. And I've got some wine."

"Sounds good. About that nurse's uniform."

"It's at the cleaners."

"Damn. Bad timing."

She smiled at his back as he went out. He didn't run for the hills when a sick boy was involved, he made her stomach flutter when he kissed her. And, he knew who Deadpool was.

Yeah, she was a goner.

Upstairs, Beckett walked into Clare's room, and thought how small the boy looked in her bed.

"How's it going, kid?"

"I threw up two times."

"That's what you get for eating all those oysters and drinking all that whiskey."

"I didn't!"

"Yeah, you say that now."

He hugged a worn stuffed dog hard. "I didn't mean to throw up on you."

"These things happen between men." Beckett sat on the side of the bed, offered the cup and bowl.

"They do?"

"Ask me again in about ten years. I bet Deadpool's puked on Wolverine before."

"No, he . . . Really?"

"Wouldn't surprise me."

Intrigued, Liam picked up Deadpool and made puking noises.

"Nice. Your mom said she'd make you scrambled eggs if you're up for it."

"Maybe. Will you watch TV with me?"

"For a couple minutes." Though it wasn't the way he'd envisioned getting into Clare's bed, Beckett shifted, settled back against the headboard. The boy shifted, too, settled his head in the crook of Beckett's arm.

And glanced up. There it was, that angel smile, just like his younger brother.

❦

HE PLAYED BENDOMINOES—cool game—while she scrambled eggs for Liam. He watched a fun flick with the kids while she sat with the sick boy. He waited while she put the other two boys to bed, checked on Liam.

"He's sleeping," she told Beckett when she came back down. "And his forehead's cooler. So, I'd say that crisis is over. Harry'll be next, and he'll have it worse."

"That's optimistic."

"I know what I know. So. Scrambled eggs in the kitchen?"

"You don't have to bother. You must be tired."

"I'm starving, and I really want a glass of wine."

"Talked me into it."

It wasn't such a bad deal, sitting in the kitchen drinking a glass of wine while she scrambled eggs at the stove. Inspired, he went into the living room, gathered a trio of tea lights she had in dark blue cups.

"You mind? I had a candlelight dinner in my head for tonight." ·

"I love it." She opened a drawer, passed him a lighter.

They sat in the kitchen with tea lights and pink roses and ate scrambled eggs and toast.

"I'm glad you stayed."

"So am I. And you look just as beautiful in candlelight as I imagined. Do you want to try for a meal you don't have to cook next weekend?"

"Friday night?"

"Same time, same channel."

"You're a glutton for punishment. I'm in. Okay, the question has to be asked. Yes, you were once a boy, but all men were, and not all men are as easy and natural with kids as you are. Why don't you have some of your own?"

"I never got serious enough about anybody, I guess. You started younger than most."

"It was exactly what I wanted, and I didn't want to wait. It was the same for Clint. We just knew."

"What was it like, the military life?"

"There's a lot of waiting, if you're a military spouse. I saw parts of the world I never would have seen, learned how to organize, how to let things go. I did miss home. Not all the time, but there were moments, I missed it so much. When Clint was killed, I knew I had to come back, bring the boys here. For family, and for the sense of continuity."

She shook her head. "I wouldn't have made it without my parents, without his parents. They were, are, wonderful. You know how that is, working with your brothers, your mother, the family business."

"Yeah, I do."

"Some people need to step away from family, and others need to stick. I've done both, I suppose. This is home now, or again. Did you ever consider living somewhere else?"

"Thought about it, but there's nowhere else I wanted to be."

He made her laugh, talking about people she knew, people she'd never met. And when he rose with her when she cleared the table, when he drew her close, kissed her, he made her pulse jump.

"Maybe we could sit on the couch," he murmured in her ear. "Drink another glass of wine. Neck."

Oh yes, please, she thought. "You pour the wine. I'll just go check on Liam, then—Harry."

Sheet white, a little glassy-eyed, he stood in the doorway. "I got sick." .

"Oh, baby." She went to him quickly, felt his forehead. "Yeah, you're a little warm. We'll fix you up. Beckett."

"It's okay. Do you need any help?"

"No, I've got this."

"Go ahead. I'll let myself out. Feel better, big guy."

"Thanks. Come on, baby."

"Can I get in your bed, too? Liam did."

"Sure."

She sent Beckett an apologetic look, then led her sick boy upstairs.

CHAPTER TEN

THE WEEKEND PASSED IN A BLUR OF SICKBEDS, SOUP, AND scrambled eggs. By Sunday morning, both Liam and Harry felt well enough to be bored and cranky. She'd thought her idea to make camp in the living room where the two boys could have each other and an assortment of books and DVDs for company inspired. But the novelty wore off as Harry, no longer feverish but still a bit peaked, also became thoroughly sick of his brothers.

She had to sympathize, as she was fairly sick of them herself.

She solved the last shouting match over which DVD to watch by walking in, picking up the remote, and switching off the TV.

"Mom!"

The single word blasted in three-part harmony.

"Since all you can do is bicker and complain about the movies, we'll take a break from them."

"Harry started it," Liam began.

"I did not! You—"

"I don't care who started it." Sick kids or not, Clare pulled out the Mom Voice. "It appears I've finished it. Now you can all stay here and read, or color, or play quietly with your toys. Or you can go to your room and sulk. And if you argue with me," she said anticipating, "*all* the DVDs go away until next weekend."

"It's his fault," Liam said under his breath.

"Liam Edward Brewster, you're on notice. Not another word."

His eyes filled, tears and temper. She felt a little like a crying jag herself. "Now I want everyone to be quiet for ten minutes."

"Mom."

"Harry," she said with a warning note in her voice.

"I'm hungry. I want my soup."

Getting his appetite back was a good sign. However. "Harry, I told you, we're out. Marmie and Granddad are bringing more."

"But I'm hungry now."

"I can fix you something else. I have Chicken Noodle or Alphabet soup."

"I don't want those. I want Chicken and Stars."

"Then you have to wait. They'll be here soon."

"Why can't they be here *now*?" Fatigue and sheer pissyness turned his voice into a whiny toddler's.

Feeling her patience fray, Clare reminded herself how pale and pitiful he'd looked the night before. "They'll be here soon. It's the best I can do, Harry. Ten minutes of quiet now. I have to check the laundry."

She figured she'd be lucky to get five minutes of quiet, and didn't rate that as Murphy followed her into the kitchen.

"I'm hungry, too. I want a peanut butter and jelly sandwich."

"Honey, we're out of bread. More's coming."

"How come we don't have anything I want?"

"Because your brothers got sick, ate all the eggs, bread, and soup, and I couldn't go to the store yesterday."

"Why?"

"Because Harry and Liam got sick." While her head began to throb, she dumped the load of dry sheets in the basket.

"If they get to stay home from school tomorrow, I'm staying home, too."

"First, you don't get to decide. I do. And, no, you're not staying home tomorrow, and as neither of them has a fever, odds are they're not staying home either."

Please God, have pity on me.

"Nobody'll play with me."

"Murphy, I played games with you half the morning."

"With *all* of us. Why can't you play with just me?"

She closed her eyes until the urge to snap passed. She got it, she really did, and she tried hard to give each of them some one-on-one time. But God, not now.

"Why don't you get your Power Rangers? You can play upstairs while I make the beds."

"You *have* to play with me."

"No, I don't. And while I might like to, I don't have time. Why, you ask?" she continued, knowing he would have if given half a chance. "Because I have to do the rest of the laundry I didn't get to yesterday because I was taking care of Liam and Harry. I have to put clean sheets on the beds, which I didn't get to yesterday either, which is just as well as Harry got sick on his in the middle of the night. Would you like the list of everything else I have to do today?"

"Okay."

She stopped, rubbed her hands over her face, and laughed. "Murphy, you kill me."

"Don't get killed."

"It's just an expression." She leaned down, gave him a hug mostly because she really needed one.

"Can we get a puppy?"

Done in, she just dropped her head on his little shoulder. "Oh, Murphy."

"Harry and Liam would feel better if we had a puppy. My new best, best, best, *best* friend in school Jeremy has a puppy named Spike. We could get a puppy and name him Spike."

"Timing counts, kid, and this isn't a good time to ask for a puppy. Please don't ask me why. Just let me get myself together, Murphy. Let's go upstairs. You and the Power Rangers can help me make the beds."

"Power Rangers fight bad guys."

"Well, they have to sleep sometime, don't they?" She hefted the laundry basket. Since she hadn't taken any out of the linen closet, she'd save a step and put the freshly washed ones back on.

No folding. Woo-hoo, she thought as Murphy chattered his way into the living room. Where she found a miracle. Both boys had passed out.

"Shh. Quiet now. They're sleeping, so let's be sneaky."

Nobody'd gotten much sleep the last two nights—which didn't seem to bother Murphy the Mouth—though he did chatter in a whisper as they went upstairs.

She'd barely reached the top when someone banged the door knocker.

"Go get your Power Rangers," she told Murphy, and raced down. She'd kill anyone who woke her two sleeping kids. Strangle them with her bare hands.

She yanked open the door, and language she'd trained herself not to use because of the children ripped through her head. "Sam."

"Hello, gorgeous! I was in the area, thought I'd stop by, and sweep you off for brunch. I'm meeting my parents at the club. We'll make a party of it."

"This is a bad time. My two oldest boys have been sick all weekend, and they're sleeping."

"Sounds like you need a break. Call your sitter." He added that broad smile and wink. "I'll take you away from all this."

"All this is my life, and I'm not leaving my children when they're not well."

"Mom!"

"Murphy, quiet. You'll wake your brothers." She sensed Sam moving forward behind her, shifted to block.

"But I got my Power Rangers, and you said—"

"I'll be right up. I'm sorry, Sam, but I'm very busy. I have to go."

"I'll have my mother call you about that au pair."

Lack of sleep, lack of patience, lack of goddamn Chicken and Stars just snapped it. "I'm not getting a damn au pair, for God's sake. I'm not interested in brunches at the stupid country club. I'm interested in getting the beds made. Now, I have a lot to do, so you'll have to excuse me."

Rude wasn't her default, but she shut the door in his face.

Outside it, Sam balled his hands into fists. He'd had enough, just about enough of her games. Smiling and flirting with him one minute, brushing him off the next. Just about enough of her using those three brats to hold him off.

More than enough, he thought as he strode to his car, especially since he'd seen Beckett Montgomery walk out of her house the night before—at nearly eleven.

She wanted to make him jealous, he decided. Well, he'd about finished being Mr. Nice Guy. It was high time Clare Brewster learned who was in charge.

He pulled his car out of her drive and to the curb. As he had the evening before, he sat, watched the house, and stewed.

❦

INSIDE, CLARE BURNED off the temper Sam had ignited by wiping down the kids' room with disinfectant. She left the windows open to freshen the air, and felt the heat cooling in her brain and belly as she worked.

What was wrong with that man? she wondered. Nobody could be that dense, that egotistical and clueless all at the same time. And add in annoying.

It had gotten to the point where she could barely manage to be polite to him, and *still* he kept coming back. Maybe she'd cured him this time.

Lord, she'd literally shut the door in his face. That was a first, she decided. Surely no one could mistake that for anything but "leave me the hell alone."

She was on her hands and knees, scrubbing down the bathroom, when Murphy tapped her shoulder.

"Are you still apart?"

"Apart from what?"

"You said you had to get yourself together. Are you still apart?"

Charmed, she sat back on her heels, hugged him hard. Au pair, her ass. "Just a little bit. Nearly there."

"How come you didn't make the beds?"

"Because I wanted to clean first. I'm battling germs. I'm killing them dead. Can't you hear them screaming?"

His eyes rounded. "I want to kill germs!"

She dumped another rag in the bucket, squeezed it out. "There's some over there, there in that corner! Get them, Murph."

"I don't see them."

"They have the cloak of invisibility, don't be fooled. Scrub 'em out!"

Not bad, she decided as he attacked the floor with a vengeance.

She let him have at it, braced her tired back against the door frame while he made bomb and battle noises. Alerted by the sound of padding feet, she turned to Liam.

"Did you have a good nap?"

"I guess. We woke up. Can we watch a movie now? We're going to watch *Star Wars*."

"I killed the germs." Murphy waved the rag like a flag. "I wanna watch, too."

"All right. Let's go set it up."

When she got downstairs, Harry—and he looked so much better—gave her a pleading look. "I'm really hungry."

"Why don't I fix you some cereal to hold you off until— Wait a minute." She held up a hand as she heard the front door open. "Provisions have arrived. We're saved!"

"There's my guys." Rosie Murphy, with Ed just behind her, strode in, arms loaded. She winked at her daughter, passed her a grocery bag. "Look what we've got here for two sick boys and their brother."

She pulled action figures out of a separate bag. In the ensuing pandemonium, Clare smiled at her father. "She raided her bribery stash."

"You know your mom."

"Yes, I do. I'm going to get this stuff in the kitchen. Harry's withering away from a lack of Chicken and Stars."

Tall, beefy, his sandy hair streaked with silver, Ed carried his bags in, set them on the counter. "I'll get the rest."

"More? I just asked for—"

He wagged a finger, grinned in the way that crinkled his mossy green eyes at the corners. "You know your mother."

She wouldn't have to squeeze in a stop at the store tomorrow, Clare thought as she put away a week's worth of groceries, which included, from the indulgent grandparents, Popsicles, gummy worms, potato chips, and ice cream bars.

"Popsicles *and* ice cream bars?" Clare said when Rosie came in.

"They've been sick."

"Just don't tell them until they've had some lunch. The receipt wasn't in any of the bags."

"Consider it your reward for dealing with two sick boys and I imagine their pesky little brother all weekend, with no casualties."

"It was close. But I don't want you to pay for——"

"Never argue with a woman giving you food."

"Murphy's law?" She turned and put her arms around her mother. "Thanks." Then laid her head on Rosie's shoulder a moment.

Always there, Clare thought.

"My baby's tired," Rosie murmured.

"Some." She eased back.

She'd gotten her sunny hair from her mother, though Rosie wore it short and sassy, and cleverly low-lighted. It suited her angular face, the delicate-as-a-tea-rose skin.

"You look so good."

"New moisturizer. And a good night's sleep, which I don't imagine you've had lately. Oh, be sure to ask your father if he's lost weight."

"Has he?"

"Three pounds. I've nagged him into exercising with me. I'm shooting for ten. Now, what can I do for you?"

"You did it, and possibly saved lives." She picked up the soup can. "Harry was getting desperate."

"They all want grilled cheese sandwiches. I'll make them. You, take a break. Get some air, take a walk. Get out of the house."

Clare started to protest, then saved her breath. Besides, she could use a walk. "I owe you."

"Give me three grandsons. Oh, wait, you already have. Take an hour."

"Half hour, and I'll have my cell phone in case."

"I think we can handle things. We're watching *Star Wars*. Oh, and the boys want a sleepover. Is Friday night all right?"

"Yeah, sure, if you want."

"We want. And maybe your night out with Beckett Montgomery will go a little smoother."

"It would have to. Though I told you, he was great about it."

"I always liked the Montgomery boys." Rosie assembled ingredients for grilled cheese sandwiches. "And I'm glad you're dating someone—and someone I know."

"We're not really dating. I mean, obviously we would have, but . . . It feels a little strange yet."

"You like him."

"I've always . . . Yes, I do."

"Then give him a test-drive, honey. But drive safe."

"Mom, are you having the kids over so I can take the wheel?"

"Just clearing the road," Rosie said cheerfully.

Clare shook her head. "I'm definitely taking a walk."

***

MIDDLE OF THE week, Beckett thought, and though they'd run into countless glitches, they'd made some decent progress. The gas lines were in, and that was a huge headache behind them. He'd spent the weekend in the shop, working with Ryder on the bookcases and the arches while Owen built the counter his mother wanted for the gift shop.

The extra project wasn't as much of a time suck as he'd feared. And he had to admit, seeing the building painted in the warm cream and sage gave him a nice lift.

Plus, checking the progress there made it handy to drop in and see Clare.

Most of the work he focused on was behind the tarp, and he was as ready as the rest of the town to see it come down. Not much longer now, he calculated as he set another plank on the main porch. Maybe next week if they clicked along.

He and his two-man crew worked steadily through the morning. Just as they broke for lunch, Owen came to the doorway.

"Looks good. That's damn pretty wood."

"It'll be prettier yet when we get poly on it. This mahogany's going to gleam."

"It'll make a statement. We need you out back."

Beckett stepped inside, checking as he went. Progress, he thought again.

"We're working on the back steps. We want to go over the landings one more time, the columns, the paint. Once it's done, it's done."

"You've got the drawing."

"Yeah, and we've got a couple questions on tying it in, and how it's going to work with the pavers, the stone walls around The Courtyard. They're going to start that as soon as they finish the patio deal at the gift shop."

"We haven't settled on the pavers yet."

"Yeah, and that's another thing."

He walked out. He could see it. The ground still rough, the stairs half done, with rails and pickets yet to come. But he could see it.

Ryder stood, hands on hips, looking up. "Are you sure you want those angles on the second floor?"

"Yeah."

"A straight run would be easier."

"And not as aesthetically pleasing."

"Told you he'd say that," Owen put in.

"Yeah, yeah. About this planting wall."

They discussed, wrangled about parking and access until Beckett stepped it off. "Paved walkway here, running from the sidewalk, past Reception, then right around the side and to the lobby porch. Handicapped parking there, regular parking there."

"We'd have more parking without the plantings."

Beckett shook his head at Ryder. "You're sitting out here at one of the tables, having a drink. Do you really want to stare out at a parking lot, or be stared at by people pulling in?"

"You're still going to see the lot. It's not like we're planting a run of oak trees."

"You have the feel of private, and that's what a courtyard's about.

There's no place for a garden, which is what Mom really wanted. This
works. You've got some nice raised beds, and with the arch over the
entrance there, some sort of flowering vine. Like the main porch, it
makes a statement."

"Fine, fine, you're the 'aesthetically pleasing' guy."

"And I'm right."

Ryder's lips twitched. "You'd better be. I'm going to grab some lunch."

"I think I'll get a sub at Vesta," Owen said. "I've got some calls to
make."

"Sounds good."

"I'll catch up with you," Beckett told them. "I'm going to check
in at the gift shop."

Owen snorted. "Tell Clare hi."

"I will, but I'm still checking on the gift shop."

He felt a hint of fall in the air—something changing. He caught a
whiff of burgers grilling in Crawford's as somebody came out the
door. Then the smell of paint, fresh and new.

Things were headed that way, he thought. Fresh and new.

He noted the gift shop crew had already broken for lunch. Tarps
covered the floors, and tape ran in front of the steps still wet with the
dark green contrast paint.

He walked through, down the steps into the office area. They'd
need a desk, a computer, office supplies, shelves. God knew what else.
But that was Owen's area.

Apparently the hardscape crew heard the lunch bell, but they'd
put in a solid morning's work first. Pavers replaced the narrow gravel
walkway that had bisected the scruffy grass. They'd hauled out rocks,
cleverly using them to build a low wall around the Rose of Sharon—
still blooming madly.

Tools and supplies sat in piles, and with the materials and space
left, the fencing to be replaced, he calculated they'd be done by the
following week.

He could report to his brothers, if all continued smoothly, work on The Courtyard could begin within two weeks.

Not bad.

He rounded the old fence, and went through the back door of the bookstore.

He heard kids in the children's section, saw a couple of them poking at each other in the main store while their mother—he assumed—browsed the shelves. Cassie waited on a customer at the counter while Laurie manned the computer station.

"Busy," he commented.

"We just finished our first Story Time of the fall." Laurie stopped keyboarding to give him a thumbs-up. "Had a nice turnout. Avery should, too. Most of them plan on hitting Vesta for lunch."

"I'm probably heading up there myself. Is Clare around?"

"Down in the annex, putting things back together. Don't step on the toddlers."

In the annex, Clare packed art supplies into a chest. She wore black pants today, snug through the butt with a white, lacy blouse that cuffed at her elbows.

He thought he'd like to kiss her there, in that tender crease at her elbow. He thought he'd like to kiss her anywhere. Everywhere.

A couple of women chatted as they considered a display of candles, one rocking a stroller back and forth with the kid inside it sucking its thumb with fierce intensity. The other woman carried an infant sleeping in one of those slings across her chest.

The stroller kid gave Beckett a hard, suspicious stare, as if he might steal the precious thumb. Probably not the optimum time for kissing the inside of Clare's elbow, Beckett decided.

"Hiya."

She looked over, colorful strips of felt in her hand. "Hiya back."

"I heard you had a successful return to Story Time."

"We did, a sure sign summer's over. It's the first one I've done without one of my own kids here, and that's another transition. How are things going?"

"Moving along. You should come over later, see the changes."

"I'd like to if I can manage it. I'm going to email you the file on the copy once I finish up here. I think we can do better, once we see everything in place. But I tried to make it fun and appealing."

"Great. I'll take a look. Here, I'll get that." He picked up the case before she could.

"It's not heavy. I'm just going to put it in the back." Since he didn't give it back, she glanced at the customers. "I'll show you where it goes. Are you finding everything all right?" she asked the women.

"Yeah, thanks. I'm crazy about these handbags."

"Made from recycled video tape, plastic bags. Clever, pretty, and green. Just let me know if you need any help."

She led Beckett around to the little alcove outside the back room. "I keep it on the top shelf there since I only use it once a month. I always thought I'd be crafty, like one of those mothers who can make a toy car out of a cereal box and rubber bands."

"MacGyver Mom."

"Exactly. But that didn't work out."

"I always thought I'd pitch a no-hitter for the O's. That didn't work out either."

"Life's a series of disappointments." She smiled when he gave the dangle of her earring a flick. "And surprises."

"Kids okay?"

"Back to normal *and* in school. Praise Jesus."

"Why don't we have a dry run of Friday night? I'll buy you lunch."

She thought of Sam Freemont and his damn country club, and how much she'd have preferred to grab a hot dog at Crawford's or a slice at Vesta with Beckett.

"That's a nice offer, and I wish I could. The girls and I are getting delivery and finalizing our holiday orders. Christmas," she explained.

"Christmas? We just had Labor Day five minutes ago."

"Which shows you've never worked in retail. We need to get the card order in this afternoon."

"There's that series of disappointments again, so I'll have to settle for this."

He leaned down, found her mouth with his. With the women on the other side of the wall laughing, the phone ringing, the infant squalling awake, he sank in.

Too long, he thought. Too long until Friday when he could, for a few hours at least, have her to himself. Everything about her called to him, her taste, her scent, the shape of her body as he drew her closer.

"Hey, Clare, there's a—Oops, sorry."

Laurie cast her eyes, very deliberately, at the ceiling when Clare and Beckett broke apart.

"Is there a problem?" Clare thought she pulled off casual. Or nearly.

"There's a man on the phone who insists on speaking to the owner. I could tell him you . . . stepped out, take his number."

"That's all right. I'll take it in the back room."

"All right. Get you anything, Beckett?" Laurie batted her eyelashes. "A cold drink?"

"No, I'm good. I'd better get going."

"See you soon." Laurie walked off humming.

"Sorry," Clare told him. "I'd better take care of this."

"I'll head out the back. Come on over if you get a chance."

"I'll try." She watched him go, wished, as he had, for Friday. She laid one hand on her fluttering stomach, the other on the phone. Maybe he was good, but she could use that cold drink.

"Sorry to keep you waiting," she said into the phone. "This is Clare Brewster."

When she finished the call, she walked back to the main store. After the bustle and noise of the morning, she found the quiet lull welcome.

Until she saw the gleam in Cassie's eye.

"I called in our lunch order," Laurie told her.

"Great. Let's get the catalog and order sheet so we—Stop," she demanded as both women grinned at her.

"I can't help it." Laurie bounced in her chair. "You can't expect me to walk into you and Beckett Montgomery in a major lip-lock and not react."

"I wished I'd answered the phone, then I'd have come looking for you," Cassie complained. "Damn customers. I knew there was sparkage, and everybody knows you were going out last week before the kids got sick."

"Booted right on his shoes."

Clare winced. "And everybody knows that, too?"

"I ran into Mrs. Ridenour in the park on Sunday and asked how the date went. She told me. Sucks for everybody. Anyway, we can't miss how he comes in here pretty much every day—nothing new there—but lately the two of you have been flirty."

"Flirty?"

"Discreetly flirty. Or so I thought until I find you sneaking off to the back room to fool around."

"We weren't fooling around. It was . . . It was just a kiss."

"Smoking-hot kiss." Laurie waved her hand in front of her face. "So, is it serious or just a little thing?"

"Laurie, we haven't even officially gone out yet."

"If a guy kissed me like that, I wouldn't go out either. We'd stay home. But then, you've got the kids so—And I'm being really nosy. I'll zip it." She mimed zipping her lips. "I just liked seeing the two of you together. Plus, smoking."

"And on that note, I'm getting a soda."

She didn't snicker until she was out of range. She imagined her rep had just taken a huge leap.

And Laurie was right. It had been a smoking-hot kiss.

She'd like more of the same. Soon.

CHAPTER ELEVEN

TAKE TWO, BECKETT THOUGHT AS HE BANGED THE knocker on Clare's door. This time he carried a cheerful bouquet of white daisies. No point in jinxing things by bringing her the same flowers as last week.

It struck him as a little weird, not just the deja vu, but especially the intense anticipation for the evening because of the postponement.

Just dinner, he reminded himself. He had to stop making such a big deal out of it in his head, or he'd screw up. He'd played it all over in his mind so often you'd think they were winging off to Paris to dine at . . . wherever people dined in Paris.

He'd have to ask her if she'd been there. She'd done so much more traveling than he had. Maybe she spoke French. Hadn't she taken French in high school? He seemed to remember—

Good God, cut it out, he ordered himself.

He didn't know whether to cheer or run when she opened the door.

She hadn't wanted to jinx it either, he decided. She wore a differ-ent dress, this one with pink and white swirls topped with a thin pink sweater that stopped at her elbows. And made him think about kiss-ing that spot again.

Should he have brought the pink roses? Was this a signal?

"I'm going to get spoiled." She reached for the flowers. "I'll start expecting flowers every Friday night."

"Thought I'd mix it up."

"Good plan, and thanks. Come on in. I'll put them in water before we go." As he did, she eyed the little shopping bag in his hand. "More?"

"Not for you." As if to keep it out of reach, he shifted it to his other hand. "You've had enough. It's a bribe so nobody pukes on me. A game for the PlayStation. I got a pretty good look at what they've got when I hung out with them, and I didn't see this one. Where are they? Did you lock them in a closet?"

"No, but my parents may have by now. They're having a sleepover at Marmie's and Granddad's."

"Oh." His mind instantly landed on all the things they could do to each other, alone in the house.

Slow down, buddy, that's not what this is about. Slow and steady, a step at a time. He followed her into the kitchen, watched as she dealt with the flowers.

"Quiet in here," he commented.

"I know. I can never decide if it's spooky or bliss when they have a sleepover. I guess it's spooky bliss."

"You're not afraid to stay in the house alone, are you?" He could offer to stay over, sleep in the kids' room.

Or somewhere.

"Not as long as I don't cave and read a horror novel. It's a weakness, and then I sleep with the light on. I've never figured out how leaving the light on saves you from the vampires or ghosts or demons. There." She stepped back to examine the flowers. "They're so pretty. Should we go?"

"Yeah, I guess we'd better." So he'd stop thinking of her bed upstairs, no kids in the house.

"That's not your truck," she said when they walked outside.

"No. Mom refused to let me take you out, at least this time, in a pickup, so she handed me the keys. Felt like high school."

"When's your curfew?"

"I know all the ways to sneak into the house."

She pondered that while he slid behind the wheel. "Did you really? Sneak into the house as a kid?"

"Sure. I didn't always get away with it, none of us did, but you had to try." He glanced at her as he drove. "No?"

"No, I didn't, and now I feel deprived."

"If you want, when we get back, I'll help you climb in through a window."

"Tempting, but just not the same when I have the key. What did you do that you had to sneak in?"

He took a long pause. "Stuff."

"Hmmm. Now I have to worry if one day the boys will decide to do *stuff*, then sneak into the house. But not tonight. My biggest problem with them at the moment is Murphy's decided his life is unfulfilled unless he has a puppy, and they've joined forces against me."

"You don't like dogs?"

"I like dogs, and they should have a dog. Eventually."

"Is that like Mom for *we'll see?*

"It's in the neighborhood," she admitted. "I think about it because they ought to have a dog. They adore my parents' pug, Lucy, and Fido the cat."

"Your parents have a cat named Fido? Why didn't I know that?"

"He thinks he's a dog, so we don't spread it around. Anyway, I think they should have one, feel guilty they don't. Then I think, oh God, who's going to housebreak it, train it, haul it to the vet, feed it and walk it and all the rest? I tried to talk them into a kitten, but they're not having it. Kittens, Liam informed me, with no little disgust, are for girls. I don't know where they get that."

She arched her eyebrows at his profile. "You agree with him?"

"Kittens are for girls. Cats now, they can go either way."

"You know that's ridiculous."

"I don't make the rules. What kind of dog do they want?"

"They don't know." She sighed because the boys were wearing her down on the subject. "It's the idea of a dog they're in love with. I'm also told a dog would protect me from the bad guys when they're not around." She shrugged. "I'd go to the pound and adopt one, save a life, but how can you be sure the puppy you save won't turn into a big, mean dog that barks at the mail carrier and terrorizes the neighbors? I need to research family-friendly breeds."

He pulled into the restaurant parking lot. "You know Ry's dog."

"Everybody knows D.A." She shifted to study his profile. "Ryder takes him everywhere. He's a sweetheart."

"Hell of a good dog. You know how Ry got him?"

"No, I guess I don't."

They got out of either side of the car, then he walked around to take her hand.

"He was a stray, six or seven months old, the vet figured. Ryder's out at his place one night after work, putting some time into the house he built. It's getting on dark, he's knocking off, and this dog comes crawling in. Bone thin, his paws bleeding, shivering. It's pretty clear he'd been out in the woods awhile. More than likely, somebody dumped him."

Instantly her affection for D.A. doubled. "Poor thing."

"Ryder figures he can't just leave him there, so he'll take him back home—he stayed with Mom a lot until he had the house closed in. So, he'd feed him, clean him up a little, give him a place to flop for the night. He'd take him to the pound in the morning.

"That was six years ago."

Sweet, she thought—not the usual adjective applied to Ryder Montgomery. "I guess it was love at first sight."

"I know we asked around, in case he'd run away, gotten lost. No collar, no tag, and nobody claimed him. By the morning, I can tell you, Ry would've been brokenhearted if someone had."

"And yet, he named him Dumbass."

"Affectionately, and all too often accurately. Montgomery, seven thirty reservation," he told the hostess when they went inside.

Clare thought it over as they were escorted to the table. "You're telling me this to illustrate pedigree doesn't really matter."

"People or dogs, I'd say it's more about how you're raised than bloodlines."

Oddly that made her think of Sam Freemont, and just thinking about him annoyed her.

"But I get some breeds are better for kids," Beckett added.

"It's funny, Clint and I talked about getting a dog right after Harry was born. We thought we'd wait maybe a year, let them grow up together. Then, what do you know, Liam's on the way, and we're dealing with Clint's next deployment, so it got put off."

He started to speak, but the waiter arrived with the menus, the list of specials, offers for cocktails.

They studied the menus a moment in silence.

"Does it bother you when I talk about Clint?"

"No. It's just I never know what to say. He was a good guy."

"He was." She made a decision. Lay it out, say what should be said. Nothing would be real between them unless she did.

"It was love at first sight," she said. "He always said it was the same for him. Just instant, just . . . there you are, now let's start planning the rest of our lives together. Heady stuff for a girl of fifteen."

"Heady at any age, but yeah, especially."

"I never had a single doubt. Never worried, never wondered. We argued sometimes, had more than a few scenes of high drama. But still, I never worried. My parents did; I certainly understand that better now than then. But he was a good guy, and they saw that. They loved him, too."

"You were like the golden couple in high school. C and C. The cheerleader and the football star."

"Heady stuff," she repeated. "We were together two years before . . . we were together. Again, I was sure. I never worried. When he left for basic, I cried all night. Not because I was worried, but because I missed him like a limb."

The waiter came back, took their orders.

"You were so young," Beckett prompted.

"And bold. Fearless. I married him, went off with him, left my home, my family and friends without a single twinge of doubt or regret." She laughed. "Who was that girl?"

"I've always thought of you as pretty fearless."

"Well, I learned about fear when Harry came along. What's this little person? What if I make a mistake? What if he gets sick, gets hurt? But even then, I didn't doubt we'd manage it all."

She picked up her water glass, smiled as she sipped. "We wanted four, with an option for five. Crazy. A potential of *five* children. I imagine we'd have done that if he'd lived."

"You were happy."

"Oh yes. And sometimes brutally lonely, overwhelmed. That's when fear would sneak in. But I was too busy for that, I told myself. I was proud of him. I hated being without him, hated knowing what he faced every day, every night. But he was made to be a soldier, like his father, like his brother. I knew it when I married him."

The waiter brought the wine, and after the ritual, Clare sipped. "It's good. Even better when it signals someone's going to bring me food I didn't have to cook."

"You have more. You should finish."

"Yes, I should finish." And be grateful he was willing to let her.

"Harry was playing, and Liam was crying in his crib. I had morning sickness, so I had to let him cry until I'd finished. I knew I was pregnant. I hadn't taken the test yet, but I knew."

She paused for a moment, just a moment. "He'd only been back in Iraq three weeks. I never got to tell him we were having another child. It's my biggest regret. I never got the chance to tell him. He never got to see Murphy, touch his face, smell his hair, hear his laugh. Murphy never had him. Liam doesn't remember his father. Harry, at best, has some dim memories. Clint was a good father. Loving, fun, attentive. But they didn't have time."

"You never have enough."

Understanding, she nodded, put a hand over his. He'd lost his father, too. "No, I don't guess you do.

"They came to the door that morning. You know when you see them. The officer, the chaplain. You know without a word being said. The lights dim; the air goes out. For a little while there's nothing at all."

Beckett squeezed her hand. "I'm sorry, Clare."

"I was holding Liam. I'd forgotten I'd picked him up when the knock came. He's crying—teething and fussy, a little feverish with it. Harry's hugging my leg. He must have sensed something because he started crying, too. And the baby's inside me. Clint's gone.

"The other wives came, to help, to comfort. I broke, a million pieces. There was fear and doubt and worry, and such horrible, horrible grief. I didn't think I'd live through it."

He thought of her, alone, two babies, newly pregnant, and widowed. "Who could? How did you?"

"All I knew was I needed to come home. They needed to come home. It was the only clear answer for all of us, and it was the right one. I can think about Clint here, how much I loved him, and I've been able to accept that we had what we were meant to have. No more, no less. Now I have something else. I can think about him, talk about him. I have to, the boys deserve that. Just as they, and I, deserve the life we've made now."

"I don't know if it helps, but I know when we lost Dad, we were all just numb, I guess. Just taking a step at a time dealing with all the horrible, practical things you have to deal with. Eventually you find yourself in another place. Some of it's familiar, some of it's not. You make something else out of it, and you know you couldn't have without the person you lost."

"Yes." Now she could be grateful he understood. "When you think of your dad, or talk about him, it reminds you of that. It's the same for me. You knew Clint. We have a history that includes him, so since we're seeing each other I don't want you to feel awkward or uncomfortable."

Beckett considered, went with impulse. "Do you remember Mr. Schroder?"

"I had him for U.S. history. I hated Mr. Schroder."

"Everybody did. He was a dick. Clint and I, and some other guys TP'd his house."

"That was you? Clint was in on that?" She sat back and laughed. "Oh my God, I remember that so well. You must've used a hundred rolls. It looked like a cargo ship of Charmin exploded."

"No point in doing something if you do it half-assed."

"You sure didn't go half-assed on Mr. Schroder. And he was a dick."

"Owen organized it, as you'd expect. Me, Owen, Ry. Two other guys whose names I must protect, as we swore an oath."

"Clint never told me, and everybody talked about that hit for weeks."

"An oath's an oath. We had about fifty rolls, and it took forever to accumulate that much. If a bunch of guys walked into Sheetz or wherever and bought that much at a time, you'd be busted. So we bought a little at a time, in different places, snuck some out of the house, a roll or two each time. We had time lines and maps and lookouts, escape routes. It was a major campaign, and it was beautiful."

"You were the unsung heroes of Boonsboro High. If we'd known we'd have thrown a party for you."

"We had our own about a month later. Camped out in the woods near our place and got wasted on Budweiser and peach schnapps."

"That's disgusting."

"Yeah, it was. Good times."

"Charlie Reeder." She pointed, got an *aha* glimmer in her eyes that sparkled green. "One of the others had to be Charlie. He and Clint were tight."

"I'm unable to confirm or deny."

"Charlie Reeder," she repeated. "He was always up for trouble back then. Now he's a town cop. You just never know. He likes men's adventure novels and black coffee with a shot of espresso."

"I guess you get to know people by what they look for in the bookstore."

"I also have secrets. I know, for instance, that all the Montgomery boys like to read—and what they like to read. That you all drink too much coffee. I know that you and Owen go for sentimental cards for your mom for Mother's Day and her birthday, and Ryder goes for funny."

Lifting her wine, she shot him a knowing glance. "That's just the tip of the iceberg."

"A side benefit of the small-town merchant."

"You bet. And I know of at least half a dozen customers who are planning to book a night at the inn for a special occasion, even though they live locally. You're going to have a hit, Beckett."

"It'll be nice for Lizzy to have company."

"Who? Oh, your ghost. She's Lizzy now?"

"Well, we've gotten close. How do you think Hope's going to deal with that?"

"Hope deals, that's part of who she is." Ghosts, Clare thought, were fanciful nonsense—and deliberately shifted the subject. "How's the apartment coming?"

"Should be ready next week. Lizzy could take lessons from Avery, as she's been haunting the place. She nagged—let's say she persuaded Owen that the place needed a little more than paint, so it's taken a little longer."

They talked throughout the meal. A nice next step, Beckett thought, in the slow-and-steady plan. Maybe he'd suggest a movie next time, with a casual meal after. Keep it easy and traditional.

"This was wonderful." She made a quiet sound of pleasure as they walked back to the car. "I can't think of the last time I had an adult dinner out."

"We can do it again." He opened the car door for her. "As soon as you want."

Tomorrow, she thought, then felt a little pang of guilt. She couldn't spend two evenings in a row away from her kids. So she'd better make the most of the one she had. "I'll check the schedule, see what I can work out."

She turned, giving him the perfect opening to kiss her. When he didn't, she slid into the car.

Maybe the dinner had decided for him that he wanted to stay friends. Take her out now and then, be a pal to the kids when he had the time and inclination.

She couldn't fault him for that. Dating was meant to let people figure out if they wanted a relationship, and what they wanted from one. And a relationship with her had multiple complications, she thought as they started the drive home.

Which she'd certainly reminded him of by talking about the kids. She'd probably talked about the kids too much. What guy wanted to hear a bunch of kid stories out on a date?

And all she'd told him about Clint. She'd hoped to give him a clear picture of why she'd gone, why she'd come back. Who she'd been, who she'd become. And to be honest with him about how deeply she'd loved Clint Brewster.

And what man wanted to hear about a woman's dead husband on a date?

Why couldn't she have talked about books? Well, they had, she remembered. But just books or movies, or anything breezy and datelike?

Maybe, if they did go out again, she'd think of a list of appropriate topics beforehand. It surprised her just how much she wanted more, from Beckett, with Beckett. He'd made her feel like a woman again, with all those nerves, all those needs.

Safe topics, she decided. Start now.

"I meant to tell you, I read a review copy of Michael Connelly's latest."

"Harry Bosch?"

"That's right. I think you'll love it. And I've got a debut thriller author booked for an event next month. You might want to check it out. She's good, and we have a local author signed up for the event, too."

They talked books all the way home. Better, Clare told herself. She'd work on her dating chops. She knew how to have conversations that didn't involve her children.

She just didn't have many opportunities for them.

When he pulled up at her house, she thought of the quiet. She could work on the website for an hour undisturbed. She could have the unspeakable luxury of a long bath. She could do absolutely anything she wanted to do without any other responsibility or concern.

"Nights are getting cool," she murmured as he walked her to the door. "Almost chilly. Summers never last long enough."

"And winter's too long."

"But this one will be special. The inn," she said when he gave her a puzzled look. "It'll open this winter."

"That's right. The way it looks, we'll be freezing our asses off when we load in."

"It'll be worth it. I'd love to help. In fact, I'm dying to."

"The more hands and asses, the better."

"Then I'll plan on it. I had the best time."

"So did I." He leaned in, a light touch on her shoulders, a long, slow, dreamy kiss.

No, oh no, she thought as her skin went to humming. A man didn't kiss a woman like that when he just wanted to be good friends. She wasn't that out of the loop.

"Better go in," he said quietly, "before you get cold."

She smiled at him, unlocked the door.

"I'll call you." She stared at him, flummoxed when he stepped back.

He wasn't coming inside? Had *all* the signals changed while she'd been in dating retirement?

"Make sure you lock up," he added.

"I will. 'Night." She opened the door.

Wait a minute. Proactive, isn't that what Avery said? Going in alone when she damn well didn't want to be alone wasn't being proactive.

"Um, Beckett, I'm sorry, and I know it's silly, but would you mind coming in? Empty house." She gave a helpless shrug that embarrassed her.

"Sure. I should've offered. Spooky bliss," he added when he stepped inside. "I'll check the back door."

She'd manipulated him and she wasn't sorry. She'd be sorry, she admitted, if she turned out to be wrong and he didn't want to stay with her. To be with her.

She'd be humiliated.

But if she didn't find out now, she'd go crazy wondering.

She hated wondering.

"All clear." He walked back from the kitchen. "Not a bad guy in sight. But you should still get a dog. A house never feels empty with a dog. Are you going to be okay?"

"Yeah, thanks. Can I get you a drink?"

"Better not. I should get going."

"I have to ask you something."

"What?"

"When you kissed me at the door, was that a let's-have-dinner-again-sometime kiss, or was it something else? Because it felt like something else to me."

"Something else?"

She slid her arms up his back, took his mouth as she wanted to.

"It felt like that."

He dropped his brow to hers. "Clare."

"Beckett, don't make me ask you to come upstairs and check in the closets." She laid her hands on his cheeks. "Just come upstairs."

She stepped away, offered her hand. He took it, held firm. "I've wanted to be with you when I didn't have the right to."

"As long as you want to be with me now."

They started up together.

"I didn't want to rush you. I figured you'd need time to get used to the idea, to be sure."

"I tend to make up my mind quickly." In the bedroom, she turned to face him. "We've been friends a long time, but I have a confession to make. You know I can see the inn from my office window."

"Yeah."

"When we had that hot spell in the spring, you'd be working outside now and then, up on that scaffolding, on the roof. With your shirt off. I'd watch you."

She laughed a little, her eyes on his. "And I'd think about you and wonder what it would be like. Now I can find out."

She laid her hands on his chest. "Here's something I haven't done in quite a while."

"It'll come back to you."

She laughed again, relaxed and easy. "That, too, but I meant it's been a while since I undressed a man. Let's see if I remember how this part goes."

She slipped the jacket off his shoulders, eased it down his arms, then tossed it on the little chair beside her closet. "So far, so good," she decided. She unfastened the first button of his shirt, the second.

And he found himself trapped between pleasure and desperation.

"I thought you'd be shy."

She opened the shirt. "You did?" She angled her head. "I haven't been fifteen and innocent for a long time either."

"It's not that, or not just."

"Ah, the mother of three, the young widow." She drew the shirt off, tossed it over the jacket. "You've probably heard how little boys are made."

"Rumors."

"I love my boys, so much." She ran her hands slowly up his bare chest, closing her eyes at the sensation. "I really loved the process of making them."

She turned, lifted the hair she'd left loose around her shoulders. "Would you mind?"

He drew down the zipper, inch by inch. It was like a dream, he thought, just that filmy and sweet. And like the most intense of realities. Hot and stirring.

She stepped out of the dress when it fell to the floor, turned to him again. And reached out for him.

No dream, no longer, but real and wanting him as he wanted her. No dream when he could, at last, feel that smooth skin, the way her heart beat strong and fast under his hand.

It was she who drew him to the bed. Her fingers combed through his hair, ran down his back while their lips clung. Under him she moved, sexy and sinuous, impossibly seductive. He'd thought he knew her, had been sure of it. But he never knew this open and eager woman lived inside her. That woman caught him by the throat, could have driven him to heaven or hell at her whim.

Alive. Everything in her alive and beating, and hungry. Those rough-palmed hands stroked over her, waking her skin, her pulse, her senses. She couldn't get enough—the muscles in his arms, the press, the weight, the shape of his body. The way their breath mingled in another drowning kiss before he took his mouth to her breast.

Her breath exploded in a gasp. Delight, desire—she let herself go, fall heedlessly into both.

They stripped each other. Not a word, too frantic for words before they tumbled back down. She wrapped around him; rose to him. An offer. A demand.

When he buried himself in her she cried out, a sound of relief and release. He struggled for control as he felt her shudder, shudder, shudder. But she rose to him again, and in that single, powerful surge, snapped his will.

He took her, riding on that hot, rising wave of need until his own release ripped through him, emptied him.

She couldn't get her breath, and wasn't sure—if she ever did—if she'd let it out with weeping or cheering. She felt foolishly like doing both.

"I can do better," he mumbled with his face buried in her hair.

"Hmm?"

"I can do better. I kind of rushed that."

"No, I rushed it, and thanks very much for keeping up the pace. Oh my God, Beckett." Ah, she realized, she let it out on a long purr. Even better. "Please don't move yet. Stay." She wrapped her arms around him to make sure he did.

He stayed—happy to—but rose up to his elbows. "Look at you, Clare Murphy—sorry, Brewster—all mussed and flushed. You're so damn pretty."

"I like feeling mussed and flushed and damn pretty. And look at you, Beckett Montgomery, all smug and pleased with yourself."

"Sure. I just nailed the neighborhood bookseller and town sweetheart."

She choked out a laugh, pinched his butt. "You'd better not go bragging to the crew."

"I was going to take out an ad in the *Citizen*."

She liked looking into his face, so relaxed now, into his eyes, so deep and blue. "Make sure you say I was amazing."

"Nothing but the truth." He bent down to kiss her. "You destroyed me."

"It's good to know I haven't lost my touch."

He pressed a kiss to the side of her neck, to give himself a moment. He didn't want to think of her with someone else, not even the man she'd married. Stupid of him, maybe; selfish, certainly. But right then and there, he just didn't.

He lay quietly awhile until the feeling passed. "I want to see you tomorrow."

"Oh, Beckett, I can't go out again tomorrow. The boys."

"We don't have to go out. Or we can take them somewhere."

"They have a birthday party to go to tomorrow afternoon. That's something that starts now and goes on forever on Saturdays. You could come to dinner on Sunday. It has to be a little early because it's a school night."

"What time?"

"Five thirty?"

"I'll be here."

He rolled off, took her hand as he sat up. "I should go."

She wrapped her arms around herself, faked a little shudder. "And leave me in this empty house all alone—without a dog."

He grinned. "You're not afraid."

"No, I tricked you, but I had to get you in bed somehow."

"And thanks."

"And now you're going to make me work to keep you here?"

"The car's outside in the drive. You know people are going to see it, especially if it's still there in the morning."

Amused he'd be concerned for her reputation, she sat up with him. "Beckett?"

"Yeah?"

"Let's give them something to talk about."

CHAPTER TWELVE

MONDAY MORNING, WELL SHY OF OPENING, CLARE USED her key to get into Vesta. She heard the enormous mixer chugging along, and went straight back where she knew Avery would be making dough.

"Hi! I wanted to talk to you before—" She stopped dead, stared as Avery rolled already mixed and cut dough into balls. "Your hair! It's . . . Is that magenta? You dyed your hair."

"You had sex."

"I—You dyed your hair because I had sex?"

"No. I dyed it because *I* didn't have sex. Okay, not really." She huffed out a breath as she rolled. "Maybe a little. Mostly I just wanted a change. Something to stir things up."

"You definitely stirred."

Avery looked down at her far from spotless baker's apron all the way to her Old Navy sneakers with their gel inserts. "I'm in a rut, Clare. No, I *am* the rut."

"You're not the rut. I like it. It's . . . fun."

"I think I like it. Sort of." Her hands coated with flour and dough, Avery rubbed an itch on her chin with her shoulder. "I scared myself this morning when I looked in the bathroom mirror. I forgot about it, then it was like *eek*, who the hell is that! Anyway, it's just one of those wash-in-and-out rinses. I'll live with it awhile and see."

Privately, Clare thought: Thank God.

Movements practiced and quick, Avery began placing the rolled dough in rising pans. "Now, about that sex. You had sex Friday night and—"

"And into Saturday morning."

"Bragging is the tool of the small and the petty. Am I or am I not your best friend?"

"BFF." Clare tapped a finger on her heart.

"And what do I get, a measly little text message. *Spent night with B. Fabulous.*"

"Didn't I leave that bit of Shania Twain on your answering machine, the 'I Feel Like a Woman' cut?"

"Okay, that made me laugh, but these are not the details given to the BFF."

"Birthday party Saturday, and you worked here until what, midnight?"

"About."

"I'm not used to having lots of sex. I went to bed Saturday right after the kids. Then Sunday, it's enough to say I didn't have any privacy, and you were working again."

"See. I am the rut."

"You're not." Clare laid her hands on Avery's shoulders, gave them a good rub and shake. "But I came in early especially to talk to you. God, I really want to talk to my BFF."

"You're sucking up. I like it. Please continue while I deal with the rest of this dough."

"That's an awful lot of dough for a Monday, isn't it?"

"Private party tonight, and I've got a lunchtime delivery on the books for six large. Now talk."

"It was great. Everything. Dinner—"

"I've had dinner recently. I haven't had sex. Move along."

"Well . . ."

Clare told her about her concerns when she and Beckett left the restaurant and on to her change of plans at the door.

"You pulled the 'oh, I need a big, brave man to walk through my scary, empty house'?"

"I did."

"I'm proud to know you."

"He had the idea I needed everything to go slow. I realized if I didn't do something we could still be on phase one at Christmas. So I gave it a jump start, and took him for a drive."

The blue of Avery's eyes brightened with laughter, and a little pride. "Listen to you."

"I *know*." Delighted with herself and the world in general, Clare wiggled her shoulders. "I feel like part of my life that's been on hold is back. I feel things with him I haven't felt in so long. Not just the physical, though that was pretty damn perfect."

"Slow and easy or wild and crazy?"

"I think by the time he left Saturday morning, we'd managed both, all, and some combinations."

"Okay, now I'm jealous." After covering the pans, Avery moved to the sink to wash dough off her hands. "Happy for you, but jealous. Happy for him, too. Beck's always had a thing for you."

"That's the only problem. I'm not the Clare Murphy he had a thing for. He has to want to be with the person I am now."

"Do you think he's living out an old fantasy?"

"I'm not sure, not sure if he's sure either. I'm not going to worry about it yet. I like getting to know each other as we are now. Things are changing. I want to see what they become."

⌇

BECKETT SPENT THE next two weeks bouncing from project to project, from shop work to inspecting deliveries and carving out time when he could manage it to be with Clare. While the installers laid the tile on the main floor, the crew focused primarily on exterior work.

Then came the day when he and his brothers stood at the front doorway, studying the completed entrance porch and steps.

"What did I tell you?" Beckett said. "She gleams."

"She ought to with all those coats of poly." Ryder crouched down, ran a hand over the wood. "Smooth as glass. Hard dry, too."

"You know skateboarders are going to see this run and go for it."

Ryder glanced up at Owen. "Then we'll kick some asses, and we'll make sure word goes out on that. I say we pull this bastard down." He jerked a thumb at the big blue tarp. "Give everybody a look at what Inn BoonsBoro's crew pulled off."

"Let's do it—and," Beckett added, "let's run some tape between the posts to keep people from coming up this way."

It may have been one of the most satisfying moments of his life, Beckett decided, when they dropped that tarp on a cool September morning with fall spiced in the air.

School buses lumbered out to pick up their load as he and his brothers crossed the street for a full-on view. Cars slowed as the drivers' heads swiveled to look toward the unveiled building.

And she was beautiful—still not fully dressed for the party, Beckett thought, but beautiful. The deep, rich color of the wood gleamed against the old stone walls, drawing out the hints of gold and umber.

Generous in size, its steps spanning the length, it stood out against the softer colors of the rails and pickets. Rising over it, the upper porch added grace and charm to dignity.

"You know, you work on it," Owen began, "and you see it change. But you're inside it or on it, so you don't really *see*. Fucking A, we did good."

"Damn right. It's a moment." Ryder pulled out his phone, framed the building in, took a picture. "And the moment's immortalized. Back to work."

"Better send that to Mom."

Owen shook his head at Beckett. "I've already talked to her this morning. She's coming in anyway. Let's give her the full impact."

"Better idea," Beckett agreed. "Talk of the town." He studied the lines and colors as they crossed back over.

Inside, they split off, Owen to check on the progress of the tile install, Ryder to begin work on the coffered ceiling in the dining room. Beckett headed up to the third floor, but paused on two when he smelled honeysuckle.

"Like that, do you?" he murmured, and walked down to Elizabeth and Darcy. "She doesn't look sad anymore."

On impulse, he walked into the room, then out onto the porch. He looked out on the town, the line of Main Street with its shops and houses, its covered porches and bricked sidewalks. And beyond it to the glint of fields, the rise of hills, the ring of mountains rolling to the blue autumn sky.

"This is good." He didn't know if he spoke to himself, the building, or the ghost. It didn't matter. "This feels right."

Others had stood on this spot when the street had been a wide dirt road carrying horses, carriages. When soldiers came to fight in those fields, those hills and mountains. It stood while the dead were buried, and the grass grew green over them.

"Did you?" he wondered, thinking of the honeysuckle. "Did you stand here? When? Did you come in a carriage or in a car? How did you die? Why do you stay?"

Not ready to share, he thought. Women knew how to keep their secrets.

He glanced down toward Turn The Page. Too early for Clare to be in, he thought. She'd be getting the boys ready for school, dealing with breakfast and backpacks.

Did she think of him during her morning routine? Would she look out her office window and wonder what he was doing, how soon they'd see each other?

Did she sometimes ache at night wishing for him the way he wished for her?

He liked to think so.

He saw one of the operators unlock the front door of Sherry's Salon, then glance over—then simply stand and stare. It made him grin as pride rushed into him.

We're not done yet, he thought. She needs lights and benches, planters—and so much more. But when she's dressed for the party, she'll be the belle of the ball.

As he walked back in, he caught a movement out of the corner of his eye. Just a blur that seemed to shimmer in the air—there, then gone—as he turned toward it.

The door he'd secured swung back open.

He took a quick step back as his heart jolted. He'd have sworn he heard the faintest whisper of a laugh.

"Yeah, funny." He moved over, shut the door again. The minute he started out, it opened again.

He closed it; it opened.

Maybe she liked the fresh air, or the view, but he couldn't play this game all morning.

"Okay, look, I can't leave it open. Remember the pigeons—and the pigeon shit? Let's not give them an invitation to move back in."

As he watched, the door opened a couple inches—like a tease—then shut.

"Thanks." He waited a moment to be sure before backing out of the room.

He'd just won an argument with a ghost, he decided on his way upstairs. That had to be one for the books.

Just after nine, his day got another boost when his cell phone rang and he saw the bookstore on the display. He set his measuring tape aside.

"Hi."

"Oh, Beckett, it's beautiful. I just got in, came up to my office and glanced out the window. I swear I did a double take."

"We took the tarp down a couple hours ago."

"I know you told me what it would look like, and I saw a little, but it's just so much more. I'm watching people walking or driving by stopping to stare."

"So am I. I just walked out on the second-floor porch." He lifted his hand, grinned.

"Hold on a minute."

He heard some rustling, a muttered curse. He heard—and saw—her office window open. She leaned out—pretty as a sunflower—and made his grin widen.

"Hi, Beckett," she said in his ear.

"Hi, Clare."

"You must be on top of the world."

"On top of Main Street, anyway. Come on over, see it from here, because it's pretty damn terrific. And you've got to see downstairs, the tile work."

"I can't this morning. I've got a ton of paperwork I didn't get done last night due to a history project, multiplication tables, a science quiz, and a bad dream."

"Science quizzes give me bad dreams, too."

"It wasn't that. It was the aliens with octopus arms."

"That'd do it, too."

"Liam. He was freaked enough to wake his brothers, and Murphy decided that made it a fine time to play. Anyway, I have to catch up this morning. Then we have a bus tour coming in, so I'll just have to admire the fabulous Inn BoonsBoro from here."

It just wasn't enough, he realized. Seeing her, talking to her, with Main Street between them. "Tell you what, bring the kids in after school. We'll give them a tour, then take them for pizza."

"Homework."

"You're such a mom. After homework."

"They'd love it, but the way things have been going, it could be around four thirty before we make it."

"I'll wait."

Ryder's voice boomed up the stairs. "Beckett, goddamn it, where are those measurements?"

"Looks like we both better get to work. Thanks for the great view. I'll talk to you later."

"Clare. It was nice seeing you."

HE SPENT THE entire day on a high, and the high kicked up a notch every time he had to go out and someone stopped him to talk about the inn. He continued to ride it at the end of the day when the crew knocked off.

He held the usual end-of-day meeting with his brothers to confirm the next day's business and strategies.

"Let's take this over to Vesta," Owen suggested. "A day like this deserves pizza and beer."

"Can't. Clare's bringing the kids in to take a tour, then we're heading over for pizza."

"See what happens when you get hooked up?" Ryder shook his head, sadly. "No more time for pizza and beer with your brothers."

"Beck's a family man now," Owen said soberly. "You'd better start thinking about beefing up your retirement plan and life insurance."

"Kiss my ass. And I'm not a—"

"No more poker tournaments, no more partying." Ryder gave Beckett a sympathetic rap on the shoulder. "And you can forget the tittie bars, man. It's all about saving for that vacation at Disney World now. Poor bastard. Come on, Owen, we'll eat and drink his share."

"His oats." Owen sighed as he walked out. "They have all been sowed."

"Assholes," Beckett called out, laughing it off. But the ragging comments gave him a little twinge between the shoulder blades.

"Just jealous because I have a woman."

He looked down at his clipboard, tried to concentrate on what needed to be done the next day, and through the week.

He wasn't a "family man." Jesus. He liked the kids, a lot. They were great—interesting, fun, smart—and he liked hanging out with them. But he didn't know anything about being a family man. He knew about being a brother, a son, so he knew about family, and how vital it was. But he didn't know anything about being, sort of, in charge of one.

He was just seeing Clare, just in the beginnings of a relationship with Clare. Sure, her kids were part of that—he wasn't an idiot. But they were just pals, he and the kids.

Just pals.

And making him chew over it was exactly what his brothers intended when they'd started poking at him.

He told himself to put it away, forget it, but was grateful for the knock on the door of Reception for distracting him.

He went out, passed the kitchen area, saw Clare and the boys through the door—which he opened with a flourish.

"Welcome to Inn BoonsBoro. Do you have a reservation?"

"We have a personal invitation from the owner."

"In that case——" He stepped back, gave a sweeping gesture that made the boys laugh.

"You said to come to this door, right? I'm so used to—— Oh, the tiles are just great! It's all right to walk on them?"

"Here, and through the kitchen and down the hall. Lobby's off-limits. They'll grout that tomorrow."

"It looks so big. Don't touch anything," she added quickly. "Remember? And stay with me. We can only go where Beckett says we can go."

"Do you really own this whole place?" Liam asked him.

"My family does." There was that word again. "This is where people will come in, check in. Hope's going to sit right there."

"There's no place to sit."

"There will be," he told Harry. "Chairs for people to sit, too, in front of the fireplace."

"Mom wishes she had a fireplace." Murphy looked up at him. "You build stuff, so you could make her one."

"How come you got all those old bricks?" Harry poked at them. "Where's the wall for the inside?"

"That is the wall for the inside. They've been there a really long time, so we wanted people to see them. It shows respect for the building. Down here's the kitchen." He glanced at Clare. "They're going to start installing the cabinets soon. That'll be another big corner turned."

"I'll say. See, guys? This is where Hope's going to fix breakfast."

"Don't walk past the tape, Harry." Beckett started down to where Harry stood at the edge of the completed tile.

"I'm not. What're all those little things sticking up?"

"Spacers. See how straight all the lines are between the tiles?" He started explaining grout, then wondered if he was too technical.

"Why are there smaller pieces?"

"At that edge there? They have to cut the tiles to fit." So the kid was interested. "They have a special tool for that."

"Where?"

"I'll show you before we go."

"The tile rug." Clare kept a firm hand on Murphy, just in case. "It's fabulous."

"What rug?"

So Beckett explained about tile rugs before taking them around to the dining room.

"You've started on the ceiling!"

"We wanted to see if the plan worked," Beckett told her. "And with it done, there'll be less chance of messing up the hardwood when that's installed."

Harry pointed at the arch of stone in the wall. "Is that stone for respect?"

"That's right. This was the first stone building in town. It's important."

"My mom's bookstore place is old. The stairs creak."

"That'll happen."

"If it's old, how come you got a new porch?"

"Someone took the one that used to be here away a long time ago. We put one back." Beckett went out, opened the door. "It's not exactly the way it used to be, but I think the building likes it. I have copies of old pictures Mr. Bast gave us. I'll show you sometime."

"He has a furniture store and a museum." Liam danced out on the porch. "He has all *kinds* of stuff in the museum. But he doesn't have any mummies."

"Maybe he can work on that."

"It's beautiful from this angle, too." Clare stepped out, looked over to Vesta, down to her own shop. "Everyone who came in the bookstore today talked about it. I must've walked out on my own porch a half dozen times to look over and— Murphy!"

She whipped back inside in time to see him halfway up the stairs. "Come down here. I told you not to go upstairs alone."

"I was just going to talk to the lady." He looked up, smiled that angel's smile. "Okay, 'bye."

"What lady? Who are you talking to?" Clare rushed in, scooped him right off the steps and into her arms.

"The lady upstairs. She said hi, and she guessed my name."

"Beckett, if there's someone upstairs—"

"I'll go up." But he already knew.

For Clare's peace of mind, he did a quick walk-through.

"Nobody here," he said when he came back down.

"I guess she had to go to the party. Is she gonna live here with Hope?" Murphy wondered.

"Maybe." Speculating, Beckett glanced back up. "She was going to a party?"

"I guess. She had a long dress. Ladies wear long dresses to parties sometimes. Can we see upstairs now?"

"Sure. Okay?" Beckett said to Clare.

"Fine, but . . . we'll talk about things later. Murphy, you stay with me."

❦

SINCE SHE WOULDN'T let the boys out of her sight, he had to wait until they went for pizza. Getting her alone, more or less, at that point came easy. All it took was a pocketful of quarters.

"Okay, I get you don't want to talk about it in front of them, but we could be talking about a plague of two-headed frogs and they wouldn't cop to it now. That was something else."

"I don't know what happened, or what this is. All I know is whatever it is had my little boy going upstairs, by himself, to. . . whatever it is."

"She's not dangerous."

"There is no she," Clare insisted. "And how can you be sure, if there were, she isn't dangerous?"

"We're all over that place every day."

"Grown men."

"I've been in there countless times on my own. Just today she and I had this little negotiation about leaving the porch door open."

"Maybe because she wanted to push you over the rail."

He would've laughed, but clearly this wasn't a joke to her. "Why would she?"

"How do I know why?" Irritation bubbled in her voice. "I can't believe I'm having this conversation. We're sitting here talking about a ghost. For God's sake, Beckett." She grabbed the glass of soda the minute the waitress set it down.

"Everything okay?"

"Everything's fine, Heather." Beckett sent her an easy smile. "Thanks."

He waited until Heather moved off again. "We're having the conversation because you're upset about it. Murphy wasn't scared."

"He's a child."

"Yeah, and I figure that's why he actually saw her. They say, don't they, kids are more open to stuff like this."

"How do I know? I don't—didn't—*don't*—believe in stuff like this. It's crazy."

Gauging her mood, he tried to lighten it. "You can be Scully and I can be Mulder. Maybe I do want to believe, but the fact is Murphy saw her. Hair like yours, he said, so she's a blonde. Wearing a long dress. I'd say she's from back when women wore long dresses. Eighteenth or nineteenth century."

"God."

Now he put a hand over hers, held it firm. "I wouldn't let anything happen to him, to them, to you. Clare, if I thought for a second Lizzy wanted to hurt anyone, I'd find a way to—I don't know—exorcise her. I guess it's exorcism. Here's the thing." He shifted forward a little. "You're thinking she's all *Blair Witch* or *Poltergeist*. Because you dig on horror novels. So you think ghost equals evil."

"Ghosts aren't always evil in fiction."

"There you go."

"In *fiction*. I've never dealt with one in reality. It scared me, seeing Murphy going up those stairs, smiling up at thin air."

"I have a theory. Quick version before the quarters run out, and the pizza gets here. She likes what we're doing, likes that we're fixing the building. Bringing it back to life, you could say. I think she likes having people around."

"Now you want to believe you not only have a ghost, but a sociable ghost."

"Why not?"

"Oh, so many reasons."

"Try this, Agent Scully. The more we do over there, the more she comes out. When we first went through, I got nothing. But later, when we started taking measurements, when I started doing some sketches, I got this sense. Like being watched. Now that was spooky. As things progressed, I started smelling honeysuckle. Not every time, but more and more often. Now today, we take the tarp down, and that's a big deal. We have this."

"I don't want her screwing around with my kids."

"Who?" Murphy crawled into her lap.

"Anybody." Clare wrapped her arms around him, nuzzled his neck until he laughed. "Nobody messes with the Brewster boys."

And that, Beckett thought as the pie arrived, was that.

After she took the boys home, Beckett went back over. He had the pleasure of walking over the stretch of finished floor, thinking about the permanent steps that would go in before much longer.

And waited to see what might happen.

Nothing.

Maybe they hurt her feelings, he thought. Dead or alive, women could be pretty damn touchy.

"You scared her. Her kids are number one with her, and Murphy's the baby on top of it. So she's a little freaked out, that's all."

Still nothing.

"I don't know why I'm getting the silent treatment. I didn't do anything. And you ought to cut her a break. Most people get a little freaked out. I'm used to you, and I still get jumpy sometimes."

And again, he thought, nothing.

"You should give her a little time to adjust, especially since she'll probably be around a lot while we're working on the place, after we finish.

"One of her friends is going to run the inn. Hope'll be living up on three, so Clare and Avery are bound to hang around. Once we finish, and Hope's living here, you won't have to be alone."

The door to the porch in E&D opened, and Beckett realized it was a little disconcerting at night without the crew around.

"Sure, a little fresh air'd be good."

He walked out, smelled the honeysuckle.

"You'll like her when you get to know her. She's great. She was afraid you might hurt the boy, so—"

He broke off when the door slammed.

"Whoa. Temper." He opened the door again. "I didn't say I thought it. Look, maybe she's a little overprotective. Her husband was killed. Damn, stupid war. He never got to meet Murphy. So, the way she sees it, she's all they've got, and she needs to make sure they're safe. Who can argue with that?"

The door opened another inch, and he took it as a sign of apology or understanding.

"Just give her some time. I've got some work to do over at my place." He gestured across the street. "It's going to be busy around here tomorrow when they start tiling the bathrooms. It's going to take some time, but it'll be worth it. I'll be back in the morning."

He walked in, shut the door, considered.

"You've really got to keep the door closed."

He waited a moment, then, satisfied, went down, walked out, and locked up.

Across the street he stopped and turned to look, and thought he saw, just for a moment, the shadowy form of a woman at the porch rail.

But the door stayed closed.

CHAPTER THIRTEEN

RAZZLED, IRRITABLE, AND DESPERATE FOR TEN MINUTES of peace, Clare dragged herself into the bookstore. For a moment, she indulged in some much-needed self-pity.

She owned the damn place, didn't she? She ought to be able to just take the day off, go do something fun like . . . she couldn't think of a thing.

Because she wasn't in the mood for fun. She was in the mood to sit alone, blissfully alone in a quiet room, and stare at nothing for a couple hours.

"Morning!" Laurie sat cheerfully at the computer station. Her wide, bright smile gave Clare an instant headache. "How's everything?"

"As you'd expect after hauling three kids to the dentist, listening to the bickering and whining all the way there and back. They were still at it when I dumped them at school. Their teachers may send out a warrant for my arrest."

Laurie's smile dimmed toward a look of sympathy. "Not a great way to start the day."

"For any of us." Clare dumped her purse and briefcase on the steps. Since taking the day off for a quiet room didn't make the slate, at least she needed coffee before she got started on work.

And really, work climbed several rungs up the ladder from three battling boys.

"I'm going up to sulk for a while," she said as she poured a mug. "And try not to think about the fact they have their checkups at the pediatrician next week. Maybe I'll just run away from home."

"You work too hard."

"I'm not in the mood to disagree. Or remind myself that dentists and doctors insist on payment for services rendered."

"I hate to tell you, you've got three messages."

"Three?" That called for a shot of caramel in the coffee. "We've only been open a half hour."

"Sorry. Um, plus we've got some sort of leak in the stockroom bathroom. Really sorry."

Potential plumbing bill. No amount of caramel could ease the pain. "Oh well."

"Maybe you're getting all the crap stuff out of the way at once."

"By the time you shovel up the crap, more materializes. It's like the loaves and fishes. So I'd better get to it."

Laurie waved the yellow message pad, smiled expectantly.

"I'll take care of those first. I'll be upstairs if you need me, and I sincerely hope you don't for the next hour." She reached for the messages, found herself in a little tug-of-war. "I actually need these to return the calls."

"I know, but . . ." Doing a quick chair dance, Laurie jiggled the pad between their hands, tilted her head in a downward jerk.

"Laurie, for heaven's sake. What's going on with you? You're officially cut off from caffeine until— Oh! Oh my God." Clare released the pad to grab Laurie's hand. The one sporting a sweet, sparkling engagement ring.

"I'm getting married!"

"I see that. Oh, Laurie, it's a beautiful ring."

"Isn't it? I can't stop looking at it. I love it. I just *love* it. I thought you'd never see it."

"I was blinded by self-pity and leaky pipes. When did this happen?"

"Tyler asked me last night. He's been acting so weird the last week or so, I was worried he wanted to break up."

"Laurie, he's crazy about you. Obviously," she added turning Laurie's hand to study the ring from another angle.

"Yeah, but he'd just been so weird. Then last night he's like so super serious and he said we needed to take a walk in the park. I didn't know what was up."

"I'm so happy for you." Clare set the coffee aside to free her arms for the hug. "You had no idea?"

"Zero. I mean, we've been together for two years now, and we've sort of poked around the edges of maybe. But I didn't see it coming." Her brown eyes glistened with happy tears. "Clare, he actually got down on one knee, right there in the bandstand at Shafer Park."

"Seriously? Aw, Laurie."

"I know! Who'd have thought? I love him so much, and I was going to be so mad at him for breaking up with me. And now, look!" She waved her hand around again. "We're getting married. I almost burst waiting for you to get in so I could show you."

"Let me see it again."

Thrilled to oblige, Laurie held out her hand. "He picked it out himself."

"It's just beautiful. It's just perfect. When are you—"

The door jangled as two customers came in. "We'll talk more later," Clare told her.

It took another half hour before she could get upstairs, organize, and settle herself. Once she'd returned the calls, she remembered the leak and hurried down to check it out.

She was crouched on the restroom floor, a bucket under the slow drip, when Avery came in.

"I've sent you a zillion texts this morning."

"Dentist, trauma, engagement, work. And now plumbing. God, what a day, and it's not even noon."

"Laurie told me about her and Tyler—with sparkly rainbows shooting out of her eyes. And it's nearly one."

"It can't be."

"It is, and I've only got a minute. Hope's here."

"What? When?"

"She got here about eleven, which you'd know if you checked your phone. A couple of the guys from the inn crew carried up the furniture she brought with her. She's here!"

"Does she need any help with the rest of her things?"

"I haven't really had a chance to talk with her yet. I'm going to try to go over, help her set up, unpack and all that after the lunch rush. Can you come over?"

"I . . ." Already one in the afternoon. "Let me see if Mazie can watch the kids after school for a while."

"If she can't, I bet Beckett would. Unless you're still having your lovers' spat."

"Lovers' spat?"

"That's the word I got. You were in my place a couple nights ago, arguing."

"We were not arguing. For God's sake." Even though he was just wrong. "But I'm not asking Beckett to watch the kids after he's worked all day."

"Whatever. Try to make it, even if you can't stay long. She's a stranger in a strange land, after all."

"I'll work something out."

"Cool." Avery glanced toward the drip plopping musically in the bucket. "You ought to have Beckett fix that leak."

Clare scowled up at Avery, whose hair edged closer to maroon now with thick gold streaks. "What is he, my man of all work?"

"Hey, a nice benefit of sleeping with a handyman who seems to like your kids is using him when you need him. I've got to get back. I'll see you at Hope's apartment."

She wasn't going to *use* Beckett. She'd handled everything that came along for six years without a man, handy or otherwise. Just because she'd started seeing Beckett didn't mean she'd suddenly become incompetent.

Annoyed, she dashed back upstairs, where she kept a basic tool kit. She just needed a wrench, just needed to tighten the pipe joint. Anybody could do that.

"I'm going to take care of the leak," she told Laurie when she came down again. "If anyone calls for me, just take a message. This shouldn't take long."

"Are you sure? I could call over. They'd send one of the men from the inn."

"I'm getting you your own tool kit for an engagement present."

"I'd rather have a sexy nightie."

"Tool kit." She shook the one she carried. "Men aren't always around, you know. Women have to know how to handle basic household repairs."

"If you say so."

"And I do."

Now more determined than ever, Clare marched to the restroom. She sat on the floor, opened the tool kit. She'd dealt with plumbing issues before—with squeaky doors, drawers that stuck. She'd dealt with the epitome of parental frustration. Toys labeled *some assembly required.* When she'd been married, she'd had to learn to do what needed doing as she'd so often been on her own. And since, she'd continued to learn.

She could hardly afford to call a plumber every time something dripped. She'd be damned if she called her father when the gutters were clogged, or her lawn mower started sputtering—which it was— or some other minor annoyance cropped up.

She could certainly fix a little drip without issuing a help wanted bulletin. She picked up a wrench and got to work.

Within ten frustrating minutes the little drip became a slow but steady stream of water.

But that was okay, that was all right. She knew where she'd gone wrong. All she had to do was—

"Have you got a license for that?"

Flushed and struggling not to be furious, she looked over at Beckett. "I've nearly got it."

"Let me take a look."

"I've nearly got it," she repeated.

He just hunkered down, took the wrench out of her hand. "Looks like you need a washer. I probably have something that'll fit it out in the truck. I'll need to turn the water off for a few minutes."

"I know how to turn the water off."

"Okay, why don't you go do that while I get the washer?"

He straightened, drew her to her feet.

He hadn't shaved that morning, she noted, plus his hair needed trimming. *And* he smelled of sawdust. Which all added up, in her mind, to smug, let me handle that for you, little lady, male.

"Did Laurie call you?"

"No. Why?"

Clare just shook her head and went out to turn off the water.

So it needed a washer, she thought as she watched him quickly, competently make the repair. She'd have figured it out—and she knew where to buy a stupid washer for the stupid pipe.

"That should do it. Let me turn the water back on and—"

"I'll turn it on."

He only lifted his brows when she swung around and walked out.

He ran the water in the sink, checked the pipes, packed up her tools. "That'll cost ya." In a casual move, he tipped up her chin, kissed her. "Paid in full. Why didn't you call me?"

"Because I was *fixing* it myself."

He searched her face, deep blue eyes puzzled and patient. "Are you pissed at me or the pipe?"

"I'm—" She made herself stop short of the fresh rant building in her throat. It was hardly Beckett's fault. "It's been a crappy day, that's all. I appreciate the help."

"Anytime. Speaking of which, I can hang with the boys after school so you can give Hope a hand settling in."

"Is this place bugged?" she demanded. "Is there a town intercom running from here to the inn?"

"Not that I know of, but I saw Avery when I went over to get a panini for lunch."

"And I told her I was going to call Mazie."

"So I have to ask again if you're pissed at me."

"No, why would I be?" But she ground the words out because she was, for no good reason she could name. "I just don't want you to feel like you're on call for repairs, child care, and whatever else might come up. I know how to work these things out. I've been working these things out for years."

"No question about that." He spoke coolly, watching her face. "Is there any reason you can't take an assist when it's offered, or is it just an assist from me in particular?"

"No. Yes. Oh for—" She pressed her fingers to her eyes. "God, crappy day, starting with dragging three irritable boys to the dentist."

"Cavities?"

"No, so it could've been worse. Fine, I'm sure the boys would be happy to see you, if you're sure you've got the time."

"I can clear my busy social schedule."

"Um, I'll pick them up, get them started on their homework. I promised to make tacos if they were good at the dentist, which they weren't particularly. But we'll give that a pass as they're quick, and easier for me."

"How about I come by about four? Does that work?"

"Yes, thanks."

"See you then."

"Beckett. I'm sorry I snapped at you, and I do appreciate you fixing the leak."

"No problem." He started out, stopped. "You know, Clare, being able to do everything doesn't mean you have to."

Maybe not, she thought. But she didn't want to forget how.

❧

RYDER WATCHED BECKETT packing it up for the day. He knew when his brother was in a mood, and decided to poke at it to get to the root.

"You know, we could use a hand in the shop."

"My talents are required elsewhere."

"Babysitting. She's got you whipped, bro."

Beckett just shot up his middle finger.

"I guess you've got to make nice if you want some touch since you had that fight at Vesta."

"What fight?" Now he looked over, and with a scowl. "We didn't have a fight."

"That's not what I heard."

"We had a *discussion*. If people can't tell the difference—shit." He kicked the front tire of the truck. "Maybe she can't tell the difference. What do I know?"

"Trying to figure her out's your first mistake. Nobody figures women out."

"Something's up with her. She nearly took my head off when I fixed a leak over at TTP. It's Lizzy, that's what it is."

"Clare thinks you're making time with your ghost?"

"She's not my ghost. Clare got freaked the other night when I took her and the kids through, and Murphy saw Lizzy."

"Now you've got kids sharing your delusion?"

"And it's not a delusion, you damn well know." He jerked a thumb at D.A. while the dog peed on the tire he'd just kicked. "How come your dog goes upstairs and hangs out in that room every day?"

"He's a dog, Beck. I don't try to figure him out either." But this was interesting, he had to admit. "The kid said he saw her."

"He did see her. I never mentioned her to any of the kids." He told Ryder about the incident. "Then Clare's wigged out, and pissed off. Seems like she still is."

"She'll get over it. Take her some flowers or something."

"I don't have time to get her flowers. Besides." He kicked the tire again. "I didn't do anything."

"Yeah, that matters." Ryder shook his head in pity. He leaned in the truck window when Beckett got in. "They're always going to figure you did something, so the easiest way around it is to distract them with flowers. Then you're more likely to get laid."

"You're a cynical bastard."

"I'm a realist, son. Go babysit, maybe that's the same as flowers to a woman like Clare."

Maybe it was, Beckett thought as he drove away. But he wasn't hanging out with the kids because he'd done something. He was just helping her out.

He liked helping her out. He *wanted* to help her out.

Sooner or later she'd have to get used to it.

When he got there, the crowd went wild. Both his ego and his mood took a boost when the kids raced around, vying for attention, assailing him with questions and pleas to play.

"Take a breath," Clare ordered, then laid a hand on Harry's

shoulder as she turned to Beckett. "We just have to finish up some math homework."

"Math, huh? That happens to be my best thing."

"I've been doing homework *forever*."

"It certainly seems like it. We just have to finish this worksheet, then you're free."

"Go on," Beckett told her. "We got this."

"Oh, but—"

"We have no time for women here."

"It's Man Night!" Murphy flexed his little biceps the way Beckett had shown him.

"Man Hour and a Half," Clare corrected, then eyed the bag Beckett set on the counter.

"That's of no concern to you. It holds manly things." He snatched it up again, gave her a light kiss that inspired Liam to make gagging noises while Harry stared at his worksheet and Murphy tried to climb Beckett's leg like a monkey.

"All right." She sent Harry a long look, then brushed her hand over his hair. "Don't do the math for him. And you guys, give your brother a little quiet so he can finish up. Then you can all play. I won't be long."

"Have a good time." Beckett sat at the table. "So what have we got here?"

Clare gave Harry one more long look, then left them.

"You have to add the three numbers and write the answer. I don't know why there are so many of them."

"You've got a good start."

"Can we have the bag now?" Liam asked. "Is it cookies?"

"No and no. You two hit the playroom. I need you to separate all the action figures into good guys and bad guys, then put them into teams."

"What for?"

Beckett drilled a finger into Murphy's belly. "For the war."

The prospect of war sent them both racing away with blood-curdling screams.

"So," Beckett began, "fifty plus eight plus two hundred."

It didn't take long, and Beckett discovered Harry didn't need help so much as someone to keep him focused.

"Good deal. You aced that sucker." From the sounds coming from the playroom, they'd started the war without him. He got the bag, brought it to the table. "Now for math homework, over and above the call of duty, this seems fitting."

He took out a measuring tape. "This is the real deal, not a toy. It's one of mine. There's probably tons of stuff that needs measuring around here."

Harry pulled the tape out, let it snap back.

"When you need it to stay out, you push this—then it sticks. Just push it back to release."

Saying nothing, Harry tried it a few times. Then he looked at Beckett. "How come I get this?"

"You seemed interested in how to build things, and fix them, how it works when we were at the inn the other day. You can't build anything without a measuring tape. My dad gave me a measuring tape when—"

"You're not my dad."

"No," Beckett said, and thought *uh-oh*. "I just remembered getting one when I was a kid, and figured you'd like one."

"I saw you kiss my mom. I saw you kiss her before, too."

"Yeah."

After setting the measuring tape down, Harry folded his arms. "Why are you kissing her?"

"Because I like her. Maybe you should talk to your mom about it."

"I'm talking to *you*."

"Okay, fair enough." So the answer, Beckett decided, had to be fair enough, too. "I like your mom a lot. Kissing's a way to show it."

"Are you getting married?"

Whoa. How did he explain to an eight-year-old the long, sticky stretch between kissing and marriage? "We like each other, Harry, and we like being with each other, doing stuff together."

"Laurie's getting married, Mom said."

"Yeah, but—"

"You can't ask her to get married unless you ask me first. I'm the oldest."

"Okay."

"And you can't kiss her if she doesn't want to."

"All right."

"You have to *swear*." Though his eyes and voice went fierce, Beckett saw his bottom lip tremble a little.

Brave boy, he thought. Damn brave boy. "You know, I lost my dad, too."

Harry nodded. "Sorry."

"Yeah, it's hard. Sons have to take care of their mothers. It's our job. You're doing a good job, Harry. I won't kiss your mom if she doesn't want to. I won't ask her to marry me until I ask you about it first." Beckett held out a hand. "I swear."

Harry studied the hand a moment, studied Beckett's face. Then shook.

"Are we okay, you and me?"

Harry jerked a shoulder. "I guess. Do you come over to play with us so you can kiss Mom?"

"That's a nice benefit, but I come over to play because it's fun, and I like you. But I'm not going to kiss you."

That made Harry snort out a laugh before he picked up the tape again. "Did everybody get a measuring tape?"

"No, everybody got something different."

"Can I see?"

"Sure. I got this little level for Murphy. See when you set it down, you check these bubbles here in the middle. See the lines there, and the way the bubbles sit in between them? This table's pretty level. Otherwise." He lifted one end of the level so the bubbles tipped. "See?"

"Yeah." Fascinated, Harry tried it himself. "That's awesome."

"And this is a Phillips-head screwdriver."

"Who's Phillips?"

"Good question. I've got no clue." He'd have to look it up. "They call it a Phillips-head because, see it's got ridges in the point instead of being a flat-head like a regular one. This one's small enough so Liam can unscrew the battery cases on your toys when they need changing."

"It's pretty cool."

"If we had some more tools and some materials, we could build something, sometime."

The boy perked up. "Like what?"

"We'll think of something."

"Okay. I like the measuring tape. I like it's real and all. I'm going to show Liam and Murphy, and measure something."

"Good idea. I'll be right there."

Beckett sat for a moment when the boy ran off. He hoped he'd handled that thorny matter the right way. He felt like he had, but, *whew*, he was damn glad to set it down again.

CLARE SIPPED THE champagne Avery provided and studied Hope's apartment. Clean, she thought, serviceable—and temporary. Obviously Hope felt the same, as she'd kept the furniture move to a minimum.

"I sold a lot, gave some things to my sister. My brother took the bed. I didn't want it, and he didn't have any qualms about sleeping where I used to sleep with Jonathan." She shrugged.

"Better for you," Avery agreed. "Fresh start, fresh place, fresh everything."

"I figured I'd wait until I move into the apartment across the street before I bought a new one. For now, I'll be fine on just the new mattresses."

"Smart." Avery toasted her. "You should look at Bast, down on Main. Most of the furniture for the inn's coming from there. And Owen told me they'd hold anything that comes in until they're ready to load in. I'm sure they'd do the same for the innkeeper."

"Maybe. I'll take a look anyway." Hope studied the packing boxes, the bare walls, the bare floor. "Oh God, what have I done?"

She turned a quick circle, eyes wide and a little wild. "I've sold half my things, I have stuff I don't know what to do with in storage. I've moved from a place I loved, and I won't have a real job for God knows how long. Why did I do this?"

"You're just anxious," Clare began.

"Anxious? Anxious isn't in the same hemisphere with what I am. This is crazy. This isn't like me. I don't even know where I am."

"You're in Boonsboro." Avery turned her toward the window overlooking Main Street. "You've been here dozens of times. See, there's my restaurant."

"You know what I mean."

"What I know is you're about to start a job that's perfect for you in a place where you have friends. The best of all possible friends, who are smart and sexy, beautiful and wise."

"And modest and loving," Clare added, but Hope didn't laugh.

"How do I know it's the perfect job for me? I haven't done it yet."

Avery gave her a quick one-armed hug. "I know what you need."

"You're right. You are wise. I need a lot more champagne."

"No—well, later for that. Now." Avery dug in her pocket. "Owen gave me the key. Your key to the inn. We're going over now so you can remember why you're here."

"I haven't finished unpacking. I may never. There's not enough room for all my clothes in here." Hope squeezed her hands on either side of her head. "What am I going to do with my clothes?"

"We'll figure it out. But right now we're going to explore your future domain."

"Avery's right." Though going inside the building, just the three of them, made Clare a little uneasy, she put all the enthusiasm she could muster in her voice. "You said you haven't been over since you got here."

"I've been trying to organize."

"I'll help you later."

"And I'll come by tomorrow," Clare promised. "At least for a little while."

"Okay, all right. Let's go."

"You couldn't help but see the entrance." Clare grabbed her jacket as they headed out, and down the back stairs.

"And it's beautiful. It's a great building, no argument. I just can't figure out why I thought I should be in charge of it."

"Because you're smart, self-aware—which is the same as wise, really. And this is just the kind of challenge you thrive on."

Hope stared at Avery, blew out a breath as they crossed the side street. "Big talk. And you forgot sexy and beautiful."

"Goes without saying, Miss Philadelphia County."

"Sexy and beautiful always go *with* saying."

"They're prepping the ground for the pavers." Avery gestured. "You should take a look behind the gift shop, see what they've done there. It's just great. Here." She handed Hope the key. "You should unlock it."

Here goes, she thought, sliding the key into the lock.

CHAPTER FOURTEEN

HOPE SAID NOTHING WHEN THEY WALKED IN. CLARE started to speak, but Avery shook her head. Understanding, Clare kept her silence.

Boxes were stacked everywhere with barely a pathway between. Kitchen cabinets, Clare noted. So that installation would begin soon, but she worried Hope might not appreciate the lovely tiles since the boxes and tarps hid so much of them.

They snaked their way through to the wide archway.

"The colors are good." Hope's tone stayed noncommittal, but she stood in the cluttered space for several moments before continuing down the short hall into the lobby area.

There she made a little sound—pleasure and surprise.

"All right, gorgeous. Elegant and unique without being fussy. Do you know if it's safe to walk on this part, too?"

"Owen said anything we couldn't walk on would be taped off."

Wanting to see for herself, Avery crossed the tile and flipped on the work light inside one of the restrooms. "Big wow."

"What? Oh." Hope stepped in, ran her fingers over the stylized pattern of the wall tiles. "Look how it picks up the details in the tile rug but doesn't duplicate it. I love this."

"Want it?"

Hope merely gave Avery an arch look. "I'm sure there's more to see."

She wandered to the first guest room, and stood at the taped doorway of the bathroom.

They'd laid the floor, Clare noted, and thought of that first moment with Beckett, right there. Of the sudden, surprising awareness. Of the scent of honeysuckle.

She backed out, left her friends cooing over colors and tile details to go to the dining room.

"That's a great look," Hope said when she joined Clare. She continued to study the ceiling a moment before she wandered to the front windows.

"Are you really not sure?"

Still looking out, Hope lifted her shoulders. "I guess I feel out of my element, and that's unnerving. This, all of this, is such a big change, and I want that—I think I need that. But now that I've done it I wonder if I'm ready for this big a change."

She turned back. "Still, there's something about this place. It just speaks to me, and makes me think maybe this *is* my element now. It feels right when I'm in here. I'll probably go back across the street and panic again, but it feels right when I'm in here."

She looked up to the coffered ceiling again when she heard the sound of footsteps overhead. "Avery must've gone up without us."

"No, I didn't." Her gaze angled up as well, Avery walked in.

"It's probably Ryder or Owen," Clare began.

"Could be, but I didn't see their trucks out front or out back."

"Well, somebody's up there, and since the doors are locked, it's somebody with a key." To solve the matter, Hope walked out to the hall, stood at the base of the steps. "Hello!"

Her voice echoed back; silence followed.

"Must be the ghost." Avery grinned, her face full of fun. "Let's check it out."

"Avery—" But she was already jogging upstairs. Resigned, Clare followed with Hope beside her as Avery continued to call out.

"Is this cool or what?" Avery stood in the doorway of E&D. "Can you smell it?" She breathed in deep. "Summertime. Honeysuckle."

"It's just your imagination." But Clare folded her arms, chilled, because she smelled it, too.

"Then my imagination took the same trip. It's fascinating." Hope moved into the room. "Has anyone done any research to try to find out who she was? That would be . . ." She jumped as the porch door opened. "Look at that!"

"The door wasn't latched and locked. That's how someone got in," Clare insisted.

"Someone carrying an armload of honeysuckle? I don't think so." Avery went to the door, opened it wider. Closed it again. "And it wouldn't be easy to access that porch from the outside, when it's still light out on top of it."

"It doesn't feel sad, does it?" Hope circled the room, opened the door again, stepped out. "Whatever, whoever—it feels friendly."

"It can't *feel* anything, because it's stone and brick and wood." Temper snapped in Clare's voice.

"So was Hill House." Avery lowered and deepened her voice. "And whatever walked there walked alone."

"Oh, stop it." This time, Clare rounded on her. "Just stop it. It's an old building. Floors creak. They need to fix the door. That's all."

"Honey." Avery reached for her hand. "Why are you so upset?"

"You're standing here making this place out to be the haunted hotel and you wonder why I'm upset?"

"Yeah." She tightened her grip on Clare's hand. "If you don't believe in spooks, you'd just think we're being silly. But you wouldn't be mad."

"I'm not mad. I'm just tired of being pulled into talking about ghosts as if they existed."

"Okay. I'm not upset if you don't believe. Why should you be upset if I do?"

"You're right. Absolutely. It's been a hard day, and I've still got to fix dinner. I should get home."

"We'll go back," Hope began.

"No, you should stay, go through the rest. I'm sorry. I really am tired. I just—" Her voice broke, undoing her. "I don't believe in all this."

"Fine, no problem." Avery gave an irritated shrug. "We should go up so Hope can see her apartment."

"I don't want to believe in all of this." Tears clogged her throat, stung her eyes. "If it's possible, why didn't Clint come back?"

"Clare." Before Clare could evade, Avery had her wrapped in a hug. "I'm sorry. I never even thought."

"It's stupid. I'm stupid." Giving in, giving up, Clare let the tears come. "And it's stupid to get mad, but why does she get to come back? Why does she get to stay?"

"I wish I knew."

"Murphy saw her."

Avery jerked back. "What? When?"

"When we were here with Beckett. It scared me, seeing him starting upstairs, smiling at . . . her. And it made me furious. Why should he see her, Avery? Shouldn't he have had the chance to see his father? Just once? Just once. Hell."

She walked out onto the porch, into the air. As she stood at the rail, Hope pushed a tissue into her hand. Then Hope's arm came around one side of her, Avery's on the other.

"It is stupid to be mad." A sigh trembled out as she wiped at her eyes. "Useless to ask why. I've done all that already, and I got past it. When they first started talking about ghosts, I didn't believe it, so it was interesting. The way a novel is. Just a good story, that's all. But then, Murphy."

"You're allowed to ask why," Hope murmured. "Even when there's no answer."

"I didn't know why it twisted me up this way, until now. Or maybe I couldn't admit it."

"We'll get out of here," Avery suggested. "We'll go back over to Hope's, just sit and talk awhile."

"No, I'm all right now. It's better to know, to admit it, then deal with it."

Clare turned, watching the door open wider. And let out a long breath.

"I'd better deal, because it doesn't look like she's going anywhere."

IN THE MORNING, Beckett huddled with his brothers in the laundry room. If Owen hadn't called the meeting, he could've gotten another hour of sleep—maybe two—since he planned to work at home through the morning.

But Owen was Owen, he decided, and meetings and agendas were his cotton candy.

"The electrician's coming in this morning to install the exterior lights here, and the new interiors over at the gift shop. The boxes are marked, but you need to double-check the fixtures, Beck. And before you ask why," Owen continued, "we've got close to two hundred light fixtures between here and across the street. We don't want to waste time, money, and man-hours switching something out if it got mismarked."

"Fine. I'll do it before I go over to my office. And before *you* ask, yes, I have my checklist."

"While you're at it . . ." He added a half dozen tasks and calls to Beckett's list.

"What the hell are you doing while I'm on the fucking phone?"

Owen turned his clipboard around. The length of the list shut Beckett up.

"Why aren't you giving a chunk of that to the innkeeper?" Ryder asked.

"Because we're giving her a couple days to move in, for God's sake. She'll earn her rent next week, believe me." Owen flipped a page on his clipboard. "That's a list I've started for her. While I'm installing the counter across the street, what's your plan?"

"Two men over there, punching out." Ryder checked his own list. "When it opens, they'll go pick up the desk Mom settled on down at the flea market, haul it up to the office there. Exterior painting continues, probably forever, and I'm going to have them start inside, get going on The Lobby since the floor's done."

He ran it down while Beckett drank his coffee, and the radio switched on to country rock with the crew's arrival.

"Mom's got an appointment in Hagerstown," Owen reminded them. "So she'll swing through on her way home. Tell the crew the big boss is coming in. That's all I've got."

"Thank Christ."

When Beckett yawned, Ryder smirked. "Babysitting wear you out last night?"

"Is that code for sex?" Owen wondered. "I need to be updated if we're using codes."

"No, it's not a code, and no, it didn't wear me out. I just didn't get a lot of sleep. Probably since babysitting isn't code for sex."

Ryder kept smirking. "She have a headache?"

"You're such an asshole," Beckett said mildly. "It's not time—it'd be weird to sleep with her with the kids right down the hall. They're not ready for that, especially since Harry grilled me over kissing his mom."

"No shit?" Now Ryder's smirk bloomed into a full, appreciative grin. "Good for him."

"Yeah, you've got to admire him, looking out for her. They're great kids. Murphy wants me to build coffins for his action figures, for when they die in battle. Who thinks of that?"

"I wish we had," Owen mused. "That would've been cool. We could've buried them out back, made little headstones with their emblems on them."

Brilliant, Beckett thought. "Then they'd rise again, recharged by some supernatural force, to seek revenge."

"You could burn in their emblems on the coffin lids, too. Every man should have his own coffin. You've still got your wood-burning kit, right?"

"Sure. Man, he'd love that."

"While you two are playing with your toys, I'm going to work." Ryder strapped on his tool belt. "Plenty of scrap plywood around," he added as he walked out.

Owen waited until Ryder was out of earshot and shouting to the crew. "You know if you build them, he's going to want in, and he's going to call dibs on Wolverine and Venom, just like always."

"Yeah, he will. You?"

"Damn straight I want in. I get—"

"Dibs on Spidey and Moon Knight."

"Damn it. I was going to call Spider-Man."

"Too late."

"Batman and Joker."

"It's a start."

He intended to go directly home, straight to his office, but got roped in to pulling on work gloves and helping tear down the old fencing. Then he answered the call across the street to consult with Madeline on the display shelves she wanted to stagger on the left wall of the gift shop.

On his way out, he spotted the barber on the bench outside of Sherry's, stopped to talk.

"Looks real good." Together they watched the electrician install one of the big carriage lights flanking the doors. "I hear you're going to have a big party when it's done."

"That's what I hear, too."

"People driving by break their necks looking at it."

"They haven't got your view, Dick." The phone jingled in his pocket. "I'll see you later." He pulled it out as he walked. "What's the matter, Ry? Did you miss me?"

"Like a butt rash. Tile guys have a question on the wall pattern down here. Mom's in Hagerstown, so you're elected to answer."

"On my way."

He finally walked into his office closer to ten than the nine o'clock start time he'd planned on. But he didn't mind. Every step, he thought—and poured the last of the morning's coffee in a mug—was a step.

He dealt with the calls first because he hated them most, then settled down to update the plans for furniture placement with some additional purchases.

Once he shot the updates to everyone's email, he opened a file.

He was damn well going to finalize the signage today—and they'd better like it.

They'd whittled it down to three possible fonts because nobody wanted to commit. Well, today he committed for all of them.

He fiddled around with all of them, with spacing, size, color tones. Got up, walked around, went to the window and stared out at the building, trying to see it. Went back, rechecked measurement, math, fiddled some more.

Food, he decided, and called downstairs for a calzone.

This is it, he told himself, and printed out a copy. He took it to the window, held it up with one eye closed. Smiled.

"And he deems it good."

To add impact and persuasion, he sat again, worked on a sign for the gift shop using the same palette and font.

"Yeah, it's open," he called out at the knock on the door. He started to rise, reach for his wallet. And his day got just a little brighter when Clare came in with a take-out box.

"Moonlighting at Vesta? I bet you make great tips."

"I'm saving up for a new car." She offered the box and a smile. "I was downstairs when they boxed it up, so I said I'd bring it since I wanted to talk to you. It's on your tab."

"Good deal." He set it aside. "I'll split it with you."

"Thanks, but I'm just going to grab a quick salad, then give Hope a hand for an hour. But I wanted to—"

"I didn't give you your tip." He braced his hands on her hips, drew her in. "You smell great."

And looked, he thought, a lot more relaxed and happy than she had since their *discussion* about Lizzy.

"I've been sampling some new body lotions we're thinking of carrying. This one's apricot and honey."

"Sold."

He leaned down, slid into the kiss, into apricots and honey and Clare. Too long, he thought, as her arms linked around his neck. Too long since he'd really held her, really had her.

"You're an excellent tipper."

"That's just the down payment." He backed her toward the door. "You have to come with me for the rest."

He backed her out, and into his apartment.

"Beckett." She laughed, but he heard the hitch in her breath, felt her quiver when he grazed her bottom lip with his teeth. "I can't. We can't. It's the middle of the day."

"Lunch break."

"Yes, but—"

"I think about you all the time." He kept backing her up, his lips gliding over her neck, back to hers. "About being with you again, like this. It's hard seeing you and not being able to touch you."

"I know. I—"

"Let me touch you."

He already was, his hands roaming, molding, spreading needs to smother common sense.

"I guess I could be a little late."

He slid his hand under the skirt of her dress, trailed it up her leg, over her, down again.

"I can definitely be late."

She fell back on the bed, her heart already racing, her body already revved. Crazy, irresponsible, wonderful, she thought when his mouth pressed, his teeth nipped at her breast—somehow wildly sexy with the material between them.

She let out a gasp of shock when his fingers snaked under the dress again, and into her.

"God. Oh God."

"Just go." Crazed now, he drove her higher while he feasted on the warm skin of her throat. "Just go."

She bucked under him, her hands clutching at the tangle of sheets, her eyes dazed. When she came, the long, shuddering moan arrowed straight to his loins.

And when she went limp, when her eyes closed, he yanked down his jeans, tossed up her skirt. And plunged into her.

The cry of shock sounded again, and now her hands clutched at his hips, nails digging in. His name trembled from her lips as she stared into his eyes.

Then she wrapped her legs around his waist and matched him beat for frantic beat.

Spent, they lay together, still half dressed, breath whistling.

"I should always deliver your calzones."

"Works for me."

She closed her eyes, wanting just another moment to bask. "That goes on my list of firsts."

He lifted his head. "During the day, you mean?"

"No, but in the middle of a workday—and I'm still wearing my clothes. Nearly all of them."

"I was in kind of a hurry." He lowered, rubbed his lips over hers. "But I can get you undressed now and start over again."

"I don't think my system or my schedule can handle another tip. But thanks very much for your patronage."

"Best calzones in the county. Shit, I'll get it," he said at the knock on the apartment door.

Which of course wasn't locked, he remembered when he heard Avery's call. He dragged on his jeans as Clare sprang up, began trying to straighten and smooth her dress.

"Hold on! Be right out."

But she'd already made it to the door, where she stood, mouth dropping open, finger pointing. "You had a nooner! Look at the two of you all sex-eyed and guilty. My body can't hold any more of this jealousy. I'm going to have to hire a man. What do you charge?"

"Funny."

Clare tugged the band out of her hair, then realized she'd left her purse—with her brush in it—in Beckett's office. "We were just coming—"

"Evidence indicates you've already done that."

"She's a riot." Turning to Clare, he jerked a thumb at Avery.

Then the two of them just smiled at each other like, Avery thought, two people who'd had a nooner.

"I knocked," she told them. "On the office first because that's where you wanted the calzone delivered—and where Clare said she'd take it because she wanted to"—Avery inserted air quotes—" 'talk to you.' "

"I did, and I haven't. Look, I need to get my brush—my hair. I'll be over at Hope's in a few minutes."

"You can't have any more sex now. I'm putting my foot down. I'll know if you do, then I'll cry, and cut my own hair. You don't want to be responsible for that."

"I'm just going to put myself back together. I'll be right there. Promise."

Avery said nothing, just pointed her finger at both of them, added a narrowed look, then left.

"I thought she'd never leave. Why don't we—"

"No." Clare tossed up a hand, palm out. "Absolutely not. I promised. I've got to get my purse. I wanted to talk to you, to apologize."

"For what?" He followed her back into the office.

"For being so distracted I didn't even really thank you for watching the kids yesterday, for being bitchy when you fixed my sink, and for snapping at you the night we went to the inn and had dinner— which is the reason for the rest of it."

She grabbed her purse, glanced around. "I don't think I've ever been in here before—in the office. It's nice. It's you. Is that a bathroom?"

"Yeah."

"I need the mirror." She stepped in, left the door open as she brushed her hair back into order. "Avery, Hope, and I went over to the inn while you were with the boys. And, well, we heard something upstairs, like footsteps. And we smelled her up there. The door to the porch opened."

She took the band off her wrist, twisted her hair into a smooth tail. "I jumped all over them, like I did with you. No," she decided. "Even more. I was so angry."

She pulled out lipstick, repaired the damage there.

"Why?"

"That's the question. And I realized why, or let myself. I realized I was angry because if it's possible, if this is really happening, if it's really possible to come back, then—"

"Oh shit. Clint. I never thought of it, of him. I'm sorry."

"No, *I'm* sorry. There's no reason for you to think of it. And none for me to take it out on you, on Avery and Hope. Except that's what you do when you're upset. Take it out on the people who care." To finish the job, she dug out her compact.

"It hurt you, and I wouldn't let it alone."

"You didn't hurt me, the situation did. And now that I know why I felt that way, it won't hurt."

"Just like that?"

"I had a good cry after I put the boys to bed, and did a lot of thinking. No, it won't hurt anymore." She tossed the compact back in her purse as she came back out. "I don't know why some people come back—at least you hear stories about it. So I can't know why Clint didn't. Or maybe he did, and I wasn't ready or open so I didn't see him or feel him. But I know he's gone, and I can't be angry with him, or you, or . . . whatever is over there. So I'm sorry, and thank you for taking the boys through, for fixing that damn sink, and watching them yesterday so I could start working this out."

"You're welcome."

"Now I really have to go."

"I want to see you this weekend."

"I want you to see me this weekend." She moved into his arms, just held for a moment. "Let me check the schedule."

"I'll call you later."

"Okay." She went to the door, opened it. "Oh, one more thing. Thanks for the tip."

He walked to the window, waited so he could watch her cross the street. She did it at a run, skirts flying, legs flashing. When she reached the opposite corner, she looked back, saw him there and waved before hurrying to the back of the building.

He thought about her, about love. What it cost, what it offered. Then he took his take-out box to his office microwave to heat up his very cold calzone.

❧

IT WAS NEAR the end of the workday by the time he made it back to the inn. His mind on other things, he smelled the paint before he saw it.

They'd need another coat, but the quiet straw color already picked up the light, played with the tones in the tile. He heard the grind of the tile saw, the thump of hammers. When he got to the base of the stairs, his mother's voice carried down to him.

Perfect, he'd get them all at once.

He found his mother and Carolee on two in the Eve and Roarke room.

"Hey. I was hoping I'd catch you." He crossed back to the bath.

"Look at this!" His mother thrust a cut sheet at him. "It's the perfect towel warmer for this room."

"You already—"

"I didn't order the other one because I wasn't a hundred percent. This is a hundred percent. Heated glass."

"It's kind of—"

"Pricey, I know, but it's exactly right. It looks futuristic."

"It is pretty cool." Studying it, he brought the rest of the room's features into his head. "It works with the lights, the fixtures we're putting in here."

"Good, because I already ordered it. But that's not the big news."

"You're not pregnant, are you?"

She slapped his arm. "Carolee—"

"Carolee's pregnant?"

"Aren't you in a good mood? No, and it's a good thing she's not, because Carolee is going to be our assistant innkeeper."

"That is big." Surprised, he looked at his aunt. "I didn't know you wanted to work here."

"I'm dying to." Carolee's eyes sparkled with the thought of it. "I love this place, and giving up my part-time job at the outlet won't hurt my feelings a bit. I'm good with people, and you know how I love to entertain. I wrote up a resume."

"As if." Justine bumped her sister with her elbow.

"It's business, Justine. Family business, but still business."

"My vote is you're hired," Beckett said. "You'll be terrific."

"See? That makes it unanimous."

"I'm so excited! I really love this place. I'll be able to walk to work instead of driving all the way to—" She stopped, shook her head. "But we have to see how Hope and I get along." Carolee held up her fingers, crossed them. "Then we'll make it official."

"Well, this news blows my news out of the water."

"Clare's pregnant."

Beckett's mouth dropped open. "Jesus, Mom."

"Tit for tat, my baby boy. What's the news?"

"Where's the rest of us?"

"Upstairs in Hope's apartment. They went ahead and laid the tile in her kitchen and bath since it's simple."

"Let's get them down here, so we can all do this together."

He went out, yelled up. "Family meeting, ASAP. Eve and Roarke."

"What's this about, Beckett?" Justine asked.

"Something I finished up today. Oh, I need to use the shop for a while, just FYI. I have to build some coffins."

Not much surprised Justine Montgomery, especially when it came to her boys, but this one had her blinking. "Coffins?"

"For the kids, for action figures who've fallen in battle. I'm probably going to head over there when— Okay, here they come."

"What's up?" Owen demanded. "We're just knocking off."

"And I want a beer," Ryder added.

D.A. moseyed in behind him, circled the room to sniff everyone hello.

"You can buy me one." Beckett opened his folder, took out the mock-up of the sign. "This is it. Anybody doesn't like it, I'll kill them with a sledge-hammer. I'll feel bad if it's Mom or Carolee, but I'll still do it."

Ryder studied it, said, "Huh."

"What font is that?"

"The one I picked," Beckett told Owen. "I can kill you. I have a spare brother."

"Justine, look at the colors." Carolee laid a hand on Beckett's arm as she leaned in.

"They're exactly what I wanted, that rich brown on creamy, beigy tan."

"It's to scale. Plenty of room for the website and the phone numbers without crowding the name."

"Not bad." Ryder nodded, scratching D.A.'s ears while he shot Beckett a grin. "Not bad at all."

"I still need the font. If we're sticking with this—"

"We're sticking with it," Beckett insisted.

"I need it for the stationery, business cards, room plaques, key fob—"

"Okay, shut up." Beckett took a disk out of the file, handed it to Owen. "Everything's on here."

"It's like the towel warmer." Justine wrapped her arm around Beckett's waist. "It's a hundred percent."

"I made one up for the gift shop, figured we'd go vertical there, hang it out on a bracket, print on both sides."

"I love it!" Justine took it. "Carolee, let's go see if Madeline's still over there. She'll want to see this. Good job." She gave Beckett a squeeze. "Really good."

"I guess I'll buy you a beer," Ryder decided.

"I guess you will."

"Meet you there. I need to clean up since I wasn't riding a desk all day."

"Did you give me the point size on the—"

"It's all there, Owen," Beckett assured him.

"I'll check it out. After Ry buys me a beer."

"Why am I buying your beer?"

"It's your turn."

"Bullshit."

They argued about it on the way out.

CHAPTER FIFTEEN

CLARE BARELY HAD THE COFFEE STARTED AND THE computer booted on her preopening routine when the bookstore doorknob rattled. She glanced over, saw Sam Freemont through the glass panel. Too late to hide, she decided as he'd spotted her, gave her that sly wink and smile.

She considered just shaking her head, but he'd only knock, wink, smile. She'd never been able to figure out why Sam thought he was so charming.

Unlocking the door, she angled herself in the narrow opening. "I'm sorry, Sam. I'm not open yet."

"I smell coffee."

"Yes, I just started it, but I'm not open for an hour. I really need to—"

"I could sure use a cup. You can spare a cup for a friend now, can't you?"

He didn't exactly muscle his way in, but she found herself backing up. Easier to just pour the damn coffee, she thought, and slipped behind the counter.

Sam had given her the mild creeps since middle school.

"How do you want it?"

"Hot and sweet. Why don't you just tip your finger in it. That's all the sugar I need."

Maybe more than mild these days, she decided.

"I saw your car in the back, and thought, Clare's getting an early start today. Honey, you work too hard."

"Can't run a business without working." Unless your daddy owned the car dealership where you put in time when it suited you. She set the go-cup on the counter. "Sugar's on the shelf right over there."

He only leaned on the counter. "How are things going with you, sweetheart?"

"Busy. In fact, I've really got to get to work. So—"

"You've got to take time for yourself. Isn't that what I always tell you?"

"Yes, you do. But right now—"

"Did you see the demo I'm driving? She's one sweet ride."

"I'm sure it is."

"Come take a look. In fact, let me take you for a spin." He gave her that wink again.

"I have work to do." She slapped the top on the cup since he'd made no move to doctor it. "Coffee's on the house."

"Now you can't buy yourself pretty things if you give it away." With that sly look on his face he reached in the inside jacket pocket of his gray pinstripe suit, flashed gold cuff links and monogrammed French cuffs.

He took a twenty out of his wallet, set it on the counter.

"You keep the change, buy yourself a little something."

She came around, intending to get to the door, get him out. He timed it well, turning into her so she ended up trapped between him and the counter.

Enough, Clare decided. Just enough.

"You're in my way, and you need to leave."

"I tell you what we'll do. We'll go for a drive tonight."

"No, we won't."

"A long, pretty drive," he said, trailing a finger down the side of her throat before she slapped it aside. "I'll treat you to a nice dinner. And then—"

"I don't know how to make this any more clear. I have a business to run. I have children to raise. And I'm not interested in going for a drive with you, a dinner. Or lunch. Or brunch." That got through, she thought as the smile fell away from his face. "Now I'm telling you to get out of my store."

"You should be nicer to me, Clare. You should stop playing games with me. I could do things for you."

"I can do for myself." She started to step to the side, but he shot out his arm, slapped a hand on the counter and blocked her.

The first prickle of fear scraped the surface of sheer annoyance. "Stop it. What's wrong with you?"

"You're always too busy to spend a little time with me. But not too busy to spend plenty with Beckett Montgomery."

"That's my business."

"You're wasting your time with him. The Montgomerys, they're nothing but blue-collar punks. I could buy and sell Beckett Montgomery." He stepped in, put a hand on her hip, and shot twin spears of temper and fear through her when he slid it around, squeezed her ass. "I just want you to take a drive with me. Let me show you a good time."

"Get your hands off me." She hated the jerky sound of her voice, fought to steady it. "I'm never going to take a drive with you. I'm not interested in you or what you can buy and sell. I want you to get out of my store, and I don't want you to come back."

The pseudo charm switched to a bright, sharp anger that sent her heart on a gallop. "That's no way to talk to me. It's past time you realize a woman like you needs to be grateful, needs to show some appreciation."

She thought of the coffee behind her, slapped one hand on his chest, reaching for the cup with the other.

Someone banged hard on the door. "Clare!" Avery, her face furious through the glass, banged again. "I need you to open the door." She turned her head, raised a hand. "Hey, Owen! Come over here."

Sam stepped back, shot his cuffs. "You think about what I said."

Because her legs trembled, she pressed back against the counter. "Don't come back here. Don't come to my house again. Stay away from me."

He walked to the door, flipped open the lock she didn't realize he'd turned.

Avery bolted in when he went out. "Creep," she yelled behind him, then shut the door hard, locked it again. "Are you okay?"

"Yeah. Yes. Yeah."

"Was he actually putting moves on you? Stupid, pin-striped bastard. How many times do you have to turn him down?"

"Apparently I haven't reached the magic number."

"Clare, you're shaking." Instantly, Avery moved over to hug her, to rub her arms as she felt how cold they were. "Damn it, what did he do? He really scared you."

"A little. Maybe a lot. Don't tell Owen—where is Owen?"

"How the hell do I know? I just used him as a threat of a beat-down. Sam's always been scared of the Montgomerys. What the hell was he doing in here?"

"I'm stupid, just stupid." She went behind the counter, got a bottle of water out of the little cooler. "He said he wanted coffee, and

I figured it was easier to give it to him than argue about being closed. He usually just makes a pest of himself. Today was different. He got mad, and pushy."

She remembered the feel of his hands on her, let herself shudder it away.

"He knows I'm seeing Beckett, and that seemed to set him off."

"Sam the creep Freemont always gets what he wants, and you're screwing with his record. His mother just indulges the crap out of him; always has. You know there was talk about him and some woman he was dating a couple years ago."

Clare nodded, soothed her throat with water. "That he'd knocked her around, and his mother paid her off. I thought it was just gossip. Now . . . I'm inclined to believe it."

"You should've kneed him in the balls."

"I was stupid there, too. He just took me by surprise. I was going to toss his damn coffee in his face, which wouldn't have worked very well since I capped it."

"Do you want to call the cops?"

"No. No, he was just being obnoxious, and creepy. He's bound to be embarrassed since you scared him off. And I told him not to come back. He'll have to get his damn coffee and books somewhere else."

"Like he reads."

Clare took the cap off the cup, deliberately poured it down the drain in the under-counter sink. "He left his damn twenty. Keep the change, he says, buy yourself a little something. He *is* an asshole."

"Tear it up."

"I'm not tearing up a twenty-dollar bill."

"Then I will."

"No." Laughing now, Clare slapped a hand on it as Avery reached for it. "I'll just mail it to him."

"You will not." Face flushed with temper, Avery slapped a hand over Clare's. "No contact. I mean it, Clare. Contact of any kind encourages his type of obsession or whatever it is."

"Where do you get that?"

"I watch a lot of cop shows since I'm not currently spending any time dating and having sex. Seriously, Clare, tear it up, give it away, spend it, but don't send it to him."

"Okay, you're probably right. I'll give it to the church or something." She jammed it in her pocket. "I'm really glad you came by."

"So am I."

"Why did you come by?"

"I saw the asshole's car when I was walking to the shop. Flashy car, dealer tag, so who else could it be? I thought I'd stop in, keep you from being bored to death. I didn't expect to find him practically assaulting you."

"Thanks. A lot."

"When's one of the girls getting in?"

Clare glanced at her watch. "Any minute. God, now I'm behind."

"You'll catch up. Go on and get started. Since I'm here, I think I'll browse for a couple minutes."

"Avery, he's not coming back—and I wouldn't let him in if he did."

"I'm forced to remind you—not dating or having sex currently. I could use a good book."

Hands in her pockets, Avery studied the shelves of new releases.

Clare sighed, got out two cups. Since her friend decided to be her sword and shield, they might as well have some coffee.

❧

BECKETT LIKED HIS timing. The way he calculated it, he'd get to Clare's right after homework, and before dinner. So maybe he could wrangle an invite to stay. He liked his chances. They'd had a good time Saturday night, spent some time with the kids in the park on Sunday afternoon.

He'd had a good week so far with no major glitches on the job, so he figured his luck was in—right up to when he pulled up to Clare's and didn't see her car. But he did see Harry on the little porch with his measuring tape.

He got out of the truck, hefted the box he'd brought with him.

"I'm measuring to see how big a pumpkin we should get for Halloween. We put it on the post."

"Good idea. What're you going to be?"

"I'm either going to be Wolverine or the Joker."

"Hero or villain. Tough choice."

"We got a catalog with all kinds of costumes, but we have to pick soon. Mom gives out candy at the store on trick-or-treat night."

"Oh yeah? I'll have to get me some. Where's your mom?"

"She had to go back to work for something. Mrs. Ridenour's here until she gets back. What's in the box?"

"Something for you guys my brothers and I made."

"For us? What is it?"

"Let's go in. I'll show all of you."

Harry bolted to the door, shouting as he shoved it open. "Beckett's here! He's got something for us in a box."

It sounded like a stampede. Alva came out from the kitchen as the boys raced from different directions to surround him.

"Isn't this a nice surprise? Boys, inside voices. Clare had to run to the bookstore. You just missed her."

"I'm just dropping something off for the kids."

"He made it with his brothers," Harry said. "What is it?"

"Let's take a look." He crouched on the floor, put the box down, took off the lid.

"Wow." Liam's tone was reverent.

"Those look like . . ." Alva shook her head at Beckett.

"You made coffins?"

"Yeah." He grinned at Harry. "Heroes and villains all deserve a decent burial, right, guys?"

"What are these?" Liam picked up a miniature headstone. "Like their shields?"

"Not exactly. Those are the headstones. You mark the grave with them so you know who's buried where."

Liam stared at Beckett with a nearly religious fever. "This is *awesome*."

"They have their symbols on them and everything." Murphy lifted a coffin out, opened and closed the lid on its tiny hinges. "This is for Batman."

"This is the Hulk's. See, it's bigger like he is." Harry studied it, then Beckett. "How did you know how big?"

"Measured." He poked Harry in the belly.

"This is the coolest *ever*." Overcome, Liam launched himself at Beckett. "We never had *anything* like this. Can we bury them? For real?"

"That's the idea."

"In the sandbox, for now," Alva warned. "No digging in the yard."

"We gotta go get the dead guys." Harry dashed to the playroom.

"We got more upstairs." Liam charged up the steps.

Murphy took out coffins, headstones, examining each one. "Here's for Moon Knight and for Captain America and the Green Lantern."

"Bad guys in there, too."

"Mrs. Ridenour?" Harry poked out of the playroom. "Can we have something to carry them all out? The ones who aren't dead have to go to the burying."

"Yes, I'm sure they'd want to pay their respects. I'll get you something." She shook her head at Beckett again, walked back to the kitchen.

Murphy stacked coffins, opened and closed lids. "We have to decide who got killed in the war and who didn't. My daddy got killed in the war."

"I know." What did he say, how did he say it? Jesus, what had he been thinking, making coffins for kids with a dead father? "I'm sorry."

"He was a hero."

"Yeah, he was."

"I didn't get to meet him first 'cause I wasn't borned yet. Mom says he loves me anyway."

"Count on it. I knew your dad."

Somber interest gazed out of Murphy's eyes. "You did?"

"We went to school together."

"Were you his friend?"

They hadn't really hung out together, but Beckett thought of the night they'd TP'd Mr. Schroder's house, and the night they'd celebrated the event. "Yeah."

"Did you go when they buried him?"

"Yeah, I did." Horrible day, Beckett remembered. In every possible way.

"That's good, 'cause your friends are supposed to be there." He smiled, beautifully, then clambered up. "I'm gonna take them outside to the sandbox." He tried to lift the box, gave a puppy-dog look. "It's too heavy."

"I'll get it."

"I got them, Harry!" Liam ran down with a small red basket, loaded with figures.

"Get your jackets." Alva stood outside the playroom. "There's a nip in the air."

"Beckett's bringing the coffins!" Murphy ran after his brothers. "I wanna dig! I get to dig!"

Beckett picked up the box. "I guess you heard that."

"It breaks your heart."

"I didn't think when we made these they'd make him think about what happened to Clint. I should have."

"Nonsense. Those boys have a normal fascination with war and death, villainy. They know it's just pretend. They're well-adjusted, healthy young boys. Clare's a fine, fine mother."

"I know. She really is."

"Being a fine mother, she makes sure those boys know their father was a good man, a loving father, and that he died in the service of his country. And now Murphy knows that you were there when his daddy was laid to rest. That his father's friend is his friend, too. That's a good thing, Beckett."

"I just don't want to make a mistake."

"Even superheroes make mistakes, or they wouldn't have to be buried in handmade coffins in the sandbox. Do you plan to wait for Clare?"

"Yeah, since I'm here anyway, I thought I would."

"That's another good thing. I'll just go on home then, and leave the boys and the funeral arrangements to you."

She patted his cheek on the way to the door. "She's got chicken thawing. I'd say there's enough to stretch for one more."

"Thanks, Mrs. Ridenour."

"You can start calling me Alva now. School's been out a long time."

❧

AVERY CHEWED OVER the incident with Sam Freemont all day, and the more she chewed, the more she worried.

"He's always been arrogant," she told Hope. "Even as a kid."

Hope held out her hand for another picture hanger. "She should've reported it." Setting it on the mark she'd made, Hope nailed the hanger on the wall.

"Maybe. Yeah, the more I think about it, the more I realize she should have. I get why she didn't, didn't want to." Uneasy, Avery paced to the window just as Hope held out her hand for the print she wanted to hang. "It's weird calling the cops on somebody you've known most of your life. Even if he is a flaming asshole."

Hope stepped off the stool, picked up the print, climbed back up to hang it. "From what you've told me, he sounds like a stalker."

"I don't know, that sounds extreme." But worry took on jagged edges that churned in her stomach.

Hope retrieved a small level. After setting it on the top of the frame, she tapped the right side until the bubbles lined up. "You said he's asked her out again and again, drops by her house, by the store at closing when she's there. What else? Oh yeah, flowers on her birthday, and he just happened to be on the spot a couple times when she's hauling groceries in the house."

" 'Let me help you with those, little lady.' " Avery nodded. "That's true. But it's not like he's got a shrine to her in his bedroom closet."

"How do you know?"

"If he has a shrine, trust me, it's to himself. But still, he scared her today, and what I saw was definitely over the line." She rubbed her arms as she paced. "Do you really think he'd try something? I mean, something more than annoying, boring, and creepy?"

"I don't know why she'd risk it. Look, if she won't file a report, she should at least tell Beckett."

"I don't think she will. She'd worry he'd do something. He doesn't have a quick switch like Ry, but he's got one."

"Then you tell him."

"Oh God, that feels like betrayal."

"Did she ask you not to say anything to him?"

"No, but it was implied."

"Avery, ask yourself how you'd feel if something happened. If this guy hurt her—or worse."

Now Avery pressed a hand to her uneasy stomach. "You're making me feel a little bit sick."

"You're worried. Not just mad, but really worried about this. Trust your instincts. And mine," Hope added. "Because you're scaring me about this."

"I should tell Beckett. Come with me."

"Sure."

"Don't let me get distracted when we walk through the shop," she said as she got her jacket.

"We can go around, in the back."

"No, I should make sure everything's okay. I'd drive myself crazy if I lived here. I'd look out the window all the damn time to check the traffic going in and out of the shop."

"I'll pull the shades when you're here."

As they went out, Avery hooked her arm through Hope's. "I love having you so close. And I've been so obsessed about Clare and Sam Asshole Freemont I didn't even ask how things went today."

"They had everything reasonably organized."

"But not Hope organized."

Hope smiled. "It will be. I've been spending most of my time at the storage unit. It's coming along. And so's the tile work. I was in there today." She glanced back, pleased to see the exterior lights beaming. "They're working in The Penthouse. You should see the tile on the tub side of the floating wall. They've finished the main level, except for the backsplash in the kitchen. They're doing the cabinet install next week. We had a delay."

"Listen to you, all in the know."

"Owen keeps me in the loop. I barely get a grunt out of Ryder."

"A man of few words."

"Straight through," Hope said at Vesta's front door. "If you need to deal with anything, you can do it after you talk to Beckett."

"Right, straight through."

Decent enough crowd, Avery decided, and waved to her night manager with a be-right-back signal. When she glanced toward the kitchen, Hope steered her to the stairwell door.

"After."

"I wouldn't think about checking if I wasn't right here." They went out and up the stairs. "I don't even know how to put this. I should've practiced something."

"Oh, for—" Hope knocked briskly on the door.

"You know Clare's going to be mad at me—no, at us, because I'm telling her you insisted."

"We're doing this because we care about her, and we're worried. She won't stay mad."

"I don't think he's home. He could be over at his mother's, working in the shop. Hell, he could be over at Clare's. Maybe she'll break down and tell him and we won't have to. Maybe I should—"

She broke off at the sound of footsteps.

"Sounds like he's back," Hope observed, then adjusted her thoughts and attitude when she saw Ryder.

She didn't know why the man always seemed mildly annoyed with her.

"Hey. Beckett's having a party and didn't invite me."

"No." Avery tried a laugh, but it sounded false and lame even to her ears. "I just wanted—that is, Hope wanted to ask something about—something. Since we were right here . . ." She hated to lie, Avery thought, because she so totally sucked at it. "Anyway, he's not home."

"I was wondering if I could look for a coffee urn for the dining room. And chafing dishes. I'll need two."

Ryder spared Hope a glance. "You're good at it, she's not."

"Excuse me?"

"Coming up with bullshit. Talk to my mother about coffeepots. Now, what's up?" he asked Avery.

"Nothing."

"How long have I known you?"

"Look, it's just . . ."

"Oh, for God's sake," Hope said impatiently, then spoke directly to Ryder. "Do you have a key?"

"Yeah."

"If you don't think Beckett would mind, can we go inside? We really shouldn't discuss this in the stairwell."

He nudged by her, pulled out his key ring.

"Want a beer?"

"No." Avery folded her arms over her chest as she followed him inside.

"I'm getting a beer." Making himself at home, Ryder switched on lights as he walked back to the kitchen. "Now, spill it."

"Do you want me to tell him?" Hope suggested when Avery stayed silent.

"No." She dragged a hand through her hair. "I have to. Okay, look, it's about Sam Freemont."

"That asshole?"

"Yeah, that asshole. I saw his car outside TTP this morning, before opening."

Hope studied Ryder as Avery told the story. He didn't react, just nodded, sipped at his beer. If you weren't looking closely, she realized, you wouldn't notice how tight his jaw got, how his eyes chilled.

She'd expected heat—a flash and boom—and found the ice more lethal.

"And I decided Hope was right," Avery finished. "If—on the off chance, the slim chance I really think—anything happened, I couldn't stand it. So we were going to tell Beckett."

"Okay, we'll take care of it."

"You're not going to go beat him up." Now Avery pulled at her hair. "Not that he doesn't deserve an ass-kicking for scaring her, but if you do that, she'll only be more upset. And people are bound to hear about it, and talk about it. Talk about her. She'll hate that."

"He doesn't care about any of that," Hope observed. "He cares about kicking this jerk's ass for scaring Clare. And I agree with him, on principle."

"Common sense and a quick mind for bullshit. Not bad," Ryder commented.

"In principle. What I'd worry about, and I don't know this guy, but I'd worry that he'd take it out on Clare. That pounding on him might make the situation worse for her. So you'd have the satisfaction of making him pay, and risk her paying more."

Ryder took a contemplative pull on his beer. "We'll take care of it," he repeated, "one way or the other."

"Ryder—"

"Avery. You're a good friend, and you did the right thing, the smart thing. Now you can stop worrying. We'll look out for Clare."

They would, Avery thought. Of course they would. "All right. If you get arrested for assault over this, I'll get your bail."

"Always good to know. Why don't you send up a Warrior's pizza."

"Sure. Well, okay."

He waited until they'd gone out to take out his phone. "Need you at Beck's," he told Owen. "No, I don't care what you're doing."

He hung up, settled down to wait.

⤜⤛

BECKETT JOGGED UP the stairs, light on his feet. Damn good day, he decided—and a most excellent funeral. When Clare got home, she'd called the coffins gruesome little works of art, and he'd earned a very nice chicken dinner.

He decided he'd cap off the very good day with a little work, a little ESPN.

The minute he opened the door, he smelled the pizza.

"Jesus, make yourselves the fuck at home. Is that my beer?"

"It's ours now. One slice left." Ryder indicated the pizza box. "If you want it."

"I had dinner at Clare's. What's going on?"

"Why don't you sit down?" Owen suggested.

He did. "If something was wrong with Mom, you wouldn't be having pizza and beer, but something's wrong."

"Here's the deal. I found Avery and the brunette at your door earlier. After a little dancing around, Avery told me what she'd come to tell you. Sam Freemont talked himself into the bookstore this morning before Clare opened. He got pushy."

Beckett's eyes narrowed. "What do you mean, he got pushy? Be specific."

"I wasn't there, but according to Avery, when she looked in—spotted his car outside and decided to check—he had Clare pinned against the counter."

Beckett got to his feet, slowly. "He put his hands on her?"

"He scared her," Owen said. "Wouldn't leave when she told him to leave, wouldn't back off when she told him to back off. Then Avery pounded on the door, faked like she was calling me over, and he took off. Hold it!" he ordered when Beckett turned back toward the door. "Do you even know where he lives?"

He couldn't think, not with the red haze in front and in back of his eyes.

"I found his address." Owen tapped his phone. "But I don't think going over there and smashing his face into bloody pulp is the best idea."

"I do," Ryder put in.

"You would. And if that's what Beckett wants after we talk this through, well, majority rules, and I'm in."

"Give me the fucking address."

"I'll give you the fucking address after you give me five minutes. If you kick his ass, he's the type who'll charge you with assault."

"Avery said she'd make the bail."

"Shut up, Ry. You're not worried about that now because kicking his ass is what you want. Can't blame you," Owen added with a glint in his eye that belied the mild tone.

"But you'll be in jail or facing charges, and Clare's going to be more upset. The kids, too. He's also the type—I've always hated that smug bastard—to take it out on Clare. Scare her again, or threaten her, or just badmouth her like he did to Darla back in the day."

"Ry kicked his ass over that, didn't he?" Beckett demanded.

"Yeah, but Darla didn't have kids who'd end up hearing the kind of crap he might spread about their mother. You know that's just the sort of thing he'd do."

"And you expect me to do nothing?"

"I expect you to pay a visit to his daddy's dealership tomorrow and have a talk with him. If you can't intimidate that weasly son of a bitch, you're no brother of mine. You scare him, maybe he stops this shit. If he doesn't, since we—and the crew—will be looking out for Clare, we deal with him."

"It's the roundabout way of kicking his ass," Ryder commented. "When there are witnesses."

"If it comes to that, and we deal with him in public, or in front of people, he's humiliated. Side benefit there."

"Maybe." Calmer now, Beckett picked up Owen's half-finished beer. "Maybe."

"You need to talk to Clare."

Fury surged back. "Believe me, I'll be talking to Clare. Why the hell didn't she tell me this herself?"

"That'd be my first question," Ryder agreed. "And I have to agree with what Owen said before you got here. She's got to file a complaint or report or whatever with the town cops so they've got it on record. So do we talk to him or punch his face in?"

Beckett understood the "we," though he'd be the one taking the action.

"Talk first, punch later."

"Good. Get your own beer," Owen said and took his back.

CHAPTER SIXTEEN

FOR THE SECOND TIME IN TWO DAYS, CLARE OPENED THE door of the bookstore early. But this time she did it with a smile on her face.

"Hi. I just got in. It'll be a couple minutes yet for coffee."

"That's not why I'm here." Beckett shut the door behind him.

"Oh, something's wrong." Instinctively she reached for his hand. "Is there trouble at the inn?"

"No. I want to know why you didn't tell me about Sam Freemont."

Damn it, Avery. Resentment laced with irritation rolled in first. "It wasn't something I wanted to talk about."

She moved behind the counter. Maybe he didn't want coffee, but she did. Plus it gave her both a little distance and something to do with her hands.

"You mean it wasn't something you wanted to talk about with *me*."

"Or at all. It was an uncomfortable situation. Dealing with the public means I deal with uncomfortable situations from time to time."

"How many times do you have a customer trap you in here alone and put his hands on you?"

"I wasn't trapped." She refused to think of herself that way. Trapped or helpless. "And it was my own fault for opening the door in the first place."

"Why the hell did you?"

Since she'd berated herself a dozen times since, the sharp, sharp question struck like a slap. She responded in kind. "Look, Beckett, it was knee-jerk. A customer at the door, and someone I knew."

"Someone you know who'd already been coming on to you, annoying you."

"Yes, and in hindsight I shouldn't have let him in. You'd better believe I won't make that mistake again. I made that clear to him, and to Avery. She shouldn't have gone running to you about this. It's my business."

"Is that how it is? I'm supposed to stay out of your business?"

She let out a sound of impatience. "That's not what I meant."

"That's what you said, and that's how it strikes me, all the way through."

She felt trapped again, this time by too much concern and what she judged as out-of-place anger.

"You're blowing this way out of proportion."

"I don't think so. Anytime I want to give you a hand with something, I have to talk you into it."

"I don't want to take advantage of—"

"Why the hell not? We're sleeping together—when we get the chance."

"That doesn't mean I want or expect you to deal with things I'm perfectly capable of dealing with myself. I appreciate your help, you know I do, but that doesn't mean I'm going to start depending on you to take care of me."

The beat of silence that followed tolled like a bell.

"Couples take care of each other, Clare, that's what makes them a couple. And couples tell each other when something happens that scares them."

"Really, Beckett, really. You're making this a bigger deal than it is. Avery—"

"Don't put this off on Avery. Did Freemont leave when you told him to leave?"

"No."

"Did he stop touching you when you told him to knock it off?"

"He didn't really—" Yes, he had, she admitted. Why compound stupidity with denial. "No. He won't come in here again. He won't be allowed. I told my staff."

That cut, he realized. Just kept slicing. "You told your staff, but you didn't tell me."

"Oh, Beckett." Frustrated, and with rising guilt she didn't want to feel, she threw up her hands. "I just told them he'd been rude and obnoxious that morning, and was banned from the store. I didn't give them chapter and verse. And you know, this really isn't about you. It's about me."

"It's about us. It's about trust."

"I trust you, of course I trust you. I guess, bottom line is I didn't tell you because I knew you'd be upset and mad, and it would become this enormous thing. Now you are, and it is, which doesn't change the fact Sam was a complete jerk, and I kicked him out of my store."

"Could you have kicked him out if Avery hadn't come to the door?"

"She did, so—"

"That doesn't answer the question. You should be able to give me that much, Clare. You should be able to give yourself that much."

It mortified her because she didn't know, just wasn't sure of the answer. "I think . . . I think the situation would have become more difficult and—and fraught, but—"

"Fraught." Eyes on hers, he nodded slowly. "That's a word for it."

"I'd have gotten him to leave, Beckett. I always do."

"Always?" Beckett laid his hands on the counter between them. "There's another word. He's done this before."

"Not exactly this, no. He makes a pest of himself, and yes, it's irritating and annoying—and maybe a little creepy, too. He's just got this idea stuck in his head that if he keeps asking me out, I'll just give in and go. Which is never going to happen."

"Has he come to your house?"

She thought of the weekend with stomach flu and bored children. And that hadn't been the first time. "Yes, but I—"

"Goddamn it."

"Beckett—"

"He's more than a pest, Clare. He's harassing you, and it needs to stop. You have to call the police."

"I don't want to do that. I just don't."

"You're smarter than this." He turned away, paced to the stacks. She could actually see him struggle for control. But there was still plenty of fire in his eyes when he walked back to her.

"Let me lay this out for you. He comes in here when you're alone."

"I let him in. I made the mistake."

"Regardless. He pressures you, as he has before, to go out with him. You decline. You ask him to leave. He won't. Then he scares and intimidates you by trapping you here at the counter. You tell him to stop, he doesn't. You tell him to leave, he doesn't. He put his hands on you, and you can't be sure what might have happened if Avery hadn't come to the door. Is that accurate?"

"Beckett—" Something in his face stopped her from making more excuses. Because he was right, she admitted. And she was smarter than this.

"Yes, accurate enough. But he didn't hurt me, or even come close to hurting me."

"If Avery hadn't come along, he might have. He comes here, he comes to your house. Think about that, then think about your kids and what it would be like for them if things had gotten more out of hand here, if anything had happened to you."

"That's not fair. It's not fair to bring the boys into this."

"The hell it isn't. If this is about you, it's about them. You call the town cops, you tell them exactly what happened. Then it's on record. You want this to stop. That's a step to making it stop. It's obvious he isn't going to listen to you. Maybe he doesn't come here to the store next time. Maybe he drops by your house again. Your kids like to answer the door. Think about what might happen if one of them lets him in."

"Now *you're* trying to scare me. Good job," she muttered. "All right, I'll call the police, tell them what happened. Mostly because you're right—he doesn't listen to me. He doesn't take my refusals and disinterest seriously. I guess if I do this, he might."

"Good, and I have a feeling he'll take me more seriously."

"I knew it." She jabbed a finger at him. "You've just got to go confront him. Make it an issue."

"Clare, for Christ's sake."

The tone, a kind of weary patience she often heard in her own voice when her children behaved like morons, might have amused her under any other circumstances.

"It is an issue. You think I'm going to go call him out? Beat him up?"

"Aren't you?" she demanded.

"It would be satisfying, and I admit it was my own knee-jerk response. But no, that's not what I'm going to do. What I am going to do is talk to him, make it clear if he bothers you again, there'll be consequences."

"So if he bothers me again, then you'll beat him up?"

He had to smile. "That's possible to likely. We're involved, you and me. You matter. I'm telling you what I'm going to do because I figure when people are involved, when they matter, they tell each other."

Something in what he said struck a chord with her, and opened a void. Think about it later, she told herself. Deal with now. "I don't see how picking a fight with him is an answer."

"Clare." Firmly, he covered her hands with his. "I didn't pick the fight. Neither did you. Now you do what you have to do. Make the call. I'll do what I have to do. Then, if Sam's got any common sense, or sense of self-preservation, he'll leave you alone." He gave her hands a light squeeze before releasing them.

"You can be pissed at me for a while," he told her. "I'm still a little pissed at you. We'll get over it."

"You know what I've always noticed about you and your brothers? The hard heads, and the unassailable certainty that you always know the answer."

"When you know the answer, it's not being hardheaded. It's just being right." He went to the door, opened it. "You're the woman in my life," he said. "Another thing about me and my brothers? We look after the women in our lives. We don't know any other way."

He went out, stuck his hands in his pockets, crossed the street. He was more than a little pissed off, he admitted. At her, at fucking Sam Freemont, at the whole screwed-up situation.

He knew how to put on the calm when he had to. Knew how to exert some self-control even when he didn't want to.

He went through the inn, looking for one or both of his brothers. His pleasure at the sight and smell of paint, of men busy at work, couldn't quite cut through the fury still balled in his gut.

He caught the scent of honeysuckle as he topped the second floor—and heard the porch door swing open in E&D.

"Not now," he muttered, and kept going up to three. He found Ryder in the innkeeper's kitchen setting the first of the cabinets.

"Good, give me a hand."

"I'm heading up to Hagerstown."

"Give me a hand anyway. Let's get this first one up. How'd it go with Clare?"

"You don't know people till you know them. Isn't that what Dad always said?" He braced the cabinet on the marks while Ryder got the drill. "She's got a bigger stubborn streak than I ever noticed."

"Let me ask you a question. How many women have you known who didn't have a stubborn streak?"

Beckett thought it over. "Good point. But she's calling the cops. She doesn't want to, and she's pissed I found the right lever to push her to do it."

Ryder drilled the first screw home. "You used the kids, didn't you?"

"That's her weak point, so yeah. Plus, I didn't say anything that wasn't true. And she's pissed I'm going up to talk to Freemont."

"Told you not to tell her."

"That's not how I work things. That's not how you build a relationship."

"Build a relationship." Ryder snorted as he sent the drill whirling. "You've been reading again."

"Blow me." He glanced around as Owen came in.

"Guys downstairs said you blew right through, so I figure you'd talked to Clare."

"Yeah, I talked to her. I'm heading up to talk to Sam."

"Good. Are you sure you don't want backup?"

"I can handle Freemont."

"He practiced fighting with Clare first," Ryder said as he checked the level of the cabinet.

"Well," Owen shrugged, "she's wrong."

"I don't know how you guys missed the memo, but it doesn't mean dick when a woman's wrong. Flowers," Ryder told Beckett.

"I'm not buying her flowers. She ought to buy *me* flowers. She screwed up, and I don't care about the goddamn memo."

Ryder just shook his head when Beckett stormed out. "You know, for twenty bucks' worth of daisies or whatever, he could smooth a lot of this over."

"He's standing on principle."

"Yeah, and a man who stands on principle doesn't get laid." He finished the first cabinet, stood back to take a look. "Let's get the rest of the top run up."

"I'm supposed to meet Hope over at Vesta at ten. Avery's letting us use the back room to go over the reservation software."

"So, she can wait a few minutes. You're not planning to bang her, are you?"

"Jesus, I'm not going to bang our innkeeper."

"Then you won't have to buy her flowers if you're late. Let's get these up."

⌁

BECKETT FOUND HIS calm again on the drive up the Sharpsburg Pike. In his experience you got more results with flat reason than angry confrontation. He just had to keep reminding himself he wanted results and not the satisfaction of a fight.

Not that he couldn't take lame-assed Sam Freemont—which he had on one memorable occasion in sophomore, no junior year, he remembered, when the bastard had tried to shake down little Denny Moser over Denny's homework.

And that, he recalled, had taken only one punch.

He remembered, too, Freemont had gone whining to Assistant Principal Klein, but with Denny backing him up, Beckett hadn't gotten in any particular trouble.

Freemont tended to steer clear of the Montgomerys, he thought as he pulled into the car dealership. Beckett doubted Freemont would be pleased to see him there, on his own turf.

Beckett headed straight into the showroom with its shiny, new, spotlighted cars. Before he'd done more than glance around, one of the salesmen hotfooted over.

"Good morning! It's a great day for a new car. What can I put you into today?"

"I'm not after a car. I'm looking for Sam Freemont."

The salesman's smile stayed in place, but his eyes lost their light. "He should be back in his office. I can have him called out."

"No, that's okay. I'll go on back. Where's his office?"

The man gestured. "Back there, turn left. He's all the way down. The corner office."

"Thanks."

Beckett worked his way down past empty offices, or others where salesmen manned phones or computers. He found Sam with his feet up on his desk, paging through a copy of GQ.

Figured.

"Sorry to interrupt since I see you're so busy."

Sam looked up. The sneer came first, just a quick twist of the mouth as he slowly set his feet on the floor. "Looking for a new pickup? We've got a basic economy model that should suit you. No frills for the working stiff."

"Nice sales pitch." Beckett stepped in, closed the door.

"Leave the door open."

"Fine, if you want everybody to hear this." Obliging, Beckett opened the door again. He thought about remaining standing, then opted for the more casual, even careless mode, and sat.

"Unless you're here to buy a car, I'm busy."

"Yeah, checking out the latest fashion in ties. This won't take long, then you can get back to it. You crossed a line with Clare yesterday."

"You don't know what you're talking about."

"I know you've been—let's just call it pestering her." Insulting word, Beckett thought. The action of a child, not a man. "And you haven't taken no for an answer. She's not interested in you."

"You're speaking for her now?"

"I'm speaking for me. She's already spoken for herself. I'm speaking for me when I tell you to leave her alone."

"Or what?" Sam flicked at his lapel. "Did you come here to threaten me? Do you think you worry me?"

"Yeah, I think I worry you. I think you're smart enough for that. It's pretty simple. You've been trying to push yourself on Clare. She doesn't want it. You're going to stop."

"You don't give orders to me."

To test, Beckett shifted in his chair, and watched Sam jerk back.

"I'm laying out the facts. Clare's off-limits. That's it."

"Because you say so? Because she's decided to try a little slumming with you?" Heat spread over his cheekbones in red patches that clashed with his tie. "It's no business of yours if Clare and I had a slight misunderstanding yesterday."

Some people don't change, Beckett realized. He was pretty sure Sam had used the *slight misunderstanding* gambit to Assistant Principal Klein to explain his harassment of Denny Moser.

"It's completely my business, and she's explaining your slight misunderstanding to the town cops right about now."

Sam's color surged hot, bright, then drained. "She'd never do that."

"Don't come around her again. You don't live in town, Sam. You've got no reason to be in Boonsboro anyway."

"You think you own the town now?"

"I think Clare means more to me than Denny Moser did. Not that I didn't like him," Beckett said easily. "Still do. But if you try anything with Clare again, you'll find out how much more she means to me."

Beckett got to his feet.

"You'll be sorry you threatened me."

"I haven't threatened you. I won't. Let's hope you don't put me in a position where I have to act. Nice tie," he added, and strolled out.

❧

HE DIDN'T BUY her flowers—that was too much of a capitulation to Ryder. He bought her a plant. A plant wasn't flowers, even if it *had* flowers.

He filled out a little card.

> *No blood spilled.*
> *Beckett*

Not an apology, he decided. A statement and a token. No point in anybody being pissed off when they'd both done what needed to be done.

He dropped it off at the bookstore, mostly he admitted, so his brothers wouldn't see it and lord it over him.

"Clare's in the back with a customer," Cassie told him. "I'll tell her you're here."

"No, I'm just dropping this off for her. I've got to get to work."

"It's so pretty. I love African violets. What's the occasion?"

"Nothing."

"Just because? Those are the best."

"Yeah, well. Gotta go."

He escaped.

When he got back up to the third floor, Ryder had nearly finished. It seemed just a little surreal, Beckett realized, like he'd passed through a small time warp.

"So?"

"He was his usual self. An asshole. But he got the message."

"Good, now maybe we can concentrate on work."

"Suits me."

They worked through the morning, into the afternoon. He paused in his install of rods and hooks in the bedroom closets of the apartment when he heard female voices.

When he stuck his head out he saw Hope, Avery, and Clare huddled in the kitchen.

"Ladies."

"Owen said you'd probably be finished with the cabinets." Hope closed the cabinet door she'd poked in. "They look nice."

"We're going to drag her down to look at furniture later," Avery told him, "but we've heard the tile work up in The Penthouse looks great so far. We want to go see."

"They're working in there now, but you can go up, take a look."

"Go ahead." Clare kept her eyes on Beckett's. "I'll be up in a minute."

Avery gave Beckett a quick thumbs-up behind Clare's back, then pulled Hope out of the apartment.

"You and Avery are okay?"

"She and Hope ganged up on me. We were worried about you, and so on. It's hard to argue with sincerity and real concern. I gave it a pretty good shot, like I did with you."

"What did the cops say?"

"I talked to Charlie Reeder. He didn't like it any more than you did. Still, there's not a lot they can do. As I said, I let him in, he didn't hurt me. He didn't threaten me. But they have it on record, and if he comes back, I can take out a restraining order. They'll talk to him if it comes to that. Actually, I have a feeling Charlie's going to talk to him anyway. I seem to have that effect on people."

"Sincere and real concern."

"Mmm-hmm. And you talked to Sam."

"We had a conversation, and he knows the way things are. It was quick, simple, to the point."

"And bloodless, according to the African violet."

"Yeah."

"Did you buy me the plant to soften me up?"

Setting the tool down, he crossed to her. "I bought it so you'd understand we don't have anything to fight about."

"It worked. So did something you said when you were lecturing me."

"I wasn't . . . maybe I was."

"You said couples tell each other their problems. I had to ask myself if I've just forgotten how to be a couple. But the fact is, Clint was gone for half our marriage. And when he was gone, he was dealing with life and death, every single day. I got out of the habit of telling him about problems on the homefront. Why should he worry, with all he dealt with, if one of the kids had a fever, or if the toilet overflowed or the roof sprang a leak?"

"You got used to running things on your own."

"What could he do about it when he's in Iraq and the car breaks down in Kansas?"

Beckett gave her a long, quiet look. "I'm not in Iraq."

"No, and it has to be said, I'm not in Kansas anymore." She lifted her hands, then let them fall. "It's not that I've forgotten how to be a couple, but that my experience in being part of one is different from yours. Maybe from most people's. And I've been on my own a long time."

"Now you're not. I'm not fighting a war, and I'm right here." Needed to be here, he realized, with her. "You know, I figure you know how to use a plunger if your toilet overflows."

She laughed a little. "Believe me."

He cupped her chin in his hand. "But if you've got a leaky roof, you don't have to be the one climbing up the ladder to patch it."

"So, there are degrees. It might take some time for me to figure them out."

"We've got time. It sounds like we're okay, too."

"Pretty close to it anyway. Fights always keep me on edge for a while. Why don't you come to dinner tonight—my version of a pretty houseplant."

"I'd like that."

He laid his hands on her shoulders. "I'm going to be there for you. I hope if you don't want to expect it, you can accept it. Maybe even like it a little."

"I like you." She rose up to kiss him. "I like us."

"That's a good start."

"I'll see you tonight." She kissed him again. "Thanks for the real and sincere concern, and the plant."

"You're welcome."

He went back to finish the closets, smiled a little when he smelled honeysuckle.

"You come in here, too? I don't mind the company. Not now anyway. Things feel right again."

His mood smooth now, he gave the closet rod a shake to check its stability. "Good and right," he decided.

❧

HIS MOOD CONTINUED smooth through the work, through a post-work meeting where his mother popped in with Carolee to check out the progress of tile and paint. It gave him a lift to hear their voices echoing through the building as they moved from room to room.

He had just enough time to run home, shower off the day before driving down to Clare's.

It was hard to beat three boys eager to play, a pretty woman fixing you a hot meal. And he thought as he drove home that night, when you added some time with that pretty woman after the kids were bunked down for the night it equaled a damn perfect way to end the day.

They'd navigated the bumps, he decided, and he realized they'd learned things about each other—maybe things neither of them had considered.

She wasn't the carefree girl she'd been when he'd taken that first fall back in high school. He'd known that, of course, how could she be? But, he understood now as he climbed the stairs to his apartment, getting to know—really know—who that girl had become made this—he supposed he could call it his second fall—a lot deeper.

At sixteen, he'd known the heartache of being in love with Clare Murphy, a girl who belonged to someone else, who looked at him as no more than the most casual of friends. He'd experienced the confusion of feelings for the young widow who'd returned home with two little boys and another growing inside her. Feelings he couldn't articulate in anything but friendship, something she'd accepted and returned.

And now, he was discovering the joys and frustrations of tripping past those careful, safe feelings, past the simple wanting and into that same bright blast he'd felt as a teenager.

It was odd, he thought, that those feelings could endure more than a decade. Feelings that had been neglected, ignored, suppressed. He supposed the foundation of those feelings had always been in place, maybe waiting. No matter how both of them had changed, evolved, restructured their lives, at the base they remained who they were.

He stood for a while, looking through his window toward the inn. Enduring, he thought. Some things were meant to. They needed care, understanding, respect, and a hell of a lot of work. Whatever changes came, the heart endured.

He went to bed eager to work on those changes—at the inn, with Clare and her boys—and to see what came.

And woke in the same smooth and optimistic mood. Right up until he carried his second cup of coffee outside to the parking lot behind his apartment and saw the four slashed tires on his truck and the vicious gouges running down the driver's side.

CHAPTER SEVENTEEN

BECKETT STOOD WITH HIS BROTHERS IN THE BRISK autumn breeze, studying the damage.

"That's not just for the hell of it," Ryder observed. "That's pissed-off personal and to the extreme."

"I got that." Beckett kicked one of his ruined tires. "I got that loud and clear."

"Then you've got who."

"Oh yeah, that's a pretty simple dot to connect. I should've smashed the son of a bitch's face in, right there in his office. Fucking coward. He had to sneak in here in the middle of the night to do this. And this? It's goddamn high school, isn't it? Keying the truck, slashing the tires."

"Some people don't grow up," Owen observed, "don't evolve. I'd say he's one of them." A quiet, simmering fury heated his voice. "He can't face you on an adult level, so he comes along and fucks up your truck. Classic payback method for the tiny-dick type."

"Thank you, Dr. Freud," Beckett muttered.

"I'm just saying. And I'm saying we may know who did it, but unless somebody saw him . . . Shit, Beck, it sucks. You could go smash his face in now."

"That gets my vote," Ryder said.

"But the same things apply as they did before. You'd get busted for assault, and his face would heal."

They looked over, turned as the town deputy pulled in. Owen laid a hand on Beckett's shoulder. "Let's see what Charlie has to say."

"That's a crappy way to start the day." Charlie Reeder, tall and lean as the beanpole who'd starred on the varsity basketball team, slid out of the car. He walked over, stuck his hands in his pockets. "Hell, Beck, that's a damn shame."

"Is that the official Boonsboro Police Department statement?"

Charlie huffed out a breath. "That's a personal note, and I'll add it's a pisser. I'll write it up. You've got insurance, right?"

"Yeah, yeah."

Frowning, Charlie walked around the truck, noted the second set of gouges on the passenger side. "You're going to want to get that claim in, get somebody out here to look at it. I'm going to take pictures for our file on it. What time did you park it here?"

"About ten I guess."

"Vesta's open another hour after that." The deputy scratched the back of his neck as he walked around to join the brothers. "Did you see anybody in the lot?"

"Some cars, no people. Ah, Dave Metzner's car—yeah, pretty sure on that. He'd be working till closing."

"I'll talk to him, anybody else who was working and would've come out this way. What time did you find it like this?"

"About quarter to seven."

"Okay. The Creamery would be closing by the time you got home." He glanced over at the ice cream shop. "It's more likely this happened later, but I'll check there. I'll talk to the people in the apartments with a view of the lot, see if they saw anything, anyone. We might get lucky."

"We all know who did it, Charlie." Ryder spoke up. "Just about everybody in town knows Beck's truck, knows where he parks it every damn night. And there's only one person he's had any trouble with."

"So you think Freemont did this because you're going out with Clare?"

"That and the fact I went to his office to see him yesterday morning, told him to steer clear."

Charlie huffed out another breath. "What did you want to go and do that for?"

"Somebody hassles Charlene, scares her, puts his hands on her, what are you going to do?"

"Same damn thing." Charlie put his hands on his bony hips. "Maybe I agree with you. It could've been kids, could've just been some drunk asshole, but nobody else reported anything like this. So it reads you were a specific target. Off the record, yeah, it looks like Sam dickhead Freemont's style to me. But unless somebody saw him, proving it's pretty damn slim."

"Maybe he left fingerprints."

Charlie eyed Owen. "Yeah, and maybe he pissed on the tires and left DNA. If this was Boonsboro CSI we'd have him locked up by end of shift. Look, I'll do everything I can, and I'll push it as much as I can. I'll go talk to Freemont myself. But I'm telling you straight, Beckett, you're pretty much screwed here."

"Yeah, I figured."

"I'm going to get pictures, take your statement, file a report. I'll talk to people—and I'll give Freemont a little nudge."

"I appreciate it. Maybe he got it out of his system. Or at least shifted his focus off Clare and onto me. That's something."

"Do us all a favor." Charlie slapped a hand on Beckett's shoulder.

"Steer clear of him. If you see him hanging around here, near Clare's, anywhere else in town, you call me. I'll deal with him. Call your insurance agent, give them my name. I'll make sure they get a copy of the police report."

With little choice, Beckett gave his official statement, then went inside to deal with the headache of insurance. By the time he finally made it over to the inn to work, word had spread through the crew. He received much sympathy and plenty of righteous anger on his behalf—and a pot load of advice. He let it all roll over him and took out his frustrations with tools. He imagined Freemont's smug face in the crown molding every time he shot in a nail.

It didn't help much, but it was something.

Having a furious Clare rush in was more, and better. She stormed over to his ladder, gripped a rung, her face sharp with temper.

He learned something new. A thoroughly pissed-off Clare's eyes glowed green as a cat's.

"I heard as soon as I got into town, but I couldn't get away until now. I went to look at your truck first. That bastard! You know Sam did that. It's just like him. Goddamn it! Now I want to punch him."

"I'd like to see that." He found his grin coming back as he came down the ladder.

"It's not funny, Beckett."

"No, it's not. But it's rubber and paint."

"That's not the point." She swung away from him, and the carpenter working with him eased out of the room.

"No, but it strikes me one of the points is this was the only way he could come at me. When I set aside being pissed off, it's kind of a boost for the ego."

"Oh for *Christ's* sake."

"There's that, too. You hardly ever swear. It's comforting for you to swear on my behalf. My ego just went up a couple more notches."

"He only did this because you went in there and confronted him."

"Yeah, so?"

"Which you didn't have to do."

"Yes, I did, Clare."

"Men." She threw up her hands, circling the room. "Men, men, men. Now I suppose you just have to go back and confront him again, escalate the whole sorry mess."

He considered. "I could let you talk me out of it." He smiled at her when she turned to glare at him. "That would be a boost to your ego, I'd say. I'm happy to reciprocate."

"You're not planning on it."

"I've had a good time picturing dragging him out into the dealership parking lot and stomping him flat in front of his coworkers and various horrified customers. Him begging for mercy, women fainting. It's a nice image."

"Men," she repeated. "You're all just boys in bigger packages."

"Maybe. But then if I did all that, Owen would get to pull the 'I told you so' when he had to come bail me out. It's not worth giving Owen the satisfaction."

She took a long, calming breath. "That's something then. I'm so sorry, Beckett."

"I guess it'll be worth it if he figures this evens the score and stays the hell away. I needed new tires before winter anyway."

She crossed to him, framed his face. "My hero," she murmured, kissing him softly.

"That's all I get? It's *four* tires, and a paint job."

She laughed a little, kissed him again. "It's the best I can do under the circumstances." She drew away, tipping her head toward the sounds of the tile crew working in the bathroom.

"We've got plenty of other rooms."

She shook her head, walked around to look at the painted walls. "I love the color in here."

Calm now, she did a slower circle of The Penthouse parlor. "I've been trying to decide which room is going to be my favorite, and I can't. And which room to treat my parents to for their anniversary next year. And I can't."

"Pick one for you and me. I'll make a reservation."

"Hard to choose, but I'd love it. I have to get back."

"How about dinner tonight? I'll take you and the boys somewhere."

"Book club, but thanks. Ah, we're decorating for Halloween tomorrow, if you want to come over."

"Are you kidding? I have major skills in this area."

"Great, you can carve the pumpkin. The boys are old enough now to realize how lousy I am at it. Come by later. I'll buy you a cup of coffee."

"I will. Oh, and thanks for the outrage."

"You're welcome."

NOT A BAD couple of days, all in all, Beckett decided. All he had to do was delete the hassle of his truck, and things looked good all around. Especially standing with his brothers across the street from the inn as they'd done the morning the tarp came down.

This time, they looked over at the finished front of the inn, including the sign.

Inn BoonsBoro
On The Square

"Looks good," Owen commented.

"Looks damn good," was Ryder's opinion.

"Now all we have to do is finish it, furnish it, outfit it, staff it, and fill it with guests." Beckett stuffed his hands in his pockets. "Should be a piece of cake, considering what we started with."

He glanced down the street, nodded to the sign outside the gift shop. "Gifts Inn BoonsBoro. It works."

"Mom and Madeline swear it'll be ready for the opening Friday night."

"As long as all we have to do is show up and eat crab balls." Ryder shifted his gaze to the building beside the inn. "You know she's already making noises about us getting to work on that place so we can get a bakery back in there."

"One thing at a time. Let's just bask," Beckett suggested.

"Time for basking when we get it finished." Ryder checked his watch. "And time's wasting."

"I need to work with Hope and the webmaster this morning."

"While you're at it, call Saville," Ryder told Owen. "We're going to be ready for them to bring in the flooring, let it acclimate."

"It's on my list. Beck, why don't you check at Gifts, see if there's anything that needs doing. Then you can grab us some coffee. It's frigging cold today."

"First hard frost forecast for tonight. We've still got exterior work to finish. Don't sneak in the back room with Clare," Ryder told Beckett as they left him to head across the street. "You're on the clock."

"Yeah, yeah." He took another moment for a solo bask, then started down to look into the gift store.

He had to admit, it looked just fine. Warm and welcoming with its sunny walls, the displays of pottery and handcrafted jewelry, the art hanging on the walls or waiting to be hung.

He checked with Madeline, who opened more boxes of stock, and took down a short list of small chores to be finished before the opening.

Tucking the clipboard under his arm, he walked into TTP.

"Hi, Romeo. Clare's upstairs."

He lifted his eyebrows at Charlene—Charlie Reeder's wife. "Romeo?"

She pursed her lips, made an exaggerated kissing sound. "You're such a sweetie."

"True. I need three coffees, large. I'll go up and say hi to Clare while you're getting that together."

"She'll be glad you did."

Beckett shook his head at Charlene's wink, wondered just what TTP put in their coffee these days. Then he climbed the creaking stairs to Clare's office.

With the phone to her ear, she held up a finger as she offered him a big, bright smile. While she finished the call, he stepped to her window, looked out at the inn again, enjoyed seeing the sign in place.

"Beckett."

He turned, found his arms full of her. "Thank you so much," she said before she caught him up in a long, dreamy kiss.

Whatever they put in the coffee, he decided, he wanted some. "Okay, you're really welcome. For what?"

"For the flowers. They're gorgeous, and such a wonderful surprise. I made what Liam called girl sounds over them until he was forced to combat them with gagging noises. We made a real scene."

She hugged him hard, rubbed her cheek against his. "But you should've come in. I'd've fixed you breakfast."

"What flowers?"

She sparkled when she eased back. "As if. The roses I found on my doorstep when I took the kids to school."

"Clare, I didn't send you any flowers."

"But they were—What?"

"I didn't bring any flowers by your place this morning."

"But the note said—"

"What did it say?"

"*Always thinking of you.* Oh God." Because her knees went shaky, she sat. "There was a box, a plain white box on the doorstep, and the roses and note inside. I worried because it was so cold, but I don't think they were there very long. They were fine. They're beautiful. They're not from you."

"Have you seen him?"

"No. Well, in the grocery store yesterday, for a second I thought I did."

"You didn't tell me."

"I wasn't sure. In fact I thought I'd just imagined it." She grabbed Beckett's hand. "Please don't do anything. I'll call Charlie, I'll call him right now and tell him. But please don't do anything. I really think the more attention we pay, the worse it'll be."

"Call Charlie. Next time, if you think you see him, you call me."

"I will. I promise. I— He's sent flowers before."

"When?"

"My birthday. Always red roses, like these, but I really thought . . . And he's always signed his name before. Beckett, he's shown up at the grocery store a few times, which was why I thought I'd imagined seeing him there—after what happened, then your truck. I thought I was just spooking myself."

"Where else?" Beckett asked, his voice deadly calm. "Where else has he just shown up?"

"Oh." Rocking a little, she rubbed her temples. "Oh God, when I think about it that way . . . Okay. I've run into him at the mall a few times, but I run into people I know there now and then, so I never thought much of it. Outside the bank, more than once."

He watched her thinking it through, watched her go pale thinking it through.

"In the pharmacy parking lot, in the nursery where I buy my plants. Other places, too, I see that now. Just like I see he always seems to show up when it's just me. Not when I have the kids along, or Avery or my mother, or anyone."

She paused a moment. "That's not coincidence."

"No, it damn well isn't. It's stalking. Tell Charlie everything. And

Clare, I'll be coming by your house every day after work until this stops."

"I'm not going to argue. The flowers." She wrapped her arms around herself. "There's something just not right about a man who'd send flowers after all this. It's not just being a pest."

"I don't think it ever was. Make sure you tell Charlene and the others about this. And don't work in the store alone."

"God." She rubbed her forehead. "No, you're right. I just need to settle down and think this through. I'll call Charlie now."

"I'm right across the street. Keep your phone with you."

"I will. Beckett? You be careful, too. He might try to do some-thing, something more than damage your truck."

"Don't worry."

But she did. Even after she'd talked to the town deputy, she wor-ried. She called Avery, and at her friend's insistence they went together to retrieve the box, the note, the flowers—all of which they took to the police station.

"Beckett's right. Sam's a gutless bastard, but it's better if you're not alone—at work, at home. Anywhere for now."

"Avery, you don't really think he'd try something?"

"I honestly don't know, so we're not taking any chances. You lock your car doors when you're in it, when it's parked—and your house, too. Not just when you leave or at night. Promise."

"You don't have to worry about that. I'm not ignoring it, but I'm going to let him think I am. The less he believes I'm affected, the sooner he'll stop."

Maybe, maybe not, Avery thought, and watched Clare walk back to the bookstore, waited until she was inside before crossing over to the inn.

She found all three Montgomery brothers in a conference in the half-finished kitchen. "Looks great," she said briefly. "We have to talk."

"We're in the middle of something here," Ryder began. "We're going to head over to your place in about an hour. What the hell color are you wearing this week?"

Avery pushed a hand over her hair. "Cherry Cola, it's a little intense."

"What's wrong with your regular hair?" Owen wanted to know.

"I've worn it nearly thirty years. Do you have anything you've worn almost thirty years? And that's not why I'm here. We have to talk now. Clare and I took those damn flowers over to the police station, but I don't know what the hell they can do about it."

"I don't know what the hell we can do about it." Owen shoved his measuring tape back in his tool belt. "What we'd like to do at this point would get us five to ten."

"Breaking his legs isn't the answer anyway, which is too bad. Look, Sam gets these obsessions. He zeroed in on me a while back."

"When?" Owen demanded. "What?"

"Back when I was just opening the shop—that was before Clare moved back. And it wasn't as whacked as this. He used to come in while I was working on the setup. People were in and out all day back then. Telling him he was in the way or I was busy wasn't enough to shake him off. He's like a frigging blood leech."

"Why didn't you say anything?"

She shrugged at Owen. "It didn't last long, maybe a couple of weeks. Listen, Clare's default is polite; my polite wears faster. I cured him one day when I told him if he didn't leave me the hell alone Luther would brand his balls. Luther," she said, speaking of the blacksmith, "was working on the vents at the time. Luther's not going to brand anybody's balls, but he looks like he could."

"Pretty good thinking," Owen decided.

"Yeah, and it worked. But this deal with Clare's gone on a lot longer, and it's a lot creepier. I've got a sick feeling about it. I trust my sick feelings."

"Every man in the crew's keeping an eye out for Freemont, and an eye on Clare. So are the town cops," Beckett added. "I warned him off. Charlie Reeder warned him off."

"I know that, just like I know doing that's caused him to escalate. Sending her flowers after she's sicced the cops on him? It's twisted. I don't know what to do about it. I hate not knowing what to do."

"Tell her neighbors. More people looking out for her."

Owen frowned at Ryder a moment. "That's good, but not just her neighbors. Spread the word in town, all through town. People like Clare, a lot. We've got a whole community here that'll look out for her."

"I always knew you had a brain," Avery observed, and felt her shoulders relax a bit for the first time in hours. "It's something. It feels positive."

"I'm going over there tonight, and I've got a couple of ideas brewing, including installing motion detector lights at her place."

Avery nodded at Beckett, and her shoulders unknotted completely. "Okay, I like that one. More positive. I've got to get back, and you can count on me spreading the word during the lunch rush."

❧

BECKETT INSTALLED THE lights himself, front and back, and calculated it only took about twice as long as it might have without the "help" the kids gave him. But he got another meal out of it, and the satisfaction of seeing Clare's relief when the job was done.

Added to it was the fun of watching the boys run outside and back a half dozen times before bedtime cheering each time the lights flashed on.

But he had to admit, he liked his couple of other ideas better, and introduced them to Clare the next afternoon at the bookstore.

He found her in the annex, restocking shelves.

"Hey, I've got a couple guys I want you to meet."

Books in her hand, Clare turned. "Oh, aren't they sweet! Where did you get them?"

Even as she asked, she set the books aside to crouch. Both dogs took that as an invitation to gambol over and lick at her hands and face. "Look at you, look at you big boys. Beckett, how are you going to keep two dogs in your apartment. Aren't these Labs?"

"Mixes, Lab-retriever mixes, like Mom's. They're brothers. They're five months old. They've had all their shots. They're house-broken."

"Yes, good boys." She ruffled chocolate brown skin, rubbed silky ears. "They're adorable, but don't they need room to run around and . . ." She trailed off, eyes narrowing at Beckett even as the dogs vied for her attention. "And you're not planning on keeping them in your apartment."

"They need kids."

"Beckett—" Her eyes narrowed to slits. "What's your middle name?"

"Ah, Riley."

"Beckett Riley Montgomery."

The grin split his face. "Wow, the whole shot, the big Mom guns."

"That's just the first volley."

"Boys need dogs, dogs need kids." He lost the grin, tried a winsome smile. "You've been thinking about getting a dog for the boys."

"Thinking, yes, and dog—as in one."

"They're brothers," he reminded her. "You can't separate brothers." He crouched as she was, scrubbed an exposed belly with his hand. "You'd break their hearts. Plus they'd keep each other company when the kids are in school. They're rescues. The people who had them just basically changed their minds. It's like evicting a couple of babies."

"Oh stop."

Okay, he thought, that might've been laying it on a little too thick. "They need a good home, together. If you don't want them, I'll keep them."

"In your apartment."

"Well." He shrugged. "I don't want to separate them, or leave them in limbo."

"This is an ambush."

"This kind of dog is great with kids. Loyal, good-natured. They love to play, and they'll take the roughhousing three boys will dish out."

"Been researching, have you?"

"Yeah, some. Mom knows people who know people. Plus, they'll let you know if anybody's coming around the house. Dogs, even friendly dogs like these, are good deterrents. I'd feel a lot better, Clare, if you had a couple of dogs in and around the house."

The smaller of the two dogs laid a paw on Clare's knee, gazed up soulfully. The sound she made—a kind of half sigh, half groan—told Beckett they had her.

"The kids are going to go crazy. God, if I do this, I have to get supplies and toys, a training manual. A psychiatric evaluation."

"I've got everything they need in the truck already. Food, dishes, beds, toys. See, they've got their collars and leashes."

"You don't miss a trick in an ambush. Housebroken, you said?"

"Yeah." He thought it best not to mention one of them had already peed on his boots. "Ah, you might have a couple mishaps, just while they're adjusting to a new place."

"What do I do when it gets cold? I'm here, the boys will be at school. They'd have to stay out in the yard."

"We need to build a doghouse."

"We do?"

"Sure. It'll be fun."

"Oh, Beckett." She gave in, nuzzled dogs. "What are their names?"

"Chauncy and Aristotle."

"You have to be kidding."

"Afraid not. They really want new names."

"Who could blame them?" The smaller one let out a high, excited bark, and bit his brother's ear. "I hope this isn't a mistake."

"It'll be great. Having them will teach the boys responsibility, how to take care of a pet."

"Right." The pups rolled between them, yipping and wrestling. "I'll remember you said that when I'm letting them in and out and cleaning up mishaps."

He leaned over the two dogs to kiss her. "Thanks, Mom."

"You had me at 'they're brothers.' Apparently I have a weakness. Let's hope my parents do, too. They want a sleepover with the boys Saturday night."

"Oh yeah?"

"Yes. Actually they'd like it better if all of us just moved in."

"They've got to be worried about you."

"I have to call home every night, check in, reassure them my doors are locked, and so on. I only got out of joining the Saturday night sleepover by telling them I'd see if you'd consider a date with me."

"I think I can clear my schedule."

"Good. I'll come by at seven."

"You're going to pick me up? Where are we going?"

"You'll find out Saturday night." She looked at the dogs, wandering now, sniffing floor and air. "You're not the only one who can spring an ambush. Now." She got to her feet. "You'll have to figure out what to do with these dogs until after school. You can bring them—and the supplies—over then."

"How about I bring pizza, too? I have a feeling everyone's going to be too busy playing to worry about dinner."

"Dogs and pizza. The kids are going to be in serious heaven."

⁂

HE HADN'T CONSIDERED the logistics of transporting dogs and pizza, but quickly realized active pups with curious noses needed to be segregated from food. It only cost him the price of a pizza and the waiting time for the second to be made to learn the valuable lesson.

He left the pizza in its borrowed insulated delivery pack in the bed of the truck, had a bit of a struggle bringing the dogs back when they sprinted to the end of their leashes, in opposing directions. But counted every bit of the hassle worthwhile when Murphy opened the door.

Even as his eyes popped wide and his mouth dropped open, both dogs leaped forward. Murphy landed on his butt, belly-laughing as the dogs ran over him, plopped on him, licked everywhere they could reach.

"Doggies! Beckett's got doggies." He rolled with them, doing his best to hug them to him as his brothers charged out of the playroom.

Chaos, probably the best possible kind in Beckett's opinion, ensued. Dogs raced, jumped, barked. Kids chased, tumbled, and shouted.

Clare came out to watch, set her hands on her hips. She started to shake her head, call some sort of order. Then found herself simply staring at Beckett.

He grinned, wide and easy, as kids and dogs wrestled and rolled around his feet. He stood, hands tucked into his front pockets, legs spread wide enough for boys and puppies to squirm through. When one of the pups tested its sharp little teeth on the toe of his boot, he just laughed and nudged it clear.

In the instant that he looked up, met her eyes, his warm, warm blue and full of fun, she fell.

Maybe she'd been sliding, she realized, inching her way along. But this was the finish line, the moment she knew—no doubts—she loved. The moment she could see herself with him next month, next year, next always.

Maybe it came with a little trickle of panic, and the uncertainty of knowing what could or would be. But the love rang as strong and as real as her children's laughter.

And that, she thought, was that.

"Mom! Mom! Did you see?" Liam staggered up, carrying a pup whose tongue hung out in a silly doggie grin. "Beckett brought puppies over."

"They like us." Harry turned his face right and left as the second pup covered it with kisses. "They really like us."

"Come see!" Murphy wrapped his arms around the one in Harry's lap. "Come see them. They're real cute, and they're soft and they don't smell bad. Can't we have a puppy? *Please*, Mom, can't we?"

"Another one?" She opened her eyes wide, feigning shock. "Two aren't enough?"

"What two?"

"Those two."

And, another moment, she thought. The moment when she told herself whatever the puppies did, however many times she had to clean up after them, roll out of a warm bed to let them out, it would be a small price to pay for the look of stunned, radiant joy on her little boy's face.

"They're *ours*?" His whisper echoed with that same joy.

"Ask Beckett. He's the one who got them—and wore me down."

Three faces turned up to his while the puppies nipped and licked. "You got them for us?" Harry managed. "For us to keep?"

"Well, they're brothers."

"Like us!" Liam shouted.

"Yeah, and they needed a good home. They needed some friends who'd take care of them, feed them, play with them, love them."

"I love them." Murphy crawled over to hug Beckett's leg. "I really, really do."

"Love takes some work." Beckett crouched down. "Even when you're tired or busy. It means making sure they get enough to eat and drink, fresh air, company. Are you up for it?"

"I promise."

"Well, I guess you get to keep them."

"This is the best ever. Thanks." Liam threw his arms around Beckett, then dashed to do the same to Clare. "Mom, we got puppies."

"You got them for us," Harry repeated, and finally gave Beckett his angel smile. "We'll take good care of them, always."

"I'm counting on it."

"Why don't you take them out back," Clare suggested. "Show them the ropes."

"Come with us." Murphy tugged on Beckett's hand. "We're going to show them ropes. What are their names?"

"They need good ones, so you guys better think about that. I've got some stuff for them out in the truck. I'll come out after I bring it in."

"I'll help you bring it in." Harry got to his feet.

"I could use a hand."

Liam and Murphy ran toward the back, calling the dogs to come, already trying out names while Harry walked out front with Beckett.

Clare stood, absorbing love—and, studying the scattered dog hair and little dribbles of pee on her floor, thought, yes. Yes, a very small price to pay.

CHAPTER EIGHTEEN

"TWO DOGS." AVERY ARRANGED CHEESE ON A PLATTER FOR the gift shop opening. "I can't get over it. Zero to sixty, Clare, that's you."

"It feels like it. Yesterday morning all I had to do was get three kids ready for school, fed, lunches or lunch money distributed. This morning, after I found them all piled—three kids, two dogs—in Murphy's bed, I had three kids to get ready for school, who all thought they really should stay home to take care of the dogs. That's after getting up twice last night to let the dogs out."

"Their bladders will get bigger."

"Let's hope. Then there's the make sure they're fed and watered, let them out, let them in, let them out. Then I feel guilty because we're leaving them alone in the backyard, so I have to go check on them before I come to work, then again at lunch. Now Mazie's dealing with all of them until I get home from the opening. I should probably run home to check again."

"They'll be fine. Kids and dogs, they're a natural unit. I'm looking forward to meeting them. What are their names again?"

"I think, after much discussion, debate, false starts, we've settled on Ben—as in Kenobi—and Yoda."

"Nice."

"Sorry I'm later than I planned." Hope hurried back to the kitchen. "We had more deliveries come in. You're busy out there," she said to Avery.

"Big Friday night crowd, punched up, I do believe, by the opening. People want to check it out, and figure they might as well grab dinner first."

"Symbiotic, as desired. What can I do?"

"I guess we can start taking the trays down, that way Madeline can have everything in place."

Trays in hand, they went out the back.

"I can't believe it's almost November." Hope shook back her hair as the evening breeze caught at it. "I feel like I just moved to town."

"We finish October with a bang with trick-or-treat night," Avery reminded her.

"Then, bang again, it's Thanksgiving, then Christmas."

"Oh, don't say Christmas." Clare shut her eyes briefly. "I have so much left to do."

"Then New Year's," Hope continued, "and we'll be fussing with the opening for the inn. They're really making progress with The Courtyard. Tile work, too. You need to see. Maybe we can run over before this starts."

"I love this space." Clare paused on the pretty patio behind the gift shop. It makes me wish I could do something like it at home."

"Why don't you?" Avery said.

"Money comes to mind first." Clare waited while Avery balanced her trays to open the back door. "But I might just start a patio savings fund."

As they went in, Madeline, chestnut hair tumbled, earrings swinging, strode down the short steps to the office. "Hi! Avery, this looks great. I'm so excited. My girls are up there—they'll give you a hand putting everything where I've set up."

"Madeline." Clare took a deep breath. "It smells wonderful in here."

"Between the candles and the diffusers—Inn BoonsBoro label there. We're featuring the Marguerite and Percy pomegranate scent tonight; we can't miss."

"Oh, talk about looking great." Clare paused in the kitchen nook. "It's so clever. It makes me want to completely re-outfit my kitchen. I love that pitcher, oh, and these bowls! I'm going to be doing a lot of my holiday shopping here."

She wandered through, passing off the tray, studying the pretty displays of jewelry, the vibrant art, the gleaming pottery. "You've done an amazing job."

"I want this." Hope stood in front of a painting where cherry blossoms in full bloom spread over a blue sky and reflected dreamily in a rippled pond. "I want this for my apartment. I want to look at spring every day."

"I love it." Avery glanced at Clare, got the nod. "It's perfect, and sold. Clare and I want to give you a housewarming present when you take up residence at the inn."

"Really? Oh boy. I'll take it." She wrapped her arms around their waists. "You're the best."

"I can put a red dot on the title card, noting it's sold—if you're sure."

"Absolutely," Clare told Madeline.

"First sale! That isn't from me, my girls, Justine or Carolee. Ladies, we're in business."

"What else can we do—besides spend money?" Avery asked.

"Honestly, we're pretty set. Nervous, excited, but set."

Avery checked her watch. "We'll come back in twenty, just in case. I've got my cell if you need anything sooner. Let's run across the street so Hope can show off."

"I'm already seeing a half a dozen things I know we're going to want at the inn when we start accessorizing." She was still trying to scan when Avery pulled her out the door. "I'm going to go back tomorrow with a notebook. Did you see that bamboo bowl? That's perfect for the kitchen island."

She dug out her keys. "We can go in the front. The doors should be in next week, and I got a look at the reclaimed teak benches Justine bought for the porch."

She locked up behind them. "Let's go up. They finished the tile in Nick and Nora. You've got to see it. I do a walk-through every night after the tile crew leaves. I know Beckett does one, but I feel like I should—plus I get to see everything that was done that day."

"Have you . . ." Clare glanced toward Elizabeth and Darcy.

"I'll catch her scent now and then, or hear a little something. But I think she's a bit shy around me yet. Just look at this. Isn't it spectacular?"

The back wall shimmered with sea blue glass tiles, floor to ceiling, a stunning contrast for the chocolate brown floor. Large tiles of brown-on-brown tuxedo stripes added a touch of sophistication to the other walls.

"I never would have thought to put these colors together," Clare realized. "They're wonderful—elegant, modern, a little glitzy, I guess."

"Exactly so, and it'll play off the chocolate brown ceiling and soft blue walls in the bedroom. And the lights? Terrific. Crystal chandelier over the tub, crystal sconces flanking the mirror."

Hope laid a hand on her heart. "I swear, I fall a little more in love with this place every day."

"I'm in love with Beckett." As her friends turned, Clare let out a half laugh. "Wow, that sort of blurted, didn't it?"

"In love, love?" Avery asked. "Like the big *L*?"

"That's the one." As Hope had, she laid a hand on her heart. "I didn't think—or believe—I'd be in love again. Not all the way through. I guess I didn't believe I could go all the way through twice. It's not the same as it was with Clint. I don't think it can be or should be. But it's just as much, as deep, as real. I can't believe how lucky I am."

"You and Beckett." Avery blinked damp blue eyes. "In big *L* love."

"Oh, I don't know about him. I think it's safe to say little *l* on his part. We're a lot to take on."

"Clare, he's been sweet on you forever."

"That's a different thing. Little *l*—that's pretty terrific. I'm not looking for more from him, for promises and absolutes. Like I said, it's different this time. I understand more than I possibly could have at sixteen. I've got more to risk."

"And to offer," Hope added.

"Yeah, I do. But . . ." She thought of Beckett's words the night before. "Love takes work. A woman, three kids—and now two dogs? A lot of work. I'm happy the way things are. I'm so happy, so grateful to *feel* this again. To know I can."

"I love that feeling." Remembering, Hope sighed. "I miss it."

"I guess I have, too, and didn't realize it. And it's a little scary this time. It may sound crazy, but I kind of like that it is. It adds an energy."

"If you're happy," Hope decided, "we're happy."

"I'm very happy. I'm in love with a really good, interesting man who enjoys my kids. That's pretty damn amazing."

"I've always admired your taste in men," Avery told her.

The bathroom window shot open, and the air that blew in carried the scent of honeysuckle.

"I'd say she does, too," Hope murmured.

JUST ONE OF the things Clare loved about Boonsboro, and that made her glad she'd brought her kids home to raise them, was the community feel. As she stood in the new gift shop, sipping wine from a little plastic cup, she saw or spoke to more than a dozen people she knew. She watched them wander, form and re-form into groups, share news, opinions.

Avery's father—a big man with his wild red hair and trim beard threaded with glints of pewter—eased his way over to her. Clare tipped her head toward his broad shoulder.

"Look at you, all dressed up."

He flushed, sweetly shy. "Justine said no work clothes."

"I should say not, when you're one of the featured artists."

His flush deepened; his big feet shuffled. "Oh, I'm no artist. Just a welder with time on his hands."

"Willy B, it takes more than some welding skill and spare time to create those metal sculptures. And the clocks are just wonderful. You know Hope's already earmarked that one"—she gestured—"and the cattails for the inn."

"She's going to put that stuff in the inn? Really?"

"She wants the clock for the dining room, in front of the stone arch. People who stay will see your work."

"Isn't that something?" He let out a short, baffled laugh.

Avery squeezed her way through the crowd. "Lay off the crab balls for now. We're nearly out. They're bringing down more."

"It's a nice crowd," Clare commented. "Madeline looks thrilled, and a little dazed."

"I should step outside. I feel like I'm taking up half the room all by myself."

"You stay right where you are," Avery ordered her father. "Madeline wants you to talk up the potential customers, tell them about your artistic process."

"Oh now, Avery."

"Oh now, Willy B." She poked him in his wide chest. "I've got to check the other trays. Don't you let him run away, Clare."

"I have my orders." She gave Willy B a shrug, but took pity on him. "We could step right outside though. Plenty of potentials out there getting fresh air."

"It's nice to see people come out like this." He took a breath when they stepped out to the sidewalk.

"It is, isn't it? I was just thinking how nice it is to see so many familiar faces, have a little time just to chat and catch up."

She scanned the little groups, so intent on the people around her she didn't notice the car parked half a block down—or Sam Freemont behind the wheel, watching her.

"How are those boys of yours? I heard you got a couple new family members. Justine mentioned it," Willy B added.

"They're in boy heaven, and for now, at least, being very responsible about taking care of the puppies. I have to admit they're more fun and less work than I imagined—again, for now."

"You won't regret it. I heard Beckett picked them up."

"Brought them into the bookstore," she confirmed. "Trapped me."

"You know, Justine's pretty pleased that you and Beckett are going around together. She's fond of you and those boys."

"I know. And speaking of them, I have to get home, relieve Mazie."

"So, the minute I turn my back, you move in on my territory." Beckett stepped out, gave Willy B a light punch on the arm.

"I've got no defense against a pretty woman. Sure looks good over there." He lifted his bearded chin toward the inn. "Tommy'd be real proud."

Willy B had been his father's best friend, since both of them had been boys. Had wept unashamed at his funeral, Beckett remembered. And very likely missed Thomas Montgomery as much as his wife and sons.

"Yeah, I think he would be. I think he'd have enjoyed a night like this."

"He'd've loved it. Wouldn't mind a chance to see what's what inside that place."

"Anytime you want," Beckett told him. "You know that."

"I'll be stopping by then, ready to gawk."

"Willy B." Justine came to the doorway, hands on hips. "You get back in here and mingle."

"Oh now, Justine." He blew out a breath. "No point arguing. Hope to hell I don't knock something over."

"He's the cutest man," Clare stated when he trudged back in.

"He's six-five and probably goes two-sixty or better. How can he be cute?"

"He just is. I've got to get home, as much as I'd like to stay. Don't forget, I'll be by at seven tomorrow."

"Wait, wait." He took her arm, shook his head. "You're not driving home by yourself."

"Beckett, it's not even a mile, straight down on Main."

"I'll follow you, make sure you get in all right, give Mazie a lift home. You heard what Willy B said. No point in arguing."

She considered it foolishly overprotective, especially when he insisted she come with him to his truck in Vesta's lot so he could drive her the short distance to her van in back of TTP.

She knew he waited while she locked up so gave the porch light a quick flick off and on. He tapped the horn before easing out of the driveway and making the turn to drop Mazie at home.

From across the street, a few doors down, Sam watched the house, noting how the front washed with light as Clare went to the door— as the babysitter came out a few minutes later.

He considered and stewed, saw the backyard flood with light. Letting the mongrels out, he mused.

Dogs and security lights. Were those for his benefit? Did she think he was a fucking burglar?

It was no way to act, no way to treat him. Montgomery's doing, he decided. She was just too soft, too accommodating to tell that interfering bastard to mind his own business.

He'd take care of that. Take care of her.

He knew what she needed. A man of means, of style, of stature. One who could put those kids in a good boarding school so she didn't have to work so hard. A man who could take her places, show her off.

She'd see. He'd make her see.

He settled in, watching the routine of lights going off, going on.

He sat for nearly an hour, watching her lighted bedroom windows, and longer still after the windows went dark.

When he drove away, he had a plan.

⌘

SINCE MOST OF the men were busy, Beckett helped muscle the first tub to the second floor. In any case, he wanted to see how Lizzy liked it. Once they'd set the white slipper tub in place, he lingered. Light, warm colors, he thought, studying the tile work, a more traditional feel than some of the rooms. A nice contrast, he decided, with the deep tone of the old rubbed-bronze fixtures, and the charm of the telephone-style floor faucet for the tub.

He waited, but apparently Lizzy was withholding judgment until the plumber finished it off.

He went down—and up again countless times, hauling tubs, toilets, faucets, shower systems. All meticulously labeled, he noted, by either his brother or Hope.

On what he prayed was nearly the last trip, he saw Hope outside the on-site storage unit with a clipboard.

"Didn't know you were here."

"I've been down at the other storage. We finally have room in there. I'm checking off here, then I'm going to go through, make sure all the fixtures are in the right rooms."

"They're marked," he reminded her. "We're putting them in the right rooms."

"So you say." She grinned at him. "I have to see for myself. There are a lot of pieces to each pie. Shower system, sink faucets, bath faucets, towel warmers, P-traps, vanity mirrors, robe hooks." She lifted one elegant eyebrow. "Should I continue?"

"No, because I've muled that and more in and up."

"It'll be worth it." She lowered her clipboard, adjusted her intricately tied scarf. "Besides, you'll be able to relax on your hot date tonight."

"Where am I going?"

She laughed. "For me to know and you to find out. Oh, I had this idea." She opened a purse the size of a small planet, pulled out what looked like a little diary or journal, with stylized fairies on the cover. "I'm going to run this past your mother, but I thought we could put a journal in each room—themed to it. I got this on loan from TTP. Guests could write comments in them."

"Fine with me."

"Good. And I thought we could get a nice registration book. I know we're not doing that sort of thing, but if we could find a classy one, put it on the desk in The Library, it's another way for guests to write something. And I got this sample today."

She reached inside the planet again, pulled out a cream-colored folder. "For the rooms—we put a nice welcome note in here on the stationery—from the staff, the list of art when we get that worked out, a menu from Avery's, other information."

"You're having entirely too much fun with this."

"I really am, and just wait until I start buying office supplies. Oh, and while I've got one of you, I thought of a few things last night."

She reached in again, pulled out an enormous notebook.

"Beckett!" Ryder yelled down from the second-floor porch. "Are you going to stand around making time with the innkeeper all day, or get any actual work done?"

"Kiss my ass," Beckett called back pleasantly.

"I'll let you go." Hope stuck the notebook back in her bag. "Tell me something first. Is he ever going to call me by name, or am I always going to be 'the innkeeper'?"

"The only time you have to worry is when he calls you that damn innkeeper."

"I suppose so."

She glanced up again, cool stare in place, but wasted it as Ryder had already gone back in.

FOR THE FIRST time in months, Beckett considered demoing his apartment bathroom and installing a hot tub. He might not have been a gym rat, but he considered himself in pretty damn good shape. Or had, until the day of hauling tubs and toilets, sinks, vanities, and Christ knew what up a couple flights of stairs—multiple times—had done him in.

Everything ached.

A hot tub, he thought as he stripped and dropped sweaty, filthy clothes on the bathroom floor. Maybe a new shower system with body jets like they were putting in the inn.

An in-house masseuse would be a nice touch.

One thing, he told himself as he got into his all-too-pedestrian shower, he'd be modifying his house plans and adding some well-deserved perks to the master bath.

Of course, the way he was going, he'd be an AARP member before he built the damn place. Really had to get on that.

But right at the moment, building anything, including the dog-house he'd promised the kids they'd start next week, seemed like the seventh level of hell.

One of these fine days he'd stick with his drawing board, his CAD, his slide rule, and blueprints, and just tell other people where to hammer, saw, and haul.

"Yeah, that's going to happen," he mumbled and tried to imagine hot jets swirling and pulsing around tired muscles. His imagination didn't quite make the grade.

He remembered to pick up the clothes, ditch the towel in the hamper when he considered Clare might use the bathroom when she came to pick him up.

His back snarled at him—he snarled back.

Since he didn't know where they were going, he considered wardrobe choices. Probably not jeans, though jeans and a sweatshirt seemed like the perfect choice for his overworked body.

He settled on black pants and a casual shirt with tiny blue and green checks. If absolutely necessary, he could dress it up with a tie and—please God, don't make me—a jacket.

If she hadn't already made plans, whatever they were, he'd have nudged her toward a quiet evening in, with delivery and DVDs.

But a woman who worked all week, at home and at business, deserved a fun evening out on a Saturday night.

If she wanted to go dancing, he might break down in tears.

He glanced around the apartment, deemed it reasonably clean, mostly because he hadn't spent enough time in it recently to mess it up. Between Clare, work, family meetings, dogs, kids, time for sprawling out with beer, chips, and ESPN had dwindled down to next to never.

He paused a moment, asking himself if he missed it, and decided not very much. Being busy had its perks, especially being busy with Clare and her engaging brood, work he genuinely loved, the regular contact with his own family. Time to stop bitching, he decided, and maybe stock up on the BenGay.

The brisk knock sounded just as he considered stretching out on the couch for five minutes. Telling himself to stop thinking like an old man, he opened the door.

Avery and Hope, arms loaded, breezed in and straight by him.

"Pretend we're not here," Avery advised as she marched back to his kitchen.

"What—"

"Hi." Clare paused long enough to offer him a kiss. "We're just going to set up. It won't take long."

"Okay. Set up what?"

"This and that. Enough of this and too much of that for me to carry up by myself."

"We're invisible." Avery cleared off the drop-leaf table he sometimes used for eating. "You can't see us."

Hope opened a white cloth, draped the table with a quick billow and snap while Avery pulled a corkscrew out of her pocket. She drew the cork on a bottle of cab, set it on a silver wine holder.

"I thought we'd have dinner in. I hope that's okay."

Baffled, Beckett followed Clare into the kitchen to watch her put a roasting pan in his oven. "You want to stay in?"

"Unless you hate the idea."

"No, but—"

She wore a dress, short and slim in a dark, deep blue, and shiny red shoes with tall, skinny heels.

"You look great." He caught the scent of something miraculous. "What's in the oven?"

"Pot roast."

"Seriously?"

Obviously pleased, she laughed. "I talked to your mother, and she said it was your favorite. Hopefully mine will measure up to hers."

"You *made* pot roast?"

"And a few other things. If that wine's breathed long enough, why don't you pour us a glass. I have a little fussing to do yet in here."

"Sure, I'm . . ." He trailed off when he saw a familiar shape on the counter. He stepped over, lifted the lid. "Apple pie? Are you kidding me? You baked a pie?"

"Also rumored to be a favorite. I like baking pies when I have time."

"Clare, this must've taken you all day to put together. I didn't expect—"

"Why?" She tipped her head at him. "Why shouldn't you expect now and then. Isn't that what you told me?"

"I guess I did. It's just . . . wow."

"You take me out. You take my kids out. You brought them dogs, and put in motion lights at my house. You give us all time and attention, Beckett. I wanted to give some back to you."

It staggered him. It moved him. "I think this is the best thing anyone's done for me in maybe ever."

"I don't know about ever, but I enjoyed doing it. How about that wine?"

"Sure."

He stepped out, saw that Hope and Avery had transformed his lowly drop leaf into a sparkling table for two, complete with candles and flowers. Music played quietly from his stereo.

He poured the wine, carried the glasses into the kitchen, where Clare put together a fancy tray of olives. "It looks pretty impressive out there. Are they really invisible, or did they leave?"

"It's just you and me." She took the glass, tapped it to his. "So, to just you and me for an evening."

"I can't think of better. Clare. Thanks."

"Beckett." She moved into his arms. "You're welcome."

She wouldn't let him help, and he had to admit it felt damn good just to sit with her, talk over wine and fancy appetizers. He felt the burden and effort of the day slip away—and pure gratitude when they sat at the table and he took his first bite of her pot roast.

"It definitely measures up."

"Your mother and I compared recipes. They were pretty close. I had to make it good," she added, "so you wouldn't be disappointed we weren't going out."

"Clare, I hauled half a ton of bathroom fixtures up those stairs today. By the time I got home I felt like an eighty-year-old man who got run over by a truck. Pot roast and apple pie at home? It's like Christmas."

"I heard you worked today. I thought you'd all take Saturday off."

"Normally, but we wanted to get the fixtures up so the plumber can start Monday morning."

"It's getting more real, isn't it? It's not just a building, however beautiful. It's form and function now, or coming to it. I remember when we put in the bookshelves, the counter, opening those first boxes of books. I remember that so well, that feeling of this is real now. This is actually a bookstore. Mine."

"Most days there's so much going on, so it's get it done and think about what's next. But yeah, there are days like this when it hits. It's real." He topped off her wine, then his own. "Right now, here with you, I can look back to beginnings, to plans, to how can we do this, and real's good. Tell me you'll stay tonight?"

She smiled at him. "I thought you'd never ask."

CHAPTER NINETEEN

H E WOULD HAVE LINGERED OVER PIE, BUT SHE INSISTED on clearing up the dishes. Since he figured she was running the show, he didn't try to persuade her into stacking them up for later. In any case, he enjoyed having her fuss around his kitchen with him with the music going, the conversation easy.

"This was a hell of a surprise, Clare."

"It may not reach the level of two puppies, but it's not bad. And for me, it's nice to have an evening where the focus of every minute isn't on costumes and candy. Plus, I know that as soon as that's done, it'll be all Santa all the time until Christmas."

"They're still believers?"

"I think Harry's copped to it, but he pretends otherwise. They've already started lists, which includes every toy they see advertised on TV."

"I remember doing the same thing. Those were the days."

"Liam wants a Barbie."

She sent him a sparkling smile as she said it. After a beat of surprise, Beckett beamed right back at her. "To use as a hostage, victim, or innocent bystander." ·

Clare fisted the hand holding a dishcloth on her hip. "That's exactly right, except he hasn't come up with innocent bystander yet. Men really are just boys in bigger packages."

"You ought to get that car she's got, too. Then she can be driving along, and get carjacked. That'd be cool."

"It used to be Winnie the Pooh and jack-in-the-boxes."

"Times change."

"Boy, they do. And just think, next year you'll be decorating the inn."

"I guess we'll have to go all-out."

"Absolutely. You'll have to seriously deck the halls. You should do a holiday tour."

"Hmm. Maybe."

"Really, Beckett. People are invested, and they really want to see what you've done in there. You should do a tour after it's all done. Hope would know just how it should be done. Avery and I could help. Think community relations, publicity, and pride."

"I'll talk it over with the family." And could already see his mother jumping all over the idea.

"Meanwhile, I'm thinking of opening the bookstore on Sundays once you're up and running. Maybe the inn will send some business my way."

She paused, glanced around. "Why don't you pour the rest of the wine? I'm going to go freshen up."

Good thing he picked up his dirty clothes and wet towels, he thought.

He poured the wine, took his to the front windows. She was probably right about the tour, the decorations, even her Sunday hours. More work for everybody, but they'd make it worthwhile. He looked at the way the building shone now, imagined it decked out for the holidays.

Definitely worthwhile.

Hardly more than a year before the building had stood sagging in the dark, and now it gleamed. Hardly more than a year from now, he thought, they'd have it sparkling with lights and wreaths and garland.

Amazing, really, what could happen in a year.

Clare was here, with him. And he could clearly see her with him next year. In fact, he realized, he couldn't see it otherwise.

"Beckett? Could you come in here a minute?"

Hell, had he left stuff tossed around in there? If so, he'd just have to distract her, so he grabbed her wine on the way.

"I haven't had a lot of time to—" He stopped speaking the minute he stepped to the bedroom door, mostly because he'd swallowed his tongue.

Clare in candlelight.

She'd scattered them around the room to create a soft and indulgent romantic glow—and added more flowers to perfume the air. She'd turned down his bed, mounded the pillows in invitation.

And she, he thought, the centerpiece. Her hair fell long and loose around bare shoulders, glinting in the soft edges of the candle glow. Her body—smooth skin, subtle curves—seemed draped in midnight that frothed at the curve of her breasts and high on her thighs.

He wasn't sure what women called what she wore—corset seemed much too ordinary and dated. He'd have dubbed it instant seduction.

"I didn't think you'd mind."

"You leave me breathless."

"I hoped I would. I hope you'll come here. Come over here, Beckett, and leave me breathless."

He set the glasses aside, crossed to her. He trailed his fingertips over her shoulders, down her arms, up again. "You know I'm going to have to get the boys a whole kennel of puppies now."

When she laughed, he swooped in, took her mouth. Took her breath.

She'd wanted so much to know this, this one vivid, intense moment, the absolute focus of body and mind. That moment that held like a diver on a cliff before the needs and sensations whipped and ripped into the heedless fall.

She'd wanted to give it to him, that moment, the ones that followed. She wrapped close, needing to seep into him as he did to her. Take him over as she was taken.

Tonight, all night, she would give everything and anything in celebration of knowing she could love.

All night, she thought again, to savor.

She pressed her cheek to his, then eased back. "It's nice"—she began unbuttoning his shirt—"to have so much time. Lingering time."

"Just tell me, were you wearing that all along?"

Her gaze slid up to his, sly as her smile. He wondered if women knew that look could make a man a slave.

"It was more efficient. And I liked knowing I'd come in here, take off my dress." She eased the shirt off his shoulders. "Call you in. I liked knowing you'd see me, and want me."

"I want you every time I see you. I want you when I don't see you. I just want you, Clare."

"You can have me. I like knowing that, too."

She drew down his zipper, making his belly quiver.

"Lingering's a challenge when you look like you do."

"I'll help you with that. You should lie down. You worked hard today." She gave him a playful nudge.

He thought it might kill him to let her take the reins and take it slow—but he'd die happy.

He lay back. She slid over him, straddled him. Shaking her hair back, she set her hands on his shoulders.

"I can feel the work you do here." She kneaded them gently, working toward his neck. "And here," she continued as she stroked down his biceps. "It's exciting. And in your hands." She took his, pressed their palms together. "Hard and strong. It's exciting to know they'll be on me, touching me, doing things to me only you and I know about."

She interlaced their fingers, then leaned down to drown them both in a kiss.

He wondered how the body could relax so utterly and churn so madly at once. She soothed him, aroused him, untied every knot of tension all the while lashing new ones as her lips brushed over his jaw, trailed in slow, silky kisses down his throat.

"I need to touch you."

"You will," she murmured. "I want you to. Soon." But she kept her fingers twined with his as she glided those lips over his chest, and slowly, torturously, down to his belly.

It was a gift, she thought, this lazy feast of his body. A gift for both of them. How good it was to have him under her, to know the shape of his body, the scent of him, the feel and taste of his skin.

To indulge herself, to gorge if she pleased, as long as she pleased. The more she consumed, the more her appetite sharpened.

Strong hands, strong arms, strong back, she thought, yet he trembled for her. His breath quickened; his workingman muscles tensed. For her. That, too, was a gift.

She took him to the edge, held him there until every labored breath burned. Then she rose up, bringing his hands with hers to breasts thinly covered with midnight lace.

She arched back at last, at last letting him touch. Sighing out her pleasure as the candlelight bathed her.

His fingers found hooks. He willed himself not to rush, not to tear and tug but to release each one carefully. And to watch the midnight shift over her skin, slide down to reveal more.

She drew him in when he bowed up to sample and to relish, pressed him to her, urging him to feast.

The air pulsed, heady with candle wax and flowers, and in the fragile light once more she eased him back, braced her hands on his shoulders. Watching him, she took him into her.

Her breath released, something like a sob. Again she laced her fingers with his, and she began to move.

Rocking, almost gently at first, her eyes on his until he saw nothing but her, felt nothing but her. Only Clare.

Time spun out, long, slow beats. Once more she took him to the edge, held him there. Held him, then drove him over into shattered dark.

IN THE MORNING, he turned the tables and brought her breakfast in bed. It wasn't pot roast with all the trimmings, but he knew how to put together a fairly decent omelette.

Her stunned surprise made him wish he could have offered her more than a couple of eggs with cheese.

"You're eating pie for breakfast?"

"It's fruit." He sat across from her so he could watch her eat. "Danishes are an accepted form of breakfast. Why not pie?"

"Don't pass that logic on to the kids. God, I'm sitting in bed drinking coffee and eating eggs. This must be an alternate universe."

"If it includes this pie, I want to live here. What have you got going today?"

"Full slate. Helping my father harvest herbs—which means I'll get some. Quick swing by the market on the way home. Some paperwork, a few things to do around the house. And so on. You?"

"I have paperwork and shop work I should get to. I'd rather spend the day with you."

"You could meet us for dinner tomorrow. We're going to grab something at Vesta before we hit the streets to beg for candy."

"I'm in. I could pick you guys up."

She shook her head as she finished the eggs. "After I pick them up from school, get them home and into costume, we're going to my parents so they can trick-or-treat them. We're Skyping Clint's parents from there, so they can see the boys in full gear. I'm hoping to get to Avery's around five, get some actual food in them."

"Okay then, I'll meet you."

He didn't want to let her go, but didn't feel right about horning in on her time with her parents. And he had told Owen he'd try to get into the shop around noon.

So he thought about her after she'd gone, and all along the drive.

SHE HEARD THE three-part harmony version of the sleepover from her boys before they raced back outside to burn off yet more energy with the puppies.

"Did they behave?" Clare asked her mother.

"They always do." At Clare's arch look, she shrugged. "Grandparents have different scales for good behavior than parents. It's our due. Those dogs are adorable, and make those kids so damn happy. Beckett's a sweetheart."

"Yes, he is."

"How did your date go?"

"Absolutely perfect. Pot roast never fails. He brought me breakfast in bed this morning."

"He sounds like a keeper." She got another look. "Don't tell me you're not thinking about it."

"We've only been seeing each other like this since the summer, and I don't want to—I'm so in love with him. Mom."

"Sweetie." Rosie stepped over to hug Clare, to hold and sway. "That's a good thing."

"It is. It feels good. I'm happy. We're happy, but that doesn't mean . . . I'm not making plans. A new approach for me—just take it a day at a time and enjoy it without thinking about . . . all the rest. I love being with him, the kids are crazy about him—and it's mutual. So I'm happy, and I don't need to make plans."

"Hey." Her father opened the door, poked his head in. "Are you going to help me out here, or what?"

"On my way," Clare promised.

"Farmer Murphy out there's got more basil and tomatoes than the two of us could use in three seasons. You're going home loaded," her mother warned.

"Then I'd better get going."

"I'll be right along."

But Rosie watched out the window for a few minutes first while her husband handed her daughter garden gloves and clippers, while her grandchildren tumbled over the yard with big brown puppies.

Her daughter was happy, she could see it. And in love. She could see that, too. She knew her girl well. Well enough to know that her Clare would always need to make plans, whether she admitted it or not.

∽

ON MONDAY BECKETT praised God he didn't have to haul anything heavy up the stairs again, even if he spent most of the day with a paintbrush and the rest of it sawing trim.

By the time he packed up, it was already five.

"Are you guys staying for trick-or-treat?" he asked his brothers.

"I am," Owen told him. "Hope's going to pass out candy in front of the inn."

"We're not open yet."

Owen spared the grousing Ryder a glance. "She got Milk Duds and Butterfingers."

"Butterfingers?" Ryder had a weakness for them. "I might stick around, see how it goes. What the hell are you doing?"

"Putting on my cape," Beckett said as he tied the bright red cloth around his shoulders. He pulled on safety goggles, work gloves before handing Owen a roll of duct tape. "Use this, put a big *X* on my shirt. Center it up."

"Who the hell are you supposed to be?" Ryder demanded.

Beckett dipped his chin, checked Owen's work. "I'm Carpenter X. Faster than a skill saw, more powerful than a nail gun. I fight for truth, justice, and plumb corners."

"That's so lame."

"I bet the kids don't think so. And I bet I get more candy than you."

"Out of pity," Ryder called out as Beckett walked out.

"Pretty good for costume on the fly," Owen commented.

"Yeah, not bad, but I'm not telling him that."

Vesta buzzed. A lot of people, Beckett noted, had the same idea. Get some pizza before hitting Main Street. He saw Avery, long blond wig tied back, tossing dough to the delight of her audience of pint-sized superheroes, fairy princesses, and ghouls.

"Hannah Montana?" he called out.

She tapped the plastic wood-grained stake in her belt before she caught the dough. "Buffy the Vampire Slayer."

"Cute."

"Not if you're a vampire."

Amused, he walked over to the booth of superheroes, checked out Clare. She made one hell of a Storm of the X-Men, he decided, in a white punk-style wig and snug black skirt and thigh-high boots.

"Excuse me, ma'am, I'm looking for three boys. They're about this high." He used his hand to measure like steps. "They go by Harry, Liam, and Murphy."

"I'm sorry, I haven't seen them. I'm Storm, and these are my friends and coworkers, Wolverine, Iron Man, and Deadpool."

"Pleased to meet you. I'm Carpenter X."

"You're Beckett!" Murphy slid off his seat, pointed up.

"By day I'm Beckett Montgomery, brilliant architect, handsome man about town. But at night, when evildoers walk the streets, I'm Carpenter X, defender of Boonsboro and the tristate area."

"Do you got superpowers?"

"I have my keen wits, my catlike agility, and super strength." He plucked up the miniature Deadpool, lifted him overhead and onto his shoulders.

"It's us." Murphy leaned down to whisper in Beckett's ear. "It's Murphy and Harry and Liam and Mom."

"Wait a minute." He lifted Murphy off, held him out. "You mean all this time you didn't tell me you were Deadpool?"

"Just for Halloween." Murphy lifted up his mask. "See?"

"How about that?" He dropped down, set Murphy on his lap. "You sure had me fooled." He gave Murphy a bounce when Heather set the pizza on the table. "Good timing."

"We have to call each other by our superhero names," Liam informed him. "Murphy keeps messing it up."

"I can tell Beckett 'cause he's with us."

"I don't want pizza." Harry scowled at the slice Clare put on his plate. "I'm not hungry."

"That's fine. I'll just hold all the candy Marmie and Granddad gave you, and what you get later until tomorrow."

"I'll take your share. I'm hungry as the Hulk." Beckett made as if to reach for Harry's plate.

"I can eat it," Harry muttered as he shifted it out of reach.

"Is it okay if I trick-or-treat with you guys?"

"You're too old to trick-or-treat."

"You, Wolverine, are mistaken." Carpenter X shook his head at Harry. "You're never too old for candy. Or pizza. Which as everybody knows is the favorite food of all superheroes."

❧

AT SIX, SUPERHEROES, villains, pop stars, fairies, and a variety of undead swarmed Main Street. Teenagers ran in packs, parents pushed strollers inhabited by bunnies, cats, puppies, and clowns. Some led or carried toddlers, others herded older kids from shop to shop, house to house.

Hope sat on the steps of the inn, a big bowl of candy in her lap. "Power rations for superheroes."

She held the bowl out as the boys shouted "trick or treat."

"Great look for you," she told Clare. "And you'd be who, Contractor X?"

"Carpenter X. My tool belt is always loaded."

"So I hear."

When Beckett laughed, poked an accusatory finger at Clare, Hope held out the bowl to the next group, answered a handful of questions about the inn.

"Everyone asks," she told Beckett. "When you can give me an absolutely we'll be done and ready date, I'm going to open reservations."

"We'll work out best calculation."

"I love this." She eased back. "I didn't know exactly what to expect, but this is fun and sweet and a great way to people watch. But I seriously underestimated on candy."

"You can get some from the bookstore," Clare told her. "Or from Avery. We always get too much."

"Mom!" Liam forgot his own directive as he tugged at Storm. "We want to go before the candy's all gone."

"Just go across the street for more supplies if you run out," Clare called as her kids towed her down the sidewalk.

"It is fun." Beckett stood with Clare while the kids dashed to the next bowl. "More fun with kids. They get such a charge."

"And a sugar rush later. I have to let them eat some, which means they'll be hyped at bedtime, then tired in school tomorrow."

"Well." He draped an arm around her as they followed the kids to the next stop. "Just make it snow a few inches, Storm. Buy yourself a delay."

They held hands as they walked, keeping pace with the boys or reining them back when someone stopped to talk. The air cooled, and dry leaves, stirred by a frisky wind, bounced along the curbs.

"I should've brought their jackets along instead of leaving them in the car."

"Are you cold? Because I've got to say, you look really hot."

She offered him a flirty smile. "Then it's worth the spandex. No, I'm not cold," she added, "but Liam has the sniffles already."

"We won't be out much longer." They'd already crossed the street, started up the other side.

"You're right, and he has a thermal shirt on under the costume. Still—"

"Tell you what, Supermom. We'll stop in the bookstore, give them a chance to warm up. I'll buy the hot chocolate."

"God, more chocolate. But that's a good idea."

When they stopped by the store, Sam Freemont stood across the street in a Jason hockey mask, sweatpants and hoodie. It gave him a thrill to stand there, in the open, watching her.

Trick or treat, he thought. He'd give her some of both, very soon now.

Satisfied with the timetable, he walked down Main with the crowd, continued on when it thinned. Porch lights gleamed as older kids ran around shouting to each other. No one paid any attention to him, strolling the sidewalk in his mask.

The power of it tangled almost erotically with the excitement of what was to come.

He walked steadily until he came to Clare's house, then took a quick, casual glance around before sliding into the shadows of the trees that bordered the side.

He'd studied the house long enough to know its weak spots. The dogs set up a stir in the backyard, but he'd come prepared for that. He tossed his pocketful of dog biscuits over the fence.

Tails wagged immediately as they chowed down.

Choosing a window, he pulled out the pry bar.

Crappy little house, he thought as the window gave with a creak and shudder. Crappy little life. He was offering her so much more, and it was past time she listened.

He tucked the tool away, boosted himself inside.

And shut the window behind him.

BY EIGHT, THE rounds complete, the boys sat in Vesta, eating and trading candy according to their mother's three-piece limit. For himself Beckett ate a Butterfinger, a Snickers, and a small pack of Skittles—and felt just a little sick.

Kids, apparently, were made of sterner stuff, as Liam was already angling for one more piece.

"Tomorrow," Clare told him to his desperate disappointment. Harry got the same treatment when he begged for quarters for the video games.

"It's already bedtime." She glanced at Murphy, who sat, focused on his third and final candy bar, as if his life had been sandwiched inside the chocolate and caramel.

"Time to go, Deadpool."

"I'll follow you home."

"Oh, Beckett. There hasn't been any . . . thing for days now. Plus—wait, there's Alva and Joe checking out. Let me see if they're going home now, and I'll have an escort. Will that do?"

"I'd settle for it."

She scooted out.

"I'm saving my gummy worms," Murphy told him.

"Worms for a rainy day."

"It doesn't gotta rain. I'm saving them for tomorrow. Can we go back to the hotel place so I can see the lady again?"

"If it's okay with your mom."

"I just want to play *one* game," Harry griped.

Beckett shifted his attention to a sulking Wolverine. "Tell you what, if it's okay, we'll go to the arcade this weekend, and we'll play like maniacs."

"Can we! But not Saturday 'cause it's Tyler's birthday. Can we go Sunday?"

"Works for me."

Clare came back with Joe, who ruffled Liam's hair. "We'll be happy to escort these fine crime-fighters home."

"We're going to the arcade on Sunday," Harry announced.

Clare lifted her eyebrows. "Oh?"

Under the table, Beckett gave Harry's foot a nudge. "We were discussing the possibility."

"It's a definite possibility, especially if three superheroes come along right now without any arguing."

Bribery worked. They were up, dashing for the door, yelling goodbye to Avery. Beckett walked them out.

"I'll see you tomorrow." He gave her a light kiss. "Happy Halloween."

Clare gave his hand a light squeeze. "Don't eat too much candy."

He watched them cross the street, turn to walk down to the parking lot. He wished he were going with them, he realized. Not just to see her safely home, but to be there. Maybe help her put the kids to bed.

He'd actually taken a step forward before he stopped himself. Stupid, he decided. She'd do it all faster without him there to hype the boys up even more. And she was probably tired, wanted some quiet time after she'd gotten them down.

He'd see her tomorrow—that was enough.

But damned if it felt like enough.

He went back inside, sat at the bar. What the hell, he'd have a beer.

"You were pretty slammed tonight," he said to Avery when she brought him a bottle.

"Always are on trick-or-treat night. Fun stuff, and God, my feet are killing me. I'm going to get off them, have Dave close out."

"Want a beer first?"

She considered. "You know, I would." Pulling off her apron, she got a beer, walked around the counter to sit beside him.

She tapped her bottle to his. "Happy Halloween."

CHAPTER TWENTY

WALKING THROUGH CLARE'S EMPTY HOUSE GAVE SAM a thrill of satisfaction. He could come and go as he pleased, anywhere he pleased and whenever he pleased. He studied the photographs she had arranged on tables and shelves, imagined himself in them.

He soon would be. It was just a matter of getting her alone until she understood what was best for her. Until she finally admitted she belonged to him.

A real man took what he wanted, and though he'd been patient with her—maybe too patient—it was time she understood that as well.

"Lessons begin tonight," he said as he walked upstairs.

Look how she lived, he thought, in this crackerbox of a house. That's what his mother would call it, a crackerbox in a one-horse town.

He'd change that.

He walked into her bathroom, gave a little sigh at the size, the simple, inexpensive fixtures. No bigger than his walk-in closet at home, he decided. It was pathetic, really, what she settled for. He poked into the medicine chest, nodded his head at the birth control pills. Good, that was good, they wouldn't want any mistakes that needed fixing.

Bad enough she already had those three brats to deal with. A decent boarding school would take care of that, a reasonable investment to clear the road.

After studying, sniffing her skin creams, body lotions, he made a note to have his mother take Clare to her day spa. A nice treat, he thought, and another lesson. Any woman attached to him had to present herself a certain way, in public and in private.

Considering that, he stepped into her bedroom.

She'd tried to make it pretty, with what she had to work with. Really, she did the best she could with her limited resources. He thought of how grateful she'd be once he took her in hand, showed her how to live well.

Had she had sex with Montgomery in that bed? They'd talk about that—oh yes, they would. Time for a firm hand there, but he'd forgive her, of course. Women were weak.

Opening her closet, he stroked dresses, blouses. He remembered her wearing most of them, thought of how she looked walking down the street or pushing a cart in the grocery store, standing behind the counter in that silly bookstore.

A whole new wardrobe was called for. He imagined how excited, how pleased she would be when he helped her select it. He should probably do the selecting himself, until she acclimated to her new status.

Yes, that would be best. He'd teach her how to dress.

Curious, he crossed to her dresser, opening drawers, touching, studying. Obviously, she needed his guidance on nightwear, on what went under her new clothes. A woman, certainly *his* woman, needed style and status even in very private moments.

He came across two pieces unlike the others—sexy, seductive. His pulse picked up as he brushed the material with his fingers, pictured her wearing them for him.

Then he realized, no, not for him. She'd worn this for Montgomery. He ripped a froth of lace from the bodice. She wouldn't wear them again, he determined. He'd make her burn them. She'd have to apologize—he'd accept no less—and burn the slutwear she'd worn for Montgomery.

Then she'd wear what he bought her, what he *told* her to wear. And be grateful.

Anger, so acute, roared in his head. He nearly missed the barking dogs.

He closed the drawer, quietly, carefully, and slipped into her closet moments before he heard the door open downstairs, and the sounds of the brats running through the house, shouting like hoodlums.

They'd be taught, too, he assured himself. They'd soon learn to live by his rules if they knew what was good for them.

⁓

HER SUPERHEROES RUSHED to the back doors as a team to let the dogs in. Five minutes, she thought, as fresh mayhem began. She'd give them another five to settle down before getting ready for bed.

They wouldn't be the only kids in Boonsboro Elementary the next day who'd gone to bed a bit late and hyped on sugar.

She put the bags of Halloween treats far back on the counter—away from curious dogs and sneaky kids—and thought just how much she wanted to yank off the wig, peel out of the costume, scrub off the Storm makeup.

Fun while it lasted, she decided. But she was ready for the fun to

end. She let them chatter about their big night, thrill the dogs with
games of tug—then brought the hammer down.

"Okay, boys, time for bed."

She got the expected *But, Moms,* the protests, excuses, negotiations—
and stood firm against them as much for herself as the boys.

She wanted her comfortable pj's, some quiet, maybe a big mug of
tea and a book.

"I guess you're not that interested in going to the arcade on Sunday."

"Yes, we are!" Harry shot her a stunned and appalled stare.

"Boys who argue with their mothers don't go to arcades. I want
you in your pajamas. And you're all going to brush your teeth extra
well tonight. Let's move out, troops."

She herded them upstairs, stood in their doorway a moment to
make sure they got started. "Don't throw your costumes on the floor.
Put them in the costume box—I mean it. I'm going to get in my
pajamas, too."

"Can we wear our costumes to the arcade?" Liam asked her.

"We'll see. Put them away for now."

She crossed to her own room, started to yank off the wig, but
caught her reflection in the mirror. The grin snuck up on her. "Well,
you're no Halle Berry, but not half bad."

Pulling off the wig, she let out a long, long sigh.

In the closet, his breath shallow, his eyes riveted to the thin opening in the slats, Sam wondered what he was doing. The moment of
clarity sent his heart into a gallop.

He'd broken into her house like a thief, and now he hid in her
closet like—it didn't bear thinking about. What if she opened the
doors? What would he say? Do?

She'd put him in this position, this terrible position, and now . . .

The moment passed as she tugged the ridiculous costume off her
shoulders, drew the snug skirt down her body. Her hair tumbled free
down her back as she folded the skirt, laid it on a little chair.

She wore a plain white bra, plain white panties. He hadn't known plain and white could be so arousing.

He knew what he was doing, he reminded himself. He was taking what he wanted.

He reached up to open the closet.

"Mom! Harry's hogging the toothpaste!"

"There's plenty for everybody. I'll be there in one minute."

The brats, he remembered, and quietly lowered his trembling hand. He'd forgotten them. He had to be patient a little longer. He had to wait until they were in bed.

Had to wait. Had to watch.

Clare stripped off her panties, tossed them in the hamper before pulling on cotton pants. She unhooked her bra, tossed that in as well, pulled on a faded T-shirt.

Hearing sounds that didn't strike as teeth-brushing, she grabbed her hairbrush on the fly.

Harry and Liam stopped their sword fight with their toothbrushes, Murphy stopped making bomb sounds as he dropped a dog ball in the sink he'd filled nearly to the rim.

Mad with excitement, dogs leaped at boy and dripping ball.

"We brushed." Murphy sent her a cherub's grin. "I'm going to wash the ball 'cause it got slobbered."

"Let the water out, Murphy." She bent down to Liam. "Open up."

She sniffed when he did, caught the distinctive scent of their bubble-gum-flavored toothpaste. "You pass. Into bed. Harry."

He rolled his eyes at her, but opened up for the sniff test. "And you're clear. Bed."

Grabbing a towel, she homed in on Murphy.

"The ball's clean now."

"I bet. And your pj's are wet." She set her brush aside to tug off the damp top, then dried his hands, his arms, his sweet little chest. "Open up."

"I brushed real good." He opened, and huffed out a big breath to prove it.

"Very nice. Go get another pajama top."

"I have to change the bottoms, too, or they won't match."

"Murphy—" She bit back the impatience. Two minutes, and they'd be tucked in. "Of course you do. Make it fast."

She used the same towel to wipe up the water on the counter, the floor, draped it over the shower bar to dry out before it went in the hamper.

When she went into the boys' bedroom she spotted Murphy in a dog's bed with Yoda, and Ben wiggling under the covers in Harry's bed. Liam sprawled in his own with the glazed, droopy eyes of the nearly passed out.

"Murphy, you're not sleeping in the dog's bed."

"But he gets lonely."

"He won't. Ben can sleep with him."

"But Mom!" Harry clutched at the dog as she wondered how many times she'd heard those two words today.

"He can't sleep on a top bunk, Harry. He could fall out, or try to jump out, and get hurt. You don't want him to hurt himself. Come on now. It's late."

She managed to get the dog down, set him in his proper bed while Murphy—executing impressive fake snoring—continued to curl up with Yoda.

"No chance." Clare hauled Murphy up, dumped him in his lower bunk. "Stay," she ordered the dogs, and kissed Murphy, then Liam, then Harry. "And that goes for boys as well as dogs. Good night."

She'd made it halfway to her bedroom when she heard the distinctive sound of puppy toenails crossing the floor, and Murphy's muffled giggle as, she imagined, the dogs joined him in bed.

Discipline started, in earnest, tomorrow, she promised herself. Remembering her brush, she backtracked to the bathroom. She brushed her hair out as she walked back. Once she got the makeup cleaned off, she'd go make that tea. Check the boys one more time, then settle down.

She really should write the copy for the store's upcoming newsletter, but she was too damn tired. She'd get an early start on it tomorrow.

She caught the movement as she crossed the bedroom toward her little bath, and whirled toward it. The hairbrush dropped with a clatter as Sam stepped out behind the bedroom door, closed it.

"You're going to want to be quiet." He spoke casually, with a smile on his face. "You wouldn't want to disturb your sons. They could get hurt."

⌒

AT VESTA, BECKETT took another pull on his beer. It felt good to kick back, hang with Avery, talk about nothing important or in particular.

"Are you heading over to Chuck and Lisa's party?" she asked him.

Only a couple blocks over, he thought, and plenty of his friends, and both of his brothers would be there. "I'm going to pass."

"Aw, no partying without your girlfriend?"

"Smartass. What's your excuse?"

"I was going to, but my feet betrayed me. What's wrong with us, Beck? We've always been up for a party."

"You're right. Tell you what. You can be my date. We'll go for an hour. Buffy and Carpenter X need to preserve their reps."

"Can I have a piggyback ride there and back?" she asked as Hope came in.

"I was hoping you were still here."

"Problem?" Beckett asked her.

"I can't get into the inn. My key won't unlock the damn door, and there are lights flashing upstairs. I was going to check, see if it's some electrical glitch, but I can't get the stupid door to open."

He got up as she spoke, looked out the front glass door of the restaurant. The glass in the doors leading from E&D to the porch flashed on and off like lightning strikes.

"She's been in a mood the last few days." At Hope's arched brow, Beckett shrugged. "I'm just saying. I'll go check it out."

"I'm coming with you. This key thing is infuriating. It worked fine a few hours ago."

"Wait for me!" Avery hurried after them. "Vampire Slayer, remember?"

"I don't think you'll find any vampires at the inn," Beckett commented as they crossed the street.

"You never know. Plus temperamental ghosts are cake for the Slayer."

Beckett pulled out his keys, jingling them in his hand while they walked down the sidewalk to the back of the building.

"Could you try mine?" Hope passed it to him.

Beckett slid it into the lock, turned it. And glanced at Hope when the lock clicked, and the door opened smoothly.

"I'm telling you it wouldn't work five minutes ago. If it's your ghost playing games, I don't know why she's mad at me."

"Like I said." Beckett flipped on the light in Reception. "She's been in a mood."

At that moment, the light he'd just turned on began to flash. Upstairs doors slammed sharp as gunshots.

"Some mood," Avery murmured.

"I'll go see what's going on. Stay here."

"Like hell." But Avery grabbed Hope's hand as they followed Beckett. "Maybe it's a Halloween thing. Her way of marking the date."

"Doesn't sound celebratory," Hope stated.

"I think she's been kind of sad the last couple days," Beckett began. As he approached, the porch doors in E&D flew open. Inside the lights flicked like a strobe.

"Maybe pissed."

"Maybe we need Ghostbusters," Avery whispered.

"Okay, Lizzy, cut it out!" Beckett raised his voice, put irritation in it. As he strode in, steam billowed in rolling clouds out of the bath. "Well, what the fuck? You don't like the tile pattern, the goddamn tub? Change rooms."

"Beckett." Hope laid a hand on his arm, squeezed hard as her voice trembled. "Look at the bathroom mirror."

Through the clouds he watched letters appear, as if someone wrote with a finger on the steamy glass.

"Help," he read. "Lizzy, if you're in trouble—" He broke off as the writing continued.

Help Clare.
Hurry!

"Oh God." Even as Avery turned to run, Beckett bulleted by her. "Call the cops. Call my brothers. Now. Tell them to get to Clare's."

"I've got the cops." Hope punched numbers into her phone as she ran.

"I've got Owen. And we're coming with you."

⁓

DON'T SCREAM, CLARE ordered herself. The boys would hear, would come. She wouldn't risk it. "You broke into my house."

"What choice did you give me? It's time you and I had a private talk, time for you to understand how things are going to be. Why don't you sit down."

"I don't want to sit down."

"I said *sit down*! One of the things you're going to understand is doing what you're told when I tell you."

She sat, braced, on the bottom edge of the bed. "You made a

mistake, Sam, breaking into my house. If you leave now we'll let it go at that. Just a mistake."

"No, *you* made the mistake when you set the cops on me." He held up his hands. "Well, I can let that go, but you're going to learn to show me respect. You're going to remember who I am."

"I know who you are."

"And I know you lack self-confidence. I know that lack caused you to play hard-to-get, make me work for it. Didn't I give you time, when you came back? I couldn't have been more considerate, more patient, given the situation you'd gotten yourself into. Running off with Clint Brewster that way."

"Clint was my husband."

"And he's dead, isn't he? Left you with two brats and another in your belly so you had to come crawling back here to this hole-in-the-wall town."

Temper wanted to war with fear, but she beat it back. If she pushed him, he might hurt her. God knew what he might do to her boys if she couldn't stop him.

"I came home. My parents are here. I—"

"You should never have left in the first place. But that's spilled milk. You led me on, Clare."

"How did I lead you on?"

"You think I didn't know what you were doing every time you smiled at me? Every time you'd tell me you couldn't go out to dinner, or just for a drive? I saw the way you looked at me. Wasn't I patient? Wasn't I?"

His voice rose to nearly a shout, so she nodded. "Please, let's not wake the children."

"Then start paying attention. I want this game to end now. I can only be pushed so far, Clare. You used Montgomery to make me jealous, and that's beneath you. I don't want you to so much as speak to him again. Is that clear?"

"Yes."

"Good. Now—"

"I'll call him right away, break it off." She rose, started toward the door.

He grabbed her arm, shoved her back. "I said you're not to speak to him. Sit down until I tell you different."

"I'm sorry." She bent down, picked up her hairbrush, took it with her back to the foot of the bed. As a weapon, she thought, staring down at her hands, it was pitiful.

"That's better." He let out a breath, smiled again. "Much better. Now, here's what we're going to do. You're going to pack a bag—you won't need much. I'll be replacing all your things right away. But you'll need your essentials for tonight. We're going on a trip, just you and me. We're going to take a few days. I've already made reservations for one of the private villas in this resort I like. They know me there, so be prepared to be treated royally."

It appalled her to see that familiar wide smile and wink.

"You're going to see how much I can give you, Clare. All you have to do is what I tell you, learn your lessons, give me what we've both wanted for so long."

"It sounds lovely. I have to arrange for someone to come take care of the children. I can call my mother. She'll—"

"The children, the children." Red rage stained his face. "I'm sick of hearing about the children. They're asleep, aren't they? Safe in bed with their drooling dogs. I'll call my own mother when we get to the resort. She'll arrange for someone to deal with them. There's an excellent boarding school in upstate New York. We'll enroll them as soon as possible. You'll learn no one comes before me. I can be generous and pay for the education of another man's children, but I won't have them put ahead of me or my needs. Do you understand me?"

"Perfectly. Should I pack now?"

"Yes. I'll show you what's appropriate." His tone changed, became sticky with indulgence. "Don't be ashamed of what you've got to choose from now. I'll take you shopping. You're going to have lots of time to enjoy yourself, to be with me, to live the life I give you without those kids and that bookstore hobby of yours in the way."

She got slowly to her feet. The fear had ebbed, and in the void fury filled her. She could only pray it didn't show. Leave her children alone? She'd see him in hell first.

"I want to thank you." She kept her gaze downcast, hoped it appeared subservient, as she took a tentative step toward him. "I've been so confused, so conflicted. But now it's all so clear."

She looked up then, into his eyes. Cocking back, she swung the brush with all her strength, all her fury into his smiling face. As blood erupted from his mouth, she leaped toward the door. Her only thought was to get to her boys, keep them safe.

Her hand closed around the doorknob as he wrenched her back. Fear sprang up again, bright as the blood on his face as he dragged her to the floor. She kicked, tried to claw at his eyes but he slapped her hard enough to have stars erupting.

"Bitch!" He used the back of his hand, shooting pain into her cheekbone. "Look what you did. Look what you did to me. I'm giving you everything, and you don't learn. You'll learn now."

When he tore at her shirt, she raked her nails down his face. He reared up, shock and pain mixed with the blood.

Rolling, she struggled to pull herself free, and suddenly his weight lifted. She crawled for the door, breath sobbing as she tried to pull to her feet, run to her boys.

Arms came around her.

"Clare, Clare, Clare." Avery held tight until Clare stopped fighting her. "You're okay now."

"My babies."

"Shh. Hope went to see. Shh."

"I have to—" The sounds finally broke through her shocked senses. Slumped against Avery, she turned her head.

At the foot of her bed, Sam sprawled on the floor with Beckett straddling him. With Beckett's fist slamming, again and again, into the already bloodied face.

"Oh God. God." Dizzy, she pushed to her feet, and Hope was there helping Avery steady her.

Seconds later, Owen and Ryder burst in, and Ryder grabbed Owen's arm when his brother started forward.

"We've got to pull him off."

Ryder shrugged. "Let's give him another minute."

"Jesus Christ, Ry."

Even as Hope sent Ryder one fierce and approving look, Owen shook him off. "Come on, Beck. Stop. Stop, goddamn it. He's done. Give me a fucking hand, Ryder, before he kills this son of a bitch."

It took both of them to drag him off. It only took one look at Clare to change his focus. "He hurt you." He moved to her slowly, touched his fingers gently to the bruises on her face. "He hurt you."

"I hurt him more. Then you—Beckett." Shaking now, she clung to him. "Oh God, Beckett."

"The cops." Hope glanced toward the windows and sounds of sirens. "I'll go down, let them know, see if they can keep it quiet and not wake the kids. Oh, and that we need an ambulance."

She glanced at the unconscious and battered Sam. "But there's no hurry on that."

She caught Ryder's hard grin before she backed out of the room.

"I'm going to take you downstairs, away from him." Beckett lifted Clare into his arms. "You can tell us what happened downstairs."

She nodded, let her head drop to his shoulder, hoping the room would stop spinning if it rested there. "Avery."

"I'll check on them again. Don't worry."

"He said we were leaving tonight," Clare told Beckett as he carried her down. "Going on a trip, just leaving the kids alone—until he put them in boarding school because they'd be in his way."

"He won't touch you or those boys. Ever again."

"When he told me that, told me to pack a few things? That's when I hit him with the hairbrush. Hard as I could. I think I knocked one of his teeth out."

"Upstairs first," he said to Charlie Reeder as they passed at the bottom on the steps. "You hit him with a hairbrush."

"It was all I had."

"No." He held her tight, sat, held her tight on his lap. "You've got a hell of a lot more."

Beckett sat beside her while she gave her statement, didn't spare a glance when they took Sam away, cuffed to a gurney. Hope brought her tea while one of the paramedics doctored his torn knuckles.

Once the cops located the jimmied window, documented it, Ryder went out for tools to repair it.

When the police left, Avery came out of the kitchen. "I made soup. When I'm upset I cook, so everybody's eating soup."

While she ladled it up in the kitchen, Ryder dropped down to a chair at the table. "Now that the law's gone, let's have it straight, what you danced around telling them. How did you know Clare was in trouble?"

"Lizzy." Beckett laid a hand over Clare's, and told the story.

"Pretty smart for a dead woman," Ryder commented with a glance at Hope. "The innkeeper's going to have her hands full."

"The innkeeper has a name," she informed him.

"I've heard that."

"Hope and I are staying tonight." Avery set soup in front of Owen. "I wouldn't sleep if I went home. We're staying."

"I'd like you to." Clare let out a long breath. "Elizabeth told you I needed help. And you came." She turned her hand under Beckett's, laced fingers. "You all came. I guess that's a lot more than a hairbrush."

Beckett didn't leave until she slept. He tossed Harry's Spider-Man sleeping bag in his truck before driving to the inn.

He spread it out on the floor of E&D.

"She's fine. She's okay, thanks to you. He hurt her a little—but he'd have done worse if you hadn't let us know."

He sat, pulled off his work boots. "He's in the hospital, under guard. He'll be in a cell as soon as the doctors clear him. One of us broke his jaw—either Clare and her trusty hairbrush or me. Lost his caps, and two teeth. Busted up his nose. I figure he got off easy."

Exhausted, wired, he stretched out. "Anyway, I thought I'd bunk here tonight, if it's okay with you. I figured you might like some company, and I'm just not in the mood to go home. I guess I'm the first guest—alive anyway—of Inn BoonsBoro."

He lay staring at the ceiling. He thought he felt something cool across his throbbing knuckles, then the light he'd neglected to shut off in the bathroom went dark.

"Thanks. 'Night." He closed his eyes, and he slept.

SUNDAY MORNING, AT his insistence, kids and dogs loaded in the van.

"We're supposed to go to the arcade," Harry reminded him. "You said."

"Yeah, this afternoon. There's just something I want to show you first. It's not far."

"It certainly is a secret."

He looked over at Clare. She'd softened the bruises with makeup, but he knew the boys had seen them. Just as he knew she'd told them the truth, if not in every detail.

He drove out of town, listening to Liam and Harry bicker and Murphy sing to the dogs, who'd already learned how to howl in harmony.

Normal, he thought. It all seemed so normal. Yet there were bruises on Clare's face.

"I can take them to the arcade if you want to stay back and rest."

"Beckett, he slapped me a few times. It hurt, and it was really scary, but that's it. And it's over." She kept her voice low, under the music from the radio.

He didn't think it would ever be over for him. Not all the way.

"Hope talked to a friend of hers, a psychiatrist in D.C.," Clare continued. "She said—best guess as she hasn't talked to him, observed him—this was classic stalker behavior, with narcissism tossed in. He'd grown more and more obsessed with me, was convinced I wanted to be with him, but kept stringing him along—adding in the kids who were an obstacle. It was one thing when I wasn't seeing anyone, but my relationship with you caused a kind of psychotic break. Basically, he went off the rails. Now he's going to jail. He'll get help. I'm not ready to care if he gets help, but he'll get it."

"As long as help comes with bars and a prison jumpsuit, he can have all he wants."

"Right there with you." She glanced around. "Doesn't your mother live over this way?"

"Not far. No, we're not going there so she can fuss over you again today."

"Thank God. I had about all the fussing over yesterday I can take from friends, family, neighbors, police. I want to feel, and be, normal and boring today."

He turned off onto a gravel lane, bore to the right and up a slope. "Ryder lives back that way, Owen over that way," he added, with gestures. "Not too far, but not too close either."

He stopped in view of a partial house, and even the partial was still unfinished.

"Eight acres. Nice little stream on the far side of the house—or what will eventually be a house."

"This is your place. It's beautiful, Beckett. You're crazy not to finish it off and live here."

"Maybe."

Kids and dogs bolted out. Lots of room to run, he noted as they did just that. He knew where he intended to put a yard, some shade trees, where he intended to put a garden—and where he intended to put a lot of things.

"This is all your trees and stuff?" Harry demanded. "We could go camping here. Can we?"

"I guess we could."

"I draw the line." Clare held up a hand. "I do not, will not camp."

"Who asked you?" Beckett plucked the ball from Harry, heaved it so all the four-legged and two-legged boys gave chase.

"This is the perfect boost," Clare told him, wandering, circling. "Better than normal and boring. It's beautiful and quiet. You have to show us the house, tell us what it's going to look like when it's finished."

He took her hand to stop her from heading over to it. "I've come out here a couple times this last week, looking at what I started and never finished. And asking myself why I didn't finish it. I love the way it feels here, the way it looks. The way it will look."

"Who wouldn't?"

His eyes, deep and blue and suddenly intense, met hers. "I hope that's true, because I figured out why I'd never finished it, what I was waiting for. I was waiting for you, Clare. For them. For us. I want to finish it for you, for them, for us."

Her hand went limp in his. "Beckett."

"I can change the plans. Add on a couple more bedrooms, a play-room."

He gestured with his free hand while the last of the season's leaves swirled around them. "I think I should pave an area over that way, for riding their bikes, maybe put up a basketball hoop. They need more room, kids and dogs. I want to give them more room. I want to give you what you want, you just have to tell me. I need to give them what they want, have what I want. I want you Clare, I want all of you. Please—Shit. You have to wait."

"What?" Her mouth fell open. "Beckett."

"Sorry, just a minute." He hurried over to the boys, who were hunting up sticks to throw for the dogs. "Harry."

"They chew them up. They chew up the sticks. Watch."

"Harry, I promised you something. I said I'd clear it with you before I asked your mom to marry me. I need you to tell me it's okay if I do."

Harry looked down at the stick while his brothers stood beside him, all eyes.

"Why do you want to?"

"Because I love her. I love her, Harry. I love you guys, too, and I want us to be a family."

"The bad man tried to hurt her," Murphy said. "But you came, and you and Mom fought him and they took him to jail."

"Yeah, and you don't have to worry about that."

"Are you going to sleep in her bed?" Liam wanted to know.

"That's part of the deal."

"Sometimes we like to, if there's thunder or we have bad dreams."

"Then we'll need a big bed."

He waited while they looked at each other. He knew how it was, the unspoken language of brothers.

"Okay, if she wants to."

"Thanks." He shook Harry's hand, then pulled him in, pulled them all in for a hug. "Thanks. Wish me luck."

"Luck!" Murphy shouted.

If he hadn't been nervous, Beckett would have laughed all the way back to Clare.

"What was that?"

"Man talk."

"Oh really, Beckett, you start all that business about bedrooms and paving, then you just walk off for man talk?"

"I couldn't finish until I'd cleared it with Harry. We had a deal, and guys have to know you keep your word."

"Well, good for you, but—"

"I had to get his okay before I asked you to marry me. He said it was okay if you want to. Please want to. Don't make me look like a loser in front of the kids."

The hand she'd lifted to push at her hair froze. "You asked my not-quite-nine-year-old son for his blessing?"

"Yeah. He's the oldest."

"I see." She turned away.

"I'm messing this up. I love you. I should've started with that. I swear I trip up more with you than anybody. I love you, Clare. I always did, but it's different loving who you are now. It's so damn solid. You're so solid, so steady, strong, smart. I love who you are, how you are. I love those boys, you have to know."

"I know you do." For a moment she stared at the trees, their bare branches soft in the shimmer of her tears. "I could love you if you didn't, because love, sometimes, just is. But I couldn't marry you unless you loved them, unless I knew you'd be good to them. I love you, Beckett." Eyes dry again, she turned back. "You brought them dogs I didn't think I wanted, and you were so busy talking me into it you didn't see me fall at your feet. I love you, Beckett, without any doubt, without any worry. And I'll marry you the same way."

She threw her arms around him. "Oh, you have no idea what you're in for."

"I bet I do."

"We're going to find out, because— What *is* that in your pocket? And don't say you're just happy to see me."

"Oh, forgot." He pulled out a small bag. "I got you a new hairbrush."

For an instant she only stared. Then she cupped his face in her hands. "Is it any wonder?"

He scooped her in, swung her around. And holding her close shot a thumbs-up to the boys.

Her boys—his boys—their boys let out whoops and cheers, and ran toward him with dogs barking at their heels.

KEEP READING FOR AN EXCERPT FROM
THE SECOND BOOK IN THE INN BOONSBORO TRILOGY
BY NORA ROBERTS

The Last Boyfriend

A FAT WINTER MOON POURED LIGHT OVER THE OLD STONE and brick of the inn on The Square. In its beams, the new porches and pickets glowed and the bright-penny copper of the roof glinted. The old and new merged there—the past and the present—in a strong and happy marriage.

Its windows stayed dark on this December night, prizing its secrets in shadows. But in a matter of weeks they would shine like others along Boonsboro's Main Street.

As he sat in his truck at the light on The Square, Owen Montgomery looked down Main at the shops and apartments draped in their holiday cheer. Lights winked and danced. To his right, a pretty tree graced the big front window of the second-floor apartment. Their future innkeeper's temporary residence reflected her style: precise elegance.

Next Christmas, he thought, they'd have Inn BoonsBoro covered with white lights and greenery. And Hope Beaumont would center her pretty little tree in the window of the innkeeper's apartment on the third floor.

He glanced to his left, where Avery McTavish, owner of Vesta Pizzeria and Family Restaurant, had the restaurant's front porch decked out in lights.

Her apartment above—formerly his brother Beckett's—also showed a tree in the window. Otherwise her windows were as dark as the inn's. She'd be working tonight, he thought, noting the movement in the restaurant. He shifted, but couldn't see her behind the work counter.

When the light changed, he turned right onto St. Paul Street, then left into the parking lot behind the inn. Then sat in his truck a moment, considering. He could walk over to Vesta, he thought, have a slice and a beer, hang out until closing. Afterward he could do his walk-through of the inn.

He didn't actually need to walk through, he reminded himself. But he hadn't been on site all day, as he'd been busy with other meetings, other details on other Montgomery Family Contractors business. He didn't want to wait until morning to see what his brothers and the crew had accomplished that day.

Besides, Vesta looked busy—and had barely thirty minutes till closing. Not that Avery would kick him out at closing—probably. More than likely, she'd sit down and have a beer with him.

Tempting, he thought, but he really should do that quick walk-through and get home. He needed to be on site, with his tools, by seven a.m.

He climbed out of the truck and into the frigid air, already pulling out his keys. Tall like his brothers, with a build leaning toward rangy, he hunched in his jacket as he walked around the stone courtyard wall toward the doors of The Lobby.

His keys were color coded—something his brothers called anal and he deemed efficient. In seconds he was out of the cold and into the building.

He hit the lights, then just stood there, grinning like a moron.

The decorative tile rug highlighted the span of the floor, added another note of charm to the softly painted walls with their custom, creamy wainscoting. Beckett had been right on target about leaving the exposed brick on the side wall. And their mother had been dead-on about the chandelier.

Not fancy, not traditional, but somehow organic with its bronzy branches and narrow, flowing globes centered over that tile rug. He glanced right, noted The Lobby restrooms, with their fancy tiles and green-veined stone sinks, had been painted.

He pulled out his notebook, jotted down the need for a few touch-ups before he walked through the stone arch to the left.

More exposed brick—yeah, Beckett had a knack. The laundry room shelves showed ruthless organization—and that would be Hope's hand. Her iron will had booted his brother Ryder out of his site office so she could start organizing.

He paused at what would be Hope's office, saw his brother's mark there: the sawhorses and a sheet of plywood forming his rough desk, the fat white binder—the job bible—some tools, cans of paint.

Wouldn't be much longer, Owen calculated, before Hope kicked Ryder out again.

He continued on, stopped to admire the open kitchen.

They'd installed the lights, the big iron fixture over the island, the smaller versions at each window. Warm wood cabinets, creamy accent pieces, and smooth granite complemented the gleaming stainless steel appliances.

He opened the fridge, started to reach for a beer. He'd be driving shortly, he reminded himself, and took a can of Pepsi instead before he made a note to call about the installation of the blinds and window treatments.

They were nearly ready for them.

He moved on to Reception, took another scan, grinned again.

The mantel Ryder had created out of a thick old plank of barn wood suited the old brick and the deep, open fireplace. At the moment, tarps, more paint cans, more tools crowded the space. He made a few more notes, wandered back, moved through the first arch, then paused on his way across The Lobby to what would be The Lounge, when he heard footsteps on the second floor.

He walked through the next arch leading down the short hallway toward the stairs. He saw Luther had been hard at work on the iron rail, and ran a hand over it as he started the climb.

"Okay, pretty damn gorgeous. Ry? You up here?"

A door shut smartly, made him jump a little. His quiet blue eyes narrowed as he finished the climb. His brothers weren't against screwing with him—and damned if he'd give either of them an excuse to snicker.

"Ooooh," he said in mock fear. "It must be the ghost. I'm *so* scared!"

He made the turn toward the front of the building, saw that the door to the Elizabeth and Darcy suite was indeed closed, unlike that of Titania and Oberon across from it.

Very funny, he thought sourly.

He crept toward the door, intending to shove it open, jump in, and possibly give whichever one of his brothers was playing games a jolt. He closed his hand on the curved handle, pulled it down smoothly, pushed.

The door didn't budge.

"Cut it out, asshole." But he laughed a little despite himself. At least until the door flew open, and both porch doors did the same.

He smelled honeysuckle, sweet as summer, on the rush of icy air.

"Well, Jesus."

He'd mostly accepted they had a ghost—mostly believed it. After all, there'd been incidents, and Beckett was adamant. Adamant enough that he'd named her Elizabeth in honor of the room she preferred.

But this was Owen's first personal, up-close and inarguable experience.

He stood, slack-jawed, as the bathroom door slammed, then flew open, then slammed again.

"Okay. Wow, okay. Um, sorry to intrude. I was just——" The door slammed in his face—or would have if he hadn't jumped back in time to avoid the bust to the nose.

"Hey, come on. You've got to know me by now. I'm here almost every day. Owen, Beck's brother. I, ah, come in peace and all that."

The bathroom door slammed again, and the sound made him wince. "Easy on the material, okay? What's the problem? I was just . . . Oh. I get it."

Clearing his throat, he pulled off his cool cap, raked his hands through his thick, bark brown hair. "Listen, I wasn't calling you an asshole. I thought it was Ry. You know my other brother. Ryder? He can be an asshole, you have to admit. And I'm standing in the hallway explaining myself to a ghost."

The door opened a crack. Cautiously, Owen eased it open. "I'm just going to close the porch doors. We really have to keep them closed."

He could admit, to himself, that the sound of his own voice echoing in the empty room gave him the jitters. But he shoved the cap in his coat pocket as he moved to the far door, shut it, locked it. When he got to the second door, he saw the lights shining in Avery's apartment over the restaurant.

He saw her, or a flash of her, move by the window.

The rush of air stilled; the scent of honeysuckle sweetened.

"I've smelled you before," he murmured, still looking out at Avery's windows. "Beckett says you warned him the night that fucker—sorry for the language—Sam Freemont went after Clare. So thanks for that. They're getting married—Beck and Clare. You probably know that. He's been stuck on her most of his life."

He shut the door now, turned around. "So thanks again."

The bathroom door stood open now, and he caught his own reflection in the mirror with its curvy iron frame over the vanity.

He could admit to himself that he looked a little wild eyed, and the hair sticking up in tufts from the rake of his fingers added to the spooked image.

Automatically, he shoved his fingers through again to try to calm it down.

"I'm just going through the place, making notes. We're down to punch-out work, essentially. Not in here though. This is done. I think the crew wanted to finish up this room. Some of them get a little spooked. No offense. So . . . I'm going to finish up and go. See you—or not see you, but . . ."

Whatever, he decided, and backed out of the room.

He spent more than thirty minutes moving from room to room, floor to floor, adding to his notes. A few times the scent of honeysuckle returned, or a door opened.

Her presence—and he couldn't deny it—seemed benign enough now. But he couldn't deny the faint sense of relief either as he locked up for the night.

⌘

FROST CRUNCHED LIGHTLY under Owen's boots as he juggled coffee and doughnuts. A half hour before sunrise, he let himself back into the inn, headed straight to the kitchen to set down the box of doughnuts, the tray of take-out coffee, and his briefcase. To brighten the mood, and because it was there, he moved to Reception, switched on the gas logs of the fireplace. Pleased by the heat and light, he stripped off his gloves, folded them into the pockets of his jacket.

Back in the kitchen, he opened his briefcase, took out his clipboard and began to review—again—the agenda for the day. The phone on his belt beeped, signaling the time for the morning meeting.

He'd finished half a glazed doughnut by the time he heard Ryder's truck pull in.

His brother wore a cap, a thick, scarred work jacket, and his need-more-coffee scowl. Dumbass, Ryder's dog, padded in, sniffed the air, then looked longingly at the second half of Owen's doughnut.

Ryder grunted, reached for a cup.

"That's Beck's," Owen told him with barely a glance. "As is clear by the *B* I wrote on the side."

Ryder grunted again, took the cup marked *R*. After one long gulp, he eyed the doughnuts, opted for a jelly-filled.

At the thump of D.A.'s tail, Ryder tossed him a chunk.

"Beck's late," Owen commented.

"You're the one who decided we needed to meet before dawn." Ryder took a huge bite of doughnut, washed it down with coffee. He hadn't shaved, so dark stubble covered the hard planes of his face. But his gold-flecked green eyes lost some of their sleepy scowl thanks to the caffeine and sugar.

"Too many interruptions once the crew's here. I looked around some on my way home last night. You had a good day."

"Damn straight. We'll finish punch-out on the third floor this morning. Some trim and crown molding, some lights and those damn heated towel racks still to go in a couple rooms on two. Luther's moving on the rails and banisters."

"So I saw. I've got some notes."

"Yeah, yeah."

"I'll have more, I expect, when I finish going over two, and head up to three."

"Why wait?" Ryder grabbed a second doughnut, started out. He tossed another chunk without bothering to glance at the dog who trotted with him.

Dumbass fielded it with Golden Glove precision.

"Beckett's not here."

"Dude's got a woman," Ryder pointed out, "and three kids. School morning. He'll be here when he is, and can catch up."

"There's some paint needs touching up down here," Owen began.

"I got eyes, too."

"I'm going to have them come in, install the blinds throughout. If three gets punched-out today, I can have them start on the window treatments by early next week."

"The men cleaned up, but it's construction clean. It needs a real cleaning, a polish. You need to get the innkeeper on that."

"I'll be talking to Hope this morning. I'm going to talk County into letting us start load-in."

Ryder slanted a look at his brother. "We've got another two weeks, easy, and that's not counting the holidays."

But Owen, as usual, had a plan. "We can get three done, Ry, start working our way down. You think Mom and Carolee—not to mention Hope—aren't going to be running around buying more stuff once we get things in place?"

"I do figure it. We don't need them underfoot any more than they already are."

They heard a door open from below as they rounded up to the third floor.

"On three," Owen called down. "Coffee's in the kitchen."

"Thank you, Jesus."

"Jesus didn't buy the coffee." Owen brushed his fingers over the oval oil-rubbed bronzed plaque with the word *Innkeeper* engraved on it. "Classy touch."

"The place is full of them." Ryder gulped more coffee as they stepped inside.

"It looks good." Owen nodded as he toured through, in and out of the little kitchen, the bath, circling the two bedrooms. "It's a nice, comfortable space. Pretty and efficient—like our innkeeper."

"She's damn near as pain-in-the-ass fussy as you are."

"Remember who keeps you in doughnuts, bro."

At the word doughnut, D.A. wagged his entire body. "You're done, pal," Ryder told him, and with a doggie sigh, D.A. sprawled on the floor.

Owen glanced over as Beckett came up the stairs.

He'd shaved, Owen noted, and looked bright-eyed. Maybe a little wild-eyed, as he imagined most men did with three kids under the age of ten and the school morning chaos that created.

He remembered his own school mornings well enough, and wondered how his parents had resisted doing major drugs.

"One of the dogs puked in Murphy's bed," Beckett announced. "I don't want to talk about it."

"Works for me. Owen's talking about window treatments and loading in."

Beckett paused as he gave Dumbass a quick head rub. "We've still got trim to run, painting, punch-out."

"Not up here." Owen crossed to the first of their two suites, The Penthouse. "*This* is what I'm talking about." He moved through, saw muted colored crystal lights, creamy trim, and the big splashy bath with its stunning tile work. He paused at the floating wall, nodded at the long counter and double vessel sinks, stepped over, scanned the large glass shower, the generous rain head, the body jets, turned toward the wide white tub.

"We could outfit this suite. Hope could move her stuff in across the hall. How about the Westley and Buttercup room?"

"It's done. We hung the bathroom mirror and lights yesterday."

"Then I'll tell Hope to break out the mop, get this level shined up." Though he trusted Ryder, he'd check the room himself. "She's got the list of what goes where, so she can run down to Bast, tell them what to deliver up here."

He made notes on his clipboard—shipment of towels and linens, purchase of light bulbs and so on. Behind his back, Beckett and Ryder exchanged looks.

"I guess we're loading in."

"I don't know who *we* is," Ryder corrected. "It's not me or the crew. We've got to finish the damn place."

"Don't bitch at me." Beckett held up his hands. "I've got to make the changes to the bakery project next door if we're going to shift the crew from here to there without much of a lag."

"I could use a lag," Ryder muttered, but headed down behind Owen.

Owen paused at Elizabeth and Darcy, gave the propped-open door a study. "Beckett, you might want to talk to your pal, Lizzy. Make sure she keeps this door open and the terrace doors shut."

"It is open. They are shut."

"Now. She got a little peeved last night."

Intrigued, Beckett lifted his brows. "Is that so?"

"I guess I had my personal close encounter. I did a walk-though last night, heard somebody up here. I figured it for one of you, messing with me. She thought I called her an asshole, and let me know she didn't care for it."

Beckett's grin spread wide and quick. "She's got a temper."

"Tell me. We made up—I think. But in case she holds a grudge . . ."

"We're done in here, too," Ryder told him. "And in Titania and Oberon. We've got to run the crown molding and baseboard in Nick and Nora, and there's some touch-ups in Eve and Roarke, and the bathroom ceiling light in there. It came in, finally, yesterday. Jane and Rochester in the back is full of boxes. Lamps, lamps, more lamps, shelves and God knows. But it's punched out."

"I've got a list, too." Ryder tapped his head while the dog walked over to sit at his side. "I just don't have to write down every freaking thing in ten places."

"Robe hooks, towel racks, TP dispensers," Owen began.

"On the slate for today."

"Mirrors, flatscreens, switch plate and outlet covers, door bumpers."

"On the slate, Owen."

"You've got the list of what goes where?"

"Nobody likes a nag, Sally."

"Exit signs need to go up." Owen continued working down his list as he walked to the Dining Room. "Wall sconces in here, and some touch-ups to the paint. The boxes we built for the fire extinguishers need to be painted and installed."

"Once you shut up, I can get started."

"Brochures, website, advertising, finalizing room rates, packages, room folders."

"Not my job."

"Exactly. Count your frigging blessings. How much longer for the revised plans on the bakery project?" Owen asked Beckett.

"I'll have them to the permit office tomorrow morning."

"Good deal." He took out his phone, switched it to calendar. "Let's nail it down. I'm going to tell Hope to open reservations for January fifteenth. We can have the grand-opening deal on the thirteenth, give it a day for putting it all back together. Then we're up."

"That's less than a month," Ryder complained.

"You know and Beck knows and I know that there's less than two weeks of work left here. You'll be done before Christmas. If we start the load-in this week, we'll be done by the first of the year, and there's no reason we won't get the Use and Occupancy right after the holidays. That gives two weeks to fiddle and fuss, work out any kinks, with Hope living here."

"I'm with Owen here. We're sliding downhill now, Ry."

Stuffing his hands in his pockets, Ryder shrugged. "It's weird, maybe, just weird thinking about actually being done."

"Cheer up," Owen told him. "A place like this? We're never going to be done."

On his nod, Ryder heard the back door open, shut, the sound of heavy boots on tile. "We've got crew. Get your tools."

❧

OWEN KEPT BUSY, and happy, running crown molding. He didn't mind the regular interruptions to answer a call, return a text, read an email. His phone served as a tool to him as much as his nail gun. The building buzzed with activity, echoed with voices and Ryder's job radio. It smelled of paint and fresh-cut wood, strong coffee. The combination said Montgomery Family Construction to him, and never failed to remind him of his father.

Everything he'd learned about carpentry and the building trade he'd learned from his father. Now, stepping off the ladder to study the work, he knew his father would be proud.

They'd taken the old building, with its sagging porches and broken windows, its scarred walls and broken floors, and transformed it into a jewel on the town square.

Beckett's vision, he thought, their mother's imagination and canny eye, Ryder's sweat and skill, and his own focus on detail—combined with a solid crew—transformed what had been an idea batted around the kitchen table into a reality.

He set down his nail gun, rolled his shoulders as he turned around the room.

Yeah, his mother's canny eye, he thought again. He could admit he'd balked at her scheme of pale aqua walls and chocolate brown ceiling—until he'd seen it finished. Glamour was the word of the day for Nick and Nora, and it reached its pinnacle in the bath. That same color scheme, including a wall of blue glass tiles contrasting with brown on brown, all sparkling under crystal lights. Chandelier in the john, he thought with a shake of his head. It sure as hell worked.

Nothing ordinary or hotel-like about it, he mused—not when Justine Montgomery took charge. He thought this room, with its Deco flair, might be his favorite.

His phone alarm told him it was time to start making some calls of his own.

He went out, then headed toward the back door for the porch as Luther worked on the rails leading down. Gritting his teeth, he jogged through the cold and bitter wind across the covered porch, down to ground level, then ducked in through Reception.

"Fucking A, it's cold." The radio blasted; nail guns thumped. And no way, he decided, would he try to do business with all this noise. He grabbed his jacket, his briefcase.

He ducked into The Lounge, where Beckett sat on the floor running trim.

"I'm heading over to Vesta."

"It's shy of ten. They're not open."

"Exactly. If you see Ry, tell him the crown's up in N&N. Somebody needs to wood putty the nail holes and touch it up."

"I don't know where the hell he is."

"No problem."

As he started out, Owen pulled his phone off his belt, sent Ry a text. Outside, he hunched against the cold at the light, cursed the fact that traffic, such as it was, paced and spaced itself so he couldn't make the dash across Main. He waited it out, his breath blowing icy clouds until the walk light flashed. He jogged diagonally, ignored the CLOSED sign on the glass front door of the restaurant, and pounded.

He saw lights on, but no movement. Once again he took out his phone, punched in Avery's number from memory.

"Damn it, Owen, now I've got dough on my phone."

"So you are in there. Open up before I get frostbite."

"Damn it," she said again, then cut him off. But seconds later he saw her, white bib apron over jeans and a black sweater shoved to her elbows. Her hair—what the hell color was it now? It struck him as very close to the bright new penny copper of the inn's roof.

She'd started changing it a few months back, going with most everything but her natural Scot warrior queen red. She'd hacked it short, too, he recalled, though it had grown long enough again for her to yank it back in a tiny stub when she worked.

Her eyes, as bright a blue as her hair was copper, glared at him as she turned the locks.

"What do you want?" she demanded. "I'm in the middle of prep."

"I just want the room and the quiet. You won't even know I'm here." He sidled in, just in case she tried to shut the door on him. "I can't talk on the phone with all the noise across the street and I have to make some calls."

She narrowed those blue eyes at his briefcase.

So he tried a winning smile. "Okay, maybe I have a little paperwork. I'll sit at the counter. I'll be very, very quiet."

"Oh, all right. But don't bother me."

"Um, just before you go back? You wouldn't happen to have any coffee?"

"No, I wouldn't happen to have. I'm prepping dough, which is now on my new phone. I worked closing last night, and Franny called in sick at eight this morning. She sounded like somebody ran her larynx through a meat grinder. I had two waitstaff out with the same thing last night, which means I'll probably be on from now until closing. Dave can't work tonight because he's getting a root canal at four. And I've got a bus tour coming it at twelve thirty."

Because she'd snapped the words out in little whiplashes, Owen just nodded. "Okay."

"Just . . ." She gestured toward the long counter. "Do whatever."

She rushed back to the kitchen on bright green Nikes.

He'd have offered to help, but he could tell she wasn't in the mood. He knew her moods—he'd known her forever—and recognized harried, impatient and stressed.

She'd roll with it, he thought. She always did. The sassy little redhead from his childhood, the former Boonsboro High cheerleader—cocaptain with Beckett's Clare—had become a hard-working restaurateur. Who made exceptional pizza.

She'd left a light, lemony scent behind her, along with a frisson of energy. He heard the faint thump and rattle of her work as he took a stool at the counter. He found it soothing, somewhat rhythmic.

He opened his briefcase, took out his iPad, his clipboard, unclipped his phone from his belt.

He made his calls, sent emails, texts, reworked his calendar, and calculated.

He steeped himself in the details, surfacing when a coffee mug slid under his nose.

He looked up into Avery's pretty face.

"Thanks. You didn't have to bother. I won't be long."

"Owen, you've already been here forty minutes."

"Really? Lost track. You want me go?"

"Doesn't matter." Though she pressed a fist into the small of her back, she spoke easily now. "I've got it under control."

He caught another scent and, glancing to the big stove, saw she'd put her sauces on.

The red hair, milk-white skin and dash of freckles might declare her Scot heritage, but her marinara was as gloriously Italian as an Armani suit.

He'd often wondered where she'd gotten the knack, and the drive, but both seemed as innate a part of her as her big, bold blue eyes.

Crouching, she opened the cooler under the counter for tubs, and began filling the toppings containers.

"Sorry about Franny."

"Me, too. She's really sick. And Dave's miserable. He's only coming in for a couple hours this afternoon because I'm so shorthanded. I hate asking him."

He studied her face as she worked. Now that he really looked, he noted the pale purple shadows under her eyes.

"You look tired."

She shot him a disgusted look over the tub of black olives she was holding. "Thanks. That's what every girl loves to hear." Then she shrugged. "I am tired. I thought I'd sleep in this morning. Franny would open, I'd come in about eleven thirty. Not much of a commute since I moved right upstairs. So I watched some Jimmy Fallon, finished a book I've been trying to squeeze out time to read all week. I didn't go down until nearly two. Then Franny calls at eight. Six hours isn't bad, unless you worked a double and you're going to work another."

"Bright side? Business is good."

"I'll think about bright side after the bus tour. Anyway, enough. How's it going at the inn?"

"So good we're going to start loading in the third floor tomorrow."

"Loading in what?"

"Furniture, Avery."

She set down the tub, goggled at him. "Seriously? *Seriously?*"

"The inspector's going to take a look this afternoon, give us the go or no. I'm saying go because there's no reason for no. I just talked to Hope. She's going to start cleaning up there. My mother and my aunt are coming in—maybe are in already, since it's going on eleven now—to pitch in."

"I wanted to do that. I can't."

"Don't worry about that. We've got plenty of hands."

"I wanted mine to be two of them. Maybe tomorrow, depending on sickness and root canals. Jeez, Owen, this is major." She did a little heel-toe dance on her green hightops. "And you wait almost an hour to spill it?"

"You were too busy bitching at me."

"If you'd spilled, I'd've been too excited to bitch. Your own fault."

She smiled at him, pretty Avery McTavish with the tired eyes.

"Why don't you sit down for a few minutes?"

"I've got to keep moving today, like a shark." She snapped the lid on the tub, replaced it, then went over to check her sauces.

He watched her work. She always seemed to be doing a half dozen things at once, like a constant juggling act with balls hanging in the air, others bouncing madly until she managed to grab and toss them again.

It amazed his organized mind.

"I'd better get back. Thanks for the coffee."

"No problem. If any of the crew are thinking about lunch here today, tell them to wait until one thirty. The rush'll be over."

"Okay." He gathered his things, then paused at the door. "Avery? What color is that? The hair."

"This? Copper Penny."

He grinned, shook his head. "I knew it. See you later."

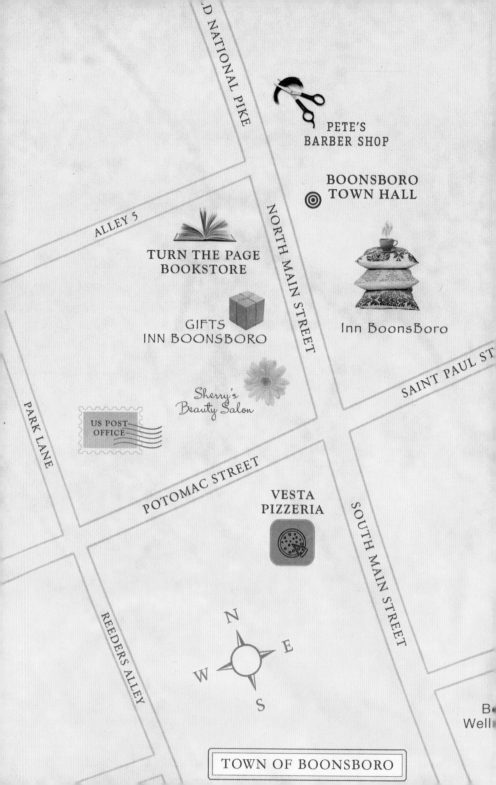